ORDEAL BY TERROR

BOOKS BY LLOYD BIGGLE, JR.

SCIENCE FICTION

The Angry Espers
The Fury Out Of Time
The Light That Never Was
Monument
Alien Main (with T. L. Sherred)

Jan Darzek Novels

All the Colors of Darkness
Watchers of the Dark
This Darkening Universe
Silence Is Deadly
The Whirligig of Time

Cultural Survey Novels

The Still, Small Voice of Trumpets
The World Menders

Short Story Collections

The Rule of the Door
The Metallic Muse
A Galaxy of Strangers
Nebula Award Stories Seven (Editor)

MYSTERY AND SUSPENSE

Pletcher and Lambert Novels

Interface for Murder
A Hazard of Losers
Where Dead Soldiers Walk
Murder Jambalaya

Memoirs of Sherlock Holmes

The Quallsford Inheritance
The Glendower Conspiracy

ORDEAL BY TERROR

LLOYD BIGGLE, JR.

*Edited by Kenneth Lloyd Biggle
and Donna Biggle Emerson*

WILDSIDE PRESS

ORDEAL BY TERROR

In Memory of

Dr. James V. McConnell

The generous interest, assistance, and encouragement he gave to projects such as this one are sorely missed.

CHAPTER 1

The grandfather clock in the hallway struck eleven. It was a Friday morning in early July, and for Adelle Gernyan the moment was one she had commemorated. Three weeks earlier, an interview with an odd little woman whose name Adelle still did not know had resulted in her being hired as a Researcher/Word Processor by an even odder business establishment called Z-R Publications. The building she worked in and the room that served as her office were the quintessence of oddness. Oddest of all was her salary, which was fantastic.

Only the work was mundane. Z-R Publications used "Researcher/Word Processor" as a euphemism for typist. For eight hours each day, minus whatever breaks she decided to give herself, Adelle sat in front of a computer copying handwritten or typewritten material supplied by the firm's other two employees and arranging it in attractive page formats for eventual publication.

She was doing excellent work, but any competent typist could have done as well. That was what made her salary so unbelievable. As a bonus, she had this incredible office and an entire unoccupied wing of the building to shield her from interruptions. Such splendid isolation would have been a distraction to some employees, but Adelle had always been able to work diligently without supervision.

On this particular morning, however, her concentration faltered. She sat frowning at her computer screen, fingers poised rigidly above its keyboard, while the clatter of a tractor lawn mower swelled to a sputtering roar. It was her fourteenth day of typing statistics—Z-R Publications had given its staff the 4th of July off—and she could copy scrawled numerals almost without thinking. She was oblivious to most disturbances, but the tractor defeated her. Its explosive pulsations sounded like an evil spirit frothing in frustration before gates where spirits of whatever intent were forbidden to enter.

As the racket continued, with the tractor roaming among the hedges of a charming formal garden and circling its large, sculpture-cluttered, unused fountain, Adelle left her desk and went to one of the room's windows to look out. They were oriel windows, with stained glass in delicately leaded patterns that converted the outside world into a jigsaw mosaic of contrasting tints. The tractor, snorting its way from one color segment to another, looked out of place in all of them.

Its driver was known to Adelle only as Goon 2. Like the other Z-R Publications maintenance men, he wore a dark green shirt and trousers and was as incongruously neat and clean in appearance when shoveling dirt as when vacuuming plush carpets or fastidiously wielding a feather duster. Despite striking individual differences, all of the goons seemed cut from the same mold—large and hulking—and all of them were strangely inarticulate and anonymous. They neither introduced themselves nor were given in introductions. They did not speak even when spoken to. After enduring a week of that peculiar anonymity, Adelle dubbed them goons and assigned numbers to them.

Goon 2 was the eldest of the five. He had a circle of baldness on his head surrounded by a fringe of surprisingly black hair, and he was the only goon who wore glasses. The formidable disapproval with which he gazed at her when he thought she wasn't looking had disturbed her until she noticed that he disapproved of everyone and everything else just as formidably. He was one of those unfortunate individuals who moved through life with the conviction that whoever was responsible for the universe hadn't quite got it right.

Adelle was about to turn away when she saw two people standing in an opposite doorway. The starkly beautiful Romanesque contours of that wing made it her favorite, but she had never seen anyone using its entrance. Now the maintenance worker she called Goon 1 stood at the bottom of the steps, and above him, holding the door open, stood the little woman who was his boss—and Adelle's.

Goon 1 was Adelle's personal goon. He could be surprised watching her surreptitiously whenever she went anywhere—home, or to lunch, or to the rest room down the hall. Her two coworkers also had personal goons spying on them, which seemed ridiculous. If the firm wanted to know whether they were working, Adelle thought, all it had to do was study their productivity.

Goon 1 had a large, beefy face, a crew cut, and the sternest blue eyes she had ever encountered. She called him number one because he looked like a top sergeant and giver of orders. He was taking orders now and not liking them. He stood rigid with resentment, fists clenched, arms partially bent and held out from his sides.

The plump little woman who hovered above him, gesticulating impatiently, was known to Adelle only as Madam. She bustled about absent-mindedly and seemed like the most improbable person imaginable to be entrusted with running a business. Perhaps she didn't run it. The indecipherable signature on the firm's checks bore no resemblance to her handwriting, and the firm's conspicuous prosperity and grandiose planning suggested clouds of invisible corporate officers and incognito directors.

But this odd creature was the boss, unmistakably. She hired and fired, she passed out work assignments, and she gave orders. Especially to the goons she gave orders.

Adelle couldn't make out expressions at such a distance, but she had no difficulty imagining them. Goon 1's face would be livid. As for Madam, her streaky gray hair always hung in a straight droop, and her wrinkled face was testimony to a lifetime of virginity at least from cosmetics. She would be peering down at Goon 1 through the thick, ugly, bespattered horn-rimmed glasses that always perched precariously on her monstrously oversized nose, talking at him cheerfully, calling him "Darlink" in every other sentence even though each word stung like a lash. She called everyone "Darlink." Probably it was because she never remembered names. In return, she didn't expect anyone to remember hers. Her first words to Adelle had been, "Call me Madam, Darlink. Everyone else does." So Adelle did, and so did everyone else, and it hadn't occurred to Adelle until a week later that Madam was as nameless as the maintenance workers.

Abruptly Madam turned and tiptoed away. She always tiptoed. The door swung shut behind her, but Goon 1 remained motionless, fists still clenched. Adelle wondered what kind of maintenance problem could have produced such a dramatic clash of personalities and such taut emotions. Had Goon 1 put tulip bulbs in the wrong place?

In its normal, everyday operations, Z-R Publications seemed odd enough, but a totally inexplicable incident such as this one took the firm beyond oddness and into the realm of the strange or eerie.

The tractor, having attended to the grass in the formal garden, moved off. Goon 1 finally stirred and disappeared around the corner. The threatening evil spirit fled with the mower's fading clatter, but it had been doomed to frustration in any case. This magnificently sprawling Feinstwaller Manor was phony from one end to the other, a sham environment that would repel evil spirits in any guise. Further, it was headquarters for that most unhauntable of Earthly institutions, a corporation.

"Z-R Publications," Adelle murmured, "hail." During her job interview she had asked what the letters stood for, and Madam shrugged and told her, "It's just a name, Darlink." At first she had thought it was a word, spelled something like *Zeeare*. Either way, it was immune to specters. A sign that read, "Z-R Publications, Inc.," would have banished ghosts from a mausoleum.

Adelle returned to her desk, which was the type normally occupied by whatever executive officer of a firm had the least work to put on it—enormous, ornate, expensive, and totally inappropriate for a Researcher/ Word Processor—but then, so was the room Adelle worked in. To go with the oriel windows and their tinted jigsaw puzzle view of garden and fountain, it had fielded paneling and a high, fan vaulted ceiling. Computer, desk, and oversized, plushly upholstered office chair—like the desk, more suitable for a corporation president than a mere employee of whatever status—looked like brash intruders, and Adelle felt like one. The room was otherwise furnished with pseudo-antique chairs, tables, bureaus, and sofas. On the floor was a thick pseudo-oriental carpet.

Adelle resumed typing, and row after row of crisp numbers took their places on the computer screen in orderly columns:

1975	12,472	127,896	921
1976	14,798	124,310	1,014
1977	19,490	125,747	1,823
1978	20,244	128,165	1,769
1979	22,314	130,002	1,854
1980	23,562	129,773	2,331

Madam tiptoed silently into the room. Adelle finished the column she was typing before looking up. By that time, Madam had placed Adelle's paycheck on the corner of her desk.

She stood beaming down at her. Today she was wearing what Adelle called her alternate dress, which was less baggy and more flowery than the one she usually wore. Her face, seen from close up, looked like the side of a house from which paint had just been removed with a blow-torch. Adelle also shunned cosmetics, but Madam's peeling visage was almost enough to convert her to the use of lipstick, rouge, nail polish, and eye shadow in clashing colors. Madam's other outstanding features, in addition to her two dresses, were her one pair of shoes with badly worn, flat heels—one of the many mysteries about her was how she could wear out heels when she always tiptoed, but Kevin Mondor, one of Adelle's two coworkers, maintained that she tiptoed *because* her heels were worn; her neck, which always was slightly dirty but never got dirtier; her manner of squinting nearsightedly through bespattered glasses; and, of course, the exceptionally broad nose upon which the glasses rode so precariously. She was infuriatingly absent-minded and fluttered about hysterically when she mislaid something, which happened frequently.

She stood for a moment studying the computer screen. "That's nice, Darlink. I like wide margins. I like your new clothes, too. Pants. That's different. So attractive. Did you hear what Write said about Add?"

Madam's failure to remember names resulted in a cryptic speech of her own fabrication. Adelle, called "Darlink" to her face, knew she was "Type" behind her back. Kevin Mondor, with an official title of Researcher/Statistician, was "Darlink" and "Add." And Craig Dolan, the concern's Researcher/Writer, was "Darlink" and "Write."

Adelle smiled. "No. What did he say?"

"He said Add's parents fed him nothing but alphabet soup—made with numbers instead of letters!" Madam cackled shrilly.

Adelle feigned another smile and asked calmly, "But did you hear what Add said about Write?"

"No!"

"Write grew up on a farm, you know. They didn't have indoor plumbing. Instead of catalogs, they used old dictionaries for toilet paper."

All of that was sheer improvisation on Adelle's part. Madam threw up both hands and quickly tiptoed away, laughing convulsively. Adelle wondered if she repeated these stories to the goons and if they found them as hilarious as Madam did. Adelle couldn't imagine the goons laughing at anything.

Of course Madam would tell Dolan what Mondor was supposed to have said about him, and Dolan would quickly discover that the remark came from Adelle. Before another day passed, Madam would be back with some tale from Dolan, attributed to Mondor, about an alleged peculiar habit of Adelle's. Such silly by-play, nourished by Madam's childish tattling, had puzzled Adelle when she first came to work there. Now she felt splendidly indifferent to it. She disliked Mondor thoroughly and despised Dolan, and she knew the two of them scorned her and hated each other, but their offices were in three different wings of the sprawling building, and they were able to keep personal contacts to a minimum.

Further, all three of them were in this together and doing good work, however silly that work might be. Her own names for Mondor and Dolan were Cad and Clod, and her job would have been much pleasanter with more congenial people to work with, but she could have put up with Dracula and Frankenstein's monster for the fabulous dimensions of her salary.

She picked up her check and regarded it with the same studious disbelief she had directed at the first two. More than nine hundred dollars in take-home pay for doing a week of—what? She had put in her time faithfully, she had worked steadily and well, she had followed instructions scrupulously, and she knew she hadn't earned half than that. Supposedly the salary was justified by her highfalutin title, Researcher/Word Processor, but the only research she did was with a dictionary, correcting Dolan's spelling errors.

"Mine not to reason why," she murmured. But she couldn't suppress her feeling that something was very wrong about this job. No honest business could afford to pay its employees so well to work in such a costly environment and produce so little.

"Just getting started, Darlink," Madam had said cheerfully. "Books aren't made in a day. All of ours will be annuals, and the business firms we serve will be buying replacements every year or two." Adelle wanted to ask how many firms were likely to buy the books in the first place, but of course that wasn't her problem. Perhaps it wasn't Madam's problem, either.

Paychecks were delivered promptly just before noon on Friday—a truly generous gesture since they weren't due until the end of the day. "In case you want to shop during lunch hour," Madam said. The Z-R Publications logo on the checks was both stylish and dignified, the checks were prepared on a check writer and looked thoroughly professional—corporate, in fact—and despite the interminable, scrawling, illegible signature, neither of Adelle's two previous checks had bounced. The solvency of Z-R Publications could not be challenged by anything she had observed.

Even so, she couldn't shrug off that feeling of uneasiness.

"If they're smuggling heroin or running a numbers racket, the police can hardly blame me for something I know nothing about," she told herself philosophically. The numbers racket seemed the more obvious guess—she certainly had typed enough of them in the past three weeks—and unemployment was the worst thing that could happen to her if Z-R Publications collapsed, whether due to a police raid or bankruptcy. With each passing week, as her nest egg became larger, that possibility seemed less menacing.

She was a recent graduate of Darwood College, a small, non-sectarian school located in Darwood, Illinois, where she was born and grew up. She had lost her parents, one after the other, when she was still in high school, and then, in her third year of college, her guardian died, leaving her entirely alone in the world. In both high school and college she made the mistake of taking courses that interested her rather than those that were practical, but the solid common sense of her guardian kept the error from being a fatal one. He insisted that she attend a business school during her summer vacations. Typing came easy for her—she'd had ten years of piano lessons—and she thought computers were fun.

She finished college on a scholarship and the last of her father's insurance money, and she chose Ann Arbor, Michigan as a place to look for work because a friend at the University of Michigan sent her an exaggerated description of employment opportunities there. Her first reaction to the city was one of shock. The cost of living there was wildly exorbitant compared with Darwood. After she paid a deposit and a month's rental on a cramped apartment in a garish tower called Chateau Arb, whose name enabled its promoters to add twenty dollars monthly to its already inflated rates, and bought an overly used, used car from a kindly-looking salesman who reminded her of a favorite college professor, she barely had enough money left to keep going until her first paycheck. Fortunately the car ran and continued to run. She was completely dependent on it—first to find a job, and then to drive to work.

She had been too intelligent to waste time looking for a position that would make use of her small college bachelor's degree in English Literature. The day after her arrival she answered an ad for a Researcher/Word Processor, and Z-R Publications hired her. She began work the following Monday, and now she was about to cash a third fantastic paycheck.

She gave the check another disbelieving glance, and then she returned to her computer and the columns of figures with the nice wide margins.

When the grandfather clock in the hallway outside her door struck noon, Adelle finished the page she was typing, saved it, and made a backup copy. Then she picked up her purse and coat—although the day was sunny, the weather was unexpectedly cool for mid-summer—and stepped into the hallway.

As she started for the stairs, she glanced back over her shoulder. Goon 1, ever faithful, was watching from the remote end of the hall. She smiled and waved to him; as usual, he made no response. She shrugged and began her descent of a lovely, curved, hanging staircase. She always found it delightful because it gave her a sense of flying. Craig Dolan, with a writer's gift for polluting the poetic with the mundane, said the sensation was one of sliding down a fire pole in slow motion. At the bottom she turned into the broad main corridor that led to the massive front door.

It was a pleasant day for the half-mile walk to the Arbor Vista Shopping Mall, so she left her car in the mansion's parking lot and moved briskly along the left edge of the neat, crushed-rock drive that led out to the highway. A thick grove of trees screened the building from passing motorists.

A car approached from the rear, but Adelle didn't bother to look back. She knew the sound of its motor only too well. As it zoomed past, it swerved close enough to her to whip her coat in the breeze it stirred up. Adelle made no response, but inwardly she was seething.

The driver was Kevin Mondor, and that was his juvenile notion of a joke. His squat little deep blue foreign convertible, which looked much the same coming and going because it was rounded on either end, screeched to a stop at the highway and then made its turn in a swirl of dust and roared out of sight. Fortunately Craig Dolan had already left. Dolan's maliciousness was more imaginative. If he saw her walking ahead of him, he would slow down until he could catch her at the muddy spot between the end of the crushed rock and the highway and spatter her when he passed.

When she reached the highway, she saw a goon at work beside the road, poking with a shovel at something in a wheelbarrow. She identified him from his pot belly and his hat—it was Goon 4—and he seemed seemed to be mixing cement. Madam had mentioned putting up a sign by the highway, and the pole-like object lying on the ground beside him probably was the support to attach the sign to. Z-R Publications, which thus far had lurked invisibly behind the trees, was about to lose its anonymity.

She continued to walk briskly, and—since there was little traffic to distract her—she thought about her coming weekend. Because she had never been in Michigan before, she planned something touristy each week to familiarize herself with her new home. The previous Saturday, she had visited the Dossin Great Lakes Museum, the Detroit Institute of Arts, and the Detroit Historical Museum. This Saturday, it would be Henry Ford's Greenfield Village. On Sunday afternoon, she would attend a concert with a young man who also lived at Chateau Arb—her first date in Ann Arbor. It would be an eventful weekend, and she was looking forward to both days.

In the shopping mall parking lot, Mondor's convertible stood beside Dolan's wreck of a car. The latter's junkyard appearance was as distinctive as that of Mondor's exotic import. Dolan would be taking his repast at a place called Barney's Pub, swilling beer with a sandwich. Mondor, a food faddist who believed all meat was poisonous, ate at The Greenry, where the salad bar was reputed to be the most lavish in Washtenaw County. Adelle had never seen the inside of either establishment. She went to her bank's branch office and split her paycheck into three parts— savings, checking, and a small amount of cash for pocket money. Then she treated herself to a light lunch, without soup, at a tidy little restaurant that called itself The Soup Kettle.

When she finished, Mondor's silly little foreign car was gone, but not Dolan's rusted junker—he would stay with the beer until the last minute of his lunch hour if not beyond it. His lateness is returning from lunch was the subject of some of the jokes Mondor told Madam about him. Madam gleefully relayed them to both Dolan and Adelle, but—as far as Adelle knew—her cackle was Dolan's only reprimand. Dolan's excuse for every tardiness, which he would tell with a straight face even when surrounded by clocks, was that he didn't have a watch.

Goon 4 was still at work when Adelle turned in at the meandering, crushed rock drive to the manor. The pole had been erected, and he was mixing the last of the cement needed to fill its hole. She waved at him, and as usual she was ignored. She walked on, maintaining a steady pace until she abruptly emerged from the trees that screened the manor from the road. There she halted. The building was a familiar sight to her by now, but she always stopped to admire it.

It seemed to sprawl endlessly, with bulging wings in a conglomerate of architectural styles and materials that was at once breathtaking and hilarious. Oddly enough, there seemed to be a weird kind of logic about it. Only when one considered that this building was also the editorial and production headquarters of Z-R Publications did it become preposterous.

The south wing, on the left, was a miniature Gothic cathedral, complete with flying buttresses. The large portico was from ancient Greece, a miniature Parthenon complete with sculptured friezes, but its imposing effect had been spoiled somewhat by the insect screening that had been added between the fluted shafts. Behind the portico, the upper story's facade could have been lifted intact from Shakespeare's Tudor Stratford. The wing beyond was imitation Georgian.

The same hodgepodge continued all around the building, with incongruities at the sides and rear that Adelle was still discovering. On her first puzzled glimpse of it, the structure had seemed like a montage of illustrations from a textbook on the history of architecture. She learned later that it actually was a textbook. The strange, extremely wealthy professor of architecture who created it, Adolph Feinstwaller, intended it to illustrate different types and styles of buildings and their construction problems. The project was a lifelong obsession with him. There always was one more wing and one more interior to design, and in the end it became an architect's dream turned nightmare.

Adelle usually brought her lunch from her apartment, and on pleasant days she ate it in a neatly kept French jardin from which she could look at a miniature palace of Versailles on one side and the simple beauty of the Romanesque wing on the other. While she ate, she wondered about the builder—whether he was genius or crackpot to sink a fortune into such a monstrous mutation and whether he had accomplished what he wanted and got his money's worth. Probably the fun had been more in the doing of it than in having done it, the traveling hopefully rather than arriving, which was why he continued to add wings as long as he lived.

Adelle had no idea what his heirs had made or tried to make of such a white elephant, or how Z-R Publications came to locate there. If the firm flourished as Madam predicted, the stained glass, the fan and ribbed vaultings, the bay and oriel windows, the linenfold and fielded and sunken panels, the hammerbeam roofs, the sculpture ornamented domes and cupolas, the hard carved balustrades, and all the rest were forever doomed to look down on humming and purring and clanking business machines and offset presses. Even a crackpot's dream, she thought, deserved a better fate.

But even if this gloomy future was not irrevocable, Adelle still had the uneasy foreboding that something was very wrong about Z-R Publications.

CHAPTER 2

At ten minutes before one o'clock, Adelle seated herself at her desk to begin a new page of statistics. She was being extravagantly overpaid. Giving Z-R Publications a generous measure of whatever it was they thought they were paying her for was the least she could do in return.

Madam's cheerful voice sounded in the hallway as she tiptoed past Adelle's open door. "Back at it already, Darlink? Those pants look nice."

Adelle waved without looking up. Apparently Madam had never seen a pants suit before, and she was still grappling with the idea of a dressed up woman in trousers. Her blank expression when Adelle walked in that morning—wearing the first new outfit she had bought in more than a year—was a memory to be cherished.

She typed one seven-digit number and paused to frown at the next. The copy was in pencil, and the figures had been corrected without erasing—an eight changed to a six, she thought, followed by a five corrected to a three or vice versa.

She glanced at her watch and then picked up the copy. When she stepped into the hallway, she caught sight of Goon 1 vanishing around a corner. Smiling, she headed in the opposite direction, descended the hanging staircase, and turned away from the main corridor toward the sound of splashing water.

At the end of a short intersecting hallway, a massive door stood ajar. Beyond it, the oversized opening had been screened around the framing of a normal-sized screen door. Adelle emerged in a small courtyard surrounded by a stone-faced gothic exterior. The fountain was a hideous gargoyle on the wall that spat a stream of water into an equally hideous sculpture whose mouth served as a basin. On a stone bench in one corner, knees drawn up and clasped, placidly puffing on a cigarette, was Kevin Mondor.

He was slender, dark, clean-shaven, and dressy-looking—he always wore a sport jacket and tie to work—and ridiculously finicky about his appearance. One of Craig Dolan's insults, told to Madam as coming from Adelle, was that Mondor pressed his own permanent press slacks each night. Mondor also had his hair cut weekly, but for some reason he left it long in front to tumble down over his face. His thick glasses were an indication of the havoc that could be wreaked on one's eyesight by a lifelong fascination with mathematics. The lenses gave his brown eyes a perpetual wildly-staring look. In any rational organization, his title of Researcher/Statistician would have ranked him far above Adelle in both status and salary. At Z-R Publications, there was no status, and their salaries were the same. He was the senior member of the production staff—he had been employed three weeks longer than Adelle and two weeks longer than Craig Dolan.

Adelle preferred the French jardin for her lunch hour. Mondor favored this medieval courtyard, and though he never brought his lunch from home, he came here daily the moment he returned from The Greenry. Perhaps the surroundings put him in mind of a happier age when mathematics had not yet got cluttered up with computers and pocket calculators.

She thrust the copy under his nose. "Pity they don't teach mathematics students to write legible numerals," she said.

"Pity they don't teach liberal arts students to read them," he answered without looking up. He exhaled a cloud of smoke.

"Well—what is it?" she demanded. "I'm assuming the first numeral is a six. Is the next one a five or a three?"

Mondor studied the page for a moment. "Yes," he answered.

"Yes, what?"

"It's a five or a three. I'll check after the lunch hour."

"It's after the lunch hour."

He turned her wrist so he could see her watch. "I have two more minutes."

"Why don't you get your watch fixed?" she asked disgustedly. "You're as bad as Dolan."

"I resent that insult. At least I own a watch, even if it doesn't run, and I keep it in a safe place at home. I have a high regard for anything involving numbers. But who needs a timepiece in this building? There are clocks striking everywhere." He settled back to enjoy his two minutes. "I never thought I'd learn to hate an Eighteenth Century drawing room. But then, I never expected to work in one. What's the hurry? Dolan's always late, and no one says anything. It isn't as though we have a deadline."

"How do you know?" she asked.

He flipped the cigarette in the direction of the fountain and missed. "Tell me honestly," he said, lowering his voice. "Don't you think there's something loony about this place?"

"Everything is loony about it, including the building."

"There's an explanation for the building," he said, still keeping his voice low. "Granted the explanation is loony, too, but the building has been here for a long time, and looniness half-a-century old has a certain patina. Z-R Publications and its alleged books are unequivocally loony. Does anyone really care how many refrigerators were sold in Istanbul in 1981 or how many automobiles were sold in Algiers in this year or that?"

"Manufacturers and exporters ought to."

Mondor shook his head. "No. They care about how many they can sell next year, which may have no connection whatsoever with 1981. And they have local contacts of their own who no doubt are capable of giving them all the past statistics and future prognostications they want. I figure Z-R Publications is going to sell a maximum fifty copies per book to the sales departments of giant corporations that can afford to buy things and not use them. Is it loony, or isn't it?"

"Loony or not, I'm going to take the money as long as it's offered."

"Aren't we all? But I prefer a job that makes sense. There's something about this setup I can't get a grip on. Loony isn't quite the word for it. I'd ask Dolan for a better one, but he'd have to look it up. Try 'sinister.' The way Madam snoops around gives me the creeps. Does she go through your stuff during the noon hour?"

"Is it Madam? I thought it might be my pet Goon 1. Is Goon 3 still spying on you?"

"Goon 3 or Goon 4. I think they change off on me."

"On my first day here, I learned to take my purse when I go to lunch," Adelle said.

"Was anything missing?"

"No. But things couldn't have been stirred more thoroughly with an egg beater. That's why I thought it was a man. Men think all women's purses are miniature trash containers and any amount of pawing won't be noticed. I keep mine organized." She glanced at her watch. "You're a fraud. You can't hear clocks striking out here. It is now one minute after the lunch hour."

"I worked three minutes overtime this morning." Mondor transferred his gaze to the fountain and resumed his speculation about looniness. "Would any sane management hire three such incompatible people as us? The girl you replaced was comparatively human. You're just an accessory to your computer. And look at that slob Dolan. I got along fine with the writers that worked here before him."

"Were they vegetarians?" Adelle asked maliciously.

"No, but they weren't slobs. Each one lasted a week. Then they hired him. And then they hired you. A writing slob and a word machine."

"To work with a calculating cad," Adelle suggested.

"If you say so," Mondor said imperturbably. "If we three had to occupy the same office, there'd be murder before the end of a week. We survive only because we work so far apart, but that's another thing that's loony. This setup would give an efficiency expert apoplexy." He got to his feet resignedly and turned off the fountain. "I'll call you about those figures."

She turned and went back into the building without waiting for him. Word machine, indeed! When she reached her office, the phone was ringing. She hurried to answer it.

"Six, three," Mondor said. "Did I muck up anything else?"

She glanced over the next six pages and told him most of the figures were half legible.

Craig Dolan came in a few minutes later, grinning broadly and waving some typewritten sheets of copy. Mondor had once said Dolan could pass for Santa Claus if the padding was moved from his head to his stomach, but this was an exaggeration on several counts. He was an inch or two taller than six feet and large framed, but thus far the beer that he drank had put very little fat on him—perhaps because he consumed so few calories from other sources. Adelle thought his twinkling blue eyes indicated malice rather than mischief, and if she had heard him exclaim, "Ho! Ho! Ho!" she would have looked quickly to see whose leg had just been broken. His blond beard was medium length and neatly trimmed, and he wore bushy sideburns and kept his hair long. His trousers and open sport shirt always looked in need of pressing and cleaning. With a protruding jaw, he could have posed in a museum's Neanderthal exhibit. Give Neanderthal Man long hair, a beard, sideburns, and sloppy modern dress, and—presto! Craig Dolan.

Gerald Wyman, the young man she had a date with, also had blond hair and blue eyes, and the contrast between him and Dolan had been a revelation to her. Because there had been so few men in her life, she was guilty of generalizing from insufficient evidence.

Dolan flourished the copy he was carrying. "Madam lost it. Then she insisted I'd never done it. I found it on her desk under umpteen dozen other things including that suitcase she calls a purse."

"Handbag," Adelle said. "I've never heard her call it a purse."

"It's certainly a bag," Dolan agreed. "Hand, overnight, weekend, nose—take your pick. For that matter, so is she. A bit unhinged, too. Have you talked with the nicotine fiend today?" Dolan, who didn't smoke, enjoyed razzing Mondor about his noon hour indulgence in a cigarette or two.

"Not willingly," Adelle said.

"No one talks with Mondor willingly. Did he give you his lecture about this setup being loony?"

"He did. And it is, isn't it?"

"Of course, but it isn't politic to say so. If he's right, our rooms probably are bugged."

"In that case, we ought to do our work and shut up," Adelle said politely. She took the copy from him. "I suppose this has to be done at once."

"It was supposed to be done yesterday, but I told Madam I didn't think you could manage that. 'Loony' is far too mild a word, but Mondor is only a Researcher/Statistician. Probably it was the best he could do."

"As I remember it, he also mentioned 'sinister.'"

"Then he's found a thesaurus since I talked with him. 'Sinister' comes closer. Why are we called researchers when none of us researches anything? Someone furnishes the figures Mondor does his statistical stuff on, and the notes I base my copy on, and when I need a stray fact I telephone Madam, and she calls me back and tells me. The goons must look things up for her in their spare time, of which they seem to have quite a lot. I'll swear she couldn't find a fact or anything else all by herself. But why call me a researcher, and pay me for it, when all I do is write? Why call you one when you don't do anything but massage a computer keyboard?"

"Future anticipation, maybe," Adelle said. "Why are the three of us spread all over the building? Maybe each of these wings is going to be a separate department."

"I hope you're right. A couple more weeks of this, and my paychecks will become a habit. The setup is loony and also sinister, and when I have time, I'll teach Mondor a few new words. On the other hand, Z-R Publications does show indications of actually intending to publish something. Madam just asked me what I thought of some offset pages of one of your lovely printouts."

"Really?" Adelle exclaimed. "Do the goons have a press to play with?"

"I think Madam had someone offset a few pages to see how your copy would look. It looks good. When you finish that stuff, give her a buzz."

"I'll do it as soon as I finish this page," Adelle promised.

Dolan pulled up a chair, a spindly item that looked much too small for his bulk and too fragile for his weight. "This place is double-phony," he said. "Have you noticed how the interior of every wing is in a different style from the exterior? Tell me this. Did Mondor ever try to date you?"

Adelle sat frowning at the copy he had brought. Who had tried to date her, Mondor or anyone else, certainly was none of Dolan's business. She said, "Of course. He's a normal male—lecherous and obnoxious."

"And you consider me abnormal?"

"Supernormal. Lecherous, obnoxious, and nauseating."

"But only in the presence of a two-legged refrigerator," Dolan grinned.

She shook her head. "Freezer. When you're around, any respectable refrigerator becomes one. Now if you don't mind—"

"Tell me why you hate men."

"I don't. That'd be silly. Why hate half the human race? It's just that at the moment I don't care to own one."

"One more question. Have you dated anyone at all since you came to Ann Arbor?"

Adelle smiled at him. She felt immensely grateful to Gerald Wyman, the nice young man in her apartment building. Thanks to his concert invitation, she could answer truthfully, "Of course I have."

Dolan stared at her for a moment. Then he got to his feet, returned the chair to its original position, and strode away. Adelle's smile broadened. In one afternoon she'd been called a word machine and a two-legged refrigerator. It made her day a double success.

Whether Z-R Publications was loony and sinister, or one or the other, or neither, she was being paid an extraordinary salary for a simple typing job, and she intended to work as enthusiastically as she could while it lasted and ask no questions. She finished the page of statistics. Then she typed Dolan's copy and telephoned Madam.

A short time later Madam tiptoed in, beaming with pride and bringing the offset pages to show to Adelle. Adelle agreed that they looked excellent. Madam complimented Adelle's typing, and Adelle generously gave the credit to her computer and printer, especially the printer, which produced even, crisp letters that looked very much like printed material.

"Those pants really are lovely, Darlink," Madam said. She took the copy and departed, tossing a last, superfluous "Darlink" over her shoulder as she went out the door. Adelle wearily returned to Mondor's statistics.

While she typed, she thought about the evening ahead of her: bath, book, and bed. Tomorrow, the visit to Greenfield Village. She was amused at the number of people she encountered who had lived in Southeastern Michigan all their lives and never seen it.

And then her Sunday date. She had met Gerald Wyman in the apartment building's laundry room, and they chatted while their laundry was being done. She enjoyed talking with him, and they seemed to have a great deal in common, but she was far too practical to spin a fantasy on the basis of half an hour's conversation. One date did not, as Dolan thought, constitute a relationship.

She began new columns of figures: Mondor's figures, based on information Z-R Publications had obtained from—where? There was indeed something peculiar about a company that lodged itself in such sumptuous surroundings, produced so little, and paid its employees with insane generosity. On the other hand, a new publisher had to expect to make a substantial outlay in order to get its first books into print, and Z-R Publications might be paying ridiculously low rent for the preposterous building it occupied. There couldn't be much commercial demand for a place like Feinstwaller Manor.

The one totally inexplicable item was their salaries. Adelle could think of no rationalization at all for them. She would have been willing and eager to work for less. So would hundreds of others.

The afternoon passed without further incident. When the grandfather clock in the hallway struck five, Adelle finished the page she was working on, saved her material, and copied it onto a backup disk. She filed the disk, covered her computer, picked up her purse and coat, and glanced around the room to make certain she hadn't inadvertently moved a chair out of line or committed some other trivial outrage to the pseudo-antique decor.

When she reached the stairway, she saw Goon 1 standing at the far end of the hallway. She called, "Did you want something?" For a moment she thought he was going to speak, but he turned and disappeared into a side hall.

"Oh, well—he works here, too." she said and shrugged.

At the massive front door, she paused to put on her coat and slip her purse strap over her shoulder. She was reaching for the door knob when she heard Madam's voice. "Darlink!"

Madam came hurrying toward her on tiptoe. "You look nice today, Darlink. Such a practical thing to wear!"

Adelle murmured her thanks for the fifth or sixth time and wondered if Madam were enthusiastic enough to imitate her. The sight of this odd little woman in a pants suit would be one to cherish.

"I need a folder, Darlink. The one on automobile tires. Would you get it for me? I know it's after hours, but—"

"Of course," Adelle said. "Where is it?"

"In the basement. Down the stairs, straight ahead, and there are some black filing cabinets against the far wall. It's in number two. Second from the left." Madam paused. "I can't remember which drawer. Sure you don't mind? I've got to have the figures ready for Add to start on next week. You're not in a hurry?"

"Not at all. Is the folder labeled, 'Tires'?"

"'Tires—Europe,'" Madam said. She sighed. "It's supposed to be. It ought to be. It's a folder that was used for something else, so the something else is crossed out and the 'Tires—Europe' is on the right hand side of the tab if someone hasn't messed it up. I'm sure it'll be easy to find. Second black filing cabinet from the left. 'Tires—Europe.'"

"I'll be back in a jiffy," Adelle promised.

She flipped the light switch and moved quickly down the basement stairs. It was an enormously deep basement, and Adelle didn't blame Madam not wanting to negotiate the long stairway with her worn heels. The scene at the bottom, with concrete pillars and cement block partitions, looked more like a parking garage than the basement of a mansion. There was nothing else visible in the lighted area except groups of filing cabinets in various colors.

But none of them were black. "Down the stairs and straight ahead" lay beyond the lighted area, and the dimness in that remote part of the enormous room was punctuated only by a single high, small window.

Adelle had been downstairs several times on errands but never to that part of the basement. She paused and looked about her. A metal pipe descended a concrete column and terminated in a box with two switches. The first turned off the lights behind her. She turned them on again and tried the second switch. Lights came on ahead of her, illuminating the basement to its far wall, and against it she saw the row of black four-drawer cabinets.

She walked forward confidently. "Second from the left," Madam had said. A folder with something crossed out and "Tires—Europe" on the right. If the drawers were full, finding one folder might take time.

They weren't full. The top drawer of the second cabinet felt empty as she began to pull it open, but she never saw its interior.

The floor dropped from under her. As she fell, she clutched wildly at the handle of the cabinet's drawer, but her grip had been too loose. It slipped through her fingers, and for an instant she fell into nothingness. Then she landed on a steep incline of smooth metal. Her feet hit first and instantly shot out from under her, and she fell backward with a thud that stunned her. She caught a glimpse of a trap door closing over her head as she slid rapidly down the incline into darkness.

CHAPTER 3

Adelle tried frantically to stop herself, but her elbows banged hollowly on metal and her hands clutched at emptiness. She shot downward, flat on her back and enfolded in darkness, until she skidded to a stop on a smooth cement floor. For a few moments she lay there idiotically worrying about her new pants suit. Then she decided she was fortunate to have worn it. In a dress, she probably would have lost skin.

Something above her head rattled and creaked. There was a faint, prolonged swish; then silence. Staring upward, she saw no crack of light to indicate where the trap had been. She got to her feet and felt about her blindly. A step forward, two steps—her hands encountered an obstacle, a smooth surface of metal that felt cold and gave off a solid whang when she thumped on it. She ran her hands along it, first sideways and then vertically. It was a wall. She turned in the opposite direction, and after four cautious steps she encountered another wall. She stood with her back against it trying to figure out what had happened.

She knew there was no point in calling for help. Madam was two stories above her, and the fact that the lights had been out in the basement meant all of the goons were elsewhere. If one of them had been available, Madam wouldn't have sent Adelle after the folder.

She seated herself on the hard, cold floor, embraced her knees, and thought furiously. She had been given precise instructions for finding a folder on tires. That meant someone had put the folder in the cabinet— but no one could have done that without stepping on the trap, just as no one could remove it without stepping on the trap.

The top drawer, at least, had seemed empty.

"Something," she announced to herself, "is decidedly fishy, but the problem is how to get out."

She cautiously got to her feet. Her first thought was to find out where she was. Since it was too dark to see anything, the Braille system was the only tool available. She turned to her right and edged forward, hands in front of her.

A dim light flickered on. She dropped her hands with a sigh of relief, but as she looked about her, she knew instantly that Mondor's words "loony" and "sinister" had been understatements. She was in a small room, perhaps six or seven feet square, with gray metal walls and ceiling. The tiny, recessed light at the center of the ceiling was no brighter than a night light, but she noticed at once that the ramp she arrived on had vanished. There was no opening in the walls or ceiling that she could have passed through, and that baffled her completely.

Each wall was in three sections, with braces reinforcing the seams. There was a horizontal reinforcement about six feet from the floor. The ceiling consisted of strips of riveted sheet metal. It was a bare room with a cement floor, but there was one remarkable feature: Above Adelle's head on three of the walls were incomplete, upside down baseball scoreboards. The inning numbers were in the bottom row instead of on top—white numerals, one through zero placed on square black protrusions about the size of her hand. Above each row of black squares was a row of bulging white squares. When the game started, she thought, the white squares would show the runs scored in each inning, but she had no idea why all three scoreboards had space for only one team.

She abandoned the scoreboards and gave the room another puzzled scrutiny. There was no possible way she could have entered it, but here she was. She must have passed through a wall or the ceiling, but she could see no trace of an opening.

She called out, "Hey! Anyone here?"

Her voice echoed thunderously in the metal room.

Suddenly one white square on each of the scoreboards—the square for the third inning—showed a brightly illuminated numeral three.

As Adelle stood looking bewilderedly from one scoreboard to another, the lighted squares went dark, and the white squares for the sixth inning showed brightly illuminated numeral sixes. They were followed by numeral nines in the ninth inning squares. Then the threes came on again and went out; the sixes, out; the nines, out. Pause. Threes, out; sixes, out; nines, out.

"I can do even better than that," Adelle announced caustically. "Twelve, fifteen, eighteen, twenty-one, twenty-four."

The pattern kept repeating: threes, out; sixes, out; nines, out.

She walked over to one wall and looked up at the scoreboard. The numbered black squares in the lower row looked like control buttons similar to those found on many electronic devices. Adelle reached up and punched them in turn as the numerals in the upper row lighted: three, six, nine.

The ceiling light went out. The lighted numerals faded. For a moment she stood blinking in darkness. Then, with a sustained swish, a section of wall below one of the the horizontal supports slowly sank into the floor. Beyond it was a well-lighted passageway the same width as the room, with gray metal walls and a high ceiling of translucent squares that glowed with light. It was an explosion of illumination, and Adelle had to shade her eyes as she sprang through the opening.

She heard another sustained swish. The doorway was closing after her.

When her eyes became adjusted to the flood of light, she looked about her. The metal walls were similar to those of the room she had just emerged from. At the foot of each wall, at regular intervals, steel brackets were bolted to the unpainted cement floor. At longer intervals, grooves on opposite sides of the corridor ran all the way to the top of the walls, and they were connected by inch-wide strips of black rubber or plastic material that crossed the cement floor from one side of the corridor to the other.

None of this signified anything at all to her. "So where am I?" she demanded. "And why?"

She thought she heard a subdued murmur of talk coming from somewhere. She called out, "Is anyone here?"

A response echoed along the passageway, faint but understandable. "Is that you, Adelle?" It was Craig Dolan. She called back sarcastically, "No. It's Dracula's mother."

"You could be, at that. Come and join us."

She walked toward the distant end of the corridor. Before she reached it, she saw an opening on the left that led into an even longer corridor, identical to the other except for length. She called, got another response, and turned. At the end of that corridor she found yet another opening on the left; and, after a short distance, another. A dozen more steps, and she stopped to stare through an opening on her right. She was looking into a narrow kitchen where Dolan and Mondor sat at a small table. Dolan was tilting a can of beer. Mondor, who had his back to her, clutched a can of his own with both hands and leaned forward as though praying over it.

After the long succession of identical blank walls, this was too much detail to take in with one glance. Adelle found herself speechless.

Dolan set his can down, carefully wiped foam from his beard with a paper towel he was using for a napkin, and grinned at her. "So they suckered you, too."

Mondor spoke gloomily without looking around. "We figured you'd be along. Pull up a chair." He waved at one that stood against the wall.

Still too astonished to speak, Adelle slumped into it. Suddenly she turned toward the stove and sniffed.

"I'm broiling some steaks," Dolan explained. "I found a package of three in the refrigerator, which is why we thought someone would be joining us. They look pretty good."

Whatever the peculiarities of their situation, Dolan seemed expansive, perfectly relaxed, a man who had been caught up in adversity all of his life and took it for granted. He sipped beer again, wiped his beard, and grinned across the table at Mondor.

Mondor had not looked up since Adelle arrived. He remained hunched over the clutched can, lips set in a firm line, hair disheveled, his manner that of a mourner at a funeral he would have preferred not to attend.

Adelle remarked disbelievingly, "The pure food addict and vegetarian is drinking beer and eating steak?"

"When a great mathematician gets bamboozled by a kindergarten trick, it breaks his spirit," Dolan said, grinning again. Mondor grunted. Dolan went on, "Madam told him the firm had bought a computer for him to use. She invited him to help unpack it. Naturally he couldn't resist a computer, so he blunderingly galloped to her assistance and fell through the floor. After that brilliant display of stupidity, it wasn't difficult to convince him that brain cells need meat occasionally to keep their clutches from slipping. Anyway, there aren't enough vegetables to make up a meal. He drew the line at the beer, though—that's Red Pop he's drinking."

Mondor grunted again and raised his can.

"Stupidity's the word," Adelle agreed. "What would Z-R Publications want with another computer when it has him? What bamboozled you?"

"Madam asked me to help a goon unload their panel truck. Reasonable request, considering what she's been paying me. I carried some boxes down to the basement, put them on a shelf, and suddenly I wasn't there any more."

"You should have been suspicious. Madam may be half blind, but the goons aren't, and they'd know you couldn't perform manual labor without getting your beard tangled in it. How long ago did this happen?"

"About four o'clock. Mondor took his dive about four-thirty—he says. What time is it now?"

Adelle looked at her watch. "Almost five-thirty."

"What's your excuse for being stupid?" Mondor demanded.

"Madam sent me to the basement to get a folder on tires. I marched up to a filing cabinet, opened one of the drawers, and the floor dropped away."

Dolan nodded gravely and drained his beer can. "Sounds almost reasonable. You couldn't expect Madam to tiptoe down the basement stairs for a folder, and it wouldn't have been polite—or politic—to tell the boss to shove it when she asked you to perform a simple errand."

"Face it," Mondor said bitterly. "All three of us were conned from the moment we were hired—first by the money they were paying us, second by the stupid work we were pretending to do to earn it, and third by the flimflam they pulled to get us down here. If they'd told you to go look at a computer and help unpack the thing, you'd have gone. My thirty-five dollar calculator is far too sophisticated for the work I've been doing, but it didn't surprise me in the least that a screwy outfit like Z-R Publications would invest in a computer for me." He raised his can and drank deeply. Then he turned to Adelle. "How long did it take you to solve the psychological test?"

"Psychological test?" she echoed blankly.

"Didn't they dump you into a room with rows of numbers and response buttons?"

"Oh, that. Is that what it was? I was curious about the buttons, so I pushed three of them, and a door opened."

Mondor turned his chair sideways and regarded her with astonishment. "You were curious about the buttons, so you pushed three of them. In order to get out of there, you had to push the numbers they were flashing in the correct sequence. Didn't you figure that out?"

"I didn't figure anything out. I just pushed the buttons under the lighted numbers without thinking."

Mondor tossed his head back and roared with laughter. "You've wrecked their experiment! You've utterly demolished it! You've shattered all of their scientific calibrations! You were supposed to figure it out!"

"Why?" Adelle asked.

"Good question. The goons probably are asking themselves the same thing. I hope someone will have to sit up all night working out an answer." He waved a hand. "Have a look around. Get acquainted with your home away from home."

"Thanks, Adelle said, "but no, thanks. I don't need a home away from home. I don't want dinner, either, even if it is a steak. I'd rather eat at home. So why don't we do something about getting out of here."

"We'd all rather eat at home," Mondor said morosely. "It's my night to savor my landlady's vegetarian cuisine. Every Friday she fixes an absolutely remarkable vegetarian meal for the two of us, and then I give her a lesson in bookkeeping. She's a harpy of a person and an absolute dunce of a bookkeeper, but neither Heifetz, nor Perlman, nor anyone else ever played the violin half as well as she performs in the kitchen. I've been looking forward to that meal all day. Instead, I'm stuck with Dolan's steaks. Heaven to hell in one move, and unless you have a miracle up your sleeve, this is where we're going to eat."

"Madam is waiting for me at the top of the stairs. Surely she'll send someone—" Adelle broke off. Mondor was shaking his head forebodingly.

"Goons saw both of us hit the chutes," he said. "Almost an hour and a half ago for Dolan and an hour ago for me. If they'd wanted us out, we'd be out. It isn't as though we'd tumbled into an unknown pit in the middle of a jungle with no witnesses. This is just a sub-basement, and they know exactly where we are. Have a look at the setup. Go ahead. Everything in the place is in threes—three beds, three chairs, three table settings. There's food for dinner and breakfast for three people. Whoever furnished and supplied this place expected three guests. Go ahead, have a look. Then you tell us whether we're likely to get home for dinner."

Adelle got to her feet and looked about her. On one side, the narrow kitchen contained an electric stove, a refrigerator, a sink, and a full complement of cupboards. The blank wall opposite, of the same gray metal she had encountered in the corridors, had four openings.

She squeezed past the table and went to investigate.

Three of the openings led into small rooms that were just deep enough to contain narrow beds. Each bed was made up with sheets, one thin blanket, and a single, miniature pillow. On the wall opposite was a row of hooks. Gray plastic curtains that slid across the openings on rods provided a smidgeon of privacy.

The last of the openings, at the far end of the kitchen, led into a room that contained a toilet and a lavatory. Its entrance was curtained like those of the bedrooms. Beyond the kitchen was a corridor identical to those she had already traveled. She turned. Dolan was getting a can of beer and one of pop from the refrigerator. "Where does this lead to?" she asked.

"More corridors," he said.

"Alleys," Mondor corrected sharply.

"Corridors, passageways, call them what you like," Dolan said. "Mondor thinks we should call them alleys. We're in the middle of a maze, a fact he and I discovered by trying to find a way out. After we'd explored a series of dead ends and nearly lost ourselves, we decided to have dinner and think the whole thing over."

Adelle squeezed past the table again and returned to her chair. "And what have you concluded?"

"I've concluded that Mondor once took a college course in which mazes were mentioned. He passed it by learning to say 'alley' instead of 'corridor.' I don't know what he's concluded. He hasn't been his obnoxious self since he got duped by that nonexistent computer."

"There isn't any way out," Mondor said gloomily. "That's what I've concluded. On the side where we landed, the alleys lead directly to this place. The only exit would be through the ceiling, which we have no way of reaching, and we probably couldn't find the traps if we did. The other side is a labyrinth. There's no way out there, either."

"Don't labyrinths have exits?" Adelle asked.

"Only when the builder wants them to," Mondor said.

Dolan set his beer can down with a thump. "As our mathematician has already pointed out, we have three bedrooms, three chairs, three everything, with food supplied for three people. Therefore Madam and her goons intend to keep us down here at least until after breakfast tomorrow. Since they've already made that decision, and gone to considerable trouble and expense to implement it, Mondor thinks it unlikely that they'd absent-mindedly leave us a running escalator marked 'Exit.' He reached that abstruse conclusion all by himself. Aren't we lucky he can count to three?"

"Crap on your counting!" Mondor exploded. "The moment I realized I'd been dropped into some kind of psychological hell, I knew I'd find Dolan here."

Adelle got up, squeezed past the table again, and began opening cupboards. A large bowl was filled with foil and paper containers of the type dispensed by airlines and fast-food restaurants. There was coffee, sugar, tea bags, chocolate, powdered non-dairy creamer, salt, pepper, mustard, ketchup, steak sauce. There was a small box of dehydrated potatoes and a foil container of gravy mix—enough of each, she reflected, for about three people. There were three individually boxed servings of breakfast cereal.

In a lower cabinet, behind a roll of paper towels and a plastic container of dish washing detergent, she saw a box of sanitary napkins. Someone certainly was planning on their staying and had thought of everything.

But the scantness of the food seemed puzzling. She turned to examine the contents of the refrigerator. In the freezer compartment, she found a package of mixed vegetables and a fruit pie. Presumably the steaks had been in the meat container, which now held only a pound of bacon. The other items were a quart carton of milk, a dozen eggs, and numerous cans of beer and pop. They had adequate food for dinner and breakfast but virtually nothing for subsequent meals.

In the cabinet under the sink there was an enormous reserve of beer and soft drinks along with more kinds of alcoholic beverages than Adelle had ever seen outside a liquor store.

She entered the end bedroom, the one farthest from the toilet, and hung her coat on one of the hooks. She tossed her purse onto the bed. Then she returned to the kitchen and sat down.

She remarked, "Kevin is right. Someone planned this carefully and invested a lot of time and money on it. Why? What do they want with us?"

Dolan spoke to Mondor. "You've been saying there's something loony or sinister about Z-R Publications. Did you suspect anything like this?"

"Would I have hung around if I did?"

"No," Dolan agreed. "It was a silly question. Adelle's was better. What do they want with us? What's the point? In a sense, all three of us have been kidnapped. Surely they aren't holding me for ransom. The only money I have is what's left of the salary they've been paying me, and why pay it in the first place if they want it that badly?"

Mondor gestured at their surroundings. "Whoever arranged this setup had an unlimited budget. Even if the sub-basement was part of the original building, installing an automated maze with a fancy complication like that psychological testing room was a huge expense. If they had to dig the basement under another basement without disturbing the building's foundations and supports, it cost a fortune."

"I think the sub-basement was part of the original building," Dolan reflected. "The excavation for it, anyway. It'd be difficult to surreptitiously put a basement under a basement, especially one this big. I mean, what do you do with the dirt? There'd be truck loads and truck loads of it. If Mondor had his pocket calculator, he'd tell us how many cubic yards they'd have to remove. Sooner or later someone would get curious about where it was coming from, and whoever is responsible for this caper certainly didn't want to arouse anyone's curiosity. The bartender at Barney's says there are old rumors about secret rooms and passageways and stairways in this place, so a secret basement is no surprise, but they probably added the maze themselves. I mean—if you're building a cage to keep kidnap victims in, you don't hire your work force out of the Yellow Pages or use union labor."

"The goons?" Mondor suggested.

"Why not? They're certainly in on it. But it took more than five people to do all this work, and most if not all of it was done long before we were hired. Question. If, for some extremely subtle reason I can't comprehend, they went to all this trouble just for the three of us, why didn't they sucker us Adelle's first day on the job and save the three weeks' salary they've paid us since then? Or—to take a better question—why didn't they do it my first day, with the typist they had when I came here? Or on Mondor's first day, with the typist and writer they had then? Was it because this setup wasn't finished? In that case, why hire anyone at all until they were ready? Nothing about this makes sense."

"The writer they had when they hired me had been here one week," Mondor said. "They fired him at the end of his second week and hired another. They hired a word processor when they hired me, and the two of us replaced people they fired. There may have been others before them. Why didn't they kidnap three of them? You're right—this makes no sense from any angle. But nothing about Z-R Publications has ever made any sense."

"I wonder," Adelle said.

"You wonder what?" Dolan demanded.

"I wonder if this doesn't make sense. I think Madam's flea-brained mannerisms were carefully calculated to cover up a frighteningly cold logic, and everything about Z-R Publications has had a purpose."

"I suppose Madam had a perfectly sensible reason for giving us those ridiculous jobs and paying us inflated wages," Dolan said.

"Of course she did. Just because we don't know what it was doesn't mean there wasn't one."

Dolan turned to Mondor. "We're fortunate to have such a brilliant Researcher/Word Processor. Now listen carefully, and she'll explain what we're doing down here."

"Obviously Madam wanted people who met certain requirements," Adelle said impatiently. "She kept hiring and firing until she found them, and she didn't sucker us my first day on the job because she wanted to make certain I was the person—all three of us were the persons—who met her requirements. Now she's certain, and here we are. What other reason could there be? As for what the requirements were, and why they put us down here—I wouldn't want to solve all the problems and leave you two sitting there with your brilliant minds running in neutral."

Dolan sipped his beer and carefully preened his beard. Mondor hunched over his can of pop and let his hair flop forward again.

"Touche'," Dolan said finally. "The girl has a point. They kept trying different combinations of people until they got the three they wanted, and we were the lucky winners. They paid us inflated wages to make certain we'd stick around, no matter how imbecilic the jobs seemed, until they were sure they had the right combination."

He again sipped beer. "What a devastating development this is! I was stupidly thinking they valued me for my writing talent. Before I came to Ann Arbor, I always avoided jobs involving writing, and I refused to write anything at all merely for money. Just once, when I needed cash desperately, I managed to convince myself that an integrity as noble as mine could survive the sale of a few stories to the crassly commercial fiction markets. It was as though an ugly, frigid woman were to decide that turning a trick or two in a time of dire financial necessity wouldn't make her a whore. The fiction markets' lack of interest in my virtue was total, whether I was willing to prostitute myself or not."

"So how did you justify prostituting yourself with Z-R Publications?" Mondor asked.

"My motives were pure. I only intended to work long enough to earn the money I needed to drive back to Chicago. The job was a revelation. I found to my surprise that with very little effort I can turn out expository prose that's a model of clarity. I don't even have to put my mind in gear to do it. I was afraid it would sap my creative energy, but I've been able to work evenings on my novel and fatten my bank balance during the day. This is the first time I've ever held a job for four consecutive weeks. Now it's gone. So are those huge paychecks. Regardless of what happens, I'm sure none of us will ever work for Z-R Publications again." He shrugged resignedly. "What were we talking about?"

"Why they chose us," Adelle said. "I know one of their requirements. They wanted three people who didn't like each other. Look how Madam tiptoed around trying to stir up trouble between us with her malicious gossip."

"Right on," Dolan agreed. "Would you like some beer?"

"No, thanks," Adelle said. "Beer short circuits the brain's power supply, and you're the horrible example that proves it. I'll stick to pop."

"Assorted flavors in the refrigerator," Dolan said, gesturing. "Help yourself. I'm a firm believer in Women's Lib. Did you notice the reserve stock under the sink? Along with the wine, scotch, bourbon, vodka, gin, and several liqueurs? They didn't leave us much food, but they certainly provided for drowning our sorrows."

Adelle went to the refrigerator. Dolan got up and turned on the oven light to inspect the steaks. As Adelle opened her can of cola, he said to her, "How about making like a domestic female and adding something to our dinner?"

She stared at him—not from resentment, since he was broiling the steaks, but because the situation was so unreal. She should have been home by this time even if traffic was unusually heavy. She probably wouldn't have felt like cooking—she usually didn't. Right now she would be putting a frozen TV dinner or pizza in the microwave. Then bath, book, and bed. Instead, she had this.

She sipped her pop for a moment. Then she went to the refrigerator, and from the freezer compartment she took the package of frozen vegetables and the pie. The pie she put into the oven in its aluminum container. She searched for cooking utensils, found a saucepan, and measured water into it for the vegetables. After looking through the cupboards again, she announced the menu.

"Steak, mixed vegetables, synthetic mashed potatoes with synthetic gravy, blueberry pie for desert. With instant coffee, tea, or cocoa. If either of you prefers creamer with your coffee, that's synthetic, too. Or you can have fresh milk."

Dolan was back at the table sipping beer. "It falls a bit short of being a feast," he observed, "but it could be much worse."

"It probably will be before they're through with us," Mondor said gloomily.

"Thanks for those cheerful words," Adelle told him. "As a reward—if we're really stuck here—you can get breakfast."

"You'll be sorry," Mondor said. He tilted his chair back, held his can of pop in front of him, gazed at it through his drooping hair as though it were a crystal ball, and directed a question at the universe. "Just what the devil are they trying to do?"

CHAPTER 4

Adelle pushed her coffee cup aside and leaned back with her eyes closed. Her grandmother, her mother's mother—of blessed memory—had preached devoutly that every dark night had, somewhere, a glowing candle, every cloud a silver lining, it was always darkest just before the dawn, good luck followed bad, providence rewarded the deserving. Adelle felt deserving enough not to have deserved this, but she had her suspicions about Mondor and Dolan.

They were arguing about mazes—open mazes, T and Y mazes, linear and circular mazes, spatial and temporal mazes. All it proved to Adelle was that Mondor had an excellent retentive memory for obscure information, and she already knew that. Also, that Dolan considered ignorance no handicap in an argument, and she already knew that, too. The pair of them made an odd study in contrasts: Dolan robust, blond, blue-eyed, heavily bearded; Mondor slight, clean-shaven, with dark complexion and dark hair and eyes. Mondor argued defensively, searching his memory for facts. Dolan argued for the fun of it, playing tricks with words.

Adelle turned her thoughts to her plans for the weekend. Bath, book, and bed. Tomorrow, Greenfield Village. Sunday, her date. These two asses were going to argue interminably while she missed all of it.

During one of their infrequent lulls, she remarked absently, "I hope this place doesn't have fleas." Dolan turned a frowning, bearded, side-burned face in her direction. "I'm thinking of the amount of acreage you'd be providing for a playground," she went on. "Why don't you two exercise your minds on something worthwhile?"

"I suppose a discussion of ways to get out of this hole isn't worthwhile," Dolan said indignantly.

"Nonsense. You're arguing about the theory of mazes, which may have nothing to do with the maze we're caught in. This one could be a conglomeration or something unique. And you're talking about mazes used for scientific experiments where there's a way in and a way out. What if the only exit is through the ceiling? Wouldn't it be more useful to figure out why we're here? If we knew that, we'd have some notion of our chances of getting out and maybe even how to go about it. Why is it that no matter how bright a man is, he has to assert his masculinity by acting stupid?"

The two men were glaring at her. "Have you got a sister?" Dolan demanded.

"No, and I wouldn't introduce you if I had."

"I merely wanted to make certain the world has only one of you. If you could find it possible to assert your femininity without arching your back and spitting—"

"Just a moment," Mondor said. He turned to Adelle. "Brothers?"

She resisted the temptation to ask him if he wanted a date. "None. Thank God."

"Mother or father living?"

"Neither. Would you like a sketch of my family tree?"

"Just a few branches. Any close relatives living?"

She shook her head.

"And you recently moved to Michigan?"

"I arrived here the day before I got my job," Adelle said. "It was the first one I applied for. Anything else you want me to confess?"

"How many friends or close acquaintances do you have in Ann Arbor?"

"One, a student at the University, but she's gone home for the summer. I came here because she told me how easy it would be to find work."

"What about all those dates?" Dolan growled.

"Since when does a date have to be a friend or an acquaintance?" Adelle asked sweetly.

"So you're a pickup," Dolan said disgustedly.

"Quiet!" Mondor snapped irritably. "This is serious and maybe even important. Same questions for you."

"Roughly the same answers. I came to Ann Arbor a month and a half ago to visit a friend, a fellow named Ed Smolett. I had just enough money for gas to get me here. I lived with my friend and did a few odd jobs, mostly manual labor, so I could pay my share of the beer bill and buy typing paper. Ed and I got along well, but he had a few irritating habits. One of them was to ceremoniously read the day's 'help wanted' ads to a jobless friend. 'Look here, Craig,' he would say. 'Starting salary thirty-eight thousand. All you need is five years' experience and a master's degree in civil engineering.' One night he chanced to see the Z-R Publications ad, and he twisted my arm until I agreed to apply. Both of us were shocked when I got the job. Then he committed matrimony and moved to Cleveland, and I took over his apartment. I spend my free time working on my novel. The few acquaintances I have, male and female, are of the beer-talk variety. I see them at the Boheme and a few other places, but I don't go out regularly, and I don't always see the same people when I do. Also, I don't even know the names of most of them, and they probably don't know mine."

"No relatives?" Mondor persisted. "No close friends at all?"

"Just the one who moved to Cleveland. Otherwise, only beer-talk acquaintances."

"Are both of you living alone?"

Adelle and Dolan nodded.

"My answers are similar," Mondor said. "No relatives, no close friends, few acquaintances. And I live alone. I came here from Nebraska to attend the University of Michigan, and the few friends I had moved on when we graduated. The one person I know well is my landlady, and that's only because we're both vegetarians and she wanted bookkeeping lessons. Right now she's probably cursing me over a warmed-up gourmet vegetarian feast. Except for her, no one will miss me if I don't go home tonight, or tomorrow, or next week. How about you two?"

Dolan gestured expansively. "It pains me to admit it, but if I fail to see the light of day again, the world will never know what it's lost. My friend in Cleveland is much too preoccupied with his new wife to waste time wondering what's happened to me. Even if he found out I was missing, he'd just assume I'd got restless and hit the road again and eventually he'll get a postcard from somewhere."

Adelle said, "I have a date with a young man in my apartment building to attend a concert on Sunday. If I stand him up, he'll wonder why."

"How long have you known him?" Mondor asked.

Adelle reflected. "I've seen him almost every day since I moved in—to say hello and mention the weather. I just got acquainted with him yesterday."

"Pickup," Dolan muttered.

"Would he be likely to go to the police because a girl stood him up?" Mondor asked.

"I wouldn't think so," Adelle said. "He'd probably draw a few apt conclusions about my character and let it go at that."

"The same applies to my landlady. She'll be furious about my not showing for dinner, and I don't blame her. But the most drastic action she's likely to take is to carefully rehearse a speech telling me off for not letting her know." He asked Dolan, "Will anyone let the police know you're missing?"

"No way," Dolan said. "It won't even be noticed, let alone reported."

"I think that's another reason we were chosen. All of your predecessors were kept for one week or at most two—just long enough for a thorough investigation—and then fired. There was a word processor who lived with her girl friend and a writer who lived in a co-op. Both of them would have been missed immediately. I must have fit the pattern they wanted, so they kept me while they hired and fired writers and word processors until they found two that matched me. Even so, they've moved carefully. It's been three weeks since they hired Adelle."

"Score one for Adelle's devastating female intuition," Dolan said with a grin and a half bow in her direction. "They wanted people who met certain requirements. When I was hired, I was living with the friend I mentioned, but he'd already made plans to move to Cleveland and get married. They didn't have to do much investigating to find out I'd soon be living by myself."

"They're being stupid if they think we're all alone in the world," Adelle said confidently. "We have landlords and landladies, and rent that comes due, and next-door neighbors who know something of our habits—" She broke off because she wasn't convincing herself. If her neighbors missed her, which was unlikely, they would think she was gone for the weekend. The landlord would respond to a missed rent payment with a reminder, and then a warning, and eventually with an eviction notice. She had no notion of how long it would take before anyone became aware that she had disappeared.

Dolan echoed her thoughts. "If your walls are thin enough for your neighbors to know anything about your habits, they'll be relieved that you're gone. If not, they'll never miss you. Anyway, on Monday morning, Madam herself will report us missing. I'd bet on it. She'll say it seems puzzling that three employees as punctual and reliable as us would neither show up nor telephone. Can't you hear her telling a detective, 'It seems so peculiar, Darlink!' Of course Madam and all five of the goons will claim they saw us leave work today promptly at five o'clock. They'll tell the police we were lined up at the door in sprinters' crouches waiting for one of the many clocks to strike so we could dash out and spend our paychecks."

"Our cars!" Adelle exclaimed. "They'll still be in the parking lot!"

"Oh, Christ, don't be so innocent," Dolan said impatiently. "You don't need keys to drive a car. They've probably been hidden already, and tonight they'll be abandoned in three different states just to give the police something to think about."

"Or peddled to a dealer in stolen cars who'll make them disappear completely," Mondor said.

"No dealer in stolen cars would have my heap as a gift," Dolan said with a grin. "Mine, at least, will be abandoned a couple of states away if they can make it run that far." He drained his beer can and slammed it down. "Whatever they're planning for us, I hope it includes restocking the refrigerator. I wonder if they'll give us steak every day." He took a deep breath and patted his stomach. "It was a good dinner. The dehydrated potatoes tasted like dehydrated potatoes, but that wasn't Adelle's fault. Who does dishes?"

"The cooks," Adelle said firmly.

"Sounds unfair. I thought they'd included you just for the dishes."

But Dolan cleared the table with surprising docility and dried the dishes while Adelle washed them. He even cleaned the tray he had used to broil the steaks. Then, while Adelle seated herself again, he went to the refrigerator for another can of beer, cocked his head inquiringly at Mondor—who nodded—and tossed a can of pop past Adelle's ear. He returned to the table, opened his beer, and announced, "I have the feeling we should try to do something."

"What?" Mondor asked, sipping pop.

"My feelings don't convey that kind of message. But I definitely have the feeling we should try to do something. I'd feel exactly the same way if we were sitting on the edge of a volcano that was trying to erupt."

When the two men resumed their argument about mazes, Adelle decided to acquire some practical experience. She asked Mondor if he had any suggestions.

"A maze is just what the word implies," he said. "It can be awfully confusing. An animal is much better equipped than a human because it has a keen sense of smell and usually knows where it's been. For example, if you walk past a number of openings and don't count them or count your steps, you won't know which one to take when you return. An animal's sense of smell probably would tell it."

"Adelle won't have any trouble," Dolan said pleasantly. "She's an alley cat."

Adelle chose to ignore him. "Which way did you go?" she asked Mondor.

"Left."

"Then I'll go right."

Feeling like an intrepid explorer venturing into terra incognita, she went to the opening at the other end of the kitchen and turned right. It would be hilarious, she thought, if she found a way out when the men had merely got themselves lost. She walked confidently along the alley until she came to an opening on her left. It led into an alley that looked exactly like the one she stood in except for its shorter length: smooth cement floor, walls of gray metal containing grooves that had black strips of rubber or plastic crossing the floor between them, and a luminescent ceiling.

"Well, here goes," she told herself. "I'll soon find out whether I'm as smart as a rat."

She started off, carefully memorizing each alley she passed through. She made alternate left and right turns, always taking the last opening before the alley came to an end. In that way, she reasoned, she could tell at a glance whether she was making the correct turn on her way back. She walked for five minutes, for ten minutes, moving slowly, carefully plotting her route on a mental map so she could remember it as she passed through one identical-looking alley after another. When she decided she had inflicted enough strain on her memory, she turned back, and she was pleased to negotiate the first intersection with no trouble.

At the second, she knew at once that something had gone wrong. The end of the alley should have been on her immediate right when she turned into it, but it was twenty feet away. She cast about and checked two more turnings before she returned to her original choice. She knew it was correct. Could the maze have changed? How could anyone move a floor-to-ceiling partition twenty feet along the alley and bolt it into place that quickly and without making a sound?

She decided to ignore the shifted wall and trust her memory. At the next intersection, instead of the expected opening on her left, she found one on her right. Either she had made a fatal error, or the way back was blocked.

She told herself, "Don't panic! The important thing is to keep going in the right direction." And of course she couldn't call for help. She wouldn't give those two clods the satisfaction of knowing she was unable to walk around in a maze for a few minutes without getting lost. She continued along the alley until she found an intersection that led in the direction she thought she should be going.

But now all of the turnings were wrong, and though she tried to keep herself oriented, she became less and less certain of where she was.

"Keep calm!" she told herself. "It's only a maze in a lousy basement."

Suddenly she heard Dolan calling. "Adelle?"

His voice came from behind her. She didn't answer, but she turned and walked toward him.

"Adelle?" he called again, louder. "Hey! Where are you?"

He called a third time before she found the correct alley. He stood at the entrance to the kitchen looking in the direction she had gone. She was returning from the opposite direction. She had almost reached him when he turned and saw her.

"I thought you went the other way," he said with a scowl.

"I did," she told him.

"You mean you found your way all around this place and came back from the other side?"

She decided to be honest. They were in serious trouble, and they wouldn't get out of it by treating it like a parlor game. "Yes," she said, "but not intentionally. When I started back, nothing was the way I remembered it. I just kept walking in what I hoped was the right direction."

"The same thing happened to us."

"What's going on?" Mondor called from the kitchen.

"Adelle has learned how easy it is to get lost in a maze," Dolan said.

Mondor was still hunched over a can of pop. "It's damned easy," he said. "I told you—Dolan and I managed it in nothing flat. We didn't go far, and we thought we were keeping careful track of all the turns, but we almost didn't make it back here. Sit down. We need to talk about something."

Adelle seated herself, and Dolan dropped onto the other chair and leaned back to balance nonchalantly on its rear legs. "Our mathematical wizard has made a deduction," Dolan said. "From now on, we'll refer to him as the Voice of Doom. But he has a point, and I think you should hear it."

"Have you figured out why we're here?" Adelle asked.

"I'd rather not know," Mondor said. "That room with the numbers game—that was a psychological test. Mazes have something to do with psychology. Obviously we're being treated like psychological specimens, but I have no idea why. What I've been thinking about is how to get out."

"There's nothing gloomy about that," Adelle said. "It's a commendable exercise, and I'll even second it. How do we get out?"

"I'm afraid we don't."

Adelle turned to Dolan. "Have you two been cooking up jokes?"

Dolan shook his head. "He's serious. Let him finish."

Mondor squared around and brushed his hair away from his glasses. "It isn't just serious, it's deadly serious. Tell me—what's the first thing you'd do if you did get out? What's the first thing any of us would do?"

"Report this to the police," Adelle said promptly.

"Right. All three of us would relish the thought of seeing Madam and her goons in the dock with a judge about to pronounce sentence."

"What does that have to do with our finding a way out?" Adelle asked. Both Mondor and Dolan looked at her silently. "I see," she said finally. "If we do find a way out, it means big trouble for Madam and her goons."

"Right," Mondor said. "Probably they're the only ones who know about this place. Certainly all the entrances and exits are carefully concealed. No matter what they tricked us down here for, they're safe as long as we're here. But they can't afford to let us get away. You see—"

"Get on with it," Dolan said. "Point two."

"Yes. We probably aren't their first psychological specimens. They wouldn't go to the trouble and expense of constructing a place like this for one experiment, and it isn't brand new. There's a scorch mark on the counter top, and the sink is yellow where someone left a faucet dripping. Probably there's other evidence around. If we aren't the first, why didn't the others go to the police? If just one person did, this place would become public knowledge, Madam and her goons would face very public criminal charges, and their scientific project would be ruined. So we can assume they've taken every precaution to make certain no one gets out."

"Which probably means there isn't any way out," Dolan put in. "If there were one, and we found it, they'd stop us. They'll be watching us all the time. Mondor is reluctant to come right out and say it, so I will. No matter what they intend to do with us, when they're finished, we're finished. They mean for us to stay here."

Adelle kept her voice steady. "You mean—murder us?"

"One way or another," Mondor said. "The only alternative would be for Madam and her goons to disappear. Disposing of us is a far simpler solution."

"You're just performing a silly exercise in logic," Adelle protested. "You can't know anything like that for certain."

"No, I can't," Mondor agreed. "I can only reason from the available facts. So I wouldn't say it's absolutely inevitable. I'd rate it about ninety-nine and a fraction per cent inevitable."

CHAPTER 5

Adelle awoke to the sound and smell of bacon frying.

She glanced at her watch. Because of the continuous glow from the ceiling, she had slept with the blanket over her head. Now it was eight o'clock on Saturday morning.

They had sat up until after midnight in quiet, spasmodic talk except when Mondor and Dolan broke into one of their silly arguments. They talked quietly because they knew Madam and her goons were listening, and they talked spasmodically because all too frequently they could think of nothing to say. They were trapped, they didn't know how to go about finding a way out, and the odds seemed very long that there wasn't any.

Adelle sat up, swung her feet to the floor, and slipped her shoes on. She had slept in her clothing because of an uneasy feeling that anything could happen, at any moment. She wanted to be fully dressed and ready for it. She even had qualms about removing her shoes.

She took a mirror from her purse—there was none in the bathless bathroom—and ran a comb through her hair. Then she pushed aside the curtain that served as a door and looked out.

Craig Dolan sat at the diminutive table with his back to Adelle, contentedly munching bacon and fried eggs. Kevin Mondor, in shirt sleeves and minus his tie and glasses, was grimacing distastefully as he transferred strips of bacon to a plate. Mondor had assumed the role of a rational fanatic—the dedicated vegetarian who would eat meat if he had to but was grimly determined not to enjoy it. The absence of his glasses added a squint to his grimace, and his hair hung down over his eyes and partially screened them from the spattering bacon. With wrinkled clothing and a face flushed and perspiring from heat and frustration, he bore no resemblance to the well-turned-out, calmly deliberative mathematician she had known. He looked like an overdressed vagrant with a hangover.

The hangover could have been genuine. Dolan had enticed him into consuming several cans of beer the night before, and Mondor wasn't accustomed to alcohol in any form.

He looked up and saw Adelle. "The next time I go expeditioning with a female," he announced, "she'll be the domestic type."

Dolan seemed oblivious to the turmoil surrounding Mondor's cooking. He gave Adelle a nod and continued to eat. "How are you on survival techniques?" he asked, speaking over his shoulder. "Like getting the cork out of a wine bottle without a corkscrew, and broiling steaks over a metal wastebasket, and breaking into bottles and cans without an opener."

"I'd flunk," Adelle said. "My survival has never depended on things like that."

"Even an undomestic female ought to have a few practical survival skills. You've led a sheltered life."

"It's been unsheltered enough to keep me from having money to buy steaks for broiling over wastebaskets," Adelle said.

"Point," Dolan conceded. "What time is it?"

"A little after eight. It seems odd that an expert steak broiler and master of survival techniques has to keep asking what time it is."

"I got my expertise broiling other people's steaks," Dolan said. "I learned to open cans and bottles because any time I had the price of a watch, I bought beer instead."

"You couldn't have bought much beer for the price of this watch. It was the simplest, cheapest one I could find. It's hand-wound and non-digital, with no calendar, no calculator, and no phases of the moon. It doesn't even have a second hand."

"Its price would have bought some beer," Dolan said. "And when there's beer, who cares what time it is?"

Adelle paid her morning visit to the bathless bathroom, where she took time to sponge off her face and hands with cold water. There was no hot water faucet. Neither was there one in the kitchen. They had to heat water on the stove for their ablutions as well as for coffee and for doing the dishes, and she hesitated to disrupt Mondor's cooking just to get hot water to splash her face and hands with.

When she rejoined the men, Mondor had her breakfast waiting. She looked at it with dismay. The bacon lay rigidly in charred strips, and the three eggs were scorched, rubbery circles.

"I told you you'd regret it," Mondor said sourly.

Adelle sat down resignedly and asked, "Did you two hear anything during the night?"

Mondor turned with the package of bacon in his hand. Dolan paused with fork halfway to his mouth. "What was there to hear?" Dolan demanded.

"A kind of thud. Not very loud. I wasn't wide awake until after I heard it. Then I listened, but I didn't hear it again."

Dolan's fork moved. Mondor returned his attention to the stove.

"No," Dolan said, chewing thoughtfully. "I didn't hear anything."

Adelle went to the stove for the pan of hot water, filled her cup, and added instant coffee. She sat down again and stirred it absently, thinking about her planned trip to Greenfield Village. She would have been starting just about now. Instead—

She looked about her at the narrow kitchen, at the bearded Dolan still contentedly eating, at the disarrayed and disgusted Mondor awkwardly separating strips of bacon and transferring them to a frying pan. The scene was so totally unreal that she wondered if she should pinch herself.

Dolan laid down his fork and carefully cleaned his beard at the corners of his mouth with a paper towel. "How would you characterize that thud?" he asked. "Metallic, or just thudish?"

Adelle reflected. "Thudish. But I was at least half asleep, so I may not be a reliable witness."

"I don't suppose it would be fraught with significance either way. We know we're not alone down here. When we've finished eating, we'll consider what we're going to do."

An hour later they were still seated at the kitchen table. Mondor had washed the breakfast dishes except for their coffee cups and heated another pan of water for coffee. He also had donned his coat, necktie, and glasses and tidied his appearance into a semblance of normality. They had sipped coffee and talked, but none of them had been able to suggest anything that seemed worth doing.

Dolan, tilted back in his chair and staring with frustration at the glowing ceiling, needed only folded hands to resemble an uncouth saint praying for divine intervention. "Are you looking to heaven for help?" Adelle asked. Mockingly she raised her own eyes and lifted her hands supplicantly. Then, continuing to gaze upward, she remarked, "We came down through the ceiling. Why don't we leave the same way?"

The front legs of Dolan's chair returned to the floor with a crash. He said resignedly, "Who could believe the mental storms that churn and fulminate behind that quiet countenance? If we give her a couple more minutes, she'll tell us how to jump through the ceiling."

"Not jump," Adelle said. "Stand on something."

"Mondor could stand on me, I suppose. Or you could. But it's a dozen feet, at least, and even if we could reach the ceiling that way—

"We could stand a bed on end," Adelle said.

"So we could. That would be better than using my shoulders. Higher, too. Let's try it."

They had to take one of the beds apart in order to move it out of a cramped bedroom. They pushed the kitchen table aside so they could reassemble it and tilt it on end. Then they regarded it with skepticism.

"If you two will keep it from tipping, I'll give it a try," Dolan said.

"Better let me," Adelle said. "I'm lightest."

"But I'm tallest. If it works, all three of us will have to use it. By the way—" He turned and scrutinized her. "You certainly dressed appropriately for this adventure. How'd you happen to wear trousers on the one day you needed them? One might almost think you were expecting this."

Adelle snapped her fingers. "Madam!"

"What about Madam?"

"All day yesterday she kept making comments about my pants suit. When I walked in yesterday morning, her jaw dropped so far I thought she was going to lose her lower plate. 'They look nice, Darlink. Such a clever thing to wear.' I thought it was because she'd never seen a pants suit before."

"Probably she wondered if you suspected something," Dolan said. "You can have it out with her the next time you meet."

"I'll have more than that out with her," Adelle promised.

"She certainly didn't give me cause for suspicion," Dolan said. "A few minutes before I hit the chute, I was joking with her. I told her we should include sections on humor in the books, giving examples of the kind of jokes the natives of each country would appreciate. I mean, if businessmen want to sell things in ridiculous places, there's nothing like a good joke for loosening up a customer. She said she thought the businessmen were funny enough already." He asked Mondor, "Did you notice anything peculiar?"

"She put on an act for me about how excited she was to be getting a new computer. Said it'd been on order for two months. Whatever else she is, she's certainly a glib liar. Let's get on with this."

Mondor and Adelle stood on opposite sides of the bed with one foot on the headboard, which was on the floor; one hand raised to support the footboard; the other hand and a knee against one of the side rails. Dolan began to pull himself up. The side rails suddenly came loose, and the whole structure collapsed as they jumped clear.

"Stand on a chair," Adelle suggested. "You won't have to climb so far."

"Point," Dolan agreed. He moved a chair while they were reassembling the bed, and a moment later he was standing upright with his head just below the ceiling. He raised a plastic panel and slid it aside. The end of a fluorescent light fixture became visible, and, just above it, a ceiling painted with a glossy white paint.

"Brace yourselves," Dolan warned them. "I'm going to jump higher and try to get a glimpse above the panels."

He landed lightly, but they had to struggle to keep the bed upright. He slipped the panel back into place and eased himself down to the chair. "It's a plywood ceiling," he said as he hopped to the floor. "It's nailed about every sixteen inches, which means there are joists or furring strips above it. The light fixtures are fastened to the plywood, and the panels are suspended about six inches below it. There'll be an air space, maybe a small one, between the wood ceiling and the basement floor above. To get out of here, we'd have to hack through wood and then cement. There must be a better way."

"If we had tools, we might have a go at it," Mondor said. "We've certainly got nothing else to do and nothing to lose."

Dolan nodded. "A sledge hammer would tear things up a bit, but we haven't got one. Anyway, the racket would attract the goons."

"So much for my bright idea," Adelle said.

"You're bright idea was admirable," Dolan said. "The reason it doesn't get us anywhere is because we're using it in the wrong place. We should put the bed under one of the openings we fell through, but how would we go about finding it?"

"Each of us landed in or near one of those silly test rooms," Mondor said. "Maybe it was the same room. That's where we should look."

They stood gazing uncertainly at the high ceiling. Adelle wondered whether they would be able to reach a trap and climb out even if they could find one.

"We've certainly go nothing else to do and nothing to lose," Mondor said finally. "That sounds familiar. Did you just say it or did I?"

"It doesn't matter," Dolan said. "A banality doesn't become wisdom through repetition, but in this case you're right. We've nothing else to do and nothing to lose. The bed will be easier to carry if we take it apart."

They quickly disassembled it and divided up the pieces. Dolan, carrying the headboard, led the way. Adelle followed with the footboard, and Mondor trailed after them, awkwardly maneuvering the two side rails. They filed into the long alley by which all three of them had arrived at the kitchen, and there they halted. The alley ended a few feet away.

"The bastards have changed it!" Dolan exclaimed.

"Calling those bastards *bastards* is an insult to illegitimate children everywhere," Mondor said sourly.

Dolan bowed an acknowledgement. "You're right. I should be able to do better than that. The putrid vermin have changed the maze."

Mondor said matter-of-factly, "We should have expected it. Scientists often change mazes to see how their subjects will react."

"I wonder if that's what I heard during the night," Adelle said.

"Probably," Mondor said. "What do we do now?"

Dolan leaned on the headboard and fingered his beard thoughtfully. "I came from that way," he said, pointing. "The opening leads into a short alley, and there's another coming in from the right—left, going the other way—just before it dead-ends. Mondor?"

Mondor pointed at the new section of wall that now closed off the alley. "My route is blocked, and it'd be silly to try to find a way around it."

"I came the same way Craig did," Adelle said, "but I don't remember any opening on the left, which would have been my right. The only ones I saw were on my left, and I took them."

"We still have two possibilities," Dolan said. "Let's have a look."

Carrying the disassembled bed, they moved along the alley and turned right; but the alley they now found themselves in was not the short section both Adelle and Dolan remembered. It seemed to stretch interminably, and they found no side openings at all as they walked along it.

"The slimy blackguards have changed this, too," Dolan observed.

Mondor exclaimed suddenly, "Let's get back to the kitchen!"

He turned and ran. Dolan and Adelle exchanged perplexed glances and then followed him. The three of them, still carrying the bed parts, burst through the opening that led to the alley by the kitchen—but there was no kitchen. The alley dead-ended a few feet ahead of them.

"Cut off!" Mondor said disgustedly. "They can change the maze any time they feel like it and do it quickly. The sections probably come out of the floor like the door on the test room."

Dolan leaned on the headboard and glared at the new wall. "The foul cullions! No, that isn't adequate. Words fail me."

"*Now* I understand why I got lost in the maze yesterday," Adelle said. "When I started back, they'd changed everything around. I thought I was just being stupid."

"They did the same to us," Mondor said. "Those black strips on the floor are located between grooves in the walls. They must be tops of partitions. They can be raised to close off an alley or lowered to extend one."

"They're playing with us," Dolan growled, his face flushed with anger. "They've cut us off from food and water, and they can starve us, or make us die of thirst, just for the fun of it. Or they can sit back and enjoy watching us frantically wander about trying to find our way back to the kitchen while they keep changing the maze all around us."

"Something like that," Mondor agreed. "We should have expected it."

Dolan was pounding soundlessly on the headboard with a clenched fist. "This isn't a psychological experiment. It's a back-alley exercise in sadism. It's on the same level with tying cans to a dog's tail or setting fire to a cat."

"So what are we going to do?" Adelle asked. "Sit down and wait for fate to intervene? Or go along with the game and hope somehow to outwit them? And if we go along with the game, do we continue to carry this stupid bed?"

"Sitting down and waiting to rot doesn't appeal to me," Mondor said.

Dolan was still pounding on the headboard. "I'm not letting anyone play games with me if I can help it. We had an idea for finding a way out of this place, so what are we waiting for? They've changed the maze, but we still may be able to find one of the test rooms."

"We're certain to find a test room sooner or later," Mondor said. "I'll give you odds they're not through testing us. And it isn't as though we were trying to climb Mount Everest. We're just walking around in someone's screwy basement, and what's a bed, more or less?"

He picked up the rails and started off. Dolan grimly hoisted the headboard onto his shoulders and followed.

Adelle called after them, "Just a moment. We dashed out of the kitchen without considering what we were doing, and look at the mess we're in. Let's think this over before we make any more dashes."

"The female," Dolan said to Mondor, "has the weird notion we should use our brains before the fact instead of afterward."

They piled the bed parts against one wall and sat down on the floor. Adelle leaned back and closed her eyes, but she found it impossible to think. She had just glimpsed the frightening specter of death from hunger and thirst in the basement of a building where they'd been working for weeks, and she found it incredible. She had slid down a chute and left reality behind.

She said slowly, "The notion that Madam and her goons might eventually be stricken with compassion for us is silly."

"Not silly," Mondor said. "Idiotic."

After a long moment of silence, Adelle got to her feet. "All right," she said determinedly. "They will or they won't. If they will, they'll know where to find us. If they won't, our sitting in a corner and looking miserable isn't likely to change their minds. We might as well go down fighting. I vote for exploring the maze, and carrying the stupid bed, and looking for traps in the ceiling even though we know they'd stop us if we tried to use one. And—if there's any possible way to do it—I vote for vandalizing this place so it'll have to be rebuilt before they can test any more victims."

Dolan was nodding approvingly. "Right on. We'll smash the place and go down fighting. I only wish we had someone or something down here to fight."

"Before we're finished," Mondor said, "there may be both."

CHAPTER 6

Dolan took out a massive pocket knife, opened the awl blade, and began gouging the gray paint on one of the alley's metal walls. "You mentioned vandalism," he said cheerfully. He carved the letters RC and the date, checked Adelle's watch and added the time, and then fashioned an arrow that pointed toward the kitchen and bedrooms beyond the new section of wall.

"'RC' means 'Rest Center,'" he said. "The arrow tells us which way to go. If it's closed off, at least we'll know we're in the vicinity, and it'll make them do some sanding and painting."

When he finished, he said to Mondor, "Want to trade?" He shouldered the bed rails and marched off into the maze. At the first turn, he paused to repeat his carving.

While Dolan was enthusiastically mutilating the wall, Mondor stood scowling at the distant end of the alley. "I wonder how large this place is."

"Having walked from one end of the building to the other several times a day—" Dolan began.

"That wouldn't give you much of an idea," Mondor said. "There are wings all over the place, and this sub-basement may be larger than the building. It might even extend out under the courtyards. In any case, it's certain to be enormously complex. We'd better be prepared for anything. What do we know about Madam and her goons?"

Dolan finished off his arrow, added the date and time, and then turned. "Very little."

"I know almost nothing," Mondor said. "That should tell us something, because I've worked here for six weeks."

"Madam had her peculiarities, such as spitefully peddling gossip, but she seemed amusing and harmless," Adelle said. "As for the others, except for Goon 1, they ignored me completely."

"Did they ever speak to you?" Mondor asked.

"Never. Not even Goon 1. I caught him watching me too frequently for it to be a coincidence, and I always spoke to him, but he never answered. It seemed odd, but so many things seemed odd about Z-R Publications."

"Adelle," Dolan remarked, "is accustomed to having men watching her."

"Did any of them ever say good morning to you, or nice day, or commit any kind of a conversational platitude?" Mondor persisted.

"Never," Adelle said. "I spoke to all of them—with conversational platitudes, of course. And I'd wave at them when I saw them at work.

Sometimes they looked at me as though they were trying to smile but couldn't remember how, and once in a while one of them did something that almost looked like a nod."

"I never noticed anything like that, and I certainly never exchanged any words with them," Dolan said. "Is this important?"

"It might help us understand the situation better if we knew why they didn't talk," Mondor said. "What were they looking for when they watched us, and why wouldn't they respond to a harmless conversational platitude? A maze, no matter what animal it's intended for, screams 'experiment'. So I think we're caught in some kind of experiment. Whether Madam is a mad scientist, or whether she just works for one, I have no idea, but I think there must be one. And I think every move we make is being observed and charted and studied."

"Then the situation can be summed up something like this," Dolan said. "We haven't got a chance, but we're going to do our damndest because the only alternative is to sit down and rot. We're completely on our own. No one knows where we are, so no one is going to rescue us. And because kidnapping is a very bad crime, Madam and her goons will take pains to make certain we don't get out of here. If the police sooner or later start looking for us, which we can't count on, and if for some irrational reason they suspect Z-R Publications, which isn't likely, it certainly won't occur to them to search for a secret sub-basement. All we can do is go down fighting and hope for an unexpected piece of luck—but fighting is what makes unexpected pieces of luck happen. Madam may have absent-mindedly left us a loophole. At the very least, we can act as unpredictably as possible and try to screw up their experiment if that's what this is. So that's what I'm going to do. You two can decide for yourselves."

"I thought we already did," Adelle said.

"We can split up and go in different directions if either of you prefer that," Dolan pointed out.

Mondor shook his head. "This isn't going to be like a Sunday stroll in the park. For one thing, we're without food and water. For another, the word 'experiment' has connotations I don't like. Arranging this setup and suckering us into it was enormous trouble and expense. It wasn't done to watch us wisecrack our way up and down alleys. There'll be plenty of surprises for us, and the last one may be a trap door that drops us into a vat of acid. We'll be better able to meet danger if we stick together, and surely all three of us would rather have company in our misery, even if we decide later to sit and rot." He got to his feet.

"One moment," Dolan said. He stooped and carefully gouged their names under the arrow he had just carved. "There. I'll do that throughout the whole damned maze. Even repainting won't obliterate it completely—they'll have to sandblast the metal first. In the meantime, we'll have left our names all over the place, and names are evidence. That's one in the eye for your mad scientist. Okay—let's go."

* * * *

It was five o'clock in the evening and long hours later when Adelle slumped wearily to the floor and announced, "If a fairy godmother had given me the option of shortening my life by one day, this is the day I would have skipped."

They had enlarged their knowledge of mazes enormously in the interim, but their newly acquired experience helped them not a jot. They continued to stumble into blind alleys, retrace their steps, march the length of long alleys that had no exit, and pass up apparent cul-de-sacs only to have to return to them later. An hour after they set out, their senses of direction were totally obliterated. Dolan stopped carving arrows because he had no notion of where to point them, but he stubbornly continued to vandalize the walls with their names and the date and time.

As he commenced his latest assault on the smooth gray paint, Dolan asked Mondor, "Is this scientist really mad, or is he merely stupid. Translation: What's the point of our wandering around in a maze like this and not getting anywhere?"

"Some scientists believe rats have the ability to acquire a cognitive map of a maze," Mondor said. "Once they've done so, they can think their way through it."

"Good idea," Dolan told him. "Go ahead and demonstrate."

"The mazes they use for rats are designed for scientific tests. God knows what this one was designed for."

Dolan got to his feet and shouldered the bed rails. "I can tell you what it wasn't designed for. Aesthetic purposes. This battleship gray is getting on my nerves. 'Water, water everything, and all the boards did shrink.' Sorry, I shouldn't have mentioned water. Gray, gray everywhere—" He kicked a wall viciously. "I wonder if they chose gray because it's psychologically depressing." He started off.

"Hold it!" Mondor snapped.

Dolan turned, scowling.

"Don't forget—they can bring a wall out of the floor wherever a black strip crosses the alley. If one of us gets too far ahead or lags behind, they can separate us."

"Right," Dolan agreed. "We'll stick together and make them work for whatever they think they're trying to prove. Now if you don't mind—we aren't likely to acquire that cognitive map by transcendental meditation."

Mondor and Adelle picked up the remainder of the bed and hurried after him.

Shortly before six o'clock, they turned into a new alley and suddenly came upon a test room that seemed identical to the room or rooms all of them had arrived in. They made no move to enter it. Dolan exclaimed, "Ah!" and began to assemble the bed.

This time they wedged the bed's feet against the wall. Dolan, with Mondor's clasped hands providing a step, hopped onto the bed, lifted a ceiling panel, and peered through. He jumped for a better look. Then he announced disgustedly, "Nothing."

"I suppose there *could* be more than three test rooms, though I don't know why they'd need so many," Mondor mused. "One should be sufficient. Maybe there are doors on all four sides, and we entered the same room on chutes coming from different directions."

"That's possible, but I see no sign of a trap door from here," Dolan said. He stood on tiptoe, and then he jumped again for a better look. "Nothing. Of course I can only see this one side. The test room's walls go all the way up to the plywood."

"Aren't there any seams?" Mondor asked.

"Sure. The plywood panels are four by eight feet, and their edges make seams, but they're very thoroughly nailed."

"Can you reach the edge of a panel?"

"Yes. And I've broken two fingernails on it already."

Mondor thought for a moment. "In that case, we might as well go through the test room and try again where we come out."

"Just a moment," Adelle said as Dolan swung down. "Those chutes were long. At least, mine was. It gave me quite a ride. Maybe we're too close to the room."

"Point," Dolan agreed. "We'll back up and try again."

They moved the bed twice, but every panel Dolan tested seemed like a solidly nailed piece of plywood. "All right," he said finally. "We'll take their dratted test and see what's on the other side."

He paused to carve their names on the wall by the door.

"Don't forget to wind that thing," he said as he got the time from Adelle's watch. "If you do, we easily could get confused about what day it is. We may anyway. Too bad you didn't have the foresight to buy a watch with a calendar."

"Too bad you were too cheap to even buy a sundial."

Dolan grinned. "That'd really be useful down here. Mondor could use your watch to calculate where the sun ought to be, and then he could check your watch by the sundial."

Carrying the disassembled bed, they marched into the test room. The opening closed after them with an almost inaudible hiss, leaving them in the dim glow of the recessed ceiling light. Numerals began flashing on the three walls where the inverted score boards were located.

The series was longer than before, and it flashed only once.

"The degenerate fiends!" Dolan exclaimed. "Now that we know how the thing works, they figure once is enough. Did either of you catch it?"

"I missed the beginning," Mondor said.

"Six, seven, nine, one, zero, four, five," Adelle recited. She punched the appropriate buttons as she spoke. With the same quiet hiss a door dropped open on the side opposite to the one they had entered.

Dolan gouged a "1" on a test room wall. He circled it. "Eventually we'll find out how many there are. How'd you manage to remember that number so easily?"

"I've been typing numbers for three weeks," Adelle said. "I couldn't help it."

They picked up the bed parts and marched out. The door swished shut behind them. Again they assembled the bed, and Dolan investigated the ceiling with the same futile result.

"They could have fastened the thing shut," he called down to them when the third check failed to find anything. "It wouldn't take much effort to bolt the trap's frame to the joists when the trap isn't in use. That'd keep us from climbing out and prevent the goons from falling through it accidentally. If they've done that, we couldn't pry it down with a crowbar."

He swung to the floor and began to carve their names on the wall.

Mondor watched him with a frown. "I should have drawn a map," he said.

"You'd need a sheet of paper twelve feet square, and the end result would look like a warren dug by drunken rabbits," Dolan told him.

"Even so—" Mondor got out a pocket notebook. "There's no harm in trying. I might accumulate enough information to help us decide which turns to take when they're generous enough to give us a choice." He drew a small square, marked it T for Test Room, and represented the alley with a straight line.

Dolan finished gouging the wall and stepped back to inspect his lettering. "Let's rest," he said. "There's no hurry to get where we're going if we aren't going anywhere."

Not until Adelle sat down did she realize how utterly exhausted she was. She had been so preoccupied with her growing hunger and thirst that she failed to notice her fatigue. The long hours of aimless wandering had left the men just as tired. Dolan's arrows became progressively less ornate as the day wore on, and now he was producing straight lines with carelessly drawn points at the ends.

He sat down beside Adelle; Mondor had seated himself on the opposite side of the alley. Adelle glanced at them before she closed her eyes. Dolan sat slumped back wearily, eyes closed, one hand cupping his hairy chin. Mondor, whose face showed faint signs of needing a shave, was bent forward, elbows on knees, and he seemed to be contemplating the toes of his shoes. This was what the bright optimism and determination of the morning had come to.

They rested in silence for a time, and Adelle tried unsuccessfully to sleep. Then Dolan asked suddenly, "Would it be a valid psychological test to observe the effects of hunger and thirst on humans?"

"I'm sure it's already been done," Mondor said.

"Then psychological tests on humans aren't unusual?"

"They're performed frequently, and they produce extremely valuable information. Reaction times, for example. How long does it take you to get your foot on the brake when you're driving and see danger ahead? That's a valid psychological test, and the data tell us things like how much distance we should maintain between us and the car ahead at different speeds. But no reputable scientist would experiment on humans without their consent."

"What stupid people would let them do it at all?"

"Haven't there been any ads for test volunteers since you hit Ann Arbor? Scientists frequently pay students to take part in experiments. If someone wanted to perform hunger tests, he wouldn't have any trouble finding volunteers. What are a few days without food to an impoverished college student—especially if he's paid well for it and fed afterward. The effect of hunger and thirst on the ability to think and remember would be a valid test subject."

"As with the number in the test room?"

"Yes. Yes, I suppose that could be one of the ways they're measuring us. They might check us again at this time tomorrow and see whether another twenty-four hours of thirst and hunger has had any effect on Adelle's ability to remember that many numerals."

"'Sadistic ghouls' is a better description of them than 'putrid vermin,'" Dolan said. "What other experiments are they likely to inflict on us?"

"I have no idea. All I had was an introductory course in psychology."

"Adelle?"

"I managed to skip psychology," she said. "I thought I already knew all about it."

"A college graduate," Dolan said bitterly, "is someone who is over-educated in everything except what he needs to know."

"And a writer," Mondor returned, "is someone who doesn't know enough about anything for it to be useful. Maybe we should ask Adelle to apply her English Literature degree."

"No way," Adelle said firmly. "Nothing about this place belongs to either literature or life. It lacks verisimilitude."

"It also lacks drinking fountains, rest rooms, and burger joints," Dolan said.

"Those things would go a long way toward giving it verisimilitude," Adelle conceded.

A gong sounded. The unexpectedness of it, the totally unreal impact of a reverberating tone with the deep quality of Big Ben, startled all of them and brought Mondor halfway to his feet.

"Interesting," Dolan remarked. "But for whom does it toll?"

With dual swishes, a wall raised out of the floor a short distance away, blocking off the alley, and a section of the wall nearby disappeared into the floor. Through the new opening, an intersecting alley was visible.

They exchanged glances. "Obviously they want us to go that way," Dolan said. "Shall we?"

"Our alternative is to sit here and rot," Mondor said gloomily. "We've already discussed that."

"Right," Dolan said. "Let's go."

The maze now seemed repentant of its former waywardness, and they encountered no more blind alleys. This made them suspicious rather than grateful. They plodded along slowly because they were tired, and they stopped twice for Dolan to repeat his carving act and once for Mondor, who was counting paces, to work on his map. It would extend from no-where to nowhere, and every time their unseen captors pressed a button and opened or closed off an alley, a portion of it would become obsolete. The maze he was mapping today would have little or no similarity to the maze they would be walking around in tomorrow, but—as Mondor kept saying—he had nothing else to do. Adelle, watching him trying to sketch the gigantic maze in a small notebook, took his grim determination as one more quirk of the mathematical mentality and said nothing.

She was about to suggest resting again when Dolan uttered a yelp. "Look!" he shouted.

He had found one of his carvings with an RC and an arrow. He rushed in that direction with the others following on his heels. They turned, turned again—and found themselves staring into the kitchen they had left that morning. Dropping their bed parts, they queued up at the sink and gulped water.

After the first long drink, Dolan urged caution. "This can be danger-ous stuff, especially when you're not used to it. I wonder if they've left us an alternative." He went to the refrigerator and opened it. "They've restocked the beer and pop. Not the food, though. And they took the three eggs that were left over from this morning. Good thing we ate well, eh? As long as there's beer, why are we drinking water?"

A resonant "pop" sounded as he opened a can.

"Did they leave the milk?" Adelle asked.

Dolan nodded. "What was left from breakfast."

Adelle began opening cupboards. "They took the breakfast cereal. And the chocolate and tea. They left us only a cup of coffee apiece."

Dolan said philosophically, "Oh, well. As long as there's beer—"

Carrying her glass of water, Adelle went to look at the bedrooms. "They've replaced the bed!" she exclaimed.

"Thoughtful of them," Dolan said, wiping foam from his beard. "They're saying, in effect, if we're stupid enough to want to carry furniture around in a maze, we're welcome to do so. If we'd taken the refrigerator, I suppose they would have replaced that."

"They didn't make the beds, though," Adelle said. "And when they brought the new bed in, they put the mattress on it, but they left the sheets and blanket and pillow in the corner where you dumped them. Give the goons a demerit—their room service is inferior." She moved over to the refrigerator and looked into the freezer compartment. "There are three small-sized TV dinners here," she announced. "Salisbury steak, string beans, and mashed potatoes. All three of them."

"Ambrosia couldn't sound better," Dolan said. "Now that we're a day older and, hopefully, wiser, do we change our plans and sit here and rot where we at least have water and beds, or do we stupidly keep wandering about in the maze and taking psychological tests?"

"As long as there's food here, we eat it," Adelle said firmly. "And we get a good night's sleep in a bed. I also want to improvise whatever kind of a bath is possible and maybe wash my socks and underwear. There'll be plenty of time in the morning to debate the wisdom of rotting here or elsewhere."

"I'll second that program," Dolan said. "I'm willing to stay here as long as the beer lasts. I'll turn on the oven."

"And I'll start heating water for that bath," Adelle said. "I don't know how you two feel, but I intend to go to bed early."

CHAPTER 7

Adelle lay in numbed, exhausted wakefulness, thinking. She should have returned from her Saturday Greenfield Village outing hours ago, book and bed, looking forward to her Sunday date. Instead, she was…

"A specimen," she murmured sleepily. "An object for scientific scrutiny. I might as well be impaled on a pin."

Again she had worn her clothing to bed. Her underwear and socks, laundered with dishwashing detergent and the limited amount of hot water available, were hung on the wall hooks to dry. She had donned her outer clothing without them. She still felt a persistent uneasiness that something was going to happen. Perhaps that was why she couldn't sleep.

Or perhaps her hunger kept her awake. The TV dinner had seemed like a mere appetizer after the long, wearisome day of maze wandering. They had finished the milk with their supper, and now there was nothing in the kitchen for breakfast except beer, soft drinks, and liquor. Dolan, at least, had chortled over the prospect of beer for breakfast.

Irritably she pulled the blanket over her face to shut out the incessant glow of light. The sleep she clutched so desperately at remained beyond her reach.

Dolan and Mondor had talked quietly for a time after she went to bed. She thought they were discussing ways and means of escaping until she heard Dolan call Mondor a procrustean right-winger. Eventually they retired, and Mondor, who still wasn't accustomed to beer, stumbled on his way to bed.

"Face it!" she told herself sternly. "Tomorrow's prospects aren't any better than today's were. They may be a lot worse. On the other hand, I hope we won't foolishly dash out of here carrying a bed and be cut off from water all day."

She pushed herself into a sitting position. "What's to prevent them from turning off the water?" she asked herself. "Nothing at all."

She slipped on her shoes and went to the kitchen, where she fished among the clutter of beer and pop cans in the garbage container. She located the empty milk carton, washed it carefully, rinsed it, and filed it with water. She put it in the refrigerator. Then she refilled the ice cube containers in the freezer compartment and, after a moment's thought, she also filled the saucepan and the frying pan that were their only cooking utensils.

"At least we'll be able to gargle for awhile," she told herself.

She returned to bed and again tried to sleep.

Suddenly she heard a faint, crescendoing, high-pitched tone like that of a malfunctioning loud speaker. Then Dolan's voice boomed, "When they're finished with us, we're finished. They mean for us to stay here."

And Mondor's: "I think we're caught in some kind of experiment."

And then her own voice: "We came down through the ceiling. Why don't we leave the same way?"

Madam and her goons had been recording everything they said. Now selected remarks were being boomed back at them. The high-pitched humming became louder. So did their voices.

Dolan: "They're playing with us...playing with us...playing with us..."

Adelle: "We might as well go down fighting...go down fighting...go down fighting...

Mondor: "I think we can plan on there not being a way out...not being a way out...not being a way out..."

The volume became thunderous, and there was no escape, not even under the blanket with hands clapped desperately over her ears. Mondor's voice sounded a climaxing blast that made Adelle cringe with pain. "The last one may be a trap door that drops us into a vat of acid...a vat of acid...a vat of acid..."

The sound cut off abruptly, but the cool restfulness of silence lasted only for a moment. Then different kinds of sounds pummeled her. A screech of brakes, followed by a crash and a clatter of breaking glass and cries for help. A jet plane zooming in suddenly, blanking out the screams of the auto victims and roaring overhead so low that she instinctively ducked. It crashed deafeningly, trailing its own pathetic wake of screams. Fire trucks, police cars, ambulances converged on Adelle's bed with sirens wailing. A train rattled past, its locomotive honking furiously.

The sudden emptiness of silence returned, and in its very abruptness it seemed to echo and crash among the maze's alleys. Adelle was panting and perspiring, and as she tried to force herself to relax, she could only pray that the sinister, unnatural seeming quiet would continue...would continue...would continue...

Faintly, as from a great distance, came the pathetic wails of a crying baby. It cried on, endlessly. The pitiable squalling crowded in on Adelle and became louder and louder.

Then the baby began to choke. Adelle had to fight her impulse to send for help, to cry out herself, to somehow find the baby and do something, do anything. Her small room was filled with convulsive sounds of a baby strangling to death. The distant wail of an ambulance could be heard. Then came turmoil, with the ambulance attendants working on the baby at Adelle's bedside. Finally, a husky voice: "It's dead."

Then the mother. "Oh, God! No! Oh, my God! No!" Her crying, her wails of grief, became louder and louder until a weeping father joined her. Adelle felt like screaming, "Shut up!" She was thoroughly ashamed of herself the moment the thought escaped her, even though the alleged mother and father whose alleged dead baby had just expired in a tumult of sound effects were certainly professional actors.

Or maybe the scene was real and a baby did die. "Madam probably strangled it herself," Adelle muttered.

Dolan's voice announced loudly, "I'm convinced. I never want children."

The lament finally faded. Silence closed in, to be shattered immediately by their own voices blasting at them.

Adelle: "Why is it that no matter how bright a man is, he has to assert his masculinity by acting stupid?"

Mondor: "I think we're caught in some kind of experiment."

Dolan: "Madam and her goons will make certain we don't get out."

It went on interminably: Their voices, followed by auto collisions, plane crashes, train wrecks, screaming ambulances, and then a repetition of the sickening melodrama of the choking baby. After a brief respite of reverberating silence, it started over again, with gusts of sound shaking the metal walls. It swelled to a hurricane of sound that shrieked furiously, and even the whispered sobs were thunderous.

Adelle got up, removed her clothing, and put on her damp underwear and socks. She dressed again and slipped her shoes on. Her instinct told her there would be no sleep on this night, and she wanted to be ready for any new maliciousness Madam and the goons inflicted on them.

Her watch said one-thirty. In a rare moment of silence she heard someone prowling in the kitchen, and the sound of an opening can suggested Dolan. As she looked out at him, the pandemonium started again. He shouted into her ear, "We have noisy neighbors. Let's order a pizza."

Mondor's fuzzily bearded face looked out through his curtain. He was glum because there was no razor available. He had remarked during supper that having the bearded Dolan constantly before him as a horrible example of the direction in which he was headed would give him nightmares.

He hadn't expected a nightmare like this. His trousers had acquired a mass of new wrinkles, and he looked a mess. Dolan, who never gave a thought to his dress, looked almost well groomed in wrinkled clothing.

Mondor shouted, "What's up?"

"We are," Dolan shouted back. "All three of us."

Screaming sirens crescendoed and then slowly faded. The baby's cries began again, and it was almost quiet enough for them to talk. Adelle asked, "What's this supposed to test?"

Mondor shrugged. "Noise certainly has a psychological effect."

"So does pulling out toenails," Dolan said, "but very few reputable researchers use it for scientific purposes."

Mondor went to get his coat and glasses. It amused Adelle that he had finally condescended to do without his necktie. As the volume of sound increased again, he went to the refrigerator and took a can of beer. Then he turned in surprise.

"Milk?" he shouted. "I thought we finished it."

"It's water," Adelle shouted back. "The pans have water, too. Just in case the faucets run dry."

Mondor arched his eyebrows. "Good thinking."

The bereaved parents now were sobbing with the intensity of locomotives. Dolan bellowed, "Anyone for ear plugs? I'll rip up a towel."

"They'd just turn up the volume," Mondor shouted back.

"Oh, well." Dolan gestured resignedly and tilted his beer can.

The sound cut off. Once again the sudden silence echoed and crashed among the surrounding alleys, but almost immediately it was broken by an audible hiss. "Tear gas!" Dolan shouted. "Let's get out of here."

He grabbed the head and footboards of the bed, which still leaned against the kitchen wall, and leaped for the doorway. Mondor, eyes streaming, picked up the side rails. Adelle's inspiration was to jerk open the refrigerator door and make a blind grab of the milk carton. On her way out of the kitchen, she snatched a clean towel.

A moment later, with a section of the alley closing behind them, the three took turns mopping their faces with the towel. "A woman's touch definitely has its uses," Dolan conceded. His remarks concerning Madam and her goons were unprintable.

"Cheer up," Mondor said. "You're the only one of us who can profit from this. It's giving you something to write about."

Dolan shook his head. "The mad scientist ploy is decades out of date except in comic books. I could do one of those, I suppose." He tossed the towel to Mondor. "That seemed like a rather mild form of tear gas, but maybe they only gave us enough to make us run."

Mondor rubbed vigorously with the towel and then put his glasses back on. "It seemed potent enough to me. Did you notice where it came from?"

Dolan shook his head. "I've experienced tear gas before. The wise recipient doesn't linger to ask whence. Hey—Adelle brought the water!

And all we managed was this stupid bed. Why didn't I grab a couple of six packs?"

Adelle regretted leaving her purse even though there was nothing in it she could have used. "What do we do now?" she asked. "Look for a hotel? Or try to find a quiet corner where we can sleep on cement?"

"This place won't have any quiet corners," Mondor said. "Not tonight." He sighed. "We should have brought the blankets."

They moved into the next alley and seated themselves against a wall. Adelle draped the towel over her head to shield her eyes from the incessant overhead glare and wondered if their tormentors would let them sleep. She had reached a level above or beyond mere exhaustion.

Then the sounds began. Sirens howled, machines roared, trains thundered, steel plates dropped from heights with reverberating crashes. During the infrequent lulls, the baby choked and died and the parents lamented.

In a moment of abrupt silence, Dolan muttered, "Pause to change tape."

It was now after three o'clock, and a new dimension of aural horrors began. Planes roared overhead, bombs shrieked down and exploded among them, victims screamed. Then the planes returned to swoop low and aim rattling machine guns and screeching rockets at them. In the background, air raid sirens wailed continuously. Finally Dolan ripped off pieces of towel for them to use as ear plugs, but the cloth was too coarse to be effective.

Again there was abrupt silence broken almost immediately by the fateful hiss of gas escaping. Mondor insisted on discovering where it came from; he searched briefly while the others were gathering up water and bed parts. In the next alley, he conveyed the cheerful news that the edges of some of the grooves in which the partitions moved up and down were perforated pipes. Since these occurred all over the maze, they could be gassed almost anywhere.

Twice more they settled themselves to rest only to be bombarded by sound and then routed by gas. Shortly after five A.M., they were chased into an alley where the light was diminished to twilight intensity. As a partition rose behind them, they stopped short, blinking into the dimness.

The alley was four or five times as wide as those they had been traveling, and a village street loomed ahead of them: a strip of asphalt flanked by sidewalks with rows of houses and stores on either side. The rears of the buildings were sliced off by the gray metal walls that rose behind them, and their upper stories and roofs were truncated by the ceiling.

"I hope there's a bar and grill," Dolan observed.

"If there is, it'll turn out to be a mirage," Mondor said. "Anyway, it's after hours."

They hurried forward.

Faintly, in the distance, they heard the roar of approaching planes. They ignored it and made their way along the narrow street to a row of store fronts. They were avidly looking into a cafe's darkened interior when they heard the first screech of falling bombs.

Suddenly bombs began to explode all around them. They flung themselves to the sidewalk as glass sprayed over them. The acrid fumes of spent explosives choked them. Buildings collapsed into the street. A metal shutter landed with a clang next to Adelle's head. Just in front of her, a wall crashed down. A heavy chunk of wood fell across her wrist, making her gasp with pain. Screams arose on all sides as a sleeping village was suddenly seized by terror. The bombs came again and again. More walls crashed down. Then a new wave of planes roared over them at treetop height with a clatter of machine guns. Bullets snapped past, rockets whooshed and exploded. Something tugged at Adelle's pant leg, and she felt a searing pain in her calf. She was too frightened to reach for her leg or try to look at it.

The sound of the planes faded away. Screams and sobbing continued to come from the wrecked houses. Dolan muttered, "Let's get out of here," and the three of them sprang up and ran, picking their way through the debris of fallen buildings. They staggered through an opening and slumped to the floor in the alley beyond.

Dolan was regarding Adelle with admiring approval. "Clever female. She didn't even spill the water, but we forgot the bed. Never mind, it was a silly idea anyway. But the water may be important."

Wincing, Adelle flexed her wrist. Then she rolled up her pant leg to examine the wound. The bullet had ripped her clothing and scraped the flesh, burning an ugly streak across it.

"What's this?" Dolan asked sharply. "A casualty?"

He got up and bent over her, clucking his tongue. "Close. A ricochet, probably. Madam and Company are through fooling around. A lot of those bullets were real. If we'd been standing when they opened up, all three of us would have been riddled."

"A lot of the explosives were real, too," Mondor said.

Dolan nodded. "A quarter stick of dynamite makes a very convincing bang in an enclosed space, and it doesn't take much to bring down one of those ersatz buildings. I think I'll drop the idea of a comic book. This situation is becoming decidedly unfunny. They didn't deliberately try to kill or injure us, not this time, but they arranged things so there was an excellent chance of it happening accidentally."

He was examining Adelle's injured leg. "That'll hurt," he observed.

"It already does," she said. She continued to flex her wrist, which hurt more than the leg.

But Dolan's attention was on the leg. "What this really needs is burn ointment. Since we haven't got any, a little moisture should help." He took a handkerchief from his pocket. "It's both dirty and salty—I cried into it— but as long as the skin isn't broken, that shouldn't matter."

He moistened it with water from the milk carton—being careful not to spill any—tied up the wound, and rolled down her pant leg.

"Makeshift first aid is all we've got," he said solemnly. "We're lucky we don't have broken bones or a punctured lung to fuss with. I'd hate to have to rely on Madam to call a doctor. I don't think she'd do it."

"No, but she'd take copious notes on our psychological reactions," Mondor said bitterly.

Dolan got out his knife. He carved their names and added the note, "Nightmare Village," with an arrow. "That's so we won't go that way again if we can help it. If I'd been drafted and sent to war, I could have accepted being shot at as part of the idiocy that's governed human affairs as long as humanity has existed. Being shot at in a psychological experiment, just to see how I'll react, is something I'm not willing to take without retaliating. We should be giving more thought to methods of messing up their experiment."

He added the date and reached for Adelle's wrist to see the time. She gasped with pain and pulled away.

"What's this?" Dolan demanded alertly.

"A piece of wood landed on my wrist," she explained.

He unfastened her watch and examined the wrist. "So it did. Gouged your watch into the flesh—see, it's bled a little. But as long as you can move it—*damnation!*"

"What's the matter?" Mondor asked.

"The watch is broken," Dolan said. "That wood must have had a nail in it. Punctured the crystal, which is plastic, and smashed the hands. The watch maybe saved Adelle from a worse injury, but it won't tell time again."

He handed it back to her. Still flexing her wrist, she stuffed it into a pocket. Dolan and Mondor were exchanging grave glances. The one fixed reference point of their existence was gone.

They were given no time to lament their loss. They heard the hiss of escaping gas, and Mondor scrambled to his feet and turned to give Adelle a hand.

Dolan resignedly pushed himself erect. "We'll have to continue this untimely discussion elsewhere."

CHAPTER 8

They strode the length of the short alley, keeping ahead of the drifting gas, and turned through an opening on their left. There they halted.

A deep pit yawned before them. It filled the alley from side to side and extended along it for more than a dozen feet. They stood staring at it and then at each other. The gas began to overtake them.

Dolan turned. "Come on!"

"We can't get out through the village," Mondor protested, hurrying after him. "The other end is closed off."

The short alley was filling with gas. They dashed through it and turned toward the wrecked village. The Nightmare Village. It, too, was filling with gas. Dolan made for the first collapsed house and began pulling a long beam from the debris. It was laminated from three thick boards nailed together, and one end was buried in a pile of window frames, broken glass, doors, smashed furniture, splintered wood. Mondor leaped to help him, and the two of them hauled on it. The gas was getting thicker. Adelle, still carefully carrying her carton of water, joined them and pulled with her good wrist.

All three were gasping when the beam finally came free.

"Is one enough?" Mondor asked.

"No time…to get two," Dolan panted.

They staggered away, pulling the beam after them.

They had no difficulty in getting it out of the wide alley, but there were anxious moments when they tried to maneuver it through the short one to the alley where the pit was. They were gasping for breath and almost blinded, and the beam was enormously heavy. They had to raise it almost to the ceiling to get around the last corner with it.

"Don't drop it in the hole!" Dolan gasped. "Never get it out if we drop it. Got to lean it against the wall, let it slide down, don't even know if it's long enough."

Gas was thick around them, now. Struggling, they finally managed to set the beam so it slanted across the alley. Its base was at the edge of the pit, but when it fell, it would fall at an angle.

"It's not long enough that way!" Mondor shouted.

They were no longer gasping. The gas was choking them. "Push it toward the wall and don't let it bounce," Dolan called. "Adelle, can you help?"

She was able to push just enough with her good wrist to get it started. As it fell, Dolan and Mondor exerted all of their strength to keep it pointed in the right direction. Then they clutched at it frantically as it landed. It bounced and came to rest a couple of feet from the wall, and it spanned the pit—barely.

"I'm first," Dolan said. "If it'll hold me, it'll hold either of you."

He stepped onto it, balanced for an instant, and then crossed swiftly to the other side.

Adelle followed. She cradled the carton of water with her injured arm and rested the other hand against the wall to keep her balance. The beam was four or five inches wide and seemed as sturdy as a sidewalk, but if she had waited much longer, she wouldn't have been able to see where she was walking. Looking down with tear-blinded eyes, she cautiously moved one foot and then the other. She worried more about dropping the precious water than falling.

"Hurry!" Dolan shouted.

She knew Mondor couldn't start until she reached the other side; the beam might not hold them both. She hurried. Dolan grabbed her as she approached the end, told her to keep going, and turned to wait for Mondor. Moments later the three of them stood in the next alley, wiping their burning eyes and listening to a partition swish shut behind them.

Dolan calmly seated himself. "Is there anything left in that carton, Adelle? Clever girl. I think a drink definitely is in order, even if it has to be water." He raised the carton to his lips, took one swallow, and passed it to Mondor.

Then he leaned back with his eyes closed, breathing heavily. "Close. Too close. If we'd let that beam bounce into the pit, we wouldn't have lasted long enough to go back for another one. Does tear gas asphyxiate?"

"Anything asphyxiates if there isn't enough oxygen in it," Mondor said.

"Would a broad jumper be able to clear that pit?"

Mondor reflected. "Not without a running approach, and I don't think anyone could get up enough speed going around those two corners."

"Certainly none of us could, and that's the only point that matters."

Adelle swallowed water and then leaned back against the wall. "Yesterday," she began. She paused. "Yesterday?"

"There was one," Dolan told her. "What about it?"

"I thought I'd never been so tired. But it was nothing compared with the way I feel now."

"You ought to be tired," Dolan said. "You've been through a war. Literally. Any combat veteran will tell you how exhausting that can be. It isn't just the physical exertion that causes it. It's the nervous strain of constant danger and the chance of being wounded or killed at any moment. Also the strain of having to make critical decisions your life depends on. Those who can't take it blow their tops." He turned to Mondor. "Could that be the kind of thing they're testing?"

Mondor reflected. "Sleeplessness, hunger, actual war effects—it certainly could."

"I wonder if this could be some idiotic project of the C.I.A. or the Pentagon," Dolan mused.

"I hope not," Mondor said. "I don't think they'd dare."

"Don't kid yourself. The United States has its own sordid history of experimentation on human subjects. German doctors who did it were brought to trial, but the U.S. Army doctors and officers who used GIs as guinea pigs in experiments with radiation, mustard gas, LSD, and various other things without their knowledge or consent weren't punished in any way. The Pentagon is still trying to cover it up."

"Somehow I can't see Madam and her goons as agents of the CIA or the Pentagon," Mondor said.

"Nor can I," Dolan said. His chest heaved as he took a deep breath. "Feels good to inhale air that's breathable. Wonder how long they'll let us sit here."

"I smell gas," Adelle said.

They were so exhausted that they remained where they were as long as they could stand it.

Time passed in a tedious succession of identical-looking alleys, and they lost count of the number of incidents when they were gassed and blasted with sound. When they reached the test room, they were arguing about whether it was noon yet. They dashed inside with the most recent cloud of gas on their heels, and the door raised behind them. Mondor had his notebook out, and as Dolan read the flashing numerals aloud, he wrote them down.

As soon as the series came to an end, Adelle recited it. "Nine, two, zero, four, seven, four, eight, six, one, nine. They're getting longer."

"They're also getting faster," Mondor said. "We need a system. From now on, Adelle's responsible for the first six numerals—grab that many and keep repeating them to yourself until there's no chance of your forgetting them. I'll take the next six, and Dolan takes whatever's left over."

"Good idea," Dolan said. "We'll try that next time and get some practice while it's still easy."

"But right now, it's nine, two, zero, four, seven, four, eight, six, one, nine," Adelle said. She reached for the protruding buttons.

Mondor grabbed her hand. "Wait. What's the hurry? It's quiet in here. There doesn't seem to be any gas except what our clothing absorbed. Why don't we rest until they make us leave?"

"Brilliant notion," Dolan said. After searching unsuccessfully for the "1" he had inscribed in the previous test room, he scratched a large and conspicuous numeral two. Then he settled himself on the floor and thumped on it. "Seems like unusually soft concrete."

A moment later all three of them were stretched out silently. The dim light was coolly refreshing after the glare from the ceiling panels outside. To Adelle's surprise, she hardly noticed the hardness of the floor. She had not slept since—eyes closed, head cushioned on her uninjured arm, she tried to think. Already her concept of time was becoming hazy, but she felt certain it was still Sunday. If she had been home, perhaps she would be getting ready for her date. The tried to focus her thoughts and remember when it was that she last got some sleep. She had awakened Saturday morning to the sound and smell of bacon frying. Since then, she had snatched occasional moments of rest, of dozing fitfully, but no real sleep. She fell asleep now with one hand touching the half-full carton of water.

She dreamed she was walking on water, but there was fire blazing up about her, and she reeled with seasickness. Faintly, from far away, someone was calling her name.

Then a hand shook her. Dolan's voice rasped, "Adelle! We've got to get out of here!"

She sat up groggily. The room was sweltering. They were in total darkness; even the numbers on the score board were invisible.

"The scoundrels turned the heat on," Dolan said. "You don't happen to remember that number, do you?"

She scrambled to her feet and stared dazedly into the darkness as though expecting to find it suspended in front of her unseeing eyes. Her mind was blank.

"If the carton hasn't melted, don't forget the water," Dolan said. "After this, we'll need it. Even hot water would taste good. Can you remember the number?"

Adelle stooped and fumbled for the carton, almost knocking it over. Her fingers were trembling when they closed on it. The number. She backed against a wall and then leaped away—it felt scorching hot. Wearily she attempted to focus her thoughts. The number.

"No," she said.

"Good thing I wrote it down," Mondor said. "Look—I'm going to strike a match, and I'll read it aloud. Both of you try to remember it. I have one book of paper matches, and it's more than half used. I don't want to waste any. Ready?"

There came the sound of a match striking but no flame. The sound came again. Then Mondor swore softly. "My pants pocket is soaked with sweat. The damn things got wet."

"I have matches," Adelle said absently.

"You have? Where?"

"In my purse. They're a souvenir from a restaurant. My purse is hanging from one of the hooks on my bedroom wall."

There was a long silence. Then Dolan growled, "If Madam hasn't swiped it. Is the match wet, or is the striking surface wet?"

"I don't know. One, or the other, or both."

"Brilliant logic. Let me have the matches. No, not the one you were trying to strike. It's probably ruined. I'll see if I can dry one. The wall might even be hot enough to ignite it."

There was another long silence, and then Dolan muttered, "This is the first time in my life I ever wished I smoked. Then I might have a lighter."

"You'd be a fire hazard with all that hay around your mouth," Mondor said sourly.

"It's wet hay now. I'm holding the book's striking surface and one of the matches against the wall. If sweat doesn't run down my fingers and keep them wet, they ought to get dry. There's a lot of heat there."

"Why don't you hold them above your fingers so the sweat can't run down on them?" Mondor asked.

Dolan swore. "We're so tired it takes all three of us to think."

They waited. The room continued to get hotter. Adelle began to wonder about sunstroke. "Not in the dark, silly," she told herself. "Some other kind of stroke. Heat stroke?"

"Ready?" Dolan asked finally. He tried the match. There was a scratch, and then another. The match sputtered and burst into flame.

Mondor was waiting with notebook open. He flipped a page. "Nine, two, zero, four, seven, four, eight, six, one, nine," he read. He repeated the series twice before the match burned down and Dolan had to drop it.

Clothing rustled in the dark as Dolan stepped to one of the rows of buttons. "Awkward without light—have to count to find each numeral. Here we go. Nine...two...zero...four...seven...four...eight...six... one...nine." He recited slowly, clicking the appropriate button as he spoke. "You two aren't the only ones who can remember numbers," he said when he finished.

Nothing happened. The heat was intolerable, now. Adelle began to feel dizzy. "You remembered the numbers, but did you press the right buttons?" She asked.

Dolan tried again. Nothing happened.

They were too stunned to speak. Finally Mondor said, "They've put in a new wrinkle. Group problem solving—that's what they did to us at the village. Now they're doing it again. Let's hit all three sets of buttons simultaneously."

They took their places. As he recited the numerals, they fumbled in the dark to count and find the right button and punch it on Mondor's order. "Nine...go. Two...go. Zero...go. Four...go. Seven...go. Four... go. Eight...go. Six...go. One...go. Nine...go."

With a hiss one of the doors opened. They staggered through it into blinding light and the cool air of the alley beyond. They rounded a corner and put two alleys between themselves and the superheated test room before they slumped to the floor.

"This calls for a drink of water," Dolan said. "But only one mouthful apiece—we don't know how long it has to last."

The water in the carton was warm. They each took a drink of it, and then Dolan leaned back, fixed his gaze on the ceiling and announced, "That was stupid of us. We're on rationed water, and we let them dehydrate us. My clothing is soaked with sweat."

"So is mine," Adelle said, "but I think it was a trade-off in our favor. We aren't that desperate for water—we had all we wanted last night, with beer and pop, and we've got what's left of this. And we did get some sleep. I don't know how much, but it was lovely while it lasted."

"True," Dolan agreed. "We may have won a few points there. Cherish them. It isn't likely to happen often." He asked Mondor, "What other peculiarities can we expect in those test rooms?"

"I can think of several," Mondor said, "but I won't say what they are. If they knew we were already onto them, they'd do something else."

"Point. Do you still consider this one long experiment?"

"I'm certain it is. They'll keep us awake, feed us very little, and test our problem solving ability under conditions of stress brought on by fatigue, lack of sleep, hunger, thirst—though Adelle messed that one up for them a bit—and very real physical danger."

Adelle's only concern at the moment was how long they would be permitted to sit there. Before she could doze off, she heard the baby crying faintly, and a moment later Mondor smelled gas. Wearily they moved on, and the baby choked, the parents wept, and the trains, planes, and fire engines roared and hooted and screamed.

It seemed like an awake form of sleepwalking. During the next lull, she asked Mondor, "How long can one go without sleep?"

"I've been trying to remember," he said. "It depends on the individual, of course. I think people have done it for ten days or more, but that would be exceptional. I dimly recall something about a person being committed to a mental hospital after going without sleep as a public relations stunt. I don't remember how long he stayed awake."

"What happens to you?" Adelle asked.

"When you go without sleep? You get confused, suffer halucinations, develop physical disorders—I don't remember all the details."

"And while this is going on, they'll keep testing us?"

Mondor shrugged. "If they're being scientific, I suppose they'll compare our performance with that of others who've had the same treatment. They won't give us tests that are impossible to solve—not if it's a genuine scientific experiment. They could do that, easily, but it wouldn't prove anything. If their science is the kind a kid practices by sticking pins in bugs, then anything goes."

Adelle said hesitantly, "And—in the end—they can't let us out, can they? Not after we've been shot at, and bombed, and gassed."

"They'd be unwise to," Mondor said.

They plodded in silence for a time with Adelle hoping the lull would continue and wishing she could lie down and rest.

Dolan said finally, "I still want to get back at these reprobates by messing up their tests. Did we do that when we used the beam to get across the hole in the floor?"

"Probably not," Mondor said. "Probably the beam was there to see whether we'd think to use it."

"You're kidding!"

"Not at all. Like I said, it was a test in group problem solving. I'll guarantee that. The tester may hide things just to see if a group will find them and figure out how to use them. Or the solution may be left in plain sight along with a lot of unworkable things to see if a group can recognize it for what it is. There are all kinds of twists that can be used. The only thing we can do is try to stay alert."

"While getting more and more tired and hungry and thirsty and shell shocked?" Dolan asked.

Mondor didn't answer.

"When I get out of here," Dolan said, "I'm going to start a campaign to make psychology and psychologists illegal."

They entered each new alley apprehensively, expecting a mock village where they would be bombed and shot at, or a test room looming at the end, or another pit in the floor, or some other fiendish hazard; but they found nothing but expanses of gray wall and, somewhere ahead of them, an opening into another alley, and then another, to be trod with intensifying exhaustion.

Sounds continued to assail them. Adelle's ears rang constantly. Whenever they tried to rest, the hiss or odor of gas drove them on. As long as they kept moving, there was no gas. Dolan, meditating this fact, passed a whispered suggestion. They began walking slower and slower.

Another whispered suggestion, this time from Mondor, and they took turns trying to sleep on their feet, the one in the center supported by the other two. Mondor and Adelle had difficulties with Dolan's large frame, but they somehow managed, and during what might have been Sunday afternoon—or Sunday night, or Monday morning, or whenever—each of them had several periods of rest while plodding slowly forward.

They had lost track of time completely—lost even their awareness of its existence—when the gong sounded and a section of wall dropped into the floor just ahead of them. Instantly wide awake, they moved in a frenzied rush. This might mean—as it had the day before—that the way was open to water, food, and beds.

But they were in a different part of the maze, or the maze was arranged differently. They blundered into blind alleys, retraced their steps, even took a wrong turning that started them back the way they had come. Finally they found the kitchen, and the first thing Adelle did—after all three of them had taken long drinks of water—was to rinse out her milk carton, refill it, and return it to the refrigerator.

The refrigerator contained three plastic-wrapped sandwiches. Otherwise, except for the pans of water Adelle had placed there, it was empty.

Dolan uttered a scream of anguish. "They took the beer! Why, those perverted, sadistic, degenerate, vermin-infested, malicious, vindictive—"

Adelle was wearily examining the cupboards. They were empty. "Our menu," she announced, "consists of luncheon meat, cheese, and stale white bread. Nothing to drink but water, and after today we shouldn't knock that. Maybe they were afraid coffee would keep us awake."

"At least the rotters left us the chairs," Dolan said. "We can eat the sandwiches comfortably."

A marvelously relaxing silence had surrounded them from the moment they entered the kitchen. They spoke in whispers as though afraid of shattering it. They ate—which didn't take long. They heated water for their ablutions, and Adelle and Mondor hung up some of their gas-permeated clothing to air.

They went to bed.

And the silence continued. Adelle fell asleep immediately.

She was awakened by Dolan's shout. "Gas!"

This time she remembered her purse. She grabbed it and her coat and whipped the blanket off the bed. She snatched the carton of water from the refrigerator before she joined the men in their rush from the kitchen.

Dolan brought the saucepan of water. "Awkward thing to carry," he said, "but there must be at least two quarts here. We can indulge ourselves for a while and then ditch the thing if it's a nuisance."

"If we do that, we won't be able to use it again," Adelle objected.

"True, oh oracle, but I'll give you fifty to one they'll never give us anything more to cook anyway. We may not have another chance to heat water. If we do, we can use the frying pan."

Adelle absently looked at her wrist where her watch had been. Not only had they lost track of time, but she felt uncertain about what day it was. Even if it was still Sunday, her date had been a thing of the past for hours. That nice-looking young man—Jerry. She had to strain her memory to recall his name. Gerald Wyman. What would Jerry be thinking of her?

She said, speaking as much to herself as to the men, "I wonder if anyone has reported us missing."

CHAPTER 9

The intense interest with which that nice young man Gerald Wyman had been following Adelle's comings and goings would have astonished her. She was missed almost the moment she failed to return from work on Friday.

Wyman had come to Ann Arbor to attend the University of Michigan's school of engineering. He, Adelle, and thousands of young people like them who arrived there in the 1980s and 1990s found a city that had long-since burst its seams.

Until World War II, it had grown slowly and solidly as a pleasant university town, spreading over the hills along the lovely valley of the Huron River. It became and remained an agreeable place to live, attracted a congenial German population that gave it a distinctive gemutlichkeit, saw spacious homes built that still would be proudly occupied a century and a half later, saw the university continue to expand, experienced the usual "town and gown" conflicts—which neither prevented the townspeople from ruthlessly exploiting the students (when the students weren't exploiting them) nor distracted them from enthusiastically supporting university-centered cultural activities and athletic events.

The end of the Second World War brought an explosive population growth. The city more than doubled its size in the next forty years, and by 1990, its population exceeded a hundred thousand. The university expanded just as rapidly and added a second campus, and its increasing prestige as a center for science and technology attracted research and development laboratories from industry as well as government and military research projects.

With the enormous influx of population came massive suburban sprawl. First it took the form of disconnected neighborhoods of small lots with slightly smaller, single-story dwellings. They were followed by a pollution of apartment buildings and condominiums, and too often these were as tinseled and glass-festooned as a Christmas tree and with the same aura of impermanence.

Occasionally a taller office or apartment building thrust a blunt silhouette above neighboring structures to blight Ann Arbor's skyline. Its incongruity provided an air of exclusiveness because its sprawl was vertical rather than horizontal. One of these apartment buildings was Chateau Arb.

When Wyman obtained his degree in engineering, he moved there from his university dormitory and got a job at an engineering research firm, hoping to save enough money for graduate study. Wyman liked Chateau Arb. After four years of dormitory living, it was pleasant to see that misplaced structure rising above the landscape like a beckoning finger as he headed for home and to be aware that somewhere in its upper reaches, albeit smeared with blatantly meretricious decorating and crammed with sleazy furnishings, was his own exclusive wedge of castle. Its closed door did not shut out his neighbors' noise or even the odors of their cooking, but at least it kept out their persons.

Shortly after he moved in, Wyman's contentment with his new home was enhanced by a growing interest in the building's parking lot—specifically, in parking space F-6. This space almost adjoined his own assigned space C-8. Further, it was visible from his window, and he found it easy to give it his unremitting attention.

F-6 belonged to the new occupant of apartment 6-6, Adelle Gernyan. The building's management had achieved the ultimate infinity of confusion by using letters in the parking lot and on mail boxes, numbers on stair exits and elevator buttons, and only the final numerical suffix on apartment doors, thus making it impossible for visitors to find anyone or anything. Wyman met Adelle fortuitously in the parking lot the morning after she moved in, and he was smitten instantly.

For almost three weeks the acquaintance progressed no further than a polite good morning exchanged as they were leaving for work—Wyman quickly learned to time his departure to coincide with hers—and an occasional "Hi!" when they chanced to arrive home at the same moment, a timing much more difficult to achieve. From his window, Wyman kept a meticulous mental log of the comings and goings of Adelle's car, which was an ancient Plymouth Horizon that one of what must have been a series of a previous owners had painted a glowing canary yellow.

It wasn't until Thursday night of the third week that he finally managed a conversation with her. They chanced to meet in the apartment's laundry room, and they sat and talked while the washers and dryers spun off their cycles—far too quickly! By the time the machines panted to a halt, Wyman had made a start at becoming much better acquainted with Adelle Gernyan.

It pained him that he couldn't offer to go along with her on her excursion to Henry Ford's Greenfield Village the following Saturday, but he had to work overtime, and the overtime was important if he was to accumulate enough money to return to school in the fall.

He did manage to invite her to attend a concert with him on Sunday afternoon, and she accepted. It was a student recital, but she was more interested in the program than in who was going to perform it, and he considered that a very rare trait.

She was a rare kind of girl. Friendly, but quiet. The bookish type—she'd brought a book to the laundry room, though their talk prevented her from reading. And the book wasn't a paperback sex thriller but a discussion of genetics and DNA.

A thoroughly nice girl. Wyman's smittenness had cubed by the time they parted, and when he arrived home the following evening, Friday, his interest in space F-6 was not merely intense but ecstatic. He lingered in the parking lot for a time, checking his oil and feigning a deep interest in his air filter and carburetor, but she didn't arrive. Finally he went up to his apartment to change and eat the pizza he had bought for supper. Occasionally he looked down at space F-6, but it remained empty.

She had gone shopping. She had decided to eat out. She was working late. She—he swallowed forlornly—she had a date with another employee at Z-R Publications, the strange firm she worked for. It was none of his business, really.

Her car still hadn't returned at nine-thirty, nor at eleven-thirty, nor at twelve-thirty. Wyman finally went to bed, but he was unable to sleep. At three-thirty he got up and looked out again, and the car was there.

He regarded it with affection when he left for work at seven thirty on Saturday morning. He regarded it the same way when he returned home. He hadn't expected her back from Greenfield Village so early, and he had a feeble excuse for telephoning her. A fellow worker who knew the graduate student giving the Sunday concert had supplied an enthusiastic description of her pianistic acrobatics. Wyman could pass that information along and confirm their date. As soon as he reached his apartment, he dialed her number.

When the phone rang unanswered, he had his first intimation that something might be extremely wrong.

He telephoned her intermittently all evening. He telephoned her the next morning—tactfully waiting until ten o'clock in case she was sleeping in. His alarm quadrupled with each unanswered call.

Finally, at two o'clock, with the date already ruined, he nerved himself to act. He descended to the apartment building's basement and rang the superintendent's bell. He was worried to distraction, but he also was afraid of being ridiculed. The superintendent, a gaunt, graying Scandinavian named Janson, opened the door and scowled at him.

"Adelle Gernyan," Wyman blurted. "She lives in F-6. She's missing."

Janson's scowl deepened. "Maybe she went somewhere."

"We had a date," Wyman said desperately. "If she'd gone somewhere, she would have told me."

Janson considered that. "Maybe she went somewhere and didn't get back when she expected."

Wyman was bright and ambitious but also shy and—as he well knew—a bit backward in personal relationships. His frantic anxiety had got him as far as the superintendent's door, but it took a valiant effort to face that dour skepticism and calmly explain himself. "Her car's in the parking lot, but she doesn't answer her phone, and she doesn't come to the door. Our date was for one-thirty. I'm telling you—something's wrong."

Janson spread his hands, palms up. "What can I do?"

"Let's take a look at her apartment."

"No," Janson said firmly.

"She could be too sick to answer the phone," Wyman pleaded. "If something were to happen to her, you'd be morally responsible and legally liable."

Janson plainly wanted no part of either one, but after a brief argument, the specter of legal liability moved him. He came with Wyman and grudgingly opened the door of the sixth floor's apartment number 6.

Wyman stepped inside; Janson positioned himself just beyond the open doorway where he could keep an eye on Wyman and at the same time avoid a charge of illegal entry. He watched uneasily while Wyman made a quick tour of the four small rooms—living room, kitchen, bath, bedroom—and then returned for a second puzzled scrutiny of the living room. If anything unfortunate had happened to Adelle Gernyan, it certainly hadn't occurred at home. She was a meticulous housekeeper. The apartment looked ready for company—nothing out of place, not so much as a pair of nylons or pantyhose hanging to dry in the bathroom. To Wyman, who had sisters, that almost seemed like a suspicious circumstance.

Janson continued to hover nervously outside the doorway, but his gaze had become a stony accusation. Wyman ignored him. He knew how preposterous it seemed, but he also knew something was very wrong. Unfortunately, no one was going to believe him without some kind of evidence, and he knew that, too.

He turned his attention to her desk. On it lay a map of the Detroit area folded to the route from Ann Arbor to Greenfield Village. A brochure that extolled the village's attractions lay beside it. Adelle had planned to go there the previous day, Saturday.

"If she'd gone," Wyman mused aloud, "would she have left these things on her desk? She had them here so she could study the route before she left. After she returned, she would have put them away." It was a feeble argument, but he embraced it fervently because it was all he had.

He opened desk drawers. Mr. Janson growled something, but Wyman was concentrating and paid no attention. In one drawer were guide booklets and souvenir postcards that identified Adelle's previous excursions to places of note in the Detroit area. There was nothing from Greenfield Village.

"So she didn't go," Wyman said, still musing aloud.

"You through?" Mr. Janson demanded.

"Just hold it a moment," Wyman said. He was thinking frantically. "Thursday night she said she'd bought a new outfit for work, her first new clothes in more than a year. That must have been what she was wearing Friday morning. She looked neat in it."

Wyman returned to the bedroom, opened the closet door, and quickly inventoried its contents. Adelle Gernyan's wardrobe was not large, and the new clothing, a light green pants suit, would have stood out conspicuously if it had been there. It was not.

Wyman went back and faced the superintendent. "She didn't come home from work Friday. Her car came back sometime between twelve-thirty and three-thirty A.M. Saturday morning, but she didn't. She was wearing new clothes Friday morning. They aren't here. If she'd been home since then, she'd have changed to something else. She planned to go to Greenfield Village on Saturday, but she didn't go. She broke our date today without letting me know, and she isn't the kind of person who'd do that. She'd have left a note in my mailbox or telephoned. Something's happened to her."

Janson altered his stance to spread his hands again with palms up. "What's to be done?"

"I'm calling the police," Wyman said. He went to Adelle's phone and did so.

A coolly impersonal male voice answered, and Wyman said uncertainly, "It's about a girl in the apartment building I live in. She's missing."

The officer, though he responded with the splendid detachment of a computer, gave every indication of taking Wyman seriously. The police of a university city like Ann Arbor have good reason to view any report of a missing young woman with concern.

As the officer asked questions, Wyman found himself making a fumbling effort to describe Adelle Gernyan, a task he hadn't believed could be so difficult. He could see her clearly—long, straight black hair, gray eyes regarding him levelly, and always the touch of a smile on her face as though life and everything in it were amusing but not worth laughing at. She was much too vital to be abstracted into a missing persons report.

"Her car came back sometime between midnight Friday and three-thirty A.M. on Saturday morning, but she didn't," Wyman said. He added lamely, "I can see her parking place from my window."

"Where was the girl employed?" the cool voice asked.

"Z-R Publications. I don't know where that is."

There was a pause at the other end of the line. "That's very interesting. And when was she last seen?"

"The last time I saw her was Friday morning," Wyman said. "She was leaving for work."

* * * *

It was only due to a flukish accident that Craig Dolan was missed at all. Dolan's habits were unpredictable. He had no favorite night-time hangout. He patronized a number of them according to chance or whimsy, and sometimes he remained home for several nights in a row while he worked on the novel he was writing. He could have dropped out of sight for weeks without anyone missing him, but on that particular Friday, Ed Smolett, his old friend and former roommate, arrived for an unannounced visit, bringing his new wife along. Originally it had been Smolett's apartment, and Dolan became the unofficial sub lessee when Smolett moved to Cleveland and got married.

When Smolett and his wife got there—shortly after six P.M.—Dolan hadn't returned from work. Smolett was astonished.

"It's still early," his wife protested.

"I know the guy," Smolett said. "He comes directly home and writes for two or three or four hours before he does any tomcatting."

"He may be having a beer with someone."

"The crowd he has beer with doesn't even get started until nine or ten," Smolett said.

"I suppose there's no one around until then to open their cages," his wife drawled. She was from Columbus, the home of the University of Michigan's arch-rival, Ohio State University, and she had known long before she reached the Ann Arbor city limits that she wasn't going to like it.

Smolett took his disappointment in stride. He parked his car in the parking space assigned to Dolan's apartment, by way of a surprise to him, and, since he still had a key to the apartment, he took his wife upstairs to wait. They watched Dolan's wreck of a television set, inherited from Smolett, and they drank his beer. Dolan stocked an incredible variety and quantity of beer, packed into the refrigerator and stowed away in various cupboards, but very little else.

At eleven o'clock, feeling hungry for something to soak up the beer, Smolett went out for a bucket of fried chicken. After they ate, Smolett's wife amused herself by trying to type something on Dolan's ancient wreck of a typewriter. Then she rummaged through his desk and found a drawer full of typewritten pages. She took one off the top and read from it oracularly.

". . . the way to filch affection without affectation, lips curved like virgin breasts, nose a question mark when not an exclamation point, eyes glowing out of the depths of time, darkly. 'Never mind the way to salvation!' he exclaimed. 'All I crave is a road map to consciousness. My dormant being is decaying in darkness, my flesh moribund, my pores exuding airs of senile afterthought, my body's nine immoral openings gaping sterilely to pour nothing into nothing.'" She turned to her husband. "You say this guy's a writer?"

"Sure, he's a writer. You don't write drawers full unless you're a writer. Don't get greasy fingerprints on his manuscript."

"And he's good, huh?"

"Sure, he's good."

"Then why don't I understand any of it?"

"Anybody can write stuff that's understood, Dolan's kind of writing takes talent."

She returned the paper to the drawer and slammed it shut.

At one A.M., having exhausted both themselves and the chicken without noticeably diminishing the stock of beer, they went to bed. In the morning, Smolett was deeply puzzled to find that Dolan still hadn't returned. Leaving a suitably insulting note for him, they went down to the parking lot.

Dolan's battered, rusty heap was parked next to their car in a space assigned to another apartment. Since parking places in the city of Ann Arbor belong to that select group of worldly possessions that are genuinely priceless, the owner of the usurped space probably was screaming a protest to the superintendent at that very moment.

Smolett contemplated Dolan's car for several minutes, walking around it and looking in. Finally he opened a door—the locks no longer worked—and snooped about the interior, stirring the dirty clothing tossed onto the back seat and glancing at the titles of paperback books scattered there.

He turned to his wife. "There's something fishy about this."

"He parked the car and went off with someone else," she suggested.

Smolett slammed the door. "Not a chance. He knows my car. He couldn't pull in here even at night and park next to it without noticing it."

"You have a point," his wife conceded. Smolett's car had been repainted by an artist friend who was into surrealism. Colors and pattern were as vividly incredible as they were unforgettable. They couldn't have faded totally from Dolan's memory in a couple of weeks.

"And if he saw it," Smolett went on, "he'd know I was upstairs wait-ing for him. He'd have taken time to come up and say hello no matter how much of a hurry he was in. I may be the only friend he's got. He'd even ditch a dame to spend an evening talking with me."

"A dame, maybe. What if it was a girl friend?"

"He'd have brought her up to meet us. Dolan's a good sort. Good company, too. Loves an audience. It's not his fault he's talented. There's something fishy about this."

They went back upstairs. Smolett took the precaution of talking with two of Dolan's neighbors, but neither of them knew much about him. Then he called the police. After describing the situation—and Dolan—and feeling more embarrassed every moment because he obviously was making a fool of himself, he suddenly turned to his wife.

"I told you about that screwy place Dolan works. Do you remember the name? Something or other publications."

"X-R," she said.

Smolett reflected. "I think is was Z-R."

"X-R," she insisted.

Smolett told the officer, "Either X-R or Z-R Publications."

"And—when was this party last seen?" the officer asked.

"One of his neighbors saw him leaving for work yesterday morning."

The officer thanked him politely, and the two of them went back to the parking lot and drove away. Smolett gave Dolan's car an angry de-parting glance as they turned into the street.

At least he had the satisfaction of having done his duty. "And," he muttered, "if that big wooly bum spent the night hanging one on and my phone call gets him picked up by the police, it'll serve him right."

* * * *

Kevin Mondor's absence was noted cholerically at six thirty on Fri-day evening, but it wasn't reported until Saturday night. Mondor's apart-ment was one of eight in a converted private dwelling that once had been a mansion. Mrs. Tinsley, his landlady, was the common, vitriolic type that thousands of students and young people in Ann Arbor come to know well and hate, but she had an uncharacteristic fondness for Mondor.

He kept his apartment neat. He did not play the saxophone, like the tenant on the third floor, nor did he vibrate the building with thunderous four-speaker stereo systems, like two other tenants. He hosted no parties; he didn't even have visitors.

Further, he was knowledgeable in a dazzling variety of ways. He could fix a leaky faucet or make electrical repairs, which startled her, because his youthful appearance and thick glasses made him look like the most bookishly impractical of students. He had a degree in mathematics, a subject Mrs. Tinsley considered one of life's ultimate mysteries. Finally, the two of them shared an idiosyncrasy that Mrs. Tinsley had refined into a vice. Mondor was the first vegetarian tenant in her memory. He also was the first tenant who never gave her trouble and the only one who had been willing to help her out when she needed it.

They quickly became friends, and out of that friendship a business arrangement emerged. Each Friday evening he had dinner with her—a special, lavishly prepared vegetarian dinner of a kind that anyone but a food faddist would have happily consigned to the world's diminishing reservoir of forbidden knowledge. Afterward, he tutored her in book-keeping and worked with her on an accounting system for running her building. She enjoyed preparing an occasional feast for a kindred and highly appreciative spirit, and with his expert guidance, she hoped to learn how to prepare her own income tax forms.

That Friday he did not come home. Mrs. Tinsley, fuming, perspiring—she was incongruously fat for a food faddist and vegetarian—stood watch over the ruined dinner until after midnight. It was not concern for Mondor's welfare that kept her from going to bed but the desire to impart a number of well-rehearsed phrases to him before her anger faded. The tenants' parking lot was immediately under her bedroom window, and she heard the distinctive engine of his little foreign car about an hour after she finally retired. She sleepily staggered to her apartment door and opened it a crack, waiting for him to enter the house, but he failed to do so. Eventually she decided she could deal with him more effectively in the morning, fully dressed, than in the middle of the night, half asleep and in her nightgown. She went back to bed.

She waited for him to come down in the morning. When he hadn't appeared by ten o'clock, she went up and rapped on his door. Getting him out of bed after the dirty trick he had pulled on her would serve him right, she thought, but there was no response.

It was midafternoon when she finally thought to open his door with her master key. He wasn't there. And his cigarettes weren't there. He only smoked at work, during his noon hours. Evenings and weekends the cigarettes always lay on the corner of his desk with his spare change. He hadn't sneaked out, because his car was still parked behind the house. Kevin Mondor never walked anywhere.

He wasn't there, and he hadn't been there. She went back downstairs and resumed her waiting, and eventually her conscience began to trouble her. Kevin was a nice lad and not at all the kind of person who would break a dinner date without telephoning. Something must have happened to him. He might be lying in a hospital at that moment.

Eventually she became sufficiently alarmed to call the police. The officer who answered the phone took her information politely and asked, almost as an afterthought, where Mr. Mondor worked.

"Z-R Publications," Mrs. Tinsley said. "He says it's a crazy place. He does something with mathematics."

"I see. And—when did you see him last?"

"Yesterday morning," Mrs. Tinsley said. "Friday. When he left for work."

CHAPTER 10

On Monday morning, Lieutenant Arthur Prehn looked through the reports the Ann Arbor Police Department had accumulated over the weekend. He detached three of them and read them again, pursing his lips thoughtfully. Then he tilted back in his chair and meditated for a few minutes before he read them a third time. Finally he turned to his telephone and dialed a number.

"Laylor, Graffington, Bartley, and Kordro," a voice responded.

"John Laylor, Jr., please," the officer said. "Lieutenant Prehn, Ann Arbor Police Department, calling."

A moment later, in a small rear office, a slender, middle-aged man with incongruously gray hair picked up his phone. "Laylor, Junior."

"Prehn," the lieutenant said. "I have three missing person reports that may interest you. They're nothing like the profile, but there are some interesting points. The odd thing is that all of them have been working for the same firm for three weeks or longer."

Laylor tilted back in his chair and looked up at the wall opposite his desk. Six framed photographs hung there. Three of them, of two girls and a boy, were unmistakable high school graduation photos. The other three, of two middle-aged men and a woman, had been enlarged from casual snapshots. Laylor studied the six faces absently while he talked. "What firm?" he asked.

"Z-R Publications."

"Never heard of it. An established business, with an address, and a listed telephone, and a bank account?"

"Right."

"That doesn't fit the profile at all, but let's have the details."

The lieutenant read from his reports; Laylor took notes.

"It sounds as though all three of them were abducted somewhere between work and home," Laylor said finally. "That's peculiar enough, but for the abductors to return the cars to their usual parking places seems astonishing. I mean—why bother?"

"It also seems unnecessarily risky," the lieutenant said. "The victims' habits must have been studied meticulously. For example, Mondor's car was left in its usual parking place even though the parking lot is the building's back yard, out of sight of the street, and no parking spaces are marked because it's unpaved. The friend from Ohio had parked in Dolan's parking place as a joke, and Dolan's car was left in the space next to it."

"Someone wanted you to think these people returned home from work safely," Laylor said.

"Someone also wanted to postpone the discovery that they were missing. One interesting point is that all three seem to have no friends, or relatives, or even close acquaintances in the area."

"Ah!"

"I said 'seem to have.'"

"I heard you."

"Gernyan and Dolan are newcomers to Ann Arbor. The third, Mondor, is an introspective type who keeps to himself. All three cashed their paychecks at the Arbor Vista Shopping Mall during the lunch hour and ate lunch there. That's the last trace we have of them. Except for three coincidences, which is almost excessive, they might not have been missed for days or even weeks. Last Thursday, Gernyan chanced to make the acquaintance of a young man in her apartment building, and she had a Sunday date with him. Mondor had a regular Friday evening date to have dinner with his landlady. Both of those social contacts were made inside the buildings where they live and would have been difficult for an outside investigator to catch. Doyle's coincidence was the unexpected arrival of his friend from Ohio."

"But surely they would have been missed this morning when they didn't show up for work," Laylor objected. "What do the people at Z-R Publications profess to know about this?"

"Nothing."

"Nothing?" Laylor echoed blankly. "At the very least, someone there should know what time they left on Friday."

"Nothing," the lieutenant said firmly, "because we can't find any of them. I had two good detectives waiting for Z-R Publications to open this morning. It didn't. At five P.M. on Friday, it went out of business."

* * * *

Monday morning had dawned eight hours earlier in Moscow. Yuri Fedorenko, who was supposed to arise with the sun but frequently overslept, arrived at the compound's main gate gasping for breath and half an hour late. From his apartment, he had to take a bus to the nearest Metro station. Then came a long subway ride with a transfer from one line to another, and finally, at the end of the line, he had more than a mile to cover on foot. He alternated running with jogging, but he was still hopelessly late. If his superiors had chosen that day to check on him, he was doomed. As far as he knew, no one had ever checked, but he worried about it constantly.

There were times when he wished he had never been honored with this special assignment. On the other hand, if he had remained a humdrum clerk in the KGB's First Chief Directorate, he certainly would have lost his job during the upheaval many were calling the Smoutnoye Vremia, the Time of Troubles, because of its similarity to the chaotic years of the early seventeenth century when Russia also was leaderless and torn by turmoil. Merely thinking about having to look for a job when so many were out of work frightened him. His background was against him. To most Russians, the KGB was history, but few employers would knowingly hire a former KGB worker, even such an innocuous one as himself.

In the old days—the good old days for members of the KGB—things had been different. Employees of the Organs of State Security could take pride in their work. They were envied and privileged. Housing assignments were theirs for the asking even at times when none were available for anyone else. In their canteens they were served foods rarely found in Moscow except at the tables of the party elite, such as fresh milk, fruit, eggs, and bacon, and all of it was inexpensive. The massive First Chief Directorate headquarters building off the Moscow Ring Road had a library, a medical clinic, a swimming pool, and a sports complex. Each morning the workers were transported to the building's location southeast of Moscow by a fleet of busses; each evening they were returned to Moscow. Police halted traffic on the outer ring road to expedite the KGB's bus service.

Then came the high honor of promotion, special responsibility, and an increase in salary for Fedorenko, but with it came exile to this forsaken place in a remote suburb. As a KGB worker, Fedorenko already had a choice apartment. Nothing comparable was available nearby, and he would have been reluctant to move anyway because he hoped his new directorate would eventually be transferred to the spacious luxury of the First Chief Directorate's headquarters building.

At first the compound had seemed rather pleasant. Its warehouses bustled with activity, and once the truckers became familiar with his plodding figure, he was offered rides in both directions. Further, he was able to take his meals with the workers. They enjoyed none of the luxuries of the KGB canteens—the food was coarse and far more expensive than Fedorenko was accustomed to—but at least it was convenient and there was plenty of it.

Then came the Smoutnoye Vremia. When there were no more goods to transport or store in the warehouses, drivers and workers, except for security personnel, were discharged. The canteen was closed. Fedorenko and the security personnel had to fend for themselves. The compound now was used for the storage of worn-out vehicles and machines for which repair parts were not available. Trucks of all sizes, cranes, earthmoving machines, and rusted monsters whose function Fedorenko could only guess at were left there in untidy rows.

Now Fedorenko had to walk the distance between the last Metro stop and the compound. In winter it was a bitter cold ordeal on a slippery road. Further, he had to carry his lunch with him—made up of whatever his wife could scrounge in a city of shortages—for there was no place near the compound where food was available.

Yuri Fedorenko was secretary of the KGB's Directorate Y. It sounded like a formidable responsibility, but in fact he was able to carry the burden of the entire directorate on his broad shoulders with very little incommodiousness. Directorate Y existed only in the limbo of Fedorenko's cramped office and in a remote location in America referred to in reports by a code name. His "work" consisted of reading and filing such papers as his superiors passed along to him concerning the directorate's experimental research. The papers were heavily laden with scientific terminology and statistics and meant little to him, but he went through the motions of reading them anyway. He had nothing else to do.

Despite the hardships he had suffered since the Smoutnoye Vremia began, the anonymity of Fedorenko's position had been a stroke of luck for him. The KGB had never been popular, and suddenly those connected with it were in danger, but even the compound's security men had no notion of who he was or what he did there. They thought he was some kind of an auditor searching for corruption in accounts relating to the compound's former activity. As long as a messenger brought his wages each month, in unidentifiable cash, he was contented to drift along with the situation. Eventually Russian society would regain its sanity, and the KGB would be able to reclaim its proper position.

In the meantime, he had to suffer daily insults from the security personnel. "Late again!" a guard had blurted when he came into view.

The massive gate, wide enough for the largest trucks, opened a mere crack, and Fedorenko had to squeeze through it. He hurried to the rear of the compound and admitted himself by key to a door at the back of a weathered two-story brick building. The door was marked "Traffic Control," and it opened onto a stairway. Fedorenko locked it behind him, clomped up the worn stair treads, and opened a second door with a different key. The building was shoddy, but the doors were of steel, and the locks were the best obtainable—they came from West Germany—and in excellent condition. He entered and locked the second door beyond him.

Directorate Y Headquarters consisted of two small, shabbily furnished rooms with a closet that contained a toilet and lavatory. The first room was barely large enough for Fedorenko's desk, chair, and a filing cabinet. His only other equipment was a typewriter that had been new at the time of his transfer and was still new because he rarely used it. The room was painted green, as was the bare room beyond, and both rooms had high ceilings and large but dim hanging globes for light fixtures. The color and the fixtures had been ubiquitous at the KGB Headquarters in Moscow's Dzerzhinsky Square in the old days, and they persisted in forgotten enclaves such as Directorate Y's headquarters. Fedorenko had long since tired of them. He had to do the routine janitor work himself, and neither walls nor globes had been cleaned in his memory.

But he was blessed with a soft job, a good salary, and as much job security and prospect for future promotion as existed anywhere in such chaotic times, which seemed astonishing when he considered that he worked for an organization that no longer existed. The abolition of the KGB had changed nothing as far as Yuri Fedorenko was concerned. Reports continued to arrive. A messenger brought his salary each month. It behooved him to keep his mouth shut and pretend to be busy.

More than once, as one week tediously followed another and the Russian states slowly emerged from the Smoutnoye Vremia into a kind of impoverished normality, he had reflected on the wisdom of his KGB masters. They must have seen the upheaval coming from far off and concealed the organization's wealth as well as a number of important departments in obscure locations such as this one. Surely no one could possibly suspect such a shabby office of being connected with a surviving—in fact, thriving—KGB Directorate.

As for KGB Headquarters, Fedorenko himself didn't have the slightest notion where that was, but it, too, survived and thrived, and even reports from America arrived there promptly and were brought to Fedorenko by messenger for filing.

On this Monday morning, he followed his usual routine. He placed the metal box containing his lunch in a desk drawer and went directly to the room beyond, which contained what appeared to be a massive old safe. It was in fact an excellent modern safe in disguise, and both a key and the correct combination were required to open it. Fedorenko checked the seal he had placed on it the night before and then he applied his key and worked the combination.

Because everything about Directorate Y was designated ultra-secret, Fedorenko dutifully consigned all of the files to the safe whenever he wasn't guarding them personally. He also sealed the safe each night. Despite these precautions—and the efficient locks and sturdy doors—the guards were too few to keep an efficient watch on the compound, and anyone with proper tools could have broken in and looted the safe. Directorate Y's real security rested in its anonymity and its unlikely location. No one would suspect that anything of value was to be found here.

He began transferring the files to the filing cabinet by his desk. Despite the fact that he rarely used them, he kept them accessible whenever he was in the office. If anyone checked on him, he wanted to create the impression that he referred to them constantly. Except for special messengers, callers of any kind were rare, and it had been years since he had seen a superior, but he never knew who might be spying on him or by what means. Safety lay in appearing to be busy. He lugged the last of the files to the outer office and closed the safe before he noticed an envelope in the "In" basket on his desk.

He opened it with trepidation, but it was only an advisory concerning field activity in America. The three high-ranking personages responsible for Directorate Y's activities had initialed it, and it had been delivered to him by the mysterious midnight messenger who brought Directorate Y's mail when there was any and left his monthly salary.

The advisory was in code and consisted of a list of numbers and colors. Fedorenko entered its number and date in his log. Then he got the code book from a special locked compartment of the safe and laboriously deciphered it.

"Project Ob," the message read. "Phase three commenced. No complications."

Federenko added his own classification label, "Vodka," which meant, "Routine."

CHAPTER 11

After the loss of Adelle's watch, they sometimes argued about what time it was. When hours became meaningless to them, they began to argue about what day it was. They measured the passage of time by the number of weary steps to the end of an alley, which was as far ahead as they cared to think. In the unrelenting glare of overhead lights, night was a myth from an almost forgotten past. Once Mondor asked Adelle for her broken watch, and he took the back off and poked at its innards with a bent nail he had picked up in a Nightmare Village. Then he snapped it together and returned it to her with a shrug.

Dolan, who had watched the operation with a grin, remarked, "If that's Mondor's notion of first aid, I hope I don't break a leg."

Another of Mondor's ideas was more successful. He devised a ploy that enabled them to rest occasionally and sometimes even to catch a few winks of sleep. When gas chased them from an alley, instead of hurrying to put it far behind them, they would move into the next alley and sit down to see what would happen. Sometimes a nearby gas vent routed them immediately. Sometimes there was none, and it took time and a large expenditure of gas before the choking cloud reached them. Once they got a long sleep that way—more than an hour, Dolan thought.

Their route moved from page to page of Mondor's small notebook in an unpatterned network of lines that looked like a web spun by a drunken spider, but he doggedly refused to give up his attempt to map the maze.

Dolan had lost interest in vandalizing the walls. There were so many of them to write on, and they happened onto his messages so rarely, that the project began to seem futile. On the rare occasions when he did make a few scrapings, he contented himself with a question mark rather than a date.

As they settled themselves one more time to wait for the gas to catch up with them, Mondor, after adding a line to his map and recording the paces he had counted, began to grumble about his cigarettes. He had left the pack on his desk when he went to inspect the "computer". Although he had never smoked more than one or two a day, the lack of them increasingly loomed as a cruel deprivation, and he complained about it constantly.

Dolan stirred himself and gouged their names on the wall. His once ornate carving had degenerated into an illegible scrawl. When he finished, he reflected for a moment, shrugged, and added a question mark with an arrow pointing in both directions.

Then he snapped his knife shut and turned savagely on Mondor. "Why don't you shut up about tobacco? This little adventure may be saving your life."

He was fond of discoursing on tobacco as one of the world's premier evils, and Adelle already knew his entire speech by heart. This time he delivered an alternate sermon in which he expounded at length and with severe indignation on the manner in which Mondor had exposed him, Dolan, to lung cancer by smoking an occasional cigarette outside the building and two wings away from Dolan's office.

"We may starve," Dolan pontificated. "We may die of thirst, but thank God Madam's goons didn't think to stock the kitchen with cigarettes. At least we're safe from emphysema."

Adelle looked irritably from one male to the other. Dolan's once neatly trimmed beard was becoming shaggy, and he had developed environs of whiskers covering his face back to his sideburns. Mondor's shallow growth had passed the stage where he looked like a bum who needed a shave. Now he looked like an adolescent trying to grow a beard. At least he had abandoned his necktie for good, but somehow that seemed to leave him perpetually in a state of undress. Their petty bickering had long since ceased to amuse her.

"Given a choice," she announced, "which, unfortunately, I'm not, I'd much rather listen to bombs and locomotives than to you two. Is it Monday or Tuesday?"

They discussed the question. Mondor argued for Tuesday and brought Einstein's Theory of Relativity into it, which infuriated Dolan. Sitting on a hot stove, Dolan said, had nothing to do with the number of times the hands on a watch worn by the sitter revolved, and its influence on Earth's period of revolution was demonstrably minute. If Mondor thought he could prove anything by it, he, Dolan, would enjoy watching Mondor sit on a hot stove the next time they got back to the kitchen. Mondor's pants probably needed changing anyway.

"If we get back," Adelle said. "When was the last time?"

They discussed that. At long intervals the Big Ben bell sounded, and they began a frantic search for the RC, the Rest Center, for food, water, and the few moments of sleep allowed them. The quantity of food was smaller on each visit and their rest period was shorter. Also, the maze had become so complicated that it took an increasing amount of time to locate the kitchen when they heard the bell, and once they failed to find it at all. They suffered acutely until it rang again.

Between bells, they continued to be gassed, wracked by air raids, run over by screaming locomotives, and tormented by dying babies. Instead of enjoying the occasional brief periods of silence, such as the one they were experiencing, they tensely awaited the crashing sounds that would follow.

The Nightmare Villages were their special nemeses. There were two of them. One had frame buildings and a street of asphalt pavement. The other had a cobblestone street and buildings of stone. The explosions were genuine in both of them, and real bullets snapped over their heads and ricocheted among them. Both villages were being reduced to piles of rubble that gradually filled the streets, and the danger from explosives and bullets and flying debris intensified each time they passed through one.

Dolan received a flesh wound in his upper arm during a scramble through the stone village, but he never said whether it bothered him. He was too angry to mention it. He wouldn't let Adelle bandage it or even look at it. That troubled her severely. He had been concerned enough to apply a bandage after the bullet scraped her leg. She felt she should be doing at least as much for him.

Further, she had an increasing awareness of how much the group needed him. He was their leader. He always seemed to know the right thing to do. They needed Mondor, too, with his astonishing command of recondite knowledge. She, with her background in English literature, was the useless one. She had never imagined a life style where physical prowess and practical thinking were so important.

She disliked the men as thoroughly as she had when their adventure began, and their silly squabbling was an increasing irritation. Too often it prevented her from taking refuge in her own inner thoughts—the one pleasure that remained to her. At the same time, she recognized that both of them had remarkable abilities, and she had a growing respect for them.

On what seemed like a regular schedule, they were routed through one of the three test rooms, and the problems there became increasingly complicated. They were given long chains of numerals and weirdly patterned solutions to be played on the three controls. They tried again to rest in one and were driven out by gas. It was an experiment they hesitated to repeat. There was difficulty enough in solving the problems without the added complications of heat, darkness, or a small room rapidly filling with choking fumes.

Each passing moment brought a new plateau of exhaustion; each new test became an obstacle that scarcely seemed worth overcoming. They were finding it difficult to concentrate.

Adelle no longer worried or even thought about a future totally beyond her control. Someone else would decide whether to lower the gunfire as they picked their way through a Nightmare Village, or whether to set off an explosion when they reached it instead of just ahead of them, or whether to block their way to the Rest Center permanently. Their destiny was oblivion, whether from catastrophe or physical degeneration, and their efforts to survive were merely postponing that.

Since she had no future, she deliberately excised from her thoughts any worry or speculation as to what might happen next. Her present was an unending, torturous exhaustion punctuated by moments of sheer terror, and she ignored it as much as she could. The only thing left for her was a return to the past. She would resurrect one small incident from her childhood—a party, an excursion with her father, a summer vacation when both of her parents were still alive—and explore it again in every small detail she could conjure out of her memory.

This was possible only when the men kept quiet long enough to allow her to think. Her fantasies were becoming increasingly important to her, and the masculine bickering was a constant irritation because it disrupted them.

She still carried the much battered milk carton, and they hoarded its precious contents. Dolan's saucepan had taken a ricocheting bullet through its bottom in one of the Nightmare Villages, and the goons had removed from the kitchen the frying pan and any dishes that could have substituted for it.

Mondor started again on the subject of tobacco; both she and Dolan ignored him. She leaned back, eyes closed, and while she waited for the hiss of gas to bring her falteringly to her feet, she began to search her memory for another incident to resurrect.

The lights went out. Even with her eyes shut, Adelle sensed the darkness immediately and sat up to stare into it. Mondor, his mind suddenly diverted from tobacco, muttered, "I've been afraid they might do that."

The dark surrounded them thickly, posing its own intangible threat to blend with the menacing silence. "Something is going to happen," Adelle thought, "and now we're completely helpless."

Mondor covered his own apprehension with sarcasm. "Isn't there a saying that what you can't see won't hurt you?"

"It's a damned silly saying if there is," Dolan said. "Staring at the dark won't give us better vision, so we might as well lie down and rest."

They moved closer together, feeling about on the cement floor to make certain there was no strip from which a partition could rise and separate them. Adelle stretched out; the darkness felt soothing and restful after so many hours of continuous light, and her tension began to drain away.

The men's voices kept her awake. They were perplexed by this new ploy and wanted to talk about it. "There's got to be some sinister purpose," Dolan said, yawning noisily. "We know we're test rats. Maybe the next test will be in Braille. What kind of psychological experiments could they inflict on us in the dark?"

Mondor thought for a moment. "Days and nights of different lengths. Adaptability of humans to darkness."

"It won't be anything that profound," Dolan said bitterly. "We're much more susceptible to their stick-a-pin-in-the-bug kind of experiments in the dark, and that's what we'll get. Have your matches ready."

"Two packages of matches won't light our way around the maze very many times," Mondor said.

"I wasn't thinking of that. We should have light available for emergencies. I'm certain there'll be emergencies."

The silence continued, and Adelle felt herself dozing off. Then Mondor said meditatively, "Maybe darkness comes in degrees. Maybe it seems darker than it is because we've been in the light for so long. Maybe our eyes will adjust. Can either of you see better now?"

Adelle wearily opened her eyes. She was straining to penetrate the darkness when the flash went off. There was no sound—just an instantaneous, blinding glare that brought an illusion of intense heat, as though the sun had shone unexpectedly into a darkened room.

Then the blackness closed in again.

Adelle sat up and rubbed her eyes.

Mondor asked, "Did either of you see anything?"

"Only the light," Dolan said. "Was there anything to see?"

It flashed again. Adelle instinctively covered her closed eyes with her hands. When she opened them, she saw only darkness.

"It was some kind of strobe light," Mondor said.

"It had a reddish tint to it," Dolan said. "Do strobe lights have a reddish tint?"

"That wasn't the light. Your eyes are still bloodshot from all that beer."

"Turn your brain on and stop acting like a moronic adolescent," Dolan snapped. "Were they flash cubes?"

"I don't think so," Mondor said. After a moment of silence, he added, "They could be photographing us, I suppose."

"Why didn't you warn us?" Dolan asked disgustedly. "Adelle could have combed her hair. If they wanted to photograph us, why would they turn out the lights? The place was bright enough to take pictures without a flash. Your brain has been unplugged so long you've lost the cord."

There was a rustle of clothing, and then Dolan's whisper sounded close to Adelle's ear. "They think we're going to sit here in the dark and let them experiment on us with flashes. So let's get moving."

He whispered to Mondor, who immediately got to his feet. Adelle reluctantly followed. She would have welcomed a longer rest or even a nap. Despite the flashes, the dark still felt cool and refreshing.

Dolan made a few vicious gouges in the wall. "Just in case we come this way again," he whispered, "those marks are vertical. Let's go three abreast. Adelle in the center. Mondor and I can feel the wall for openings. Adelle can keep a hand in front of her so we don't run into anything. Okay?"

Spotlights blinded them. Adelle instinctively turned away, but another light hit her squarely in the face. Dolan hissed, "Let's go!"

They lunged forward. They escaped the blinding glare momentarily by looking at the floor, but the next lights hit their faces from a low angle. Adelle tried to shield herself with one arm, but it was no protection from the circular glares that stabbed at her from one side. On an impulse she closed her eyes, stretched one hand out in front of her, and ran. The others kept pace with her, and a moment later they were in darkness.

"That was a silly kind of test to try on people who are free to move," Mondor said. "Why didn't they use moveable lights?"

"Don't give them ideas," Dolan said.

A few minutes later Adelle's extended hand touched a wall. There was no opening on either side.

Mondor swore softly. "Now we've got to run the gantlet again."

"Spotlights and flashes don't bite," Dolan said cheerfully. "We'll hare past them and take the first turn."

"If there is a turn," Adelle said.

They managed a stumbling run; but no spotlights came on, and no strobes flashed. Finally they slowed their pace. The only thing their reckless dash had gained for them was another increment to their exhaustion. They plodded along slowly, with Dolan and Mondor reproaching each other for the wasted effort, until Dolan suddenly announced that he had found an opening.

"Was it here before?" Adelle asked.

The two men were silent for a moment, thinking. All of them were having difficulty remembering what had happened twenty minutes earlier.

"What does it matter?" Dolan demanded finally. "We're here, and the opening's here. Do we take it, or do we sit down and rest?"

"We rest," Adelle answered firmly.

The hiss of gas brought them to their feet before they got comfortably settled. They stumbled through the opening and resumed their formation, plodding side by side through total darkness. The men continued to feel the walls for openings, and Adelle, walking with one hand clutching her milk carton, held the other extended in front of her.

They had gone only a short distance when the air raid began. Bombs screamed down on them, real explosions went off nearby with deafening blasts, and dazzling flashes of light illuminated the choking smoke that curled toward them. The men, guessing what would follow, flung themselves down. Adelle, who had been looking straight ahead when the first bomb went off, stood rigidly erect, feet frozen in place, as flash after flash blinded her.

"Get down!" Dolan shouted.

Not until the first bullet snapped past her ear did she dive to the floor. The image of what she had seen in the painfully bright light of the explosions was burned on her retinas.

It was over quickly. Dolan hauled her to her feet and demanded, "You trying to get killed, or something? Let's get out of here!"

"Wait!" she exclaimed.

Darkness had closed in instantly when the explosions stopped. The three of them stood motionless, their ears still ringing from the blasts. In that unnatural silence, Dolan's whisper sounder thunderous. "What is it?"

"There's a hole," Adelle said, speaking normally. She was surprised at the calmness of her voice. "Why whisper? They certainly know all about it."

"A hole in the floor?"

"Yes. I happened to be looking straight ahead when the first explosion went off. I caught a glimpse of it before the other explosions blinded me."

"How large a hole?" Mondor asked.

Adelle still retained the image clearly, but her uncertainty about the distance made the size difficult to estimate. "It's like a rectangle, with the narrow end across the alley," she said.

"All the way across?"

"No. There's a strip like a ledge on each side. And the long side is—" She hesitated. "It's a lot longer than the alley is wide."

The men weighed this information silently. "I guess we'll have to stop barging about in the dark," Mondor said finally. "We should have expected this. It's another exercise in group problem solving. Either we pass it, or we flunk out permanently." He reflected for a moment. "I don't suppose you could see how deep the hole is."

"All I saw was a black rectangle," Adelle said.

"Lucky you saw it at all. Probably that's part of the test—the first flash gave us one chance, and if none of us happened to be looking in the right direction, tough luck. All three of us could have fallen in."

"It could be three inches deep or thirty feet," Dolan said. "Let's get moving. I'd rather cope with this without gas on my heels. When we find out how deep it is and how wide the ledges are, we can decide what to do."

They began to edge forward, sliding one foot ahead of the other and probing before they took a step. Time passed; when questioned again, Adelle could only say she had caught a momentary glimpse of it before the flashes blinded her, and it seemed like a long way off.

"If they'd painted a black rectangle on the floor, would it have looked like what you saw?" Mondor asked.

Adelle searched her memory. "Maybe."

"Get off her back," Dolan said. "She's described it as well as she could. If she's wrong, it isn't costing us anything but a little time, and we have plenty of that. Either way we'll learn something."

They continued to edge forward.

It was Dolan, moving slightly ahead of the others, who found it. He called out, and they halted and backed off a step. He knelt and scooted forward on his knees.

"There's no doubt it's a hole," he announced. "The bottom is beyond my reach, and I'm lying down and stretching an arm into it."

"Shall I strike a match?" Mondor asked.

"We may need the matches more urgently later. Got a coin?"

Mondor's clothing rustled. His hand found Dolan's in the dark, and Dolan crept forward again. It seemed like a long time before they heard a sharp clink somewhere in the undefined darkness.

"When Adelle sees a hole, it genuinely is one," Dolan said. "At least a dozen feet, maybe deeper."

"I hope that was a penny I gave you," Mondor said.

"I hope it was a dime. One of Madam's goons might be tempted and break his neck." Dolan was edging forward again. "The ledge on the left is at least a foot wide, maybe a little wider."

Mondor knelt to investigate the other ledge. "The one on the right is about the same. Say fifteen inches."

"But they may narrow to zero before we get past the hole," Dolan said. "Adelle?"

Despite the total darkness that enveloped them, she closed her eyes. The image had faded, and she was trying to remember rather than to see. "I don't think so. The black rectangle had straight lines, and the edges were parallel to the walls."

"Sounds as if we can chance it," Mondor said. "Important question: Do we use matches? It might be easier if we can't see. Just face the wall, lean against it, and edge sideways."

"What about Adelle's carton of water?" Dolan asked.

"We'll drink that," Adelle said. "There's just enough left for one or two good swallows apiece. But I'd like to save the carton."

"We've got to save the carton," Dolan said. "Let's drink up first, and then I'll stick it inside my shirt where it'll be out of the way. Too bad we don't have a picnic lunch to go with it."

They shared out the water, passing the carton around and taking a mouthful at a time. The carton made two circuits, and Adelle, told to finish it off, found the last mouthful a generous one. Dolan took the carton.

"I'll go first," Dolan said. "Mondor can stand by with matches in case I need them. Everything else in order? What about your purse, Adelle?"

"What about it?" Adelle asked. She stubbornly continued to wear it over her shoulder even though she had no use for it. She was hardly aware of it.

"As long as it doesn't make you feel lopsided. I'll take the left ledge. Seems more natural to move to the right. Here I go."

The only sound was the shuffling of his feet.

Adelle had slumped to the floor. She meditated walking a fifteen inch ledge in the dark with a wall on one side that made it impossible to lean forward to keep her balance and a dozen foot drop on the other. Would they be able to get her out if she fell? She doubted it. They would have to leave her. If they did get her out, even a slight injury could be a fatal handicap. She remembered reading about the helplessness of injured wild animals. In a safe place and with only rudimentary care, they could recover easily. In the wild, there was neither care nor safety. The three of them were in the same situation. Any injury requiring more sophisticated first aid than Dolan could supply with a handkerchief might quickly prove disastrous.

Dolan's remote voice seemed to reach them from another dimension. "The ledge is quite a bit wider than my shoes are long, which makes it a good fifteen inches. Just face the wall and step sideways, and it's easy."

The shuffling of his feet faded into the distance. After a time he called to them again. "It works best if you slide your feet. You can kind of lean into the wall. At least, I have the sensation of leaning. Maybe it's an illusion, but it helps." Then he began to laugh. "Okay. I'm here. Let's have Adelle next. Help her get started, Mondor."

Mondor supported her until she edged out of his reach. She slid her right foot, moved her left toward it, and tried to imagine herself leaning forward into the wall. As she gained confidence, she began to move faster.

"Everything okay?" Dolan called.

"Okay," she responded breathlessly.

It went on forever: the sliding side steps, the leaning with both palms against the wall as though there might be something there to cling to. She closed her eyes, found that it made no difference, and shuffled on.

Suddenly Dolan had hold of her. "You're all right now. I didn't want to touch you until you were past the edge. Sit down and wait for Mondor."

They heard him coming. He had started shortly after Adelle, and he soon joined them. "I want to rest," he announced.

"Not here," Dolan said. "We're too close to that damned hole for comfort."

Adelle felt a sudden, numbing apprehension. "What if this is a blind alley? What if there's no exit?"

"Then," Dolan said cheerfully, "we'll go back. What we've done once, we can do again."

They resumed their formation, walking three abreast and sliding one foot ahead of the other to probe the smooth cement surface. When Dolan decided they had gone far enough, they slumped to the floor. The adrenalin that had sustained Adelle along the ledge was gone. She leaned back wearily.

Lights came on. They momentarily blinded her, but she recovered quickly and turned to look back. All three of them looked back.

The hole was closed. Black strips that outlined its edges were the only visible reminder of it.

"One of those things could be anywhere, and there's no rule that they have to have a ledge on each side or even on one side," Dolan said thoughtfully. "From now on, we'll have to feel our way even when the lights are on."

"Will that do any good?" Mondor asked. "What's to prevent them from dropping a section of the floor like a trapdoor when we're standing on it?"

Dolan didn't answer.

Adelle spoke slowly, keeping her voice steady. "There's nothing to prevent it. Any time Madam gets tired of this little game she's playing with us, all she has to do is press a button."

Neither of the men said anything. Finally, after a long moment of silence, Mondor mused, "Speaking of Madam—I wonder what she and her goons are doing right now. Gloating over us, I suppose. We may take a trick now and then, but she knows she'll take the last one."

CHAPTER 12

Madam was entertaining a visitor, a tall, dark, exotic-looking man with a touch of gray in his hair and an incongruously black mustache. Probably he had been forewarned—like everyone else, he called her Madam.

They stood before a viewing screen in the laboratory's control room, which Madam's assistants had dubbed "Mission Control." The reference to the American space program irritated her, but she had to concede its aptness. The room controlled the most lavishly equipped psychological research laboratory in the world, and Madam's visitor had been properly impressed by it.

They were watching Adelle Gernyan, Craig Dolan, and Kevin Mondor plod wearily along an alley. At the end there was an opening on either side, and Madam turned up the volume so they could listen to the argument over which turning to take. The visitor, who was calling himself Mr. Hendy—though he was no more Anglo-Saxon than Madam was Chinese—watched with elated interest. A few minutes earlier, Madam had allowed him to press the button that released tear gas and cut short the subjects' attempt to rest, and he exclaimed delightedly at their instant reaction.

"Amazing!" he murmured. "Amazing! My congratulations!"

Madam's assistants were wearing white laboratory coats for the occasion, and they were on their best behavior and listening with more interest than Madam would have thought them capable of—too much interest, in fact, so she invited the visitor to confer with her in her study, an adjoining room with a large window overlooking the control room. There they could watch and listen to everything the assistants were doing while conversing privately.

The room's walls were lined with bookcases, and it contained a desk; a table with three tape viewers where Madam could review and compare tests from the experiment's current phase with those of previous phases; and a conference table. The chairs were plushly upholstered. Madam spent most of her waking hours there, and she saw no reason why she shouldn't be comfortable.

She placed two of the chairs side by side so they could keep their eyes on the control room's main viewing screen while they talked. It now showed the subjects plodding along another alley. When they reached the end, a few squirts of tear gas hurried them around the corner and into what the subjects were calling a Nightmare Village. Bombs exploded, bullets whipped over them, ricochets whined and clattered. They weren't due for another exposure to this particular hazard, but Madam had arranged it to further impress Hendy.

He watched open-mouthed. When finally he wrenched his gaze away, all of his words were superlatives. "I'm delighted to have our causes joined," he said. "Ultimately, our goals are the same. How many have you killed?"

"We call it 'termination,'" Madam said with a smile. "We've terminated six. It'll be nine when the current phase is finished."

Hendy looked puzzled. "That isn't very many for such an elaborate laboratory."

Madam smiled again. She chose her words carefully because most laymen were unable to comprehend even an elementary discussion of psychology. "Our objective isn't to exterminate Americans but to study them. It is America that must be destroyed, not Americans, and we are learning the most effective ways to do it."

Hendy's reply was a polite murmur of puzzlement.

"A bomb on an airplane is spectacular," Madam continued, "and it may kill one or two hundred people and cost the American Government much trouble and expense in guarding airports more carefully. But in the long run it doesn't change a thing except to make the American people angry, and that can be dangerous if the source of the bomb is discovered. We don't want to anger the American people. We want to learn as much as we can about them. Especially we want to learn what frightens them, what intimidates them, what terrorizes them, what makes them panic, and how much of any of those things they can endure before their minds become impaired and they destroy themselves."

"Destroy themselves," Hendy mused. "Do you mean—all Americans—and all America…"

"Exactly," Madam said. "A few deaths caused by terrorist bombs have almost no effect on a nation—except, as I just mentioned, to anger it, and anger is not a good emotion for our purpose. The contrary—it may result in severe reprisals. We need to know what will have the greatest destructive impact on the American people. Then the deaths can be numbered in millions and the nation destroyed. Sabotage is destructive of things rather than people. Things are much more easily replaced, especially in America. We are learning how to destroy people."

"Deaths that can be numbered in millions and the nation destroyed." The idea pleased him. "But how can that be brought about? Of course atomic bombs…"

Madam shook her head. "With something far more potent than atomic bombs. With psychological bombs. We must continue our experiments so we can formulate those bombs with the greatest possible scientific efficiency."

"Ah! Scientific efficiency!" This was something Hendy could pretend to understand. Deaths in millions, the nation destroyed with scientific efficiency, and all of that somehow conected with this fantastic laboratory.

"I see," he murmured. "I like this. I am impressed. I understand. It is these psychological bombs that you need money for."

Madam thought it wise not to tax his understanding with more details. "The project is both complicated and expensive," Madam said. "A great many experiments will be required."

"Yes, complicated," Hendy agreed. He had seen the fantastic control board in use and even pressed one of its buttons. "I am sure we can continue to give you whatever support is necessary. May I come again?"

"Perhaps it would be best to wait until we are ready to start our next phase. This one won't last much longer."

"You mean these subjects are ready for death?"

"There's a Russian proverb that says one doesn't have to study death in order to learn how to die, but these three subjects are unusually resourceful. They may have to be taught. We intend to learn all we can from them, but that won't take more than another day or two. Three at the most."

"I see. And then—there will be three new subjects?"

Madam nodded. "If you can visit us at the beginning of the next phase, you'll get a much better grasp of what we are doing. I'll see that you have ample notice."

"I'll try to visit you," Hendy promised. "Perhaps the arrangements for continued financial support will be completed by then."

They exchanged pleasantries, and then Madam turned him over to her assistants. It was night outside, but Hendy would leave blindfolded, as he had arrived, and be driven back to his hotel by an involved route. No one, not even a financial benefactor, could be allowed to know where the laboratory and its secret entrances were located.

Madam remained in her study. She leaned back in her comfortable chair and focused her full attention on the experiment.

Her real name was Zinaida Sokolova. Early in her career she several times rashly permitted her distinctions and achievements—which were numerous—to be published; but the patina of time and the dust of libraries performed their own merciful effacement on youthful indiscretions, especially those committed in scientific journals in the Russian language. Except on a highly restricted level where nothing was forgotten and everything was confidential, her dossier gradually faded into oblivion.

Even her assistants knew very little about her. They sometimes argued, only half humorously, that she really was a male. Madam, who was aware of everything that went on in her domain, felt mildly flattered. It would not—could not—have occurred to her that they were considering her appearance rather than her personality and force of character. "Appearance" had been obliterated from her consciousness from the time she was an ugly little girl.

She was a doctor of both medicine and psychiatry. She had to be in order to direct this particular project. She also held high military rank in the innocuously entitled KGB, the Komitet Gosudarstvennoy Bezopasnosti, or Committee for State Security, which was known throughout the world for actions that were anything but innocuous and which had been thoroughly condemned and purged in its homeland. The collapse of the Soviet Union had seriously discommoded its activities, but in many places around the world it was alive and well and conducting business as usual, and Ann Arbor, Michigan, was one of them. Originally the KGB had been attracted to Ann Arbor by the university's scientific, technological, and military research. One of its agents had acquired Feinstwaller Manor years before when Adolph Feinstwaller's estate disposed of it—at a bargain price—and when Dr. Zinaida Sokolova needed a site for her psychological laboratory, this one was already available.

Like Zinaida Sokolova's medical credentials, a high KGB rank was implicit in her present position, though not even her assistants knew how high that rank was: full colonel.

Even if they had known her background, they wouldn't have dared to call her anything but "Madam"—she insisted on it. She differed from the Madam of Z-R Publications only in that she now wore a white laboratory coat over a dress Adelle Gernyan would have recognized instantly, and—because she had complicated reports to write and references to look up—her glasses occasionally got polished.

At one time her reports could have made or broken any of her assistants. Now they were not so sure about that, and neither was she. The power of the KGB to discipline recalcitrant or incompetent employees and agents had wilted since the events Madam and her KGB colleagues, like many Russian citizens, referred to as the Smoutnoye Vremia, the Time of Troubles. Despite the collapse of so much she had dedicated her life to preserving, she remained confident that the KGB would eventually be restored to its former eminence, and she encouraged her assistants to believe she still retained important political connections in Moscow. Like all high KGB officers, she routinely made use of anxiety and apprehension to discipline her subordinates.

Madam's long, distinguished career in teaching and research was unknown to them though they should have surmised it. They knew nothing at all about her apprenticeship under the notorious Dr. Daniil Luntz, himself a KGB colonel, at the Serbsky Institute for Forensic Psychiatry in Moscow. It was Luntz who discerned her potential and recruited her into the KGB, and she more than fulfilled that early promise by developing new techniques in what Western doctors called "drug lobotomy," the use of drug therapy to treat Soviet citizens who suffered from severe attacks of political noncomformity.

She had been rewarded for her achievements with the directorship of a special—and highly secret—KGB hospital at Kalinin, where political dissidents received the most advanced destructive drug therapy available as well as other psychiatric punishments designed to cure them of dissenting attitudes, defamations of the Soviet State and its social system, or—much worse—of harboring delusions about reforming society. Run-of-the-mill patients, those merely accused of such routine offenses as absenteeism from work, failure to carry identification papers, or complaining about the regime, were treated at sixteen other "special psychiatric hospitals." Dr. Zinaida Sokolova had made herself one of the world's leading authorities in certain types of psychiatric and psychological experimentation, though the world remained unaware of it. Expertise in this field was much more easily acquired under a state tyranny that routinely permitted experimentation on humans without risk of public investigation or damage suits and could provide an unlimited number of helpless subjects.

Because of that background, she had been ordered to design and then to carry out a lengthy series of crucially important psychological experiments—important to the KGB, to the Soviet army, and to the very survival of Marxist State Socialism—first in the Soviet Union, using Soviet citizens as controls; and then in the United States. The Time of Troubles had occurred shortly after she completed the Soviet phase of her project and began her work in America, but her orders had never been cancelled or modified, and—such was her disdain for the new governments of the Commonwealth of Independent States—she certainly would have ignored such an order if she had received it.

The world-wide disparagement and purging of the KGB had not touched Dr. Zinaida Sokolova and her project. Observers had long speculated that hidden, fearfully diseased roots of that evil growth might have a life of their own and go on fermenting abominations long after the visible plant had been cut down and destroyed. There was a Department V, for example, one of the First Chief Directorate's most secret units, also called the Executive Action Department. It was responsible for sabotage and assassinations abroad. Its personnel were carefully selected from KGB agents with outstanding physical prowess. They were trained to kill humans in every conceivable manner, beginning with conventional weapons and graduating to poisons, gases, drugs, and special techniques involving their bare hands. They also were taught ultrasophisticated methods for sabotage and subversion.

Directorate S, which controlled foreign agents, had a dark core of its own in its Department 8, which was responsible for Special Operations. The mere thought of a "Special Operation" run by the KGB held frightening implications not only for the world's governments but for the millions of people who knew the organization well. Dr. Zinaida Sokolova's project had originated under the auspices of Department 8.

The KGB mother plant had been cut back severely but not uprooted, and those roots would remain viable and ready to put forth new growth the moment local conditions became favorable. In the multi-compartmented KGB, there were cells known only to a few and kept secret even within the Moscow headquarters. They had their own personnel, their own world-wide networks, their own long-term projects and objectives, and their own financial resources based on wealth skimmed from the Russian people as well as from foreign supporters during the long years of KGB dominance. The KGB owned property in many foreign countries in the names of its local agents. It also controlled businesses, and these continued to operate and provide funds. Destruction of the mother plant would not affect the KGB root system, or Dr. Sokolova's special project, for years to come.

But it would have been wrong to say that the upheaval in the Soviet Union had left her unaffected. She was profoundly disturbed by what had happened. At the same time, she was fully confident that sanity—her conception of sanity—would eventually prevail and the Soviet Union would be reconstituted. In the meantime, it had become impossible to obtain trained replacements, and the efficiency of local KGB organizations had deteriorated markedly. That was causing severe problems for Madam. She was dependent on the local KGB personnel for security and routine services.

Further, although there was plenty of money available for present operations, the long-term future of her project was in doubt because of the uncertainty of its financing. Hence the visit of the anonymous Mr. Hendy, whose highly secret and nameless organization had already contributed half a million dollars for the continuation of Madam's experiments. The transaction had been arranged by the underground KGB Headquarters in Moscow. Madam neither knew nor wanted to know anything about Hendy's organization, but she surmised that the funds he dispensed with such a lavish hand had their origin in oil profits of states whose hatred for America had been so useful to the Soviet Union in the past—perhaps Libya or Iran. She also suspected that Hendy had been deeply involved in several notorious terrorist projects that had received KGB assistance in the past. None of that was her concern. Her project needed reliable long-term financing, and Hendy's organization welcomed a KGB connection.

The arrangement would be profitable to everyone concerned, but the necessity to cultivate and impress Hendy was another worry for Madam at a time when she should have been keeping all of her attention on the experiment—because the experiment, despite her meticulous planning, was not going well, and her moronic assistants were proving to be of no help whatsoever.

She relaxed in her comfortable chair and watched meditatively through the window while two of her assistants manned the control center. Her Soviet experiments, where workers balanced on catwalks to change the maze by cranking partitions up and down, seemed to belong to another century. Here there were viewing screens, videotape consoles, a battery of machines that produced audio, visual, and olfactory effects, banks of buttons that minutely controlled the maze and every aspect of every test. The control panel looked vastly more complicated than a spaceship's operating controls. Whatever Madam thought of American psychology—and she thought very little of it—she could not fault the technology available to its research, especially if one had unlimited funds with which to acquire it. Most of her equipment was American, purchased in widely separated locations under fictitious names.

But satisfactory experimental results required more than equipment, and something had gone peculiarly wrong with this experiment. Further, at this moment of crisis when weeks of patient labor were in danger of being wasted, her numbskulled assistants once again were proving incapable of assisting.

They had dropped their "good behavior" the moment the distinguished visitor departed. Now Pavel Derzhavin and Ilya Bychevsky sat in a far corner of the control room arguing furiously. Adelle Gernyan would have recognized them as Goons 3 and 5, and Madam—who had picked up Adelle's nomenclature by electronic eavesdropping and found it both apt and amusing—thought of them in the same terms. Those two argued about everything, from their contrasting hair styles to principles of psychology. Derzhavin wore long sideburns, and his dark hair was perpetually tousled; Bychevsky kept his blond hair short and plastered down with one of the foul smelling goops with which American drugstores seemed inordinately well supplied. Their ideas about psychology were as starkly opposed and equally ill-founded.

To further complicate matters, Goon 1, whose name was Leonid Sisovsky, had suddenly turned moody about something. First he unaccountably disputed Madam's decision to begin the experiment on the grounds that further classification study was needed, an action completely out of character. Since then he had performed his duties with more than his usual indifference, and with his mouth turned down in a pouting expression that perpetually eroded his stupidly good natured face, he exuded a miasma of gloom that Madam found irksome. She wondered if he had suddenly turned homesick. Unfortunately, she couldn't send him home. She was already short-handed, and replacements were unavailable. Sisovsky's pouting was more of a tribulation than the arguments of Derzhavin and Bychevsky.

Madam eavesdropped on them while she meditated. Earlier that day, Bychevsky had substituted compressed air for tear gas, and the subjects fled from the hissing sound, eyes tearing. Bychevsky thought he had achieved something momentous—as though Pavlov's conditioned reflex experiments needed verification at this late date. Derzhavin was arguing that one of the subjects had shouted, "Gas!" and therefore the Second Signal System was involved, the one based on linguistic and symbolic processes. Bychevsky maintained that the First Signal System, of primary conditioned responses, had been triggered by the hissing of the compressed air. The argument was becoming heated, with Derzhavin pawing at his unruly hair and sometimes lapsing into Russian, and Bychevsky's wild gesticulations threatening to become blows.

Madam pressed a button and brought the argument to a halt with one icy question. "Have you two given consideration to the impact the extra water is likely to have on deprivation stress?"

They had not, and they retired to their rooms in confusion.

Leonid Sisovsky had disappeared. Since he was assigned the next watch, Madam hoped he was getting some sleep. Mikhail Borod and Konstantin Murov, Adelle's Goons 2 and 4, were at the control panel. Their present assignment was routine: Keep the subjects moving; tire them out; record anything eventful that happened. They should be able to handle that for an hour or two without supervision, Madam thought grimly. She reached for a book.

Far too much American psychiatry and psychology—and two of Madam's bookcases were filled with it—fell depressingly short of the level of excellence that its technology made possible. Too often the rarely genuine scientific achievement had to be dissected from subjectivist rantings borrowed from Freud and his followers. Madam considered it abominable that Americans persisted in thinking of Ivan Petrovich Pavlov as a physiological experimenter on animals and remained shockingly ignorant of the fact that as early as the 1920s he had categorically stated the possibility that his experimental findings concerning the nervous systems of dogs applied equally to humans. Later, in monumental studies, he had compared the results of brain function disturbances noted in his animals with those observed in humans.

She skimmed through American books on psychology in her occasional free moments for the pleasure of sneering at them; her volumes of Pavlov were well thumbed and crammed with marginal notes and underscorings: Not the *Polnoe Sobranie Sochinenii*, but the *Lectures on Conditioned Reflexes* and *Selected Works*, for she insisted that everything in this laboratory, including the conversation, be in English.

She and her assistants were scientists, meticulously conducting their experiments with a high degree of detachment and disinterest, but if caught they would suffer the fate of any foreign agent. For this reason, she not only had to teach science to her assistants, but she also had to train them in the rudiments of intelligence work. It was essential that they fit into their background as unobtrusively as any spy.

And none of them did.

Their infuriating ineptness was one more burden on her when she had to contend with so many. Not only were they disgustingly pedestrian in their scientific skills, but their general training had been deplorably inadequate. Their English was so atrocious that she had to order them to keep their mouths shut whenever possible in the presence of a native. None of the five could pronounce the English "th", all of them had ridiculous problems with the "w", they frequently fumbled the English "r", and their "ing" words invariably ended in "k". One such assistant might have been overlooked because America was so full of refugee traitors of all nationalities. Five would have been conspicuous enough to cause comment, and comment of any kind concerning members of a secret mission could be fatal.

Since her assistants were not supposed to function as agents, but as scientists operating a highly secret and expensive testing station, the chair borne planners in Moscow had selected them as though they would be spending all of their time bent over microscopes. It hadn't occurred to those dunces that the selection and testing of human subjects was a great deal more involved than the culturing of bacteria. One had to mingle extensively with the group from which the subjects were to be drawn. Madam's assistants needed a much more thorough general training than the average agent, and they had not even mastered the rudiments.

As a result, the task of selecting subjects fell almost entirely on her, and she had to expose herself dangerously in order to carry it out. And now she sat frowning at the volume of Pavlov while the monitor screens showed her more than she cared to see of an experiment gone wrong.

Pavlov had discerned four basic temperaments in dogs: Strong Excitatory, which in Madam's reports—written in English, as was everything else in this research laboratory—she abbreviated to SE; Controlled Excitatory, CE; Phlegmatic Inhibitory, PI; and Weak Inhibitory, WI. The WI types developed neuroses far too easily, and she attempted to eliminate them from the human subjects she selected for testing.

This was the third phase of her experiments on Americans, with each phase-group containing three subjects. As with the earlier groups, she had attempted to include one representative of each of Pavlov's first three basic temperaments. There had been difficulties with the other groups because of the problem of classifying individuals on the basis of a formal interview or two and a casual investigation. One group had contained two PIs and one CE; the other, two CEs and—a very bad error in judgment—one WI. With the current group, she'd had the advantage of detailed observation over a period of time, and she had made her choices unerringly.

Craig Dolan was the classic SE, the Strong Excitatory. He was cynical, articulate, outgoing, and highly intelligent. As she had predicted, he immediately took charge of the group, and he reacted to continued stress and sudden danger with mounting excitement and increasingly aggressive behavior. He would be the first of the group to reach his breaking point.

Adelle Gernyan was the one she had been most doubtful about. The initial classification had been a tenuous PI, and since Madam already had a classic Phlegmatic Inhibitory in Kevin Mondor, her impulse was to dismiss Adelle at the end of her first week and continue searching. Unfortunately—or, in this case, fortunately—there were complications that had nothing to do with classification. The longer the experiment was delayed, the greater the risk that the plan for concealing the abduction of the subjects would miscarry. Rather than accept another postponement, Madam had kept Adelle; and the longer she observed her, the more she became convinced that the girl's inward turning was a form of control rather than evidence of temperament. Because Adelle had lost her parents at high school age and spent much of her time after that alone, loneliness was both a habit and a refuge to her. Her reactions to the same stresses that carried Dolan past his breaking point would be purposeful and controlled. Adelle was an excellent CE, Controlled Excitatory.

Kevin Mondor, the typical Phlegmatic Inhibitory, would appear calmly imperturbable in every crisis, though his response was really passive or inhibitory. His inhibition was strongly stable, however, and—like the girl—he should be able to experience continued stress far longer than Dolan.

A sharp ejaculation in Russian wrenched her mind back to the test in progress. Mikhail Borod, who was attempting unsuccessfully to adjust a videotape machine, swore a second time, and Madam pressed a button and reprimanded him. "Swear if you must, but do it in English." She returned her attention to Pavlov. When an experiment started to go wrong, she always went to the master for guidance.

Her selection of subjects had been sound—of that she was convinced. KGB agents had investigated them carefully and arranged to cover their disappearances so there would be no immediate police search—a point upon which they had erred badly with the first phase group. The actual abductions had been performed flawlessly, the subjects' initial reactions were exactly as anticipated, and everything had seemed routine; but almost at once there were totally unexpected developments.

According to plan, these three subjects were to provide—in addition to the usual test results—material for a study in intragroup relationships. There was a deep-seated antagonism in their attitudes toward each other, which was an important factor in their selection.

They still insulted each other repeatedly, but they also cooperated amazingly well under stress and made a highly effective team—so effective that they were able to deduce entirely too much about what was happening to them. Further, their teamwork was negating several important aspects of the experiment.

The girl's ingenuity in carrying a water reserve, imitated by Dolan, threatened to destroy the experiment's comparative values concerning the impact of thirst and dehydration on the subjects' responses. Their deliberately slowed pace had put the experiment behind schedule, and it was impossible to continuously fill alleys with gas in order to hurry them. The supply of tear gas was not unlimited, and there were difficulties in acquiring quantities of it anonymously.

The subjects' resourcefulness in supporting each other so they could rest or even sleep while walking was certain to introduce distortions into the experimental data. Their method of memorizing numbers in the test chambers had undermined comparison studies and resulted in their handling with ease numbers far beyond the capabilities of any other group Madam had tested. Their peculiar experiment with the bed had been unique, and the gouged walls would require tedious refinishing when the experiment was over. Mondor's attempt to map the maze also was unique.

It seemed strange that none of her other subjects, Soviet or American, had thought of any of these things. Such tactics not only complicated comparison studies, but they threatened to delay the onset of transmarginal inhibition—complete mental collapse—and prolong the experiment.

Dr. Zinaida Sokolova understood enough about human psychology to know that the unexpected had to be expected. It was impossible to learn every essential about a subject's genetic and environmental background, and what was known could be misinterpreted or misunderstood. After so much time, effort, and money had been invested in the selection of these subjects, it was silly to talk about aborting the experiment, but two of her assistants had idiotically suggested that when Adelle Gernyan carried off the milk carton of water. Every test group displayed minor disparities, and the psychologist's task was to relate them to the whole fabric of the experiment. There was much to be learned from these subjects and plenty of time in which to learn it.

Wearily she returned Pavlov to the bookshelf and went out to take a place at the control panel beside Borod and Murov. The subjects were moving slowly along one of the maze's alleys pursued by their own amplified voices. They were performing predictably according to type. The experiment had already provided invaluable data. Madam should have felt elated.

But her apprehension remained. Something had gone wrong, and she had no notion of what it was or what should be done about it.

CHAPTER 13

The Glavnoye Razvedyvatelnoye Upravleniye—the GRU, the Chief Intelligence Directorate of the Soviet General Staff—had proposed the project, the KGB had endorsed it, and Dr. Zinaida Sokolova had been chosen to direct it. She received special training from Directorate S, the KGB's Illegals Directorate, which prepared agents for activity in foreign countries. In addition, she invested three years in designing a laboratory and devising testing procedures. Finally, she tested a hundred phase-groups of Soviet citizens who served as controls.

The controls had been the principal obstacle. The non-scientist dolts in the upper regions of GRU and KGB fancied they knew everything about everything because of their lofty ranks, and they had difficulty wrapping their thick skulls around the most elementary scientific concepts, including the fact that experiments were meaningless with nothing to compare them to.

Madam finally convinced these ignoramuses that tests of American subjects, however carefully planned and carried out, would tell them nothing at all without controls, and the only way to establish controls was by extensive preliminary testing of Soviet population samples comparable to the American samples she intended to use. Unfortunately, this meant inflicting a rigorous testing ordeal on Soviet citizens and terminating them when it was over. Coddling the control group would invalidate the results, and there could be no risk of talk about the experiments afterward. But casualties had to be accepted in warfare, and the world-wide confrontation between Communism and Capitalism was war. She finally succeeded in impressing these facts upon her superiors, though they continued to chafe at the delay.

She established Project Sosva for Soviet citizens and Project Ob for Americans. The names were chosen because of their innocuousness. The Sosva and Ob Rivers were not close enough to Western Europe for projects named after them to cause apprehension and not far enough into Siberia for the names to have political implications. Further, excellent cover could be provided by assigning the same names to inland navigation projects.

While she designed the laboratory and planned the experiments, Madam also laid the groundwork for a new Directorate Y that would concern itself with the psychological study of foreign populations. Pavlov had put it succinctly: The ultimate behavior pattern of an organism reflects both its constitutional temperament and the stresses induced by its environment. Even the most fundamental instincts were adapted and readapted to changes of environment by the formation of suitable behavior patterns.

Did national populations, too, have constitutional temperaments? And did nations, with their natural resources, their philosophies, their mores, their value systems, their schools, their politics, laws, economics, sciences, technologies, religions, cultures, and all the rest—did nations provide their populations with a unique environment that would distinctively influence temperaments?

Any fool could see significant differences between citizens of different nationalities, even between those of nations as closely associated as Canada and the United States. Could these differences be generalized in terms of a national constitutional temperament and a national environment? Were such differences scientifically measurable in terms of individual citizens' reactions to experimental stress? Once measured, could those individual differences be generalized to entire populations? The questions were critical in planning for the war with the United States that Soviet leaders had long thought inevitable. The nation that won might well be the one whose citizens could best handle the enormous stresses produced by modern warfare. Which nation's citizens were best prepared? Dr. Sokolova's experiments were designed to provide the answer. When Project Sosva successfully completed Phase-Group 100, Madam closed her Soviet laboratory in order to personally launch Project Ob in America.

Now she stood in the control room of an experimental laboratory that was, despite its advanced technology, identical in layout to the one used for Soviet citizens. The Soviet laboratory had in fact been designed to fit the space available in the United States, a far simpler procedure than the reverse would have been. Before the Time of Troubles, no one in the Soviet Union spied on the KGB or even asked questions about its activities. Building a duplicate laboratory in the United States might have occasioned inquiries or investigations that made Madam's work impossible. She had been fortunate indeed that the KGB already owned this massive structure with its easily adaptable subbasement. It was ideal for her purpose. Unfortunately, the difficulty of obtaining skilled workers from the Soviet Union had slowed the completion of the laboratory, and finding suitable techniques for the abduction of American subjects had occasioned further delays. Project Ob was far behind schedule.

Its first two phases had presented no testing problems of any consequence. Each group's subjects had moved through the tests as far as their fortitude, endurance, and resourcefulness could take them, and their bodies had been disposed of. Serious errors were made in the abduction procedures for the first phase-group, however, resulting in an immediate and intense police search. This was accompanied by massive splashes of publicity in the worst American manner, as well as by press, radio, and television appeals for witnesses, and for a time it seemed that Project Ob was in jeopardy. The disappearances of the Phase-Group 2 subjects had brought another splurge of publicity merely because of their similarity to the first disappearances.

These were not Madam's errors but those of the local KGB apparatus, and they pointed to something seriously wrong with the attitude of KGB Headquarters—now underground in Moscow but still alive and well as far as Madam knew—toward its Directorate Y. Control had been vested in a committee that not only ignored her complaints and requests but attempted to dictate scientific procedures to her. She sometimes wondered whether her reports were read at all.

The local errors, at least, were correctable. Aleksei Cherkasov, the resident, had promised that the subjects of Phase-Group 3 would not be missed for a week or more and that the police would be totally mystified by their disappearances. Madam had misgivings about this, but fortunately he seemed to be right.

The selection and classification procedures had functioned flawlessly, the laboratory equipment was operating with admirable technical precision, everything was proceeding well—but Madam continued to feel decidedly uneasy about the experiment.

These subjects continued to perplex and disturb her. They were frightened only in moments of crisis, and even then they were defiant and angry. Possibly she had blundered by confronting them with a major group problem before their mental capacities had been sufficiently dulled by stress and fatigue. They solved it with what looked like ridiculous ease, and now she couldn't use it again.

Leonid Sisovsky, Adelle Gernyan's Goon 1, quietly came into the control room and settled himself in a chair from which he could watch all three of the monitor screens. "They don't act like Americans," he said complainingly. He spoke the worst English of any of the five assistants. His accent was so thick that Madam sometimes thought anything he said could have been misunderstood in either English or Russian.

An expression of intense puzzlement had replaced his usual pout. He actually seemed to have his complete attention on the experiment instead of his digestion, or his homesickness, or whatever his complaint had been.

"How do you expect them to act?" Madam asked. "Surely you, a psychologist, know better than to swallow the propaganda about soft Americans who do nothing but sit in front of television sets and eat. Didn't you watch the football games last fall?"

"Yes. But those were professionals. Even the college players were professionals."

"American boys grow up playing it, and it isn't a soft game," Madam said.

Sisovsky grappled futilely for a connection between American football and the behavior of Phase-Group 3, now staggering away from the most recent gas attack. Then he changed the subject. "They don't like each other, but they work together. Isn't that important?"

"Very," Madam said.

It might even be the basis for her own uneasiness. The schedule called for three intelligent subjects with superior educations and clashing personalities. These three fit that description perfectly, but they worked together more effectively than any other subjects she had observed. "The severest tests are ahead of them," Madam said. "Their cooperation may not last."

Sisovsky's unexpectedly avid interest both pleased and mystified Madam. She had considered him the most inept member of her staff—stolid, slow-thinking, poorly trained, and lazy. Previously, he had done only what he was asked to do and that badly, but psychiatry always had an unturned page, and what it revealed could baffle, or surprise, or shock.

The two assistants on duty were only marginally competent. Borod, the oldest, wore thick glasses and patronized American drugstores for the color lotions he used on the thinning hair around his bald spot. He had been graying when he arrived in America; since then, his hair had evolved through several deepening shades of black. Murov, his partner, found the ample supply of food to be the one irresistible aspect of capitalistic civilization, and his pot belly seemed to undergo daily expansion. He had thick hair, but for some reason not even a psychiatrist of Madam's skill could comprehend, he also had a morbid fear of baldness, and he persisted in wearing a hat everywhere he went, even in the underground laboratory. Adelle Gernyan called him the Mad Hatter and speculated as to whether he wore a hat in bed. That so amused Madam that she peeked into his room one night to find out. He did not.

Mathematical Psychology was the one subject Murov could be loquacious about. He enjoyed predicting a subject's behavior with mathematical models. Madam considered this a theoretical approach yet to be proven, and she kept him busy handling the experiment's statistics, which infuriated him. He muttered to himself in Russian while tabulating the subjects' food and water intakes and trying to guess how much water each one swallowed when they passed Adelle's carton around. He also recorded the times spent at various levels of activity and attempted to determine, by a study of respiration, whether a subject was actually asleep when walking supported by the other two. It was enough to make the most patient statistician swear, and Madam didn't reprimand him for the muttered Russian. He was at work on his statistics now.

Borod, who was an experimental psychologist, had been slouching indifferently until Madam joined them. The moment she appeared, his attitude changed to one of energetic concentration. He presumed a wholly unwarranted seniority to the other assistants because of his age and some vague relationship he claimed with an unnamed apparatchik, a Communist party functionary who certainly was no longer in power even if he existed. Borod thought himself capable not only of selecting better subjects than Madam had but of managing the entire project.

Even his casual remarks were a challenge to her. "These subjects are much too intelligent," he said.

"Every population has a percentage of intelligent individuals, Darlink," Madam told him matter-of-factly. "If our samples are to be valid, we have to include some."

"We shouldn't have taken a subject who'd had training in psychology," Borod said. "How did we happen to miss that?"

The "we" was sheer, grudging diplomacy, since Madam had made the selections. "Probably most American college graduates have some rudimentary exposure to psychology," she said patiently. She was sarcastically mimicking his accent, as she often did; strangely, he never seemed to notice. She detested him, and she would have sent him home long before if it had been possible to replace him.

Murov, hastily pouring oil before the waters became troubled, remarked, "Mondor specialized in mathematics. He couldn't have had much psychology."

"He has a remarkably retentive verbal memory," Madam observed thoughtfully. "That's strange for a mathematician. One would expect it of Dolan but not of Mondor."

She felt irritated with herself for not paying more attention to the educational backgrounds of this group's two college graduates. There were so many things to learn about an alien culture.

"I still think they're too intelligent," Borod said. "When you take subjects at random, you don't get two college graduates out of three, let alone three highly intelligent people."

"Ann Arbor is a university city, Darlink," Madam told him. "It has an unusual percentage of college graduates. And our samples aren't random. They're stratified."

In Madam's opinion, her most severe difficulties were not caused by the subjects but by assistants who weren't even qualified to function as building custodians. Borod's inane remarks were disrupting her concentration. She said, "Why don't you two get some rest? There's no need to operate more than one station when so little is happening. I'll finish your duty for you."

"They'll never separate," Borod said flatly. "They know they stand a better chance together."

"When the stress intensifies, the first crisis may break them up," Madam said. "That's one of the things we're here to study. If it doesn't, we can separate them ourselves any time we choose."

Borod and Murov left—Murov, predictably, to visit the kitchen for a snack. Madam was left to meditate in peace but only for a moment. Sisovsky, Adelle Gernyan's Goon 1, was still seated behind her.

"You'd better get some rest while you can," Madam told him. "Later, the whole staff will be needed for long periods of duty."

"But this is interesting!" Sisovsky protested. "I like to watch and plan what tests I might use next. Then, when I see your choices, I can study my errors."

"There's very little room for error. If we interpolate excessively, we destroy the bases for comparison studies. There isn't much to decide except sequence, and even that is largely dictated by the subjects' responses."

"Wouldn't their responses be more interesting if we separated them?" Sisovsky asked. When Madam didn't reply, he continued apologetically, "The subjects of our first two phases were strangers to each other. They didn't know where they were or what was happening. I can understand why they would stay together. That isn't true of these subjects. Also, they're enemies."

"Not precisely enemies," Madam said. "They never associated closely enough to become enemies. They merely disliked each other. Of course they may be bitter enemies by the time we terminate them."

"If they do, will they separate?"

"That's one of the things we want to find out."

"Isn't it true that in a real life situation, one would be more likely to experience wartime stress with one's family and friends?"

This was an objection Madam had voiced herself, but the disappearance of entire families, or groups of close friends, would have caused questions and rumors even in the Soviet Union. In America, a public uproar would have resulted. "If all goes well, we may conduct later experiments with subjects who have lived in close association," she said. "But remember this: In times of disaster, groups of strangers frequently are thrown together under stress conditions, so the relationships are realistic enough for our purpose."

"I should like to see family groups tested," Sisovsky said. "The members would have genuine concern for each other."

Madam smiled. "Would your conclusions apply equally to families on all social and economic and educational levels? Would Soviet and American families be comparable? A series of comparison tests would be required, and the subjects would be extremely difficult to obtain without undesirable complications—meaning police investigations here in America. Right now, I want you to consider how the intelligence of these subjects is affecting test results. Already they've deduced more than we thought possible. Of course that adds another dimension to our study."

The subjects had deduced entirely too much, but would that significantly alter their behavior? At one point in her career, Madam had pondered the thinking processes of animals used in psychological experiments. Did the rat in the maze ever grasp the fact that it was being experimented on? Would it behave differently if it did? The experimenter could never know. In normal laboratory procedures, humans almost always knew they were the subjects of psychological tests, which had to influence the results in many experiments.

"Perhaps both men are in love with the girl," Sisovsky suggested. "That might explain why they don't separate."

Madam was amused. "Their mutual insults make strange love talk."

"They treat her very considerately."

"All three of them have treated each other considerately—thus far. The girl brought water, and she shared it with the men. All of them drank from the same container, but none took more than the share agreed upon. They dislike each other but they cooperate fully. I don't think the men's feeling for the girl is any different from their feeling for each other."

Silently they watched the subjects plodding along an alley. They were extremely tired, but at this moment they suddenly shook off their fatigue sufficiently to exchange banter and insults. They seemed unconcerned about their hunger, and, thanks to the extra water, they had been able to avoid serious thirst pangs.

What disturbed Madam most was the way they stopped from time to time to whisper together. They had talked about finding a loophole; she wondered if she possibly could have left one for them.

"Intelligence under stress," she murmured to herself. Such a fascinating subject. The intelligent were quicker to perceive, quicker to understand problems, quicker to devise solutions—but they also would be quicker to recognize a hopeless situation when it confronted them. Would these three succumb to stress more easily than dullards who couldn't grasp what was happening? It should be interesting to watch.

"Perhaps it was a mistake to include the writer," Sisovsky said. "He imagines too well."

"All intelligent people imagine," Madam said.

Sisovsky's observations were as surprising to her as his suddenly acquired interest. "The other groups also gave us some unexpected reactions," she said. "That's why we're conducting experiments. If everything always followed our prognostications, we could dispense with laboratories and do all of our work on paper."

She added thoughtfully, "These three subjects just might be intelligent enough, and resourceful enough, to complete the entire series of tests before we terminate them."

CHAPTER 14

At three P.M. on Monday, John Laylor, Jr., picked up his telephone and told Miss Rebecca Carlyss, the receptionist, he was unavailable for the remainder of the day. "Some of my own people are coming in at four," he said. "Send them to Conference Room B, please."

He hung up, tilted back in his chair, very deliberately planted both feet on his desk, and lit his pipe. He had an uninterrupted hour for thought, and he wanted to make the most of it. The books piled in front of him were solemn tomes on psychology and philosophy, volumes few of his colleagues in this law firm of Laylor, Graffington, Bartley, and Kordro would have thought had anything to do with the law. Beside them was a folder marked MISSING PERSONS, which in those offices was a greater oddity than the books.

He was something of an oddity himself. The firm's practice was re-stricted to commercial law, and in its area of specialization, it was South-eastern Michigan's most dignified and respected law firm. John Laylor, Jr., wearing a turtleneck sweater, checkered slacks, and socks in revolt-ing color patterns, clashed with his surroundings like a circus clown on the Supreme Court. His presence there might have seemed inexplicable had he not been the son of the firm's senior partner.

He had joined the firm when he graduated from law school, starting out with his name at the bottom of the list, and at the bottom of the list it had remained. This suited him perfectly. His office was one of two small rooms on a short hallway that led to the rear exit he preferred to use. The other was a storage room. He came and went unnoticed and often unseen; dabbled unobtrusively in everyone's cases to the extent of his interest and thereby rendered uniquely valuable service to the firm—he had an uncanny knack for legal research—and he maintained an excel-lent rapport with many of the adult children of long-time clients, which insured the firm's continued growth. Because he constituted no threat to anyone's career or status, had a friendly manner and a pleasant personal-ity, kept out of his colleagues' way, did his dabbling without interfering, could be brilliantly helpful with no concern at all as to who got the credit, and was willing to take on investigative chores no one else wanted, he was popular with everyone—except, perhaps, his father, who still wist-fully hoped to make an attorney of him. His actual status with the firm, and his income, were far higher than the position of his name indicated.

But he was not an attorney and cheerfully admitted it. The books on this office shelves were tomes by and about such non-legal personali-ties as Aristotle, Plato, Spinoza, Descartes, Compte, Berkeley, Spencer, William James, Watson, Pavlov, and Skinner. Laylor was convinced that an attorney's case could not be damaged by an understanding of people and an awareness of ultimate meanings. When he needed law books, he could find them in the firm's library. His own credo was that legal principles should begin with those people the law affected.

He enjoyed the occasional investigations required by the civil litigation the firm handled. He hired a competent private detective when he needed one, and he was able to assemble a part-time staff of law students whenever additional help was required. Investigations gave him an opportunity to get out of the office and become involved with aspects of human affairs rarely encountered in the practice of commercial law.

Unfortunately, the problem described in the folder marked **MISSING PERSONS** had proved as invulnerable to Laylor's psychology, philosophy, and literature as it had to law and law enforcement. There were six entries in it, and now perhaps he had three more to add: a total of nine missing persons and no client. There never had been a client for this particular investigation, which Laylor had undertaken as a favor to an old friend and college classmate.

During more than a year of pondering the imponderable, he had memorized the entire contents of the file—the known facts were scant enough—but now he carefully reviewed it.

The first group of missing persons consisted of recent high school graduates: a boy from Indiana and girls from Texas and Oregon. Laylor's file contained a page of information on each, with photo attached, and enlargements of those photos looked down on him from the row of six on the wall opposite his desk.

Rodney Smalling, of Nortonville, Indiana. President of his senior class, president of the high school debating society, an outstanding student. Lynda Mason, of Westview, Texas. Cheerleader, president of the dramatics club, class secretary, student council president, star of her class play. Evelyn Arnett, of Elwood Park, Oregon. Editor of her high school paper, considered by her teachers to have genuine writing talent, another outstanding student.

All were intelligent, talented, personable youngsters. All came from large—and poor—families. All came from small towns where they would not be able to live at home and attend even a junior college. They'd had no expectations of continuing their education, even with the scholarships they certainly could have won. They would have had to go to work immediately in any employment they could find. Their pay checks were needed at home.

A few weeks before graduation, like the proverbial thunderbolt from a clear sky, the personnel director of a firm that later proved to be fictitious arrived in town offering a remarkable position with a six-year contract, good pay, and a college education financed by the company. In Indiana, it was the Central States Investment Company; in Texas, the Melroy Petroleum Research Corporation; in Oregon, Pacific Chemical Products. This alleged personnel director, whom later investigations identified as the same person in all three locations, interviewed the entire senior class, selected one ecstatic student for the available opening, and handed him or her a plane ticket to Detroit Metropolitan Airport, expense money, and a month's pay in advance. The money was paid in cash and the student's receipt taken; the plane tickets had been purchased with cash. The phony personnel director also paid her local expenses with cash, leaving no thread that could be unraveled later.

The students enplaned at the nearest air terminal a few days after graduation. Their planes reached Detroit Metro; presumably they did, also, but they were neither seen nor heard of again. Painstaking investigations by Laylor and several police agencies traced fellow passengers who remembered the students, but in the scramble of disembarking, all three had been lost sight of. Presumably someone else had claimed their luggage.

The families were sufficiently alarmed to notify the police immediately when their children failed to report their safe arrival in Detroit. An old friend and college classmate of Laylor's, a small-town lawyer in Nortonville, had known Rodney Smalling personally. He brought Laylor into the case at the beginning by contacting him in behalf of the missing boy's family.

The three disappearances were quickly connected. The individual who had hired the students was identified as the same person in each instance though she seemed to have made clumsy attempts to disguise herself. That was as much as could be discovered at the time. Little more than that was known now, more than a year later.

There were immediate alarms about white slave rings, but in that case why the boy, why only three, and why Detroit? This line of speculation had been thoroughly demolished by the next disappearances, which occurred in the fall. Again three people vanished, but these were middle-aged adults, two men and a woman. Otherwise, there were striking similarities.

The members of this second group also came from small towns in widely scattered states: Elmer Schmitz, from Korning Falls, Ohio; Ruth Klonder, from Pattsburg, Alabama; and Jesse Youngstrom, from Carlton, California. All three were unemployed. All were hired by the same superficially disguised woman who again represented fictitious firms: The Pacific Investment Company, in California; Central Chemical Research Corporation, in Ohio; and Delron Manufacturing Company, in Alabama.

In each community she interviewed a large number of candidates, selected one, and furnished a plane ticket to Detroit Metro that had been purchased with cash. Again she supplied expense money and a month's salary in advance, also in cash. As with the students, the three missing persons were last seen on the plane or leaving the plane. The one significant difference was that none of them had relatives awaiting word of a safe arrival. It was more than four months before all three had been reported missing.

The switch from bright youngsters living with their families to unattached middle-aged victims without relatives seemed significant to Laylor. The first disappearances had resulted in an immediate, intensive police investigation. Further, the notion that attractive young people could be abducted from Detroit Metropolitan Airport in broad daylight created an enormous publicity flap. All of the area papers had carried feature stories and photos, there had been extensive national coverage, and even after a year there was an occasional follow-up story.

The abductors learned from this. They shifted their attention to middle-aged nonentities without families. Such people were slow to be missed and unlikely to cause much fuss when they were.

The police had worked hard on the six cases and got nowhere. They never would, Laylor thought, until someone figured out the "why". Causa latet; vis est notissima. "The effect is apparent, but the cause is hidden." And, as Spinoza had put it, the knowledge of an effect depends on and involves knowledge of a cause. The police had a lengthy file concerning the effect, but they could go no further because they couldn't guess the "why". More than a year of intense investigation had turned up no clue at all as to motive.

Laylor refused to believe these abductions were the senseless crimes of a motiveless malignity—as Samuel Taylor Coleridge had once written in an entirely different connection. The victims had been selected with care from large numbers of applicants. This suggested a pattern. The Ann Arbor disappearances would, Laylor hoped, further delineate it. And—Laylor's First Law—where there was a pattern, there had to be a motive, no matter how twisted and obscure that motive might prove to be. The critical question was whether the same sloppy, plump, big-nosed, near-sighted little woman was somehow connected with these latest disappearances.

He pushed the folder aside. Cui bono? Who could have benefited from such bizarre crimes? Financially, no one. All those involved were poor, there had been no ransom notes, and none could have been paid in any case.

Why had the abductors been so stupid as to prey on prominent, highly regarded young people from small towns? It was their worst possible choice. If they wanted victims from that age group, they easily could have picked them up in large cities, runaways who wouldn't be missed because they were already missing.

Because there was a pattern, Laylor assumed it would happen again. On his own initiative, he set up a nation-wide missing person review to search for a third occurrence. His fear was that the abductors would change their methods and make their next crimes far more difficult to identify. If they dropped the job interviews, the advances in cash, and Detroit Metropolitan Airport, there would be nothing to link subsequent abductions with the six cases under investigation.

These latest disappearances might have no connection with the others. With the entire nation to choose from, why would the culprits stupidly return to Michigan and abduct three victims who not only lived in the same community but worked for the same employer? On the other hand, what outlandish coincidence could result in the simultaneous disappearances of another three persons?

From the beginning, the cases had fascinated Laylor. He was unmarried and had few close friends. For years he had enjoyed an income far in excess of his needs. He had no personal interests beyond his work and his reading. The disappearances became a hobby for him, and then an occupation, and finally an obsession. Regularly he made the rounds of the law enforcement agencies concerned, and eventually those officers assigned to the disappearances accepted him as a colleague. He hired his own investigators to follow up leads he thought the police were overlooking. In time he became the area's leading authority on the cases, and police sometimes found it convenient to use him as an information clearing house.

Month after month, he searched the backgrounds, the characters, the private lives of the missing persons, looking for quirks of personality, or skill, or aptitude that could have made someone *want* to abduct them. The phony personnel agent had conducted at least two hundred interviews to pick the six victims who vanished. What had she been looking for? Laylor pondered and analyzed everything that could be learned about each missing person, but he found no hint of a common denominator.

Those who'd had the good luck to be turned down affirmed that they had been questioned meticulously. There had been no written tests. Some applicants brought letters of recommendation and transcripts showing high school courses and grades, and this material had scarcely been glanced at. The interviewer relied on her own searching questions.

Laylor compiled a list of the questions the unsuccessful applicants remembered, and it was obvious to him that the interviewer was interested in certain undefinable aspects of personality and character. But what was she looking for? And why?

Causa latet; vis est notissima. What was the motive?

"Perhaps," Laylor told himself, "we who pass through life committing only those sins of the common, ordinary, garden variety are unable to comprehend or even recognize genuine evil when it confronts us."

CHAPTER 15

Conference Room B was a small room that had half a dozen chairs arranged around a conference table. When Laylor entered it at four o'clock, there were note pads positioned at each chair, and Miss Carlyss had sent down a pitcher of ice water and glasses. Laylor's investigative assistant, a private detective named Ray Bront, was waiting with the two law students Laylor had hired for the summer. Bront had been living with the missing persons file as long as Laylor had. The students had been introduced to it that morning.

Laylor seated himself in a chair beside Bront, dropped the file onto the table in front of him, and pushed the note pad aside to make room for his own shorthand notebook. Across the table from them, the two students edged forward and waited attentively. Jill Tabold was blond, freckled, very cute, and very, very bright. With her pert ponytail, she looked more like a high school freshman than a college law student. Bruce Kagen was an intense-looking redheaded youngster. He was as bright as Jill, but he appeared to be slower because he liked to collect all of the loose ends into a neat package before committing himself.

There were other law students working for the firm that summer— prim and properly dressed interns who were eagerly prepared to accompany their superiors to court on a moment's notice. Perhaps these two would have preferred that, but jobs were hard to find, and they needed the money. Because both of them were intelligent, they quickly inferred that little of their on-the-job training would directly concern the practice of law. They also discovered that trainees working for Laylor, Jr., were considered mavericks by the other members of the firm no matter how carefully they dressed, so they emulated their boss's informality. Jill wore jeans and a summery blouse; Bruce Kagen affected Laylor's turtleneck sweater.

Laylor greeted them with a smile and a nod and turned to Bront. The private detective dressed according to the job at hand. Today he had been in and out of police and business offices, and he wore a suit. Tomorrow's assignment might call for eavesdropping in a coal bin, and he would don appropriately begrimed overalls. He was a chameleon who needed a few minutes' notice and a place to change.

He was as unlike Laylor as a master designer could have made him— beefy looking, with coal black hair and a babyish face. Whereas Laylor looked older than his forty years and never gave it a thought, Bront looked much younger than his and worried about it.

"We all know the background," Laylor said. "Let's have some details so we can see whether these latest disappearances have anything in common with the others."

Bront took out his notebook. "The missing persons have very different backgrounds," he announced. "Two are college graduates, but one went to the University of Michigan and the other to Darwood College, which is a small school in Illinois. The third, who didn't go to college, may be the best educated of the three, but he did it on his own. The places they come from aren't as scattered as those of the first two groups, but they're too distant to be connected. The most significant thing is that all three of them came to Ann Arbor on their own initiatives, and at different times, and for different purposes. Mondor arrived more than four years ago to attend the university. He hung around after he graduated. A couple of months ago Dolan drove over from Chicago to visit a friend and stayed because he found a job. Adelle Gernyan graduated from college last month, and she came to Ann Arbor looking for work. There's absolutely no possibility that someone contrived to bring them together here."

"Already it's an entirely different situation," Laylor said. "Go ahead."

"Dolan's previous employment seems to consist of numerous odd jobs of manual labor that he held only briefly. They'd be difficult to trace. Mondor is supposed to have worked for one of those hole-in-the-wall income tax places for a couple of months during the tax rush, but the police haven't identified it. Probably it went out of business on April 16. Gernyan had part-time clerical employment in a college office while going to school. Mondor had been with Z-R Publications for six weeks. Dolan for four. Gernyan for three."

"Is one of them likely to have a fat inheritance tucked away somewhere?" Laylor asked. "I'm thinking about the possibility of ransom."

"As far as I could find out, all three were broke when they went to work for Z-R Publications."

"Would any of them have knowledge of scientific or industrial secrets?"

"Good God, no!" Bront exclaimed. "Mondor has a bachelor's degree in mathematics, but they're a dime a dozen. It might make him employable, but it's no big thing. Gernyan has one in English Literature, and when she applies for a job, she's probably better off not to mention it. Dolan seems to have read widely, but why kidnap him for that when you can get the same books at any library? He calls himself a writer, he was writing a novel, and the friend who reported him missing says he has talent—but in that case, why has he never published anything? As far as the police could find out, he hasn't, and the detective who searched his apartment and read some of his novel says he isn't likely to. The words he writes look like English, but they have to be read in some other language in order to be understood, and the detective wasn't able to figure out which one."

"Maybe you'd better give them to us one at a time," Laylor said.

Bront nodded and flipped a page in his notebook. "Kevin Mondor. Comes from a wealthy family. Had a trust fund that put him through college—extravagantly, I might add. Wears expensive clothes and owns a Mazda Miata, a Special Edition with extras, I couldn't afford one. Take that up with Laylor, Graffington, Bartley, and Kordro, will you? It gives me inferiority complex to be investigating kids who drive cars like that."

"It's good for the spirit," Laylor said. "Teaches you humility."

Bront snorted.

"Are you sure you've got the right person?" Laylor asked. "This is the first instance where we've actually had money in the picture."

"This money was gone before the picture was drawn. Mondor learned too late that trust funds can have a bottom. When he graduated from U. of M., he treated himself to the car and then discovered there wasn't enough money left for him to start graduate school. He didn't like what his bachelor's degree was worth on the job market, so he moved into cheaper quarters and did nothing at all until his money gave out completely. Then he had to take whatever work he could find—first at that income tax place, and he probably did very well there while it lasted. Then at Z-R Publications. Most of this information comes from his landlady. He doesn't seem to have talked much about himself, but she vaguely remembers some mention of a family tragedy. She can't recall whether it was financial, accidental, or a combination of things. Probably that's when he lost his parents. His only inheritance was the trust fund. He's a food faddist and vegetarian. His landlady calls it 'eating sensibly,' which means that she's one, too. He's a standoffish sort of person—a loner. When he had money, he probably was considered a snob."

"But he may actually be a shy introvert," Laylor suggested.

"No one who has had any personal contact with him calls him shy. Away from work, his only close acquaintance seems to have been the landlady. That's all I have on Mondor."

"He usually ate his lunch at the Greenry, a restaurant in the Arbor Vista Shopping Mall, which is just down the road from Z-R Publications," Bruce Kagen said. "It's famous for its salad bar, which was all he patronized. The waitresses knew him well. First, because of his car, which was conspicuous—"

"And so was the way he drove it!" Jill Tabold put in.

"And because he tipped the standard fifteen percent. Evidently few salad bar patrons tip. At least, not that much. He was quiet, gave them no trouble, and even occasionally said nice things about how crisp the lettuce was. They thought highly of him. But he always ate quickly and drove off in a rush."

"Anything else?" Laylor asked.

The students shook their heads in unison. Laylor regarded them with amusement. They were exact opposites except for their intelligence, and sometimes they clashed bitterly. He wondered if opposites really did attract and whether the summer jobs would foster an unlikely romance.

He turned to Bront. "Next?"

"Adelle Gernyan. We know very little about her because she only arrived in Ann Arbor three weeks ago last Thursday. Illinois police are interviewing people who knew her at college. She's an orphan with no known relatives. She attended college on a scholarship, a small inheritance—probably insurance money—and what she was able to earn from part-time work. Her English Literature major might have made her permanently unemployable if she hadn't taken summer courses at a business school. She got to be a rather good typist, maybe from writing all those English Literature themes. The police located only one casual acquaintance—the man in her apartment building who reported her missing. He says she's a quiet person with brains. Highly attractive. Very friendly, but she doesn't push it. A self-contained sort of person."

"What do you have on Gernyan?" Laylor asked the students.

"The acquaintance is a young man named Gerald Wyman," Jill Tabold said. "He's extremely worried about her. If it hadn't been for him, she'd never have been reported missing. Unfortunately, he doesn't know much more about her than he told the police."

"A teller at the branch bank remembers her," Bruce Kagen said. "She cashed her pay check there during the noon hour on Friday. She's thrifty—she put most of it in savings. She also ate lunch at one of the mall restaurants—a waitress there remembers a girl in a light green pants suit—but I don't think she ate there regularly. She's very attractive, and someone would have noticed her if she'd been a regular customer."

"According to Wyman, she usually took her lunch from home to save money," Jill said. "She thought her job was too good to last, and she wanted to save as much as she could."

"We'll get to the jobs later," Laylor said. "What about Dolan?"

"Again, no relatives," Bront said. "Only one close friend, the one from Cleveland who reported him missing. He may have had some casual acquaintances, but the police haven't been able to locate them. The friend, who is now back in Cleveland, says Dolan's a great guy and a very talented writer. The bartender at the Boheme, the bar where Dolan now and then met some of those casual acquaintances, remembers him vaguely and has nothing outstandingly good or bad to say about him. He drank mostly beer; like the rest of the group, he talked a lot; and he caused no trouble."

Bruce Kagen spoke up. "The people at Barney's Pub, a bar in the shopping mall, remember him well. He ate lunch there every week day. They say he was friendly, well-behaved, and extremely fond of beer. They liked him."

Bront closed his notebook. "That's it. Mostly it adds up to a lot of differences. They have two things in common."

"Three," Jill Tabold said, grinning triumphantly. Both of the students delighted in going one up on Bront, the professional. "First, none of them was a native of this area. Mondor attended U. of M. for four years, but in the eyes of Ann Arbor's more stalwart citizens, that doesn't even make him a resident except when the city counts heads for a tax rake-off. The other two arrived there recently, and anyone who has lived in Ann Arbor for less than two years is considered a vagrant. Second, they had no relatives, no local friends, almost no acquaintances. Third, all three worked for Z-R Publications."

Laylor thought for a moment. "I can give you two more from what the Ann Arbor Police told me. Gernyan's one acquaintance was someone she'd met recently and casually inside her apartment building, which resulted in her being reported missing. Mondor's one acquaintance was his landlady, and all of his contacts with her took place inside his apartment building. His Friday night dinner date with her was the only reason he was reported missing. Dolan received a chance visit from an out-of-town friend, which is why he was reported missing. That's number four, relationships that were either unexpected or inconspicuous because they occurred inside the apartment buildings. The fifth thing these people had in common is that someone knew a lot about them—their habits, where they parked their cars, and the fact that they had no friends, relatives, or acquaintances who were likely to miss them. Someone investigated them meticulously and planned their disappearances the same way, but he missed the inside contacts, and no one could anticipate a friend arriving unexpectedly from Cleveland."

"Even Dolan didn't know he was coming," Bront said.

"Right. Except for the fluke of those three coincidences, which as Lieutenant Prehn said is almost excessive, the plan to have all three of them disappear unnoticed would have worked. They might not have been reported missing for weeks. But why these three people?"

The investigation was only beginning, and already the same problem was about to stump them: Causa latet; vis est notissima.

Laylor looked from one face to another and met a trio of concentrating frowns. The pudgy Bront pursed his lips fretfully; Jill wrinkled her nose and tossed her blond pony tail; Bruce Kagen leaned forward as though straining at something just beyond his mental grasp.

Kagen was the first to speak. He said slowly, "If they were investigated like that, then they were chosen deliberately just like the other six. So they have that much in common with the other cases."

Laylor nodded. "Who chose them? That's the critical question."

"Z-R Publications brought them together by hiring them," Bront said. "As far as the police have been able to find out, they constituted the entire production staff. There was a supervisor, and there were maintenance men, but only these three worked on publications. That gives us two more highly unlikely coincidences: A firm with three employees hired only orphans with no relatives and no local friends or acquaintances. And those three employees disappeared at about the same time. Maybe at precisely the same time."

Bruce Kagen was consulting his own notebook. "According to the people at the shopping mall—especially those in the bank who cash checks and therefore know where people work—there was a constant turnover of employees at Z-R Publications. Many of them only worked long enough to cash one weekly paycheck. These three were the only employees who lasted. Another interesting thing—they were paid extremely well. Each of them received more than nine hundred dollars a week in take-home pay."

"Why such a heavy turnover of employees at a firm that paid extremely high wages for ordinary office work?" Laylor asked.

The two students began flipping pages.

Bront spoke like a man putting his words together one letter at a time. "Evidently Z-R Publications screened its prospective employees as well as it could and then gave the likely ones a tryout while conducting an intensive investigation of them. That's only an assumption, but I've bought it. So have the police. If an employee didn't fit the pattern they had in mind, they fired him—or her—and tried another."

Laylor said incredulously, "Are you saying the publishing firm abducted them? Why pick such a cumbersome and dangerous method?"

"Obviously someone wanted to observe them closely before he made up his mind," Bront said.

"Observe what?" Laylor demanded. "That's been the riddle from the beginning. The first six people were very carefully selected, but on what basis? Knowledge? Personality? Talent? Intelligence? The only thing we know for certain is that it wasn't for money. Now you're saying these latest victims were selected even more carefully—in fact, were kept under close observation for three weeks or more by giving them jobs. That's unbelievable."

Bront fished in a pocket and produced a piece of paper that he unfolded and handed to Laylor. It was a photo copy of a Z-R Publications letterhead. The firm's impressively printed logo and address stood at the top of the page. The typewritten memo was dated the previous Friday. It read:

MEMORANDUM

FROM: Z-R Publications TO: Craig Dolan

Effective this date, your employment is terminated. Your work has been highly satisfactory, but the project you have been engaged upon has not proven financially feasible. Therefore this is the last regular paycheck you will receive. Two additional weeks' pay for termination without notice will be sent to your home in checks mailed to arrive next Friday and the Friday following. We recommend you to any employer who contemplates hiring you for the type of work you have performed for us, and we thank you for your loyal service.

Z-R Publications

Laylor scrutinized the indecipherable signature for a moment, shook his head, and handed the paper across the table to the law students.

"Where was it?" he asked.

"In Dolan's glove compartment," Bront said. "It had his fingerprints—and *only* his—verified from personal items in his apartment."

"Remarkable!" Laylor exclaimed.

Bront nodded. "According to the wording of this memorandum, it was handed out with the pay checks. Presumably all three employees got one. But the pay checks were passed out before noon on Friday, and those who remember seeing this trio at the shopping mall are positive they gave no hint that they'd just been fired. The contrary. Dolan actually said something about hoping the job lasted until he finished his novel. Gernyan commented to the teller at the bank about how her nest egg was growing and she only hoped she could keep it up."

"They could have been handed the letters when they left at five," Bruce Kagen suggested.

"That isn't the way the notice reads, but it's certainly possible," Bront said.

"I suppose Dolan is the kind of person who'd shove something like that in his glove compartment and forget it," Jill said. "And the other two wouldn't."

"You're so right," Bront agreed. "It's a recommendation as well as a dismissal notice. Gernyan and Mondor are types who'd take care of something like that. Dolan would toss his copy in his car and forget it—if he didn't discard it the moment he got outside the building. He wouldn't be worried about another job. He'd work on his novel until his money ran out. Or so the police reason."

"How do you reason?" Laylor asked.

"Anyone who knows these three people well would expect them to do just what I said—so I think someone stage-managed this to make them seem to be behaving normally. It wouldn't be difficult for an employer to obtain an employee's fingerprints on a piece of stationery."

"What about the additional two weeks' pay?" Laylor asked.

"Z-R Publications closed its bank account Friday, but it left enough money for outstanding checks, including Friday's pay checks. It also arranged for the bank to mail checks to these three on the next two Thursdays."

"Only these three? What about the maintenance workers?"

"This is the only account the police have located, and Mondor, Gernyan, and Dolan were the only employees being paid out of it. Those who were fired earlier were paid from the same account."

"This gets peculiarer and peculiarer," Jill Tabold said, wrinkling her freckled nose. "But Z-R Publications was a peculiar company. All three of these people commented—Mondor to his landlady, Gernyan to Gerald Wyman, and Dolan in a letter to his friend—all three of them commented about the screwy, or crazy, or queer place they worked at."

"Have the police found anyone who saw any of the three after work on Friday?" Laylor asked.

"No," Bront said.

"Did anyone see them leave?"

"No. The police worked that over good and are still working on it. But they haven't found anyone."

"What about their cars? Someone might be able to say when they were or weren't parked in the company's parking lot."

"You can't see the lot from the road," Bront said. "Passersby are out of it unless someone happened to see one of the cars pull out."

"What an incredible blunder!" Laylor murmured. "This focuses attention squarely on the company."

"Don't forget—these three weren't supposed to be missed for weeks," Bront said. "When someone finally got around to notifying the police— maybe a landlord trying to collect overdue rent—their cars would have been parked in their assigned parking places at their apartment buildings ever since last Friday night, and everyone would assume that they disappeared after they stopped working for Z-R Publications. Maybe a long time afterward. Except for Lieutenant Prehn's three coincidences, that might have happened. Of course the police are hot after Z-R Publications now."

"Any results?" Laylor asked.

"Absolutely none. The company has vanished. There's a new sign by the highway, and a new tenant occupies the building—a real estate firm. The building, incidentally, is a subject in itself and has to be seen to be believed, but that probably has nothing to do with our problem. The real estate firm leased the place a month ago, so going out of business wasn't an abrupt decision for Z-R Publications."

"Then we have three missing employees and a missing company," Laylor said. "What do we know about the company?"

"It existed for three months," Bront said. "Its alleged purpose was to bring out books containing a lot of statistics. All three missing employees thought the books had very little commercial potential. Otherwise, the firm existed, it had a remarkable turnover of personnel, its operations seemed peculiar to its own employees, it had plenty of money, and it went out of business at the end of last week and left no forwarding address. Anything the owners wanted to salvage was packed and taken away by them. The office equipment was sold to the real estate firm that took over the building on Saturday and opened for business there this morning. And that's it."

"That isn't much," Laylor remarked.

"The police hope to learn more about it from former employees. They tracked down the first one just before I left Ann Arbor, and one interesting fact has turned up already. The description of the boss, or manager, of Z-R Publications very strongly resembles descriptions of the funny little dame with the big nose and thick glasses who hired three high school graduates a year ago and three middle-aged people last fall."

CHAPTER 16

Adelle was trying to remember something she had read years before. She asked Mondor, "If one eats little or nothing, isn't the stomach supposed to shrink?"

"So they say."

"And then it'll take less food to make one feel full?"

Mondor shrugged. "I suppose."

"It isn't true," Adelle said bitterly.

Their most recent meal had consisted of a small banana and a half pint carton of chocolate milk apiece. Adelle felt as starved afterward as she had before. The chocolate milk furnished the one bright note. When they finished, Dolan gleefully took charge of the three small milk cartons, rinsed them, and filled them with water. The extra supply would be invaluable. Adelle's quart carton was showing alarming signs of wear.

Gas routed them from a sleep that seemed to have lasted only a few minutes. Again Adelle stumbled into the alley carrying her shoes and the quart carton of water. Mondor and Dolan carried shoes and the three small cartons. Once safely around a corner, they paused to put their shoes on.

Adelle rubbed her eyes and said sleepily to Mondor, "A day or two ago, or maybe it was a week ago—have we been down here a week?"

"It certainly seems that long," Mondor answered gravely.

"You were saying something about the psychological effects of going without sleep."

"Was I?"

"Yes. I remember it as well as I'm able to remember anything. Dimly. What were they?"

Mondor reflected. "I don't remember. I wish you two would stop trying to make a psychologist out of me. I didn't even like the subject."

"What's the good of a college education if you can't remember any of it?" Dolan demanded peevishly.

"What was the question?" Mondor asked.

"What happens to you when you go forever without sleep?"

"It has serious psychological effects."

"So does death," Dolan said. "What kind of an answer is that?"

The gas was drifting out to them from the Rest Center or perhaps from another outlet nearby. As they hurried away, Adelle prodded Mondor again. "If the lack of sleep has serious effects, we ought to know what they are so we'll know what to expect."

"It's been used for torture," Mondor said. "The Fascists and Communists used it to extract phony confessions. It can lead to hallucinations and even insanity. It can cause physical disorders." He shrugged. "I don't remember. If all the garbage they're throwing at us really is some kind of scientific test, they ought to have a way to measure the results. Or think they have. Then they can write papers about what the difference would have been if we'd had five minutes sleep instead of ninety seconds or eaten two bananas instead of one."

"They're insane," Adelle said.

"Of course. If one sleepless person has a better memory for numbers than another, he'll remember them better no matter how many bananas the other person eats."

"I haven't experienced any hallucinations," Adelle said.

"How do you know?" Mondor asked. "They'd probably seem real."

"The gas I smell seems very real," Dolan said. "I think they want us to move faster."

During the next air raid, they began to smell the dead. The sickening, sweetish odor of bodies long buried in the rubble of smashed buildings permeated the alley. And the planes roared overhead, more bombs smashed down and rocked the cement floor they lay on, and bullets ricocheted, while acrid fumes and blinding smoke from nearby explosions seared their throats and made them cough convulsively.

Adelle glanced sideways at Mondor. His beard had completely darkened his face. She wondered how long it would take him to achieve an impressive thatch like Dolan's. She had never before viewed male hirsuteness as a subject for research or even speculation. She giggled, which made both men look at her reprovingly. They expected her to keep her attention on the air raid.

The sound of the planes faded; bombs and bullets ceased. The fumes, the smoke, the stench of the dead lingered. Adelle pushed herself to her feet. "If you two don't mind, the smell here—"

"Madam has a perverted taste in perfume," Dolan announced. "Madam is a pervert."

"They've tested our sight and hearing," Mondor said. "Smell had to be next. I wonder how they'll manage taste and touch."

They resumed their formation and shuffled on, feeling their way with cautious feet before they took each step. In the next alley they stopped to rest, and all three of them fell asleep at once. The alley was already thick with gas when they awoke. They fled to its far end, turned, and sat down again to wait for the gas to catch up with them.

"How are you on religion?" Dolan asked Adelle suddenly.

"I'm in favor of it."

"Blanket endorsement?"

She wanted desperately to sleep, and it took her a moment to focus her thoughts. "Depends on how you're defining 'religion'. Too many people confuse it with theology."

"I see. Religion, yes. Theology, no."

"Something like that. Why? Do you have an urge to be converted?"

"I was wondering how a deeply religious person would react to this. The fickle finger of the Almighty and that sort of thing. I suspect Job sat amidst his calamities feeling about God very much the way I do about Madam, but he had a good press agent. Is it possible to praise the wisdom of a Supreme Being from a cloud of tear gas? Mondor? Mondor!"

Mondor started and opened his eyes with a scowl. The hair that tumbled down over his glasses looked longer, now, and the glasses were filthy, but he no longer seemed to care whether his bleary vision saw anything or not.

"What?" he asked irritably.

"Is religion a factor in psychological tests?"

"Not in mine."

"Obviously. Is it in anyone's?"

"Might be. Might sustain a person in adversity. Or so I've heard."

"My guardian was Roman Catholic," Adelle said. "He wisely didn't try to convert me, but he took me to Mass. He thought if he exposed me to the truth, it would take. Like being inoculated by passing through a sick room."

Dolan chuckled.

"It left me with an impression of Catholicism I never really under-stood until I saw a photo of a piece of statuary that had been salvaged from an ancient Roman shipwreck. It was green and corroded and cov-ered with barnacles and a mess of ucky junk. After it was cleaned up, it was a beautiful statue."

"That's Catholicism?" Dolan asked doubtfully.

Adelle nodded. "It's overlaid with the clutter and untruths of centu-ries and all the corrosion of theology, but if someone would clean it up, underneath it's pure gold. Probably something similar could be said of all religions."

Dolan heaved a sigh. "Religion, yes. Theology, no. When your guard-ian was shanghaiing you to Mass, did you perchance hear anything about a patron saint of psychologists we could ask to intervene for us?"

"I don't remember any."

"Pity. Looks as if we'll have to undergo this ordeal without the sus-taining force of religion. I smell gas."

Adelle stumbled after him, thinking about her guardian. He had been a remarkably good man, a devoutly religious man. He tried to teach her to pray. "Ask, and it shall be given you." This always seemed faintly disreputable to Adelle—like begging for handouts on a street corner. Too many people were asking God for things they should have been able to do without or acquire on their own initiative.

In a totally helpless situation such as theirs, what should they pray for? That Madam and her goons be touched by grace? That would take a considerable miracle. Only a saint should have the right to make a request like that, she thought. She knew she fell far short of sainthood, and she had two additional handicaps in the form of Dolan and Mondor. Anyway, divine intervention seemed far too remote to be effectual with their problem. What they urgently needed was human intervention—someone to break in and stop what was being done to them.

In the end, that was what she prayed for—for human intervention. She even remembered to add special prayers for Dolan and Mondor.

In the next alley, the lights went out again and they encountered a garbage dump. As they cautiously made their way through the darkness, foul odors closed in and overwhelmed them. Adelle had the sensation of wallowing up to her knees in rotting debris. They dared not hurry, but they couldn't hold their breaths indefinitely. The stench became so overpowering it was difficult to breathe. Finally they found their way into another alley and fresher air, and they halted, panting.

"How the devil do they do that?" Dolan demanded. "They must have some way to pipe in odors just as they pipe in sound effects and gas. Let's move a bit further from it before we try to rest."

They shuffled along in darkness until Dolan announced, "Opening on the right." They pivoted and started off along the intersecting alley. They heard the swish of the partition rising behind them. The lights came on, and with them came the thunderous hiss of an enormous volume of gas escaping. At the same time, halfway down the alley, a partition began to rise from the floor.

"They're cutting us off!" Dolan shouted. "Let's go!"

He raced forward. Adelle, her body wracked with weariness, could manage nothing more than a stumbling lope that mocked any semblance of running. She muttered to herself, "I can't. I can't."

Dolan reached the rising partition first, leaped, hauled himself up. Seated on the slowly rising structure, he reached down an arm for Adelle to grab. She thrust the milk carton into her purse, clutched Dolan's hand, and was jerked upward. As he helped her over, Mondor's jump barely enabled him to grip the top of the wall. Struggling and kicking, he pulled himself up. The three of them hung by their arms from the other side and then dropped to the floor. The jolt of the landing staggered Adelle, and she fell heavily. Her feet had been dangling five or six feet above the floor when she finally let go.

"Now wasn't that tricky," Dolan said scornfully.

"The floor is wet," Mondor announced.

"So's my shirt," Dolan said. "I smashed my two milk cartons."

"You weren't carrying this much water," Adelle said. She was sitting in it. She got to her feet and anxiously checked her own carton. For a moment the three of them stared perplexedly. Then she became aware of the sound of running water, and at the same instant Dolan shouted, "Run!"

Far ahead of them, at the end of a long alley, water was gushing from several openings. Just beyond, another partition was rising from the floor.

Again Adelle tried to run. She could not. She called on all of her reserves of strength, but she could only stagger forward with water sloshing about her ankles. Dolan took her arm and tried to hurry her. Mondor was having his own problems. They were belaboring exhausted bodies, and the bodies did not respond.

Ahead of them, the wall rose slowly. It was waist high; then it was head high.

And the water had reached their knees.

Dolan left them and dashed, splashing, to the wall. Already he had to jump to grab the top. He pulled himself up and turned. Adelle stumbled up to the wall and stood there, panting. Dolan's slowly rising hands beckoned to her. She gazed up at him helplessly. He shouted something, and she stirred herself, made a feeble leap, and brushed his hand with her fingertips. Again she tried and missed. Mondor had leaped unsuccessfully for the top of the wall and lost his balance. He fell backward into the water. Adelle jumped again, and Dolan, hanging lower, caught her and pulled her up.

He left her unceremoniously draped over the rising wall and turned to help Mondor. "Get out of the way!" he shouted.

She slid over the wall, hung by her hands, and dropped, landing with a shock that wracked her body and sent her staggering backward. She sat down heavily, and for a moment she could do nothing more than dazedly contemplate her soaked clothing. When she looked up, Dolan and Mondor seemed about to be squeezed against the ceiling. She forced herself to scramble out of the way as both of them slipped over the top, made the long drop to the floor, and went sprawling.

They lay where they fell, and Adelle, seated nearby with her back against the wall, could neither move nor speak. The only sound was their heavy breathing.

Finally Mondor raised a hand and felt his wet shirt. "Smashed my carton," he muttered.

Dolan said nothing. Adelle shifted her position and slumped side-ways to cushion her head on her arm. Something was missing. She tried to focus her thoughts. Something—she looked doubtfully at her hands. She had been carrying something for days, and now she didn't have it.

The carton of water. Her carton. The quart carton.

She remembered jamming it into her purse, but it was gone. She wanted to tell Dolan how ironic it was. She'd lost the water in the water. "See?" she wanted to say. "Ironic."

She had to sleep. The terrifying, exhausting escapes, the hopelessness of their plight, seemed no concern of hers. All she wanted was sleep—without gas, for once; without air raid sounds; without stenches—but sleep would not come, though she felt increasingly drowsy. When finally she realized something was wrong, she was too groggy to move. She tried to cry out, to sound a warning, but she could only lie there and experi-ence the horrible sensation of dropping knowingly into unconsciousness.

She emerged slowly like a swimmer frantically struggling up from the depths. She first became aware of the lower part of her body, which felt damp. Without moving her head, she stared uncomprehendingly at the glowing ceiling and then at the drab gray walls. She had scaled a rising partition—no, two of them—with agonizing effort and with Dolan pulling her up. She had splashed through water to reach the second one. That was why she was wet.

It took intense, painful concentration to push herself into a sitting position. She clasped both hands to her throbbing forehead before she looked about her.

She was alone.

She sat staring at the short, bleak stretch of alley and its single open-ing, unable to comprehend what had happened. The men were gone. Had they recovered first and left without her? She doubted it. Madam's goons must have moved them—or her—while all of them were unconscious.

She flexed her legs and looked about her. The floor was wet under her soaked clothing, which gave her something else to be perplexed about. The men's clothing should have left similar puddles, but there were none.

She called out, "Where are you two?"

There was no answer. She called again. Then she slumped forward, hands pressed to her throbbing head, and tried to think.

She was alone. The men were gone. They wouldn't have walked off without her. Therefore they had been moved. Or she had been moved. Madam and her goons had deliberately rendered all three of them uncon-scious in order to separate them.

Should she try to find the men? Should she try to make her way back to the kitchen and water and beds and maybe food? Should she try to beat the odds and escape?

"If I start walking," she told herself, "I'll go where they want me to go and nowhere else. They'll open and close alleys and chase me with gas and lead me into traps and make me climb walls. So why should I go anywhere?"

She leaned back against the wall and dozed off almost at once. Gas awakened her—minutes later, she thought. The smashed watch that she now carried in her purse with other useless paraphernalia posed a perpetual question mark. She got to her feet and stumbled through the opening into the next alley. One of her legs was numb from lying on the hard floor, and her brief nap had left her feeling more exhausted than before.

The opening closed behind her. She took a few more steps and was about to seat herself when a voice froze her in a half crouch.

"Adelle! Adelle! Where has that bitch gone to?"

It was Dolan.

"Probably walked off and left us. Let her go. She'll fall into something and break her neck." That was Mondor.

"Look. We were doing fine as a team. We should try to find her."

Adelle called out, "Craig! Kevin!"

"Maybe she's too far away to hear us," Mondor said.

"You pound on that wall, and I'll pound on this one."

A robust thumping followed. When it stopped, Adelle called again, "Kevin! Craig!"

There was no response. She didn't hear the voices again. Or the thumping. Had it been a recording? Or had she imagined it? Mondor had said hallucinations would seem real.

"It must have been a recording," she muttered. "Otherwise, they'd have heard me. Or would they? I should have pounded back at them."

Then she saw them standing at the end of the alley. She waved and hurried toward them. Long before she reached them, they vanished, and a solitary figure, a strange, depraved-looking female, came trotting unsteadily toward her.

She was flabbergasted. Someone else in the maze? She halted. The figure halted. She started toward it, and again the figure advanced.

Finally she recognized herself: slovenly-looking, wet, tousle-haired, face smudged and taut with exhaustion—she was stumbling frantically to a rendezvous with a mirror. She stood looking at herself for a long time. She wanted to sit down, to think this thing out, to sleep.

The hiss of gas set her in motion again, and she lurched through an opening on her right. She could no longer run. Her fastest pace seemed to be a faltering stumble. She was sleep-walking her way along the alley, fleeing from the gas, but floundering more and more slowly.

"Adelle!" Dolan's voice called. "Where the hell is she?"

Adelle slumped against a wall and pounded on it feebly. "Craig! Kevin!" Again she told herself unconvincingly that it was a recording.

She stumbled on and found a test room confronting her. She would have fled from it as from a torture chamber, but she heard the hiss of gas behind her. The room might offer a brief respite, or it might offer doom. The numbers had become so long, and the multiple keyboard problem solving so complex, that it took an intense, cooperative effort from all three of them to gain a frantically fumbling solution.

Resignedly she entered, the door swished shut, and she leaned against the wall and waited for the flashing numerals. Respite, or doom?

Then she heard a gurgle. Water was gushing into the room.

She hadn't tried a test alone since that first day when she hadn't known she was being tested. Now she was much too exhausted to concentrate. With the hopelessness of total despair she watched the flashing numerals. Four, seven, nine, three, eight, two, six, zero…the board went dark. She stared in astonishment. That was all. Four, seven, nine, three, eight, two, six, zero. She had expected an interminable series that would instantly condemn her to failure. Four, seven, nine, three, eight, two, six, zero. It was simple. With water sloshing about her ankles, she went confidently to the response panels.

She tried center, left, right; center, right, left; right, center left; left, center, right. She tried the whole series on one panel after another, and then she divided the numerals. Nothing happened except that water continued to gush into the room. It had passed her knees and was half way to her hips. Four, seven, nine, three, eight, two, six, zero—had she messed it up? She was frightfully tired. If she had been a devout person, would the force of religion be sustaining her? She envisioned God wearing four, seven, nine, three, eight, two, six, zero like a convict's number. What hadn't she tried? Right, center—no, right, left, center? The water was rising faster and had passed her waist. Left, right, center—what else was there? She had to think, and there was no time for it. Four, seven nine, three, eight, two, six, zero—she must have got it wrong. God was wearing a forged number.

There were no other sequences, and the water was at her shoulders. Soon she would have to swim. Four, seven, nine, three, eight, two, six, zero?

She tried a twist that they hadn't experienced yet: Right panel, each numeral twice; central panel, each numeral twice; left panel, each numeral twice. The water had reached her throat. Should she try the same thing in other sequences? There wasn't time.

The water was at her chin. Soon it would pass the response boards. Would it short circuit something? She was tempted, so awfully tempted, to lean back and let it support her body. It would be restful. Perhaps she could even sleep that way.

She forced herself to concentrate. Four, seven, nine, three, eight, two, six, zero. God spelled backward read—suddenly alert, she began to press buttons on the central panel, desperately trying to reverse four, seven, nine, three, eight, two six, zero. Zero, six, two, eight—she faltered, she could not think—three, nine—she faltered again—seven, four.

Then she leaned back and closed her eyes, resting, floating. She no longer felt despair. She felt wonderful. There was no sound, but from somewhere below her she could feel the vibration of water still gushing in. Now, perhaps, she could sleep. This was a far better death than one from gun shots, or explosives, or being crushed at the bottom of a pit.

Her feet sank slowly, and she thrust her hands down to give herself buoyancy. She felt fully relaxed for the first time in days. She may have dozed off. When she snapped back to consciousness, she found that her feet had sunk again and were touching the floor. She thrust her hands down—her hands touched the floor. She opened her eyes.

Now she could hear the gurgle of water draining out far more swiftly than it had poured in. She sat on the floor as the last of it vanished into slots around the base of the walls. A door swished open. She would have liked to remain there in the cool, dim light. Sopping wet as she was, she could have lain on the cement floor and slept; but she knew that gas, or heat, or something worse would quickly drive her out.

She dragged her dripping figure from the test room and slumped to the floor. For a time she rested against a wall, face buried in her arms, her soaked clothing making a large puddle around her. Finally she sniffed gas, and she resignedly started off, dripping a trail of water.

As she approached the alley's end, the lights went off. She felt her way forward cautiously, found an opening, and turned into it. Immediately she wished she hadn't. Something was wrong with the floor underfoot. It felt different. It sounded different. She would have turned back, but the opening behind her was already blocked. She stood motionless in the darkness, uncertain, reluctant to move but too exhausted to be frightened.

Then the lights came on. She remained where she was, staring.

Her world had been turned on its side. She stood on one of the gray metal walls. One her left was the unpainted cement floor; a dozen feet away, on the right, were the luminous ceiling panels. Just above her head was the opposite wall. She closed her eyes, opened them again.

"Kevin said it would seem real," she told herself. "It seems real."

She stomped a foot, spattering the wall-turned-floor with water. She got back a metallic thump. She took a few tentative steps. "Either they turned the basement on its side, which seems unlikely, or gravity has flipped its lid, which seems even less likely," she mused.

She moved forward unsteadily, leaving a wavering trail of water on the misplaced wall. She had no choice. No other route was open to her, and she didn't want another serving of tear gas while she had this to figure out. As she walked, the sections of wall sagged under her weight. "Hey, goons!" she called. "The hallucination is a hoax. If you walk on a wall and it sags, that means it's the floor!" She giggled with pleasure at her ability to reason when she was too tired to think.

Twice she came to an uncertain halt, too exhausted either to continue or to sit down and rest. The hiss of gas forced her to move again, and somehow she managed to push herself to the end of the alley. When she reached it, she stood looking down into the next one.

Looking down into it. The opening was in the wall, as it should have been, but the wall was the floor, and therefore the next alley, which ran parallel to the one she was in, also had walls that were floor and ceiling and a floor and ceiling that were walls.

She rubbed her forehead fretfully. It was only a drop of six feet or so, but that would place her in a sub-sub-basement, and eventually she would have to haul herself back to the level she was on now. She doubted that she could do it. She sat on the edge of the opening and dangled her feet into it, resting and trying to think. She felt overwhelmed by loneliness, by the necessity to face dangers and make decisions by herself. Until that moment, she hadn't fully realized how much she had depended on the men.

She numbly tried to think, but no thoughts came. Finally she heard the ominous hiss of gas nearby. Resignedly she gripped the edge of the opening and swung down.

This time the alley was a long one. She was moving so slowly along the sagging wall sections that it seemed to take an eternity to reach the end. Long before she did so, the lights went out. She crept forward cautiously, fearing that this wall-turned-floor would have an opening she could fall through, but she arrived at the end of the alley without finding any.

An opening in the opposite wall would mean she had to pull herself up, and she already knew she couldn't do that. She absolutely could not do that. She backed up slowly, feeling the sections of metal above her head, but she found no opening.

Then she tried the fake cement floor that formed one of the walls, and she found an opening immediately. Heart pounding with relief, moving with infinite caution, she slipped through.

For a moment she thought things had returned to normal. The walls of this alley were the proper distance apart and made of metal—they gave off the usual metallic thump—but the floor seemed strange to her. As she knelt to examine it, the lights came on.

They came on below her. She was walking on the ceiling.

She stared down at the glowing panels for a moment, and then, in a corner of one of them, she stomped her heel. Drops of water from her sopping pant leg sprayed the plastic. Otherwise, nothing happened.

"So it's not the same stuff as the ceiling panels," she mused. "They were thin plastic, and they raised up when Craig pushed on them. They couldn't possibly hold my weight." She called out, "Another phony hallucination, goons!"

The absurdness of it roused her momentarily and fostered another illusion, one of an unsuspected reserve of energy. Nonchalantly she strolled the length of the alley, snickering over the silly contrivance someone had invested a fortune in for no better reason than to study her reactions. She wondered if she could get the creator of this stupid experiment fired by doing all the wrong things.

Again the lights went out. She found an opening and stepped through it, and the wall closed after her. When the lights came on, her world had returned to normal. She thumped on both walls and stomped on the genuine cement floor before she was convinced. She was still alone, but at least she was seeing things right side up.

Her recently-discovered reserve of energy vanished with the other illusions, leaving her as exhausted and depressed as before, and her solitude had begun to frighten her. She knew there would be obstacles she couldn't get through or over by herself. She moved ahead cautiously, testing each segment of the floor before she entrusted her weight to it.

So groggy had she become that the distant mutter of airplanes had swollen to a roar before she grasped what was happening. She threw herself down as bombs began to explode about her. She hugged the cement floor restfully, ignoring the bullets that whined and ricocheted and the stifling reek of the unburied dead. Perhaps she even dozed off between explosions. It felt reassuring to have things back to normal.

CHAPTER 17

When Laylor checked in at the Vista Motel at nine o'clock Tuesday morning, he found a note from Ray Bront waiting for him.

"12:40 A.M. Tuesday. The signature on Dolan's dismissal letter is the same as those on the Z-R checks, but no one knows whether it's hers. None of the ex-employees remembers hearing her name. Everyone called her 'Madam'."

Bront had spent Monday evening interviewing former employees of Z-R Publications who'd had the good fortune not to possess whatever special qualifications Madam was searching for.

Laylor went back to his car and drove around the building to the room assigned to him. It was what the Vista Motel called an Executive Suite: a bedroom with a double bed and a sofa bed, the latter giving the establishment an excuse to add fifty percent to the room rate. He unpacked his bag and made himself comfortable with his feet stretched out on a coffee table. He could do nothing until someone reported. He missed his pipe, but as a matter of principle he restricted his air pollution to his own office where no one but himself could be bothered by it.

The Vista Motel was adjacent to the Arbor Vista Shopping Mall. On a scale of one to ten, Laylor gave it a four for comfort, a two for ambience, a minus three for economy—it was severely overpriced—and a ten for convenience. The former home of Z-R Publications was a mere half-mile down the road.

Jill Tabold arrived at ten o'clock. Her informal costume of the previous day had been replaced by a neat business suit. Her long blonde hair had been plaited into a dignified arrangement at the back of her head. She also wore a stylish but conservative hat, and she looked a sedate ten years older.

She dropped into a chair and exclaimed, "What a place for a real estate office! That building is enormous! Wings stick out in all directions, and each one is different. I knew where your missing persons were the moment I saw it. They're lost somewhere in Feinstwaller Manor. What's the matter?"

Laylor had snapped his fingers and reached for the phone. He dialed a number, and a moment later Rebecca Carlyss's crisp voice answered, "Laylor, Graffington, Bartley, and Kordro."

"My idea of hell," Laylor announced, "is a place where I'd have to sit all day answering the telephone with the inspiring message, 'Laylor, Graffington, Bartley, and Kordro'. Law firms should have rational titles like 'Acme Legal Services'."

The receptionist, a prim, middle-aged woman whom most of the firm's employees addressed as "Miss Carlyss," giggled.

"Look, Becky," Laylor said. "Feinstwaller Manor. It's just outside Ann Arbor. I want to know who owns it, and since when, and who handles rentals. I hadn't realized that was where Z-R Publications was located. Feinstwaller. F-e-i-n-s-t-w-a-l-l-e-r. Charlie should be free by eleven. Ask him to get right on it. Yes, important. I-m-p-o-r-t—"

Miss Carlyss had hung up, something she presumed to do only with members of the firm who called her Becky.

Jill asked, "Who, or what, is Feinstwaller?"

"He was a mad architect. And a great one. That mansion was his hobby. This case certainly does get peculiarer and peculiarer. A publishing company with three employees—in that building?" He meditated for a moment. "At least this explains why Z-R Publications had such a large maintenance staff. No wonder its publications turned out not to be financially feasible. What goes with the real estate business?"

"They're actually hiring people," Jill said. "And seriously. The manager wasn't the least interested in helping out an orphan and stranger adrift in the large, unfriendly state of Michigan. He said local people with quantities of friends and relatives usually have an easier time finding prospects and listings, but he didn't insist on that. What he really wants is someone who already has a real estate license. Since I don't, he politely showed me the door. When, or if, I get one, he'll be glad to talk with me. The office is in a wing that looks like a cathedral, and they've set up shoulder-high metal partitions to make eight little offices for the agents. They can increase their staff by a hundred and fifty before they overflow into another wing. It's a bustling place. There are agents telephoning potential buyers, and people wandering about looking at photos of property for sale, and a receptionist making appointments to show the listings."

"What's the firm called?" Laylor asked.

"A&B Realty."

"Incredible! Z-R Publications. A&B Realty. Someone has a one-track mind. Maybe."

"I didn't think of that, but there's an important difference. Z-R Publications was phony. A&B Realty isn't. It actually transacts business."

Laylor reached for the phone again and dialed the number of a friend in the real estate business. After a few questions, he hung up and leaned back thoughtfully.

"Score one for you," he said. "A&B Realty isn't exactly an old, established firm, but it's been in business for several years and seems to be prospering. It doesn't operate in Detroit, but it has half-a-dozen offices in the suburbs. Now it's expanding to Ann Arbor and Pontiac. I'll have to look into this myself. I haven't anything more for you now. Go follow your nose."

"Gernyan lived at Chateau Arb for three weeks. She met Gerald Wyman in the laundry room. I'm wondering whether she met anyone else there."

Laylor nodded approvingly. "Good thought."

"Wyman will help me. He got a leave of absence from work so he could look for Adelle, but he doesn't know how to go about it. He can get me into the place, and we'll talk with everyone in the building."

She left, and Laylor followed her immediately, first stopping to leave messages with the room clerk for Bront and Kagen. He drove to downtown Detroit and maneuvered his way through one-way streets until he reached the outskirts of the business district, where he parked in an alley in front of a sign that warned, UNAUTHORIZED CARS WILL BE TOWED AT THE OWNER'S EXPENSE. He entered a rear door marked Boyd's Printing, and a moment later he was conferring with Horace Boyd over the copy of Craig Dolan's dismissal notice.

The printer, a white-haired, portly black man wearing a full length rubberized apron, regarded Laylor with affectionate wariness. "You want it today, I suppose."

"I needed it an hour ago," Laylor said, "but I can wait another ten minutes if I have to."

The printer sighed. "Someday—just once—I'd like to have you bring me a job you won't need until next month."

"If I won't need it until next month, why would I bring it in today?"

They exchanged grins, and Laylor promised to be back in half an hour. He left the same way he had entered and walked on down the alley to another rear entrance that was labeled Rolls Realty. Like most of the businesses in that area, it was struggling to survive. The present owner, whose name was Lazinski, had acquired the name "Rolls" along with the firm, but he would never drive one. His short, plump figure didn't quite match the pattern of his cheap, ready-made suit, and even his necktie seemed to be the wrong size. The office's interior looked as shabby as he did.

He greeted Laylor with a groveling smile and a handshake. The distinguished law firm sometimes had a crumb for him.

"Mort in?" Laylor asked. He already knew, from a glance at the desk in the corner, that Mort was not in.

Lazinski gestured vaguely. "Down the street seeing a client."

Laylor nodded understandingly and thanked him. He exited by way of the front door and walked along the street to a decrepit looking establishment called Lonnie's U Bar. Mort Rannon was seated in a rear booth. His eyes were fixed hypnotically on the glass in front of him as though the universe's ultimate secret was about to be unveiled there. Years of futile search for it in an unending series of glasses had not discouraged him. He was Lazinski's opposite—a tall, gaunt man with bushy hair whose clothing, though threadbare, fit him perfectly. Once he had been at the top of his profession, but a series of personal tragedies led to his spending more time at establishments like Lonnie's than with his clients. When he was sober enough to impart facts and opinions, his grasp of the real estate business was remarkable.

He grinned and extended his hand as Laylor approached, and Laylor shook it, slipped into the booth opposite him, and waved the barmaid away. As a matter of principle, he didn't drink with alcoholics. Neither did he attempt to reform them. Occasionally he helped Rannon to an appraisal fee or a commission, and the money was always well earned, but he had long since abandoned any hope that the real estate agent might thereby be encouraged to take a step toward sobriety.

"What's on your mind?" Rannon asked.

"A&B Realty," Laylor said. "Is it genuine? Is it honest? Is it competent?"

Rannon drained his glass and leaned back, eyes closed. His long, thin face and deeply shadowed eyes made him look perpetually in mourning, which he probably was. "A&B," he murmured. "It's been operating—how long? Five years, at least. It's done a lot of business, it keeps adding to its staff, it has offices scattered about the suburbs—none in Detroit that I know of—and it hasn't stirred up any scandal."

"It's opening new offices in Ann Arbor and Pontiac," Laylor said.

Rannon opened his eyes and fixed a bleary stare on Laylor. "I didn't know that."

"Tell me something I don't know," Laylor suggested.

"I was with Shaller Realty when A&B started up," Rannon said. "It hired the best salesman Shaller had—hired him by offering a guarantee that was large enough to be silly."

"Is that dishonest?"

"It isn't exactly ethical, but you can't blame the salesman for wanting to better himself. The business has its ups and downs, as you know. From a firm's point of view, guarantees are stupid. If salesmen get paid whether they produce or not, what incentive do they have to sell? How much real estate do you think I'd sell if someone put me on salary? So why would a brand new firm do an idiotic thing like that?"

"I don't know," Laylor said. "Does it prove something?"

"It does." Rannon leaned back and closed his eyes again. He counted on his fingers. "Proselytizing, it's called. Shaller's agent wasn't the only one A&B hired away from other realtors. One firm threatened to sue. Proselytizing." Rannon savored the word, his lean face tense with pleasure. "That's pretty good considering how drunk I am. Proselytizing. I make it six."

"Six top agents that A&B hired away from other firms?"

"Six that I know of," Rannon said. "Probably there were others."

"Does it prove something?" Laylor asked again.

"Someone wanted to get a business going in a hurry."

"Doesn't everyone?"

"Of course. And it worked. A&B Realty has been solid from the word go. But not many could afford to go about it like that. It means only one thing. A&B had plenty of financial backing."

"You interest me strangely."

Rannon nodded. "Plenty of financial backing. From the beginning. Virtually unlimited. Someone wanted to put a new business on solid ground in a hurry and didn't care what it cost. I'll guarantee it."

It was two o'clock when Laylor drove into the parking lot of Feinstwaller Manor. Before he headed for the main entrance, he paused for a moment, briefcase in hand, to study the building. He had seen it before, but he wanted to ponder the notion of a Z-R Publishing Company occupying this enormous structure with a few maintenance people, a manageress, and three employees. The firm's address seemed as much a mystery as the disappearances.

The same mystery applied to A&B Realty. An office in a shopping mall would have been more accessible to its customers, would have attracted far more walk-in business, and should have cost much less in rent.

At least the real estate company had taken a businesslike, no-nonsense attitude toward its grotesque surroundings. It was using only the cathedral wing and a few rooms along the wide corridor that led to it. A red rope with tassels, suspended from chrome posts, displayed a "No Admission" sign to keep customers from wandering into unused parts of the building.

The carpeting in the entrance corridor had been covered by a plastic runner that extended into the cathedral wing to protect the exquisitely polished parquet floor. Inside the door was a thick matting for customers to wipe their feet on. Laylor dutifully wiped his and moved on.

He wove his way past easels with photos of the firm's listings. At the receptionist's desk, which was located just inside the massive double doors of the cathedral entrance, he presented an expensively engraved card. The middle-aged receptionist, who obviously hadn't been hired for her looks, regarded it with eyebrows slightly raised. It read, Laylor, Graffington, Bartley, and Kordro, Attorneys-at-Law. His name, John Laylor, Jr., appeared in the lower left corner below the address and telephone number.

She said perplexedly, "Yes, sir?"

There were times when Laylor didn't mind being mistaken for his father, the distinguished head of the firm. "I'm looking for Z-R Publications," he said. "Could you direct me, please?"

"They moved out last week," the receptionist said. "I don't know where they went. There have been several inquiries about them, but we only moved in this past weekend, and I never heard of them until people started asking." The people doing the asking had been the police, but she didn't mention that.

"Incredible," Laylor murmured. "Could I speak with your manager, please?"

"Mr. Harriman doesn't know anything about them, either."

"Nevertheless—" Laylor persisted, and the receptionist resignedly buzzed a number and read the information from his card. Then she hung up and pointed back along the corridor.

"Mr. Harriman will see you."

"Thank you," Laylor said.

Harriman was waiting when Laylor stepped back through the double doors. He said, "Mr. Laylor?" shook his hand warmly, and escorted him into a sparsely furnished office. He was an elderly man with thinning gray hair and a smiling salesman's look. He was as plumply prosperous looking as his surroundings.

Harriman settled himself behind his desk while Laylor was pulling a file—conspicuously marked Z-R Publications—from his briefcase. Silently he passed a letter across the desk, and Harriman took it, glanced at it, glanced quickly at Laylor, and then began to read.

The letterhead, complete with Z-R Publications logo, had been offset by Horace Boyd from the copy of Craig Dolan's dismissal notice. The text of the letter, with appropriate modifications, had been borrowed from a query that actually had been received by Laylor, Graffington, Bartley, and Kordro from a publisher client. Laylor hoped this would provide some semblance of authenticity for what was otherwise a blatant forgery.

The letter was dated the previous week, and it read, "Gentlemen: Our first titles will be ready for publication by the end of summer, and we wish to retain you to advise us on copyright matters. Specifically, we are concerned about our right to use statistical information from copyrighted sources." From the scant details available, Laylor had deduced that Z-R

Publications would have had to cope with that particular problem. The letter continued with a list of highly technical and authentic questions and concluded by asking Laylor, Graffington, Bartley, and Kordro to kindly provide answers at its earliest convenience and bill Z-R Publications for its appropriate charges. The signature was the same that appeared on Dolan's letter, expertly forged by another of Laylor's disreputable acquaintances.

Harriman finished reading and looked up questioningly. His puzzlement was genuine, but it carried with it an expression Laylor couldn't identify.

"I'd like to know what's going on," Laylor said.

Harriman frowned and turned as though to read the letter again. "I can't tell you anything about this. Z-R Publications left before we moved in. We have no connection with them. We don't even have their forwarding address. The company that manages the building sold us some of their office equipment, but at the time I didn't know whose equipment it was."

"Why would they write a letter like this if they were going out of business in less than a week?" Laylor demanded.

"I don't know that they actually did go out of business," Harriman protested. "I only know that they moved away from this address." He passed the letter back to Laylor.

"When did your firm decide to open a branch here?" Laylor asked.

"In this area, several months ago. In this building—I don't remember the exact date the lease was signed. Several weeks ago."

"Then at the time Z-R Publications wrote this letter, someone there surely knew the firm would be moving out at the end of the week."

"Not necessarily. We'll be renting or leasing office space to other firms. It's possible that Z-R Publications originally planned to stay on here as our tenant and then changed its mind at the last moment. Or it may have assumed that your reply would be forwarded. Forwarding addresses usually are left with the post office, not with the next tenant." He was being politely sarcastic.

"The management company," Laylor said. "Could you give me its name and address?"

He already had it, but the question was one an indignant attorney would be certain to ask. Harriman found a card in his desk drawer and handed it to Laylor.

Laylor got to his feet. "Thank you for your patience. Inquiries about a former tenant you know nothing about must be tiresome for you. We find the situation tiresome, too. Someone has been playing games with us, and I intend to find out why. Playing games with a law firm is a risky pastime. I'll try the management company."

Harriman nodded pleasantly. "Yes. That would seem to be your best move. The management company should know all about Z-R Publications."

He got to his feet and shook hands with Laylor.

Laylor made an appropriately indignant exit, strode back to his car, and drove away. "I think," he mused, "that Harriman knows far more than he let on—maybe." He was trying to remember where he had seen that expression before: puzzlement, overlayed with—something. Why should a letter written by a firm Harriman knew nothing about produce that reaction?

Laylor drove to downtown Ann Arbor, negotiated the obstacle course created by the city's attempt to convert its main street into a shopping mall without diverting traffic, and parked in a parking structure. At Solstead and Company, Property Managements, he again displayed his letter and received expressions of sympathy.

Lyle Solstead, a brisk, elderly man, knew very little about Z-R Publications. "The building's owner arranged the original lease," he said. "It was for three months with an option to renew at the end of the second month. Because it was a new firm, the owner, who lives in Florida, asked for and got a substantial deposit, and he instructed us to inspect the premises weekly. And properly so, but the maintenance was excellent, and the manager seemed enthusiastic about the firm's prospects. I don't know why it failed to exercise its renewal option." He supposed it had left a forwarding address with the Postal Service.

When Laylor casually changed the subject to A&B Realty, Solstead readily supplied details about the company and its lease that clearly were none of Laylor's business.

He took his leave of Solstead and Company, and before he reached the parking structure he knew he was being followed. First, there were two pairs of eyes studying him from a nondescript parked car. The moment he passed them, the passenger scrambled out and the the driver started his motor for a quick getaway in case Laylor unexpectedly grew wheels or wings. It seemed a bit too obvious, but the operators had to pick him up without having seen him before, and probably they were jittery about following the wrong person.

"The question is, what should I do about it?" he murmured.

He decided to do nothing about it. He drove out Main Street past the huge, sunken stadium of the University of Michigan, with the driver—who had recovered his passenger along the way—following closely. Main Street became Saline Road, which was lined with heavily-trafficked shopping malls. Laylor turned toward Detroit at the I-94 intersection. After one amused glance to make certain the men were still following, Laylor forgot about them. The problem was no longer his but theirs.

He reviewed his day's activities as he drove. There was a distinct odor of overripe fish about Z-R Publications, both in the manner in which it had slipped into and out of business and in its relationship with A&B Realty, but none of that was any help to him. He still had no clue as to what had happened to the missing employees.

He had no notion at all as to why anyone would go to the outlandish rigmarole of establishing a phony firm, keeping it in business for three months, and hiring and firing a lot of people just to abduct three of them. There were so many simpler and cheaper ways. Causa latet: vis est notissima.

In downtown Detroit, he drove directly to the parking lot where he rented a space by the month. If the men tailing him had any skill, they would confirm his identity with the parking lot attendant and then doubly confirm it by following him to the law offices. He helped them out by entering the building by the front door and pausing at the newsstand to buy an afternoon paper from the long-time friend who operated it. A dozen people in the lobby exchanged nods or perfunctory greetings with him.

On the fourth floor, Miss Carlyss regarded him with mock astonishment. "Using the front entrance? Have you been demoted, or something?"

He went to his office and telephoned the Vista Motel. Bront had arrived and was waiting for orders. Laylor told him what had happened.

"First break we've had," Bront said jubilantly. "Don't leave until you hear from me. I'll have the tailers tailed. What's their license number?"

"Never thought to get it," Laylor said ruefully.

"Never mind. I'll put someone on it as soon as I can. Stay where you are until you hear from me."

"There's no rush," Laylor told him. "Since I'm making like a hard-working attorney, I'll be here until five. I might even work overtime. Now listen. I want you to change our registrations to assumed names. I want no mention in the motel's records of Laylor, Bront, and so on."

"That's illegal," Bront protested.

"That's why I'm asking you to do it. If the manager objects, Prehn will give you an imprimatur. It might spoil the fine effect I made as an angry Detroit attorney if these people were to find my name in the Vista Motel registry."

"I see. Yeah. I'll take care of it."

"When you call back, let me know what my pseudonym is."

"Yeah. Stay there until I get things arranged. By the way—today's Ann Arbor News has a feature on the missing persons. With photographs."

"It won't do any harm, and it may be helpful," Laylor said.

"It may," Bront agreed.

Laylor hung up, tilted back in his chair, and reached for a pipe.

The day's one bright idea was Jill Tabold's notion that the missing people might be hidden somewhere in sprawling Feinstwaller Manor. This seemed worth testing, but it would have to be done officially and with a warrant.

He dialed Ann Arbor Police Headquarters and explained the situation to Prehn, and Prehn said, "Feinstwaller Manor is outside the city limits, but I can ask the sheriff to send a couple of men. I suppose it's a reasonable request, since the missing people worked there. I doubt that it could be managed this afternoon, though."

"Have you had a good look at that place?" Laylor asked. "It would take two men until Christmas to go through it, and they'd be in danger of getting lost themselves. There's no point in a search unless you send enough people to do the job properly. Here's a suggestion. Let A&B know immediately that you'll be there in the morning with a warrant to perform the most thorough search you're capable of. Of course you won't interfere with the real estate business any more than necessary, but you intend to do your duty."

"What makes you think someone from A&B is tailing you?" Prehn asked.

"The tail picked me up at Solstead and Company, and only Harriman knew I was going there. I think he made two phone calls the moment I left. One was to Solstead, telling him to answer my questions and quiet any suspicions I might have. Probably he used the excuse that he didn't want to be harassed by a law firm. The other was to the persons who tailed me, telling them to pick me up when I left Solstead."

"Did Solstead show any sign of trying to detain you until the tails arrived?"

"None. Solstead may not be involved. Harriman is. He knew my letter was phony, and he was intensely curious to find out whether I'm phony, too. I'll point something out to you. Bront is going to have the tailers tailed, and he asked me to stay here until he can arrange it. I'm not to leave until he calls and says it's okay. In other words, a professional private detective, with a Detroit office, and employees, and all kinds of connections, couldn't say without checking how long it would take him to put someone on a tailing job. Harriman managed it instantaneously. In Ann Arbor, yet. I find that impressive. You'd better make an extremely thorough search."

Prehn finally agreed, and Laylor hung up and sat back to formulate a plan of his own. "For every action there's an equal and opposite reaction," he murmured, savoring the words. It was Newton's third law of motion, and there were times, Laylor thought, when a broad education had its uses. Lieutenant Prehn was about to supply the action. The equal and opposite reaction should follow quickly. The problem was to devise a method of observing it.

It was nearly five when Bront called back. "Don't leave until five-thirty," he said. "That's the best I could do. And when you leave, you're going directly home."

"Certainly. In the front door and out the back. Have a car waiting for me. I'll have to leave mine in the parking lot."

"Nothing doing. You'll have to be home."

"I'll put timers on the lights."

"What if they telephone and get your answering service?"

"Look," Laylor said impatiently. "They'll see me arrive and go into the building. My car will be in its usual parking place. My lights will go on at dark. Why would they telephone? Not to find out whether I'm home, surely. Now listen to me. We're about to pay tribute to Isaac Newton with a scientific experiment."

He gave Bront his instructions. The private detective responded with skeptical grunts. "Crazy," he said finally.

"Oh, no," Laylor said. "I've never done anything more rational. The letter puzzled Harriman. He knew it was phony. Not only that, but I saw a familiar expression in his eyes. I just remembered where I've seen it before. I should spend more time in court."

"Where'd you see it?"

"In the face of a witness who'd just been hit with an unexpected question and was about to respond with a whopper of a lie."

CHAPTER 18

Darkness, even on a night with a touch of moonlight, softened the oddities of Feinstwaller Manor, concealing the gargoyles, blurring architectural demarcations, blotting out the formal gardens with masses of shadow. The immense, rambling structure became a hulking monster of uncertain shape and features.

When Laylor was a student at the University of Michigan twenty years earlier, there had been rumors of secret stairways, hidden rooms, trap doors, concealed passageways. And why not? Old Feinstwaller was cracked, but that hadn't affected his professional skill, and he'd done some of the work on the building's interior with his own hands in order to demonstrate fine finishing techniques. He deserved a little fun with this white elephant of a hobby.

Oddly enough, no one had ever claimed to see his ghost prowling through the manor. Probably one solitary ghost wouldn't be noticed. It would take a congregation to haunt the place properly.

Following Laylor's suggestion, Lieutenant Prehn had called on A&B Realty late that afternoon to announce a police search, with warrant, the following day. Harriman's attitude was one of perplexed innocence. As far as he was concerned, no warrant was necessary. The mansion and its contents were A&B's responsibility, but as long as the police didn't break anything or inconvenience his customers, they could search as much as they liked.

When Prehn asked permission to take a preliminary look at the building, Harriman gave him the freedom of the manor with a wave of his hand. He hadn't had time to familiarize himself with the place, but he would have to do so soon in order to sublet it. He confided that the main problem in finding tenants would be the severe restrictions on alterations—even picture hangers were limited to one per wall, and carpet tacks in the fine hardwood floors were prohibited—but Harriman already had inquiries from an insurance agency and a law firm. The building was a local legend, and A&B Realty was enjoying a modest volume of business from people who visited its new office because it gave them an opportunity to see the manor.

"You were right," Prehn told Laylor afterward. "A battalion couldn't search that place thoroughly in a day. As for A&B Realty, if Harriman has guilty knowledge, either he's certain there's nothing there or he knows it's so well hidden it can't be found."

"He has guilty knowledge," Laylor said confidently. "He lied to me, and then he had me tailed. Don't overlook the possibility that his relaxed attitude was due to the fact that the search isn't to take place until tomorrow."

"So what do you expect us to find?"

"Probably nothing," Laylor said. "If the missing persons *are* hidden in the building, their abductors will have ample time to back a van up to the service entrance and remove them—and all traces of their presence—in the dead of night, after which the police can search as thoroughly as they pleased. That's why we'll be watching the building tonight—to prevent that. Also, I want to know whether there'll be any reaction at all to the fact that you're going to search the place in the morning."

Prehn said sternly, "That means trespassing."

"What harm is there in taking a shortcut through the grounds of Feinstwaller Manor?"

"Don't try to enter the building. There's a very efficient alarm system, and the sheriff would have to respond."

"I can find out as much as I need to know from the outside—I hope. Years ago, the Detroit Free Press published a floor plan of the place. One of my assistants found it and had copies made." He presented one to Prehn. "Have your men check for concealed rooms and hidden staircases. The old place deserves an opportunity to live up to its reputation."

"That'll take two battalions. What happened to your tails?"

"Saw me to my apartment. Made an inquiry or two to make certain I'm me, which they'd already established downtown, and departed, writing me off as genuine—or so I earnestly hope. Harriman probably thinks the phony letter was sent by a disgruntled former employee who stole some stationery. Bront's men followed my tails when they left."

"That might lead to something interesting."

"I doubt it," Laylor said. "Those characters started off clumsily, but once they got into the swing of it, they were slick. It was the kind of slickness that comes with plenty of experience. No one is going to stick to them very long. Good luck with your search tomorrow."

"Good luck with yours tonight," Prehn said, laughing.

Bront brought in a dozen investigators, and Laylor recruited the same number of law students. Jill Tabold brought Gerald Wyman along. He was a good-looking young man and as bright as Jill or Bruce Kagen in his chosen field of engineering, but he had no idea of how to make himself useful in a missing person search. Otherwise, Laylor was impressed with him.

Unfortunately, he was a gloomy companion. He was frantic with worry about Adelle Gernyan, and he exuded depression the way a comedian emits merriment.

Their battle stations were chosen with care. They had radios, they had cars strategically located to follow the most elaborate motorized maneuvers, and they were equipped and prepared for anything except a gun fight.

There had been one last minute complication. Bront discovered an elderly man who lived alone in a small cottage a quarter of a mile up the road. He walked his dog each night before retiring.

"He says the place has night watchmen," Bront said. "Three men and a dog. The interesting thing is that they're new. He first saw them last Friday."

"That's suggestive. I wonder what's happened recently that made the building require extra protection."

"All he could tell me is that he walks his dog down the road each evening and then circles back through the grounds behind the manor. He never saw any watchmen before Friday, but now one of them patrols outside with the dog while the other two go through the building turning lights on and off."

"How frequently?"

"He doesn't know," Bront said. "He doesn't always walk his dog at the same time, but in the course of a walk he sees them at least once. My guess is that they work from dusk to dawn and follow a regular schedule with their patroling."

"If he cuts through the grounds every night without being attacked by the watch dog, the outside search must be perfunctory."

Unfortunately, even a perfunctory search meant they couldn't perform their surveillance as close to the mansion as Laylor had planned. His own position was a narrow space between shrubs from which he had a distant, partially obstructed view across the wooded grounds to the point he was most concerned about, the delivery entrance. A van could come and go unnoticed in that neighborhood because half the suburban population seemed to own one, and an excellent driveway led from a side road to the loading platform.

The period from one to three A.M. seemed the most likely, but it could happen at any time, so there would be a long, uncomfortable night in the shrubbery for Laylor, Bront, Wyman, the investigators, and the college students. They would curse the mosquitos and hope the watchman with the dog wouldn't make a wider loop than usual on his next round. Probably nothing else would happen.

Watchman and dog began their swift circuit of the grounds regularly on the hour, with the watchman softly whistling some tuneless melody and now and then saying something in baby talk to the dog, a mangy German shepherd. They were the most unprofessional looking guardians either Laylor or Bront had ever seen, but a confrontation with them would have ruined the night's work.

Inside the manor, the other two watchmen moved in opposite directions on the ground floor, turning lights on and off in each room they passed, which made it easy to follow their progress. By the time they returned to their headquarters near the main entrance, about twenty minutes later, the outside watchman had completed his circuit. The three of them settled down to drink beer—with which they were amply supplied, according to one of Bront's men who had crept up to the window—and talk until time for their next rounds.

There was nothing for Laylor and his crew to do but keep hidden and watch nothing happen. Drifting clouds occasionally obscured the shrunken moon, at which time the only light was the occasional flicker of headlights that penetrated the trees from the highway and a distant glow from the shopping mall. By midnight, the moon seemed to have vanished permanently and the shopping mall's glow had long since been turned off. Laylor huddled in the darkness, brushing mosquitos away and wishing he didn't have hunches or at least that he lacked the means of investigating them.

Suddenly a light came on in one of the upper story rooms.

Bront, who had stationed himself nearby, sidled over to him. "See that?"

"Not being blind—" Laylor began testily.

"I think maybe you were right," Bront whispered. "Something's going on."

"Check the watchmen," Laylor suggested. "Maybe they got tired of their chairs in the office and decided to try out the pseudo antique furniture."

Bront spoke into his portable radio. Fifteen minutes later he had an answer. All three watchmen were drinking beer in the A&B office. "So there are at least four people in the building," he announced.

"Could a cleaning woman have sneaked in without our seeing her?"

"A&B's cleaning woman is a man. He comes at seven in the morning."

"Mark that room on a floor plan so the police can go over it thoroughly."

"Sure," Bront said. "But if there's anything of interest there, it'll be gone by morning. How about slipping in now? The beer drinkers wouldn't notice, and that flea hound is less of a watchdog than I am."

"They'd notice if you set off the alarm. Even if you got upstairs, whoever you found probably would have a right to be there, and you wouldn't. No, let's keep our act semi-legal."

Bront crept away. The light remained on until almost one o'clock. A short time after it was turned off, the watchmen started their rounds. Lights came on in sequence along the lower floor, flashlight beams darted about, and the watchman with the dog whistled his tuneless way through the grounds. Then all three returned to their beer, and the upstairs light came on again.

Bront crept back again. "This makes no sense at all," he muttered. "There's someone in the building who doesn't want the watchmen to know he's there, and he's turning the light off during their rounds."

"If so, he knows their schedule," Laylor said.

"Right. Every hour on the hour and don't go upstairs. So he works confidently right up to the hour, and then he turns off the light. This gets more and more interesting."

The light went off and stayed off at thirty-three minutes after one. Ten minutes later a light was turned on in an upper room of another wing. Bront spoke to his radio and verified that all three watchmen were accounted for.

Once again the upstairs light went off shortly before the hour and was turned on after the watchmen finished their rounds. Twenty minutes later it was turned off again. After a pause—Laylor could imagine someone in stocking feet treading cautiously through the mansion—a light came on in the upper story of still another wing.

Laylor said to Bront, "Got all three rooms located?"

"Located and marked."

"Good. We'll let Prehn figure it out—except that you'll have to position some people to watch the building tomorrow and find out who leaves. Would it be possible to photograph everyone who comes and goes?"

"We can try. This can't have anything to do with the A&B Realty people, you know. Why would they be sneaking around at night? They have possession of the place. If there was anything they didn't want the police to find, they could have removed it this afternoon."

"True, but I still think there's a distinctly fishy odor about them."

"Sure you don't want me to slip in and find out what's going on?"

"Too risky. Also, we don't want them to know we're interested. Even if we have no idea what they're doing, we're one up on them because we know they're doing it, and they don't know we know."

"You sound like a lawyer," Bront said.

"I'd rather not have to act like one—which I would if you got caught breaking and entering."

The third room's light went out just before the watchmen made their rounds. When they returned to their beer, it came on again. Laylor left his shrubs and crept closer to the building with Bront and Wyman following him. They moved along the drive that led to the delivery entrance, keeping on the bordering grass. The moon now shone dimly behind thinning clouds, and as they approached the building, a large shadow suddenly loomed nearby. Laylor turned aside to examine it: a cement slab with a square metal structure perched on it. Muffled pulsations of machinery came from inside.

"Air conditioning?" Laylor whispered.

"The building doesn't have central air conditioning," Bront whispered back. "The A&B rooms have individual units. New. Installed today."

The pulsations slowed and gradually faded. Laylor turned to Wyman, the engineer. "What kind of machinery would be running at night, in the summer, in a place like this?"

In a place like this stumped him. He had no answer.

They walked quickly toward the rear entrance. There seemed no likelihood of their finding a clue to the mysterious lights, but their moving about made things more interesting for the mosquitos.

When they reached the open platform that served as rear porch and loading dock, they halted and glanced about. In the moon's feeble light, Laylor caught a glimmer of a reflection near the door. He advanced cautiously, climbed steps with Bront and Wyman stumbling on his heels, reached up—and found himself examining the building's electric meter.

Using his jacket to cover his head and the meter, he turned on his flashlight. He watched for moment, and then he said softly to Wyman, "Take a look at this." While Wyman was looking, he sent Bront to see if the machinery was running again.

"No sounds at all," Bront reported. "But there's something queer—"

"Check and see how many lights are on in the building," Laylor said.

Bront used his radio. "A couple of hundred watts, at most," he reported. "The ceiling light in the room the watchmen are using and that light upstairs. As I started to say, there's something queer—"

"Just a moment," Laylor said.

Wyman had finished his own scrutiny of the meter. "Something is drawing a lot of power," he observed.

"A hell of a lot," Laylor agreed. "What could it be?"

"I haven't any idea."

Covering himself with his jacket again, Laylor copied the meter reading into his notebook. Then he switched off his flashlight and donned his jacket. "Tomorrow, we'll try to get copies of electric bills for the past couple of months and see how much Z-R Publications used. Tomorrow night, we'll come back and read the meter again."

"As I started to say," Bront resumed peevishly, "there's something queer about this place. That structure is some kind of vent, and I'll swear I smelled tear gas."

Laylor stared at him. "What in God's name would anyone be doing with tear gas in Feinstwaller Manor?"

"I don't know, but I know tear gas when I smell it. Once experienced, never forgotten."

The three of them returned to the odd-shaped structure. Laylor inhaled deeply. "I don't smell anything."

"Neither do I—now. But there was tear gas."

"If you say so."

They set out to circle the building, but the uncertainty of the footing—sometimes cement, sometimes gravel, sometimes cobblestones, sometimes grass—and the confusion of moving in darkness through the maze of formal gardens and pools and fountains and shrubbery and statuary soon defeated them.

"No wonder the watchman makes a wide circuit," Laylor remarked.

The upstairs light had gone out, and that side of the building remained dark except when the watchmen made their rounds. There were no further incidents until dawn when the three watchmen and the dog left together. Two of Bront's men followed them to find out who they were.

"Nothing about this place makes sense," Laylor observed to Bront as he studied the fantastic outlines of Feinstwaller Manor by Wednesday morning's early daylight. "The businesses don't, the night watchmen don't, a nocturnal prowler in a building with an up-to-date alarm system and three watchmen doesn't, and the missing employees make the least sense of all. We'll just have to fumble around until the mess starts adding up to something. Get going on that photography."

He went back to the Vista Motel, where he was now registered as John Brown, and went to bed. Bront woke him with a telephone call at eleven o'clock. The police search was underway, and those performing it had been given information about the mysteriously lighted upstairs rooms. Bront had placed people with cameras and telescopic lenses where they could get shots from different angles of people in cars arriving at or leaving Feinstwaller Manor, but he was making no guarantee about how the photos would turn out. The main entrance was being watched from a van parked along the highway. As cover, a woman in gypsy costume was selling woven baskets. The drive to the building's rear entrance presented no problems. There were plenty of trees and shrubs along the connecting side road.

"The rest of the news isn't good," Bront said glumly. "The men following the watchmen lost them in Detroit. They claim to have an excuse, but I think they goofed. And the license number on the car the watchmen were using is registered to an unemployed guy who moved recently. We haven't been able to trace him. He could be one of the watchmen, of course."

"Never mind," Laylor said. "Follow them tomorrow with two cars."

"Sure. The other item is worse. The men I had following those guys who tailed you haven't reported. I'm worried about them. The hell of it is, we have no idea where they went. They could be in New York or Kansas by now."

Laylor thought for a moment. "Did you mention that to Prehn?"

"No."

"Tell him. The sooner the police get onto it, the better."

Laylor hung up and then phoned room service for a combination breakfast-lunch. He hadn't eaten since the previous afternoon. He was distastefully contemplating a concoction the motel's dining room called pasta when he became aware that someone in the parking lot near his room's sliding glass door was looking in at him. He glanced at the mirror on the wall opposite—he had already noticed how well it reflected a panoramic view of the parking lot.

One glance was sufficient. He calmly set down his coffee cup, reached for the pot, and poured a refill. When he looked at the mirror again, the man was climbing into a familiar, nondescript car. As he drove off, Laylor grabbed the telephone.

He called Bront. "Pack," he said. "We're checking out."

"I just got to bed," Bront grumbled.

"You can sleep later. One of my tails just spotted me. We'll move to a motel over on Jackson Road."

Laylor packed in a rush. When he reached the the lobby, he overheard the switchboard operator saying, "No. There's no John Laylor registered here."

An hour later, he was seated in his new motel room, feet up, trying to make sense of the confused events at Feinstwaller Manor. Lieutenant Prehn interrupted him. The police officer was a tall, sturdily built man who had the perpetual air of presiding over a disaster.

"So you've changed your name again," Prehn said gloomily. "I ought to arrest you. We didn't find a thing in those three rooms."

"I didn't think you would. Too bad we couldn't catch them in the act, but it didn't seem wise to break into the place just on the chance that something important was going on."

"No. Then you would have been arrested. And negative information sometimes has its uses. We didn't find anything. Not even a fingerprint. Someone wiped the place thoroughly. Fortunately he couldn't obliterate marks on the carpet. There used to be a desk in each room and a desk chair on a plastic runner, and those three rooms are the only ones away from the cathedral area that have phone jacks."

"Interesting," Laylor said. "How do you read it?"

"It doesn't need reading. Those were the rooms where the three missing people worked. We've confirmed that with former employees. When I announced the search, someone made a very thorough search of his own to make certain we wouldn't find anything. A couple of the sofa cushions had been put back the wrong way, and one of the carpets was wrinkled where someone didn't smooth it down properly after looking under it. This is extremely important without really helping us. All it does is confirm the suspicions we already had. Otherwise, we haven't turned up a thing."

"Bront told you about the nocturnal use of electricity, didn't he? What could account for that?"

"I have no idea. I don't like this bit about Bront's men disappearing and someone dogging you. Watch yourself. I can't even guess what game these people are playing, but I'm convinced that its lethal."

The Ann Arbor News had followed its story about the missing persons with another about Feinstwaller Manor and the police search. Laylor was reading it when Bront arrived at six P.M.

"I hope this doesn't attract crowds of snoopers," Laylor said. "That would complicate things."

Bront looked like a candidate for a vagrancy charge. He was wearing soiled work clothing, and he had an unshaven face and dark circles under his eyes. His report made the situation even more perplexing. He personally had watched the A&B work force leave for the day. No one emerged from the building who hadn't been seen to enter it.

"Is it possible that someone's living there?" Laylor asked.

"Whoever was there last night certainly is still there," Bront said.

"Did you ask the police whether they found a place where someone could be eating and sleeping?"

"I did. There are bedrooms everywhere, but none of the beds seem to be in use. They're museum pieces, with fancy bedspreads and no sheets or blankets. There's a large kitchen with facilities to feed a couple of hundred, but no one can remember the last time anyone entertained there. The equipment is old and new—meaning that it's antique stuff in perfect condition because it's been used so little. Nothing is plugged in, and the place is spotless."

"Have any pizzas been delivered there recently?"

"The A&B people go out for lunch. They could have brought food back with them. I'll see if anyone noticed."

"Smell any more tear gas?"

Bront flushed. "Damn it, I know tear gas when I smell it."

"I never doubted it. What's one more peculiarity among so many? Reserve enough rooms here so your people can sleep when they're off duty, and find alternate locations for them to do their spying from. Also, you'd better warn them this job may be hazardous to their health. We'll watch the manor again tonight. Also tomorrow night and the night after that. I have a hunch we'll be watching it for a long time."

* * * *

In Moscow on Thursday morning, Yuri Fedorenko's peaceful sojourn as secretary of Directorate Y was terminated cataclysmically. When he started up the stairway to his office, he heard voices. The door was ajar, and he saw two men inside, one in his chair and the other sitting on his desk.

Fedorenko froze in horror. The man occupying his chair was Dmitri Abrasinov, who once had ranked high among the KGB's elite. After the Time of Troubles, he was rumored to have committed suicide, to have fled abroad, to have gone into hiding. He had been a slender, scholarly-looking man with a mild face, graying hair, and rimless glasses, and he reminded Fedorenko of his grandfather, a retired school teacher. Now he had dyed his hair and grown a mustache, and his face seemed oddly distorted, but Federenko recognized him immediately.

The second man, the one seated on his desk, was a stranger to him. He was powerfully-built with dirty-looking red hair, and he scowled constantly.

Fedorenko was late, as usual, and both men turned to him as though expecting an explanation. He was too frightened to say anything.

They resumed their conversation. They had opened the safe and removed the files, which were piled on the desk in front of them. Their talk—about a police search in the United States—was completely beyond Fedorenko.

"Then the only thing we're certain about is that the laboratory's security is blown and local police have searched the building," the red-haired man said. "Unless they're totally incompetent—and we'd be foolish to assume that—they'll keep it under surveillance."

"Not only that, but the abductions were discovered almost at once, and the press immediately linked them with the earlier disappearances. Frunze saw a report in the Chicago papers and sent me an alarmed message asking what was happening."

"And Cherkasov hasn't mentioned any of this?" the red-haired man asked incredulously.

"Not a word. We've relied entirely too much on individual initiative from people who don't have any. Our distinguished committee said nothing to me about the earlier blunders." He gestured disgustedly at the files.

The red-haired man got to his feet. "I suppose you want me to salvage what I can."

"No," Abrasinov said. "Project Ob is not the kind of operation that can be salvaged. It must be preserved."

"At any price?" the red-haired man asked.

"At any price," Abrasinov said firmly. "When this idiocy passes and our World Revolution can be resumed, Project Ob will be invaluable. I have immense respect for Dr. Sokolova and complete confidence in her."

The red-haired man nodded. "I'll take care of it."

He went down the stairs three at a time. Abrasinov fixed his eyes on Fedorenko. Caught in that unwavering gaze, Fedorenko was no longer reminded of his grandfather. "I suppose," Abrasinov remarked thoughtfully, "that you are only a clerk."

"Yes, sir," Fedorenko answered miserably.

"In charge of keeping the files up to date."

"Yes, sir."

"The problem with this organization is that it has too many clerks. Or too many employees with the mentalities of clerks. Now listen. I want you to go through these well-ordered files carefully. You're to study the reports on Project Ob's first two phases and prepare a summary of everything that went wrong and what explanations were given. A messenger will be here to collect it—and you—tomorrow morning. You're able to typewrite, aren't you? Of course you are, you're a clerk. I want that summary neatly and accurately typewritten."

Abrasinov got to his feet and reached the door with one stride. His final remark came over his shoulder. "And if you write it with the mentality of a clerk, I'll put you in a job where your mind won't be taxed."

* * * *

The red-haired man, whose name was Andrei Zinovyev, returned to the KGB's underground Moscow headquarters, where credentials and plane reservations were waiting for him. He became a black-haired man through the simple expedient of donning a different wig, and he flew to Frankfurt and then to Amsterdam, changing identities in each city. From Amsterdam, he took a KLM flight to New York. His Federal Republic of Germany passport bore the innocuous name of Hermann Burkel. His credentials identified him as a public relations specialist with the Volkswagen Company, on a brief American tour.

His German was flawless; his English more than adequate; his credentials impeccable; his knowledge of the American automobile industry awesome. The detailed information he possessed about Volkswagen dealers in Southeastern Michigan would have surprised those businessmen exceedingly.

At Kennedy International Airport, his customs inspection, for a visiting German businessman with a single suitcase, was routine. An hour later he was on a flight to Detroit Metro. Before midnight, Michigan time, he was in conference with three men and one elderly woman in the sound-proofed basement room of an old private dwelling situated near the University of Michigan's Central Campus. One of the men was A&B Realty's Mr. Harriman, whose real name was Aleksei Cherkasov.

Zinovyev announced coldly, "My mission has two purposes. First, I intend to eliminate the stupidity in our operations here. Then I intend to eliminate the cause of the stupidity."

CHAPTER 19

Adelle had the feeling she had been wandering forever, alone and lonely, in a sprawling, mindless entity she was calling "Maze" for want of a better name. Madam and her goons were insubstantial shadows from an almost forgotten past. So were Craig Dolan and Kevin Mondor. "Maze" was real. It was alive. Her presence irritated it, and it responded by punishing her.

Her thorough soaking in the test room had left her less begrimed and perspiration-stained than before, but her wet clothing chafed uncomfortably. She took off her outer garments and wrung them out, and then she tried to gauge the passage of time by how long it took them to dry. When hours passed—or what she thought were hours—and they still were damp, she gave it up. She continued to move when gas forced her to and collapsed and tried to sleep when it didn't.

She wondered how many hundred or thousand gas attacks there had been. When another one set her laboriously in motion, she walked as slowly as possible, placing one foot before the other with studied concentration and considering it a triumph that she remained upright and moving. At the entrance to the next alley, she halted, staring incredulously.

Its distant end was filled with a large picture window that looked onto the familiar contours of the formal garden she had admired so often from her office window: the neatly trimmed hedges, the splashes of color in the flower beds, the complicated configuration of the dry fountain. In the distance was the lovely Romanesque wing.

She rubbed her eyes disbelievingly and looked again. "Oh, no you don't!" she muttered. She knew she would have had to climb from the sub-basement all the way to the first floor before she could enjoy that view. If an alley had been tilted that steeply, she would have noticed.

The sun lay full upon the garden; branches of the shrubs stirred slightly in a light breeze. Mondor had said hallucinations would seem real, but real would seem real, too. In spite of her skepticism, she began to stumble falteringly toward it.

Then she halted. "Careful," she told herself. "It may be a trap. And if it isn't, it won't go away."

She resumed her labored plodding.

As she approached the window, it receded into the distance. The closer she came to where she thought it had been, the further away it seemed. Finally it was a tiny, oblong speck of color on the threshold of infinity.

The speck vanished, and she stood looking at a distant picture window view of another garden. Again she plodded forward, and again the window receded into the distance, becoming smaller and smaller until it was a minute speck that disappeared before she reached the end of the alley.

She slumped to the floor and remained there, resting, until gas forced her into another long alley. This time there was no window, but a black object lay on the floor at the far end. As the opening closed behind Adelle, the object suddenly ran toward her, looming larger and larger as it approached. She sank to the floor—more in stupefaction than fright, for she was too tired to be frightened. Then the thing was upon her, a gigantic tarantula, its bristling front legs spread wide to embrace her. She caught the fetid odor of some previous, decaying prey and feebly raised her arms to defend herself.

It vanished, to be replaced by a full-sized rhinoceros that thundered down the alley and, as it ran over Adelle, seemed to have the bulk and racket of a freight train. Numbly Adelle struggled to her feet and began to force herself forward again, and suddenly the zoo emptied in front of her. A gigantic boa constrictor slithered toward her along one wall. On the other side, a cobra coiled. A leopard leaped down from the top of the wall and crouched to spring at her, teeth bared in a ghastly grimace. Behind it, an African buffalo lowered its horns to charge. An elephant waved its trunk menacingly. A crocodile reared up directly in front of her, jaws agape.

She heard all of it: the hoofs, the claws scratching on cement, the roars, the hisses. And she smelled it: animal odors blending with the rotting damp of a surrounding jungle. It was real.

Then it was gone as abruptly as it had appeared, and a blank alley lay before her.

"I think," she told herself grimly, "I'd better get the hell out of here."

But she remembered to shuffle cautiously, to test every footstep. She reached the end of the alley without further incident, turned into the next one, and all but fell over the sprawling form of Kevin Mondor. He was leaning back against the wall with his eyes shut. His face was pale under his scraggly beard, his glasses had acquired another layer of smudge, and he displayed the same indescribable weariness that Adelle felt.

His eyes opened. He looked at her over his glasses. "Oh, it's you," he said. And closed his eyes again.

Adelle sat down beside him and eyed his damp trousers. "I see you survived the water torture. How wet did you get?"

"Just to my waist. I've been expecting them to pull that number-in-reverse stunt, but I was so tired I almost forgot what it was when I tried to do it backward."

"Did you enjoy the safari?"

"That was stupid."

"And the formal gardens viewed from nonexistent picture windows?"

His eyes opened. "They didn't show me that. I saw the courtyard where I used to sit after lunch."

"But did they really show us those things?" Adelle asked doubtfully. "The picture window was the sort of hallucination I'd have if I had one."

"Did you see the tarantula? And the rhino? And then a menagerie: cobra, leopard, elephant, crocodile—I forget what else."

"All of that," she agreed.

"If we both saw it, it was no hallucination. Anyway, they overdid it. There was too much realistic detail. Hallucinations tend to be on the vague side. If you were an hallucination, for example, I probably wouldn't know from looking at you that you didn't solve that idiotic reverse number test until the water got above your shoulders. Did you go through a kinky place where you walked on the wall and then the ceiling?"

"Yes."

"Have any trouble getting down through the opening in the floor?"

"You mean in the wall turned sideways. No, no trouble."

They sat for a time in silence. Adelle desperately needed sleep, but for the moment she was delighted to luxuriate in the presence of a fellow human, even one she disliked.

"After we were separated," she said slowly, "I heard you and Dolan talking. It sounded as though you were together. You were shouting back and forth and calling me and wondering where that bitch had gone to. I answered, but you didn't, and finally I decided it was a recording."

"When I came to, Dolan was in the next alley. We were able to talk by shouting, but we never did find each other. I heard you calling several times, and I called back, but you didn't answer." Mondor stretched and yawned. "I suppose they wanted to see how we'd react to things when we were alone."

"Would they have let us drown if we hadn't thought to reverse the number?" Adelle asked.

"I sort of think they would have."

"And now they want us to team up again?"

"If Dolan comes stumbling along looking like a floor mop someone forgot to shake, that'll mean they want us together. Did you hear the dinner bell while you were wandering around by yourself?"

"No."

"I just wanted to make certain I hadn't missed it. Next time it'll probably be one cube of sugar apiece with an eye dropper of fruit juice for a chaser, but I won't turn it down. Well. Whatever happens, I'm not going to move until I have to. Maybe they won't bother us until Dolan shows up. I hope the silly illusions make him think he has *delirium tremens* and keep him at the other end of that alley. We can decide what to do when he arrives. If he arrives. If they let him arrive. I'd like to see an ardent Free Will Baptist wandering around in here with a Predestination Calvinist. The place would drive both of them nuts."

Adelle looked at him doubtfully. "Maybe it's driven you nuts. Why do you sound so cheerful?"

"I've gone over to predestination, and I'm at peace with the universe. Since everything is predetermined, no decision of mine matters anyway. Except maybe one. Shall we sleep?"

"That's a decision?" Adelle asked. She stretched her legs out and closed her eyes. In the wonderful sensation of relaxing, she could ignore a minor discomfort like damp clothing. She fell asleep immediately.

Tear gas awakened her. Craig Dolan, sopping wet and furiously angry, had arrived with the gas on his heels, and Adelle and Mondor had to leap out of their comatose slumber to flee with him.

When they were able to slow their pace to the halting shuffle their weary bodies demanded, Mondor asked Dolan, "Why are you panting? Were you running from the snakes?"

"No. I was trying to stomp on them and kick a rhinoceros."

"Did they look that real to you? I thought you'd be sobered up by now. How long has it been since you had beer?"

"Please. Beer is a sacred subject."

"Did you enjoy the water treatment?" Adelle asked him.

"I darn near drowned," Dolan said frankly. "I was reading numerals from under water when I finally figured it out. What an asinine notion. Psychologists must have infantile mentalities. So here we are again. As long as we have no choice, I suggest we keep going."

"How long do you think we can?" Adelle asked.

Dolan's answer was a shrug.

Mondor weighed the question thoughtfully. "Maybe another day. Maybe two. I suppose it depends on what they make us do. If it's anything strenuous, I'm sure I won't last much longer." He looked about him uneasily. "This silence has been going on so long it's getting on my nerves."

A short time later it ended abruptly. Tear gas forced them into the wide alley where the Nightmare Village with the cobblestone street and stone buildings loomed in twilight dimness. Something new had been added: bodies, and gristly pieces of bodies, lay strewn among the rubble, and the reek of death was so strong Adelle found it difficult to breathe.

The planes came, bombs screamed down, and real explosions crumbled some of the fake building fronts that were still standing and toppled the debris onto the fake bodies. Several blasts went off so close to them that they left Adelle's ears ringing painfully. A tremendous explosion brought down an entire building at the far end of the village, spewing stones and splintered boards into the street and scattering fragments through the alley like shrapnel. Then came the low flying, strafing planes. Bullets snapped close overhead as they clung to the cobblestones, and ricochets rattled among them. Dolan got a flesh wound in the leg and swore furiously. Twice Adelle felt bullets tug at her clothing, but neither of them scratched her.

When the sounds of the raid began to fade, they hurriedly climbed over the debris and fled into the next alley. Dolan paused to examine his bleeding leg, and Adelle knelt to help him affix his dirty handkerchief to the wound. Tear gas routed them before she had quite finished. Dolan jerked the knot tight himself and impatiently brushed down his trouser leg. Their usual exit, on the right, was closed. They turned left, entered the next alley, and halted. Directly in front of them, filling the alley from wall to wall for a distance of twenty feet or more, was a shallow pool.

"What do we do—wade?" Dolan asked.

"Get back!" Mondor snapped.

He dropped to his knees and sniffed at the liquid. Then he got to his feet again, took a step backward, and spat. The pool spat back. There was a snap, a puff of vapor, an eruption where liquid struck liquid.

"It's acid," Mondor said. "Probably sulfuric in a highly potent solution. You wade that, you'll come out at the other end without shoes or feet."

They stood staring at each other; gas was creeping around them.

"Let's go back!" Dolan shouted.

The three of them turned and fled.

The wrecked village was filling with gas, and planes were approaching again. Dolan stood for a moment peering through the dim light. "There aren't any beams," he said finally. "We'll have to see if they've left us another exit. Come on!"

Bombs began to screech down on them as they ran. Explosions showered them with stinging fragments. They were almost through the village when the strafing planes approached. Dolan shouted, "Down!" Adelle dropped to the cobblestones, and bullets began to slap and whine from stone wall to stone wall.

Dolan was crawling forward, and they followed him. Adelle tried to wipe her tearing eyes with a gas-permeated sleeve, which made them smart worse.

When the raid began to taper off, Dolan scrambled along on his knees for a short distance and then jumped to his feet and ran. At the end of the alley he threw himself prone, waved at them to stay where they were, and began to crawl back.

"There's no exit," he called. "We're trapped."

For a moment the words meant nothing to Adelle. Then, as Dolan reached them, her mind seized his simple statement and shook it out as one shakes a rug. She calmly got to her feet. "The air is better up here," she announced.

The planes were gone. The wrecked village had the stillness and the stench of death underlying the hiss and choking fumes of spreading gas. "We seem to have a choice between asphyxiation and getting our feet burned off," Adelle said and wondered why her voice sounded so light.

"Some choice," Mondor growled.

Dolan was gazing at the debris that spilled into the cobblestone street and at one point almost blocked it. "Come on!" he shouted and started to run again.

Mondor hurried after him. Adelle stumbled along far behind, panting. Her lungs ached as much as her legs, and when she tried to take a deep breath, the gas smarted and choked.

Dolan picked up a large stone from one of the fallen houses. "How deep is that pool?" he called to Mondor.

"Don't know. Not very."

"Grab all the stones you can carry. Take large ones that are flat on one side. Hurry."

Adelle could carry four. Mondor had five and Dolan six. Choking, eyes streaming, they lurched through the short gas-filled alley and halted at the edge of the pool.

"Don't drop them in!" Dolan warned.

He set his stones on the floor and very carefully placed one in the acid a couple of feet from the edge. Then he took another, stepped on the first stone, and placed it in the acid ahead of him. He turned. Mondor began handing stones to Dolan. Step by step their bridge grew. When Dolan got out of reach, Adelle took her courage firmly in hand and stepped after him, letting him take the stones from her one at a time. She clutched them desperately and felt reluctant to let go when the transfer was made—a splash of acid could be as bad as stepping into it.

The pool was no more than a couple of inches deep, and its bottom was level; but the stones, even though they looked flat on one side, teetered when they were stepped on, and the sides they had to walk on were rounded. Adelle was grateful for her wide-soled shoes, and she placed her feet with meticulous care, studying each rock as well as she could through her tears. All around them their tear drops were spattering in the acid.

Mondor followed Adelle with the last of the stones, and when Adelle's were gone she began taking them from him and passing them to Dolan. Suddenly they had reached the other side, and Adelle took the last step to safety, praying she would fall forward if she stumbled. They hurried to the end of the alley, found an opening, and placed another alley between themselves and the gas before Dolan let them rest.

Adelle crumpled to the floor and lay there, panting. Mondor and Dolan sat with their backs against the walls on opposite sides of the alley and gazed moodily at each other.

"A long time ago you said something about a trap door dropping us into a vat of acid," Dolan grumbled. "Next time keep your inspirations to yourself."

"They're trying to end the experiment," Mondor said. "That acid wasn't from a kid's chemistry set. It was a high-potency commercial solution."

Dolan shook his head. "You're wrong. It was another of your damned group problem solving tests, and they left the answer there for us to fall over. The experiment is still on."

"Maybe so," Mondor said, "but I'm certain they expected at least one of us to slip in or stupidly try to wade. Everything is getting more and more dangerous. The bullets are being aimed closer to the floor—did you notice? If the experiment is still on, how much longer can it last?"

"There's just one thing I'd like to know," Dolan said.

"What?"

"You spat into the acid."

"So? It smelled like acid, and that was a quick way to prove it actually was acid."

"Do you realize how long it's been since we had anything to drink? Where'd you get the spit?"

CHAPTER 20

The longer Andrei Zinovyev considered the situation, the angrier he became. He pushed the papers aside and glared across the table at a cringing Aleksei Cherkasov. The other three agents were watching him silently with frightened eyes. It was all very well for them to lament the unpredictable, the unavoidable, the impossible-to-anticipate; but everything that had happened had been predictable, avoidable, and easily anticipated.

Their orders had been emphatically clear. Around the world, as well as in the Commonwealth of Independent Russian States, the KGB was considered as extinct as the wooly mammoth. Surviving local agents had been cautioned to take no action at all that had the slightest risk of letting the world know the KGB was alive, well, and active. Most of them had gone underground. They were on hold, so to speak, awaiting a more propitious season. Projects of such transcendent importance that their continuation and completion were imperative, like Dr. Sokolova's experiments, had to be handled with extreme care so that absolutely no publicity would result. These dourakee—these blockheads—behaved as though they were still living in a world where the KGB reigned supreme. Worse, they attempted to cover their blunders by not reporting them.

His immediate problem was to save as much as he could, and that looked like trying to put spilled molasses back in the jug: Sticky to attempt and impossible to accomplish without leaving a mess. The publicity was certain to continue. Monday's missing person speculations had become Tuesday's grim facts and Wednesday's front page sensation in the Ann Arbor News.

There was no way to put *that* back in the jug. Z-R Publications and its three employees couldn't be made to undisappear, and the fact that there were three of them instantly linked these disappearances with the earlier ones. "Stupid!" Zinovyev muttered. Why didn't they abduct five and dispose of the two they didn't need? Dr. Sokolova had in fact suggested that. Why do everything in threes, which virtually advertised the connection with the earlier phases. Why wasn't the fake publishing firm established in a suitable city safely remote from Ann Arbor? There were several only a few hours away by auto. Dr. Sokolova had suggested that, too. The training of a specialist like her was necessarily superficial, but she was a far better agent than these nincompoops.

Cherkasov stammered, "We had to be careful about the psychological effect on the subjects. Dr. Sokolova herself cautioned against that."

"Nonsense!" Zinovyev exploded. "She didn't want them drugged for an indeterminate period of time, but a few hours' ride in an automobile wouldn't have harmed them. It was unbelievably stupid to take all three subjects from the same community and idiotic to locate Z-R Publications in the building where the tests are conducted. Dr. Sokolova said as much."

"But there is no crisis!" Cherkasov protested. "The publicity is unfortunate, but it will pass. The police searched the building and found nothing. There was no risk to Madam and her experiment."

He babbled on, explaining again why there was no risk. Zinovyev ignored him. The man was so incompetent that nothing he said could be believed.

Zinovyev knew Dr. Sokolova well enough to detest her, but he respected her work. She was excessively touchy about suggestions from non-scientists; on the other hand, though she never hesitated to express her opinions, she had the good sense to restrict her activity to the area of her competence and leave matters like security to experts.

Unfortunately, the experts hadn't been expert. Projects Ob and Sosva were scientific, the new Directorate Y was scientific, and Dr. Sokolova was emphatically scientific. The non-scientists given administrative responsibility for the project had little interest in scientific matters and even less understanding of them. Further, like all KGB bureaucrats, they held a disparaging view of any undertaking that originated with the GRU.

As a result, critical decisions concerning a project of unparalleled importance were left to local agents who likewise had little interest in it.

Now the molasses was out of the jug, and those responsible were whining that there was nothing to worry about. "The first priority," Zinovyev rasped, "is the security of Dr. Sokolova's laboratory. Let's drop the nonsense about there being no risk. There's always a risk. How safe is it?"

"Completely safe," Cherkasov said. "I told you—the police searched the building for an entire day. No one could discover the concealed entrance to the laboratory without knowing where it is and how it operates. It's absolutely secure. As for Feinstwaller Manor, I manage a legitimate business there during the day, and the public comes and goes freely. What better cover could you ask for an illegal operation? I'm using guards at night, at least until the conclusion of the present tests, but they aren't necessary. No one bothers the place. No one ever has."

"What about this attorney? Isn't it strange that such a minor matter would keep him in Ann Arbor overnight?"

"He hasn't been back to Feinstwaller Manor, and the man at the motel may have been someone else. Or he could have had other business in Ann Arbor." Cherkasov leaned forward and spoke earnestly. "Sir, things are going well. Madam will complete this phase in another day or two.

The publicity is unfortunate, but it will pass. The police will make certain it passes. They don't like to have their failures publicized."

"Why was it necessary to dispose of the two private detectives? Are your operatives so inept that they can't shake a couple of tails?"

Cherkasov said weakly, "*I* didn't—they exceeded their instructions—"

"The publicity won't fade if you keep feeding it," Zinovyev said angrily. "Do you have an auto here?"

Cherkasov nodded.

"I want to see this Feinstwaller Manor."

"There's nothing to see there at night," Cherkasov protested.

For once he seemed to be right. The road was dark, and Feinstwaller Manor was invisible behind its screen of trees. Zinovyev agreed it would be unwise to drive up to the building.

Then, through the trees, he caught a gleam of light.

"The guards keep one room lighted, and they make regular inspections of the building, inside and outside," Cherkasov explained.

"Rather conspicuous guards," Zinovyev observed.

"They're supposed to be," Cherkasov said. "We aren't trying to catch anyone. We want people to know the building is watched so they'll stay away."

Zinovyev grunted but made no comment. He signaled Cherkasov to turn at the first cross road, and a short distance further on he told him to pull off the road and park. "Saw something," Zinovyev muttered in explanation. The two men got out and walked back along the road. A moment later they were studying a car that had been carefully parked out of sight behind some bushes.

"Why isn't there a security fence around the grounds?" Zinovyev demanded.

"That would make people think there's something there that needs protecting. The building has an alarm system that calls the police if anyone breaks in, which provides ample security. It's never been used. If someone did break in, he wouldn't find anything."

Zinovyev began a cautious movement through the overgrown, tree cluttered grounds that surrounded the manor. Long before he made out the building, he could see the lights that marked one of the guards' inspection rounds. He took cover and watched intently. Then he pointed. A dark shadow had flitted between the trees. Then he picked out a silhouetted figure. And another.

The lights went out, and they made a careful retreat back to Cherkasov's car. "So the laboratory is secure," Zinovyev said sarcastically when they were underway again. "The police attention is elsewhere. No one bothers the place. But someone, with a large force, is observing everything that goes on there. Who? And why?"

Cherkasov had no answer.

"When these watchers leave, I want as many of them followed as you can manage. We'll decide what's to be done about them when we find out who they are."

* * * *

There wasn't even a nocturnal prowler to relieve the tedium of those watching Feinstwaller Manor on Thursday night, the third night of Laylor's surveillance. The only apparent activity was in the electric meter.

Gerald Wyman stoically made no complaint, but he continued to look extremely worried. Ray Bront, a bloodhound straining on a leash when action loomed, quickly had his fill of waiting for nothing to happen. Several times he crept up to the strange structure behind the building and sniffed at it. Once he returned in a rush to claim he had smelled tear gas. No one else did.

Part of Bront's irritation came from worry about the two missing men who had been sent on a simple tailing job. The nine disappearances now had become eleven, and he felt responsible.

"Four men could have handled this night watch," he muttered to Laylor. "Considering how many people I'll need tomorrow to keep track of all the comings and goings—"

Laylor listened without comment, which was the prerogative of the one paying the bills. He watched the building himself until three A.M., and when he left to return to his motel, Bront was still complaining bitterly.

As Laylor drove away, he momentarily regretted his flight from the conveniently located Vista Motel. There was only one other car on the road, and he had a sympathetic feeling for its driver, another weary soul wending his way homeward at an unlikely hour. The feeling of friendliness vanished when he noticed how persistently the headlights were following him. He made an abrupt turn and swung to the curb with his car lights off. A moment later, crouched down in his seat, he watched the other car round the corner on screaming tires and speed past in obvious pursuit.

Thoughtfully he returned to Feinstwaller Manor, where he gave Bront stern instructions about the conduct of his and Laylor's employees when they went off duty. Again he headed for Jackson Road, and he found to his irritation that he had acquired another tail. This one was more competent, and it was well after four on Friday morning when Laylor finally got to bed.

* * * *

On Friday morning in Moscow, Yuri Fedorenko—and his carefully typewritten summary of Project Ob's first two phases, which he had worked on all day Thursday and much of Thursday night—were conveyed to Dmitri Abrasinov's office. An agent wearing ordinary work clothing drove him in a battered delivery van with Fedorenko riding out-of-sight in the back.

He managed to keep track of their route, and he was astonished. He had known all along that the KGB still maintained a Moscow headquarters—the reports he received, as well as his salary, had to come from somewhere—but he hadn't dreamed that it might be located in the heart of the city. A camouflaged office in a commercial structure like his own Directorate Y Headquarters, or perhaps a concealed basement location in a remote suburban apartment building, seemed likely, but they drove to the center of Moscow by the most direct route, and for a horrified moment he thought they were actually going to the Kremlin. They turned aside at the last moment, and after that, although Fedorenko knew exactly where he was and what route the van was following, he sternly ordered himself to see nothing and remember nothing. As a long-time KGB employee, he knew there were some things it was better not to know.

So he passed numbly through one of the delivery entrances of a large hotel—his mind kept it nameless—helping the driver carry a strangely weightless box down to a basement room. From that point someone else helped the driver carry the box back to the van. Federenko was guided through a series of rooms with a security check in each and then through a tunnel that led him to the crypt or undercrypt of one of the magnificent old churches in the area. Federenko's mind also kept it nameless.

The church was now a museum, and the tourists passing through its quiet interior certainly had no notion of the activity taking place beneath their feet. The old stone walls had been left bare, but the rooms were furnished comfortably enough, and Dmitri Abrasinov had a most impressive desk with red, white, and black telephones. The carpet in his office, thick and with handsomely subdued abstract designs, was the most luxurious Federenko had ever set foot on. Abrasinov nodded at a chair, and Fedorenko nervously seated himself and presented his typewritten summary.

The scowling Abrasinov began to read, asking questions as he went along. "In other words," he said finally, "Dr. Sokolova made many objections about the project's security."

"Yes, sir."

"And you brought them to the attention of no one."

Fedorenko had already decided he might as well be executed for boldness as for timidity. "Dr. Sokolova had already brought them to the attention of my superiors, sir."

Abrasinov's eyes impaled him.

"All of her reports were initialed by three persons," Fedorenko continued desperately. "The originals surely were retained by them for reference. I received copies for the Directorate Y files. If they paid no attention to Dr. Sokolova, I knew they would ignore a mere clerk like me."

"You're almost certainly right," Abrasinov said. "Unfortunately."

He pressed a button.

Three men filed in. One of them, plump with short gray hair, had an angry flush on his face. The second, incongruously thin with no hair at all, not even eyebrows, possessed the pallor of death. The third was dully indifferent. At a gesture from Abrasinov, they seated themselves on a sofa.

"This is Comrade Fedorenko," Abrasinov said. "Have you met before?"

They gazed at Fedorenko perplexedly. He eyed them in return. Two of them looked vaguely familiar. Probably he had seen them from a distance but—not knowing who they were—paid no attention to them.

"He has met you," Abrasinov said. "At least, he has met your initials. It would have been a rewarding experience for all three of you to cultivate Comrade Fedorenko. He is only a clerk, but when asked firmly, he prepares an excellent summary. He has a knack for extracting the essence of a filing cabinet of reports. He would have used his talent for you if ordered to do so, and this crisis could have been avoided. Why didn't you ask him?"

The three men suddenly became fascinated with the designs in the thick carpet.

Abrasinov picked up Fedorenko's report. "He begins with a summary of the overwhelming importance of Projects Sosva and Ob, as stated in GRU's recommendation, and of the crucial importance of their security. I remember discussing these same topics with you when I placed the projects under your supervision. You've had a number of years to meditate the matter, but all three of you demonstrate less understanding of those critical points than Comrade Fedorenko was able to acquire in one day."

"We relied on local agents!" blurted the fat man. "We accepted their recommendations. They know the situation—they're there!"

"Dr. Sokolova is there, also. Why didn't you accept—or even consider—her recommendations?"

There was no answer.

"The stakes," the Chairman said softly, "are enormous. For that reason, I'm giving you the most severe punishment I can think of. Your negligence created this mess. I've sent Zinovyev to do what he can, but I suspect it's much too late for his kind of direct action. So I pass the problem back to you. If you're lucky, you'll have until evening to resolve it. If you fail, then I'll devise a different kind of punishment."

He nodded a dismissal. As they got to their feet, he pushed Fedorenko's summation at them. "Read this," he said. "It would be unfortunate in a number of ways if your solution repeated your past errors."

They left, and Abrasinov turned to Fedorenko. "If you had protested just once, even in the most timid memorandum, I would have promoted you. The person who can't assume responsibility but handles it well when it's forced on him is not a criminal. He is merely pathetic. I'll leave you where you are for a few more days, just in case we need more summaries. Then I'll place you under a superior who'll develop your talents by insisting that you use them."

Dismissed by a nod, Fedorenko left wondering whether he had been reprieved or sentenced to death.

CHAPTER 21

The specter of death hovered very near them, now. Adelle tried not to think about it, but she knew it was on all of their minds.

She no longer plodded. It required tortuous effort and concentration for her to put one faltering, aching foot in front of the other as each alley blurred into an identical looking successor. When she thought about the walls they'd scaled, the problems they'd solved, the hazards they'd overcome, she knew they wouldn't have the stamina to do any of those things now. They were so mentally befogged from sleeplessness, from hunger, from thirst, from exhaustion, that the next test room would finish them. Miracles had kept them going, but surely they had exhausted their quota. The only question remaining was whether their tormentors would eliminate them one at a time or spring an ingenious trap that would wipe out all three of them simultaneously.

The reality of their situation was so grim, and her thoughts about it so depressing, that she tried to keep her mind focused on resurrected memories. There had been a beach with a long slide, and when she rocketed downward, her father caught her just as she plunged into the water. Screaming with delight, she splashed back to the stairway, climbed to the top, and rocketed downward again. She wondered whether there had been any other time in her life, before or since, when she enjoyed herself so much. She could have enjoyed it now—the swift, exhilarating descent, the plunge into cool water...

Dolan, dragging himself along unsteadily at her side, shattered her reverie by muttering, "What day is it?"

"I don't know," Adelle muttered back at him, "or care." All three of them were having difficulty remembering things. She couldn't have said which of the Nightmare Villages she had seen last, or what sequence of button pushing had got them out of the last test room they passed through. She knew she was negotiating entire alleys without being aware of them. Time was a theoretical speculation beyond her comprehension.

"If you hadn't been too cheap to buy a shock-proof watch—" Dolan began, "you'd know what day it is."

"Would that make any difference?"

After a moment of silence, Dolan grinned at her. "Maybe it's a good thing you're cheap. If we knew the day, what would we have to argue about?"

The hiss of gas forced them through the next opening. Adelle surveyed the new alley and thought, as she now did each time she entered one, that she could go no further. But somehow she would manage to stagger its bleak length, turn into yet another alley, and hear the muted swish of the partition rising from the floor behind her. It was a faint sound, audible only when one was close by, and she had come to hate it. It made her think of someone cutting off her past as with a meat cleaver. There was no turning back, ever, and there was no destination ahead of them.

She was so near to the end of her endurance that she knew this day, whatever it was, this day would be her last. She would collapse, gas or no gas, and tell the others to go on without her. Her legs and feet were swollen from the unending hours of walking. She was afraid to take her shoes off for fear she might not get them back on, and each step was excruciating.

Mondor and Dolan were bickering about who had drunk the largest share of water from the long-lost milk cartons. "Any time we agreed on a sip, you guzzled," Mondor said.

"If we agreed on a sip, I sipped," Dolan said. "How could I guzzle a sip?"

Mondor glared through his smudged glasses. "You not only guzzled," he said viciously, "you soaked up an extra share in your beard."

Adelle said nothing. Her parched mouth made it difficult to speak, and their petty arguments distracted her from the only pleasure remaining to her, her inward turning thoughts. She was thinking how restful it would be if she could meditate without interruptions.

"The next time we have water to share—" Mondor began.

"In my opinion," Adelle announced, hoping her speech wasn't quite as raspy as it sounded to her, "a little less talk about something we don't have would be beneficial to all three of us."

"Our Supreme Court has spoken," Dolan announced. "Turn off the water, Mondor."

They rested briefly until the gas drove them forward again. Then Dolan and Mondor resumed their discussion of what day it was. Adelle simply did not care. Except on the rare occasions when the lights were out, there was only one day, and it went on forever. Even when she closed her eyes and covered them with her hands, she never quite achieved darkness. If she hadn't been so totally exhausted she would have felt filthy, but the dirt no longer mattered. Her life was a tale of eternal, wearisome wandering from nowhere to nowhere; her world a serpentine of narrow alleys that were punctuated with terrifying sounds and nauseous or choking or poisonous odors and stabbing flashes of light that paralyzed the retinas; her companions shadowy figures she vaguely remembered from another place and time. Death showed its triumphant grimace more and more often in explosions, or bullets, or traps in the floor. The despair that had seized all of them was growing hourly.

"If we had any way to measure an hour," Adelle muttered.

The men looked and probably felt as miserable as she did. Their faces were creased with lines of dirt. They carried the same reek of unwashed body and the same stale stench of perspiration-stained clothing—in those rare moments when the tear gas had completely evaporated from it—and if this went on much longer, Adelle thought, their own odors would be strong enough to negate the gas entirely. Dolan's once neatly trimmed beard was a ragged growth that faded untidily into its bewhiskered surroundings. It was more reminiscent of a small furbearing animal that had suffered an accident than a planned part of a man's face. Mondor's beard and mustache still looked like smudges that could have been removed by washing. Both men had given up combing their hair, and Adelle, after a narrow escape when her own long hair momentarily caught in a closing partition, had tied it into a knot and forgotten there was such a thing as grooming.

There still were brief moments when all three of them were able to focus their failing energy and return to something like the banter of their first days in the maze, but such incidents were becoming rare.

"Nice of Madam," Dolan announced suddenly, "to let us have this long, pleasant stroll without any fireworks or stink bombs."

"The way we smell, who'd notice a stink bomb?" Adelle asked.

"Point," Dolan agreed. "But during this momentary lull, it occurs to me that if we have anything to talk about other than Mondor's petty complaints, it might be a good time to do it."

Neither Mondor nor Adelle offered a comment.

"No scintillating remarks? No flashes of inspiration? No cogitations?" Dolan persisted.

"Dolan thinks being a writer makes him literate," Mondor muttered.

"I'd like to sit down," Adelle announced.

"A brilliant demonstration of the difference between theoretical wit and practical logic," Dolan remarked. "Why not sit down? We're being much too cooperative about going where they want us to go. We should sit down every ten feet and rest until they make us move. They'll appreciate their achievements more if they have to work for them. We were doing that before. Why did we stop?"

"We've been too groggy and shell-shocked," Adelle said, settling to the floor.

"True. From now on we'll rest as much as we can and make them work. If they aren't alert, we might even steal an occasional nap."

Adelle leaned back against the wall and fell asleep at once. She was awakened by being roughly pushed to the floor. Guns had started firing at random, and only Mondor had heard them. They lay motionless while bullets and ricochets skipped past them. Adelle, head cushioned on her sleeve, fell asleep again.

Mondor shook her awake. "Gas. We'll rest in the next alley."

But as soon as they turned the corner, the air raid began—the screaming bombs, the flash and roar of real explosives, the fumes, the reek of unburied dead, the low-flying planes vomiting bullets. Again they lay flat on the cement, and again Adelle almost dozed off despite the racket. Finally—an ominous note—the gas came while the guns were still firing, and they had to crawl to escape it.

At the end of the alley they encountered an oddity—a choice between right and left, which hadn't happened since the early stages of their captivity. The only exception being when the dinner bell summoned them to a blundering search for the Rest Center. They paused in momentary indecision.

"Not that it matters," Dolan said. "Either way we'll end up where they want us to go. But if we make the wrong choice, we may have to walk further."

Mondor thought for a moment and then pointed. "Let's go right. It takes us back the way we came. Maybe we'll see the rhino again or even the upside down alley. That was restful."

They turned right. Gas drove them along the alley, but at the far end they were able to rest until it caught up with them. Again Adelle dozed. She awoke with gas stinging her nostrils and falteringly got to her feet. They took the single opening into the next alley, the swish sounded behind them—another cleaver slicing off their past—and the lights went out.

The darkness was momentary. A dazzling, ghostly animation of shifting, flowing lines and patterns surrounded them. The alley, which had stretched straight and level to its distant end, now—because of the upward moving illumination—seemed to rise abruptly in a steep hill, and so convincing was the illusion that Adelle stumbled when she attempted to walk forward. With gas in pursuit, they shuffled along the level cement floor while the landscape reared upward around them.

Mondor said quietly, "Watch it. They may be trying to distract us from what's underfoot."

The flowing patterns blinded Adelle. She could see nothing else, and when she closed her eyes, the dazzling streaks of movement continued to play visual tricks and make her feet stumble.

"Slide your feet," Mondor suggested.

They began a sliding, skating forward movement. It seemed silly to Adelle, but she made no protest. She closed her eyes again, and when she opened them, she decided the effect was rather pretty. She began to move with confidence. Then, abruptly, the animated lines reversed, and all three of them nearly fell. It was as though they had topped the illusory steep hill and now were headed downward just as steeply. Each footstep made contact long before their eyes told them it should.

They climbed and descended another illusory hill, and then a third. Sounds and odors began to play harassing counterpoints to the visual aberrations. When finally they reached the end of the alley, the flowing lines vanished. Moving in total darkness, they felt their way into a left turn and found a momentary blissful silence as another swish sliced off the alley behind them. In one motion they sank to the floor.

"How many times have we completely circled this place," Dolan wondered. "A hundred? Two hundred? A thousand?"

"You spent the first few days carving on the walls," Mondor said. "Have you thought about how rarely we see any of those marks? It's an enormously complex maze, and except for the villages and test rooms, they keep sending us along different routes. Even a writer who can't count to eleven should have noticed that."

They were taking their frustrations out on each other. Their good-natured, sometimes witty insults had degenerated to snarls of hatred. All three of them were near their breaking points, and Adelle thought it might be better if they split up—to escape or find death as chance or Madam ordained. They had missed an opportunity with the alley that had two exits. The next time that happened, she resolved to force a separation. They were no longer capable of helping each other anyway.

The hiss of gas brought them to their feet. As they started forward in the darkness, both Adelle and Mondor stumbled and nearly fell.

"Clumsy asses!" Dolan rasped.

Then he stumbled himself.

After the illusion of climbing and descending, they had reached an alley that actually pointed upward. It continued to get steeper and steeper until they were gasping from exhaustion and scrambling to keep from sliding backward into the cloud of gas that seemed to float about their heels. Mondor muttered something about climbing out of the place, but they were too preoccupied with remaining upright to exchange banter with him. They struggled upward until they unknowingly topped the crest, took a last, desperate step—and went, all three of them, sprawling down the opposite side.

At the bottom, Adelle—bruised and shaken but otherwise unhurt—forced herself to her feet. She heard the rustle of clothing as Mondor rose beside her. Dolan remained on the floor, swearing softly.

"Turned my ankle," he muttered.

"That's serious," Mondor said with mock sympathy. "Landing on your head wouldn't have hurt you."

"Let's rest," Adelle suggested. She sank into the darkness again. After a moment's hesitation, Mondor did the same. There were sounds of Dolan massaging his ankle.

"How is it?" Adelle asked.

"Sore. It'll be all right in a minute."

"Look," Adelle said. "We're getting on each other's nerves. We're also exhausted. We all know we can't go on much longer. I know I can't. This yapping at each other over every little thing accomplishes nothing at all, and it's going to get worse. We're too weak and tired and hungry and thirsty to be of any help to each other anyway. We might be better off alone. Think about it."

"Adelle," Dolan remarked, "does not yap. She delivers her insults in silence. They cut deeper that way."

"That's precisely what I meant," Adelle said wearily.

"Point," Dolan agreed. "We should think about it. It's only a question of whether we want to die alone or with company. The company wouldn't be much consolation anyway. Those surviving would be too close to death themselves."

It was the first time any of them had used the words 'die' or 'death.' Adelle said, "I take it you aren't afraid of dying."

Dolan's shrug was a faint rustle in the darkness. "What's to fear? Death is only the final stage of that long process of decay we call 'life.' I'm not afraid of it, but right now I resent it like hell. People our age still have a lot of decaying to do, and I'd planned to enjoy every moment of it. As for splitting up—at the moment we haven't any choice. There'll be plenty of time to decide that after we get through this mountain range."

"Can you walk?" Mondor asked.

"I can limp. It'd be easier if I could see where I was limping."

"That's another thing we should talk about," Adelle said. "Kevin, if Craig couldn't even limp, would we stay with him or walk off and leave him? Something like this could happen to any of us, and we ought to consider what we'd do."

"The one left behind would have the same chance of surviving as the other two," Mondor said. "Meaning, zero."

"I refuse to be a burden on anyone," Adelle said. "If something happens to me, I want to be left."

"You're also the one who wants to split up," Mondor remarked.

"Never mind," Dolan said. "As I already pointed out, splitting up is only a question of whether we want to die alone or with company. As for walking off and leaving one of us, when the gas gets bad enough, those who can still move won't have any choice. They'll have to leave. Right now the only question is how well I can limp. I think I smell gas."

They felt their way forward in the darkness, with Dolan half supporting himself by leaning on the others, and almost at once they encountered another steep slope.

Dolan said softly, "This time, before we fall over the top, let's reach up and see how close we are to the ceiling."

The climb was torturous, with Mondor and Adelle taking turns serving as a crutch for Dolan. They didn't come close enough to the ceiling to touch it, but they did manage the next descent without falling. After a third, equally torturous, climb and descent, they walked into the wall that terminated the alley. There was a single opening, this time on the right, and they took it.

It closed behind them, and the lights came on. They stood blinking in the sudden brightness.

"Those hills were getting redundant," Dolan said. He flexed his ankle. "Let's rest as long as we can."

Mondor was studying the stretch of alley in front of them. "This one looks uneventful."

"It looks uneventful now," Dolan said. He eased himself to the floor and continued to flex his ankle.

Adelle dropped down beside him and closed her eyes. "Better to have drowned in the test room," she muttered, "than to be driven to death from exhaustion." The same thought had occurred to her while she was frantically attempting to find the right sequence of numbers. She wondered why she hadn't succumbed to it.

They were left unmolested for a few blessed minutes, and then gas sprayed down on them from above. The droplets smarted and burned on their exposed, perspiring skin. Dolan, laboriously hauling himself to his feet, made a muttered complaint about continuing to sweat when he was dying of thirst.

They slowly made their way forward with the hobbling Dolan refusing their offers of help. He claimed his ankle was getting better. They seemed to be surrounded by a sinister calm. Adelle wondered if the others were waiting as tensely as she was for a sudden, overwhelming catastrophe that would end forever this farce of eternally wandering in a maze with no exit.

At the end of the alley there was a single opening. Just beyond it stood a test room. "No!" Adelle gasped. "I can't even remember my age!"

"What woman can?" Dolan asked.

They would have sat down and rested again, but the gas drove them into the room. It drove them out again when they tried to rest there. The number was a simple series of eight numerals that had to be repeated on each control panel, and they solved the problem quickly.

As they stumbled away with gas in pursuit, Adelle remarked, "Why so easy? Could Madam possibly be acquiring a conscience at this late date?"

"She's only applying a psychological principle I've already mentioned," Mondor said. "An experiment isn't valid if the problem greatly exceeds the capacity of the subject. They thought we were worse off than we are. Next time, they won't underestimate us."

CHAPTER 22

Jill Tabold and Bruce Kagen, neither of whom had taken part in the night watch, arrived at Laylor's motel at nine o'clock Friday morning and found him grumpily having breakfast in his dressing gown. Gerald Wyman, who had shared the all-night vigil, had been sent home to bed. His gloom was becoming funereal, and Laylor found it depressing.

Jill had reverted to jeans; Kagen wore a flowered sport shirt with shades of red that clashed violently with his red hair. Both looked alert, well rested, and far more energetic than anyone had a right to be on that particular morning. Laylor regarded them resentfully.

"You look awful," Jill told Laylor matter-of-factly. "What happened?"

"The electric meter's disk went round and round," Laylor said. "Also, a number of people didn't get any sleep, and a million mosquitoes got fed."

He telephoned room service and ordered another pot of coffee and an assortment of sweet rolls. Then he finished his breakfast while Jill and Kagen argued about a motion picture neither of them had seen. A waiter brought the coffee and rolls and took away Laylor's breakfast tray.

Laylor poured himself another cup of coffee and munched meditatively on a roll while he studied the six photographs he had brought from his Detroit office. The high school graduates made him think of Jill and Bruce and all the other bright young people who had been given summer jobs at the law offices. If the missing youngsters had gone to college, perhaps they would be enriching staid business establishments with their youthful enthusiasm. Those glowing futures had been circumscribed by picture frames: Missing, presumed dead.

Life had beaten the three middle-aged persons into a sullen unattractiveness. They were shabby in appearance and spirit, but the photos had been taken before they received the wholly unexpected job offers that promised, just once, a square deal from life. They must have felt revitalized when they deplaned at Detroit Metro. Laylor wondered whether they died before or after learning that fate had dealt them one more hand from the bottom of the deck.

The two groups of photos contrasted so starkly that they made less sense each time Laylor looked at them. "Causa latet; vis est notissima".

The students were helping themselves to coffee. When they returned to their chairs, the freckled Jill asked innocently, "About the electricity. Ray said the place is drawing enough current to run a small factory. Doesn't something actually have to use the stuff? I mean, electricity can't just leak down the drain, like water with a faucet left on, can it?"

"Something has to be using it," Laylor told her. "We don't know what it is, but we've thought of a way to find out—maybe. Last evening I remembered a friend whose brother-in-law is an executive at Detroit Edison. I pulled strings with a persuasive assist from Lieutenant Prehn. Feinstwaller Manor is going to have its power shut off this afternoon."

"Won't A&B Realty complain?" Kagen asked.

"It'll be done after closing. Harriman will be consulted as to the most convenient time. One doesn't argue when an electric company says it has to repair a transformer. If Detroit Edison is considerate enough to work its men overtime so as not to interfere with A&B's business, why should A&B complain?"

"What will it accomplish?" Jill asked.

"I don't know. We're fishing. When we told them we were going to search the place, we got a reaction. Maybe this will get another reaction."

"Maybe they'll just stop whatever it is they're doing until the electricity comes back on," Kagen said.

"They may," Laylor conceded, "and that wouldn't tell us anything. But we know *something* is going on there, and it goes on twenty-four hours a day. Bront managed several dodges to get men up to the meter yesterday, and the disc was whirling merrily every time. No flight of imagination can account for it. Feinstwaller Manor shouldn't be using much more electricity than the average home. An announced interruption of service has to bring *some* reaction if only a vigorous complaint."

He pushed his coffee cup aside and leaned back to gaze again at the six photographs. Lieutenant Prehn had given him three more the day before, Gernyan, Dolan, and Mondor, but Laylor hadn't bought frames yet.

His conscience was bothering him. These two bright youngsters were chafing to do something. So was Gerald Wyman. The three of them would work twenty-four hours a day and treat their fatigue as a joke if he said the word, but he didn't know the word. He had run out of jobs for them. Bront had the surveillance of Feinstwaller Manor well in hand. The only other task he could think of at the moment was to select the new picture frames, and for that he didn't need help.

"What do we know about Madam?" he asked.

"Everyone describes her as a strange little woman with a big nose and thick glasses," Jill said. "Careless about her appearance. Her hair style differed from place to place, but she may have worn wigs. Most of the people she talked with thought she had peculiar speech mannerisms, but none of them could offer an example."

"That's an interesting way to put it," Laylor said. "Mannerisms. Not an accent, but mannerisms."

"If she's a foreigner who knows English really well, she might speak without a noticeable accent but still do something odd once in a while with diction or syntax," Bruce Kagen suggested. "Or she might have one or two pronunciation flaws that sound like mannerisms because everything else is overly correct."

"A strange-looking little woman with a big nose and thick glasses," Laylor mused. "Careless about her appearance. Probably foreign born with quite good English that has an occasional oddity about it. What else?"

"She traveled about the country meticulously interviewing applicants for non-existent jobs," Jill said. "She was equally thorough in selecting people for the meaningless jobs at Z-R Publications."

"Meticulously interviewing applicants," Laylor echoed. "Thorough in selecting people."

"Also, she hired people in groups of three," Bruce Kagen put in eagerly. "You might almost say she was looking for matched sets. And in each instance, the matched set disappeared."

"Meticulously interviewing applicants," Laylor said again. "Thorough in selecting people. What kind of a professional background would you expect a person to have who conducts exacting interviews of large numbers of people in an attempt to find a few with special qualifications?"

"Personnel director," Bruce Kagen suggested.

"That's a job title, not a professional background," Laylor told him.

"Psychologist," Jill said. "I'd bet on it. If the job was *really* important—and with the amount of money invested, someone must have thought this job was—the psychologist would be a highly competent one."

Laylor was regarding her with interest. "Perhaps even well-known?"

Jill nodded. "Within the profession, at least."

"A well-known or at least highly competent psychologist with a foreign background. For some reason she wants groups of three persons with special qualifications. Why would she be looking for them among ordinary or nondescript Americans?"

"The more nondescript they are, the less fuss when they vanish," Kagen suggested.

"If that was her reasoning, the uproar caused by the first disappearances would have been a shock to her," Laylor said.

"It's the kind of mistake a foreigner might make," Kagen said. "She would underestimate the ability of police in widely scattered places to coordinate their information."

"Maybe so. With her next matched set she was careful to take people who weren't likely to be missed at once, and it worked. But then she changed her technique. Why?"

"It might not be all that easy to assemble a matched set when the people come from hundreds of miles apart and have never met," Jill said.

Laylor said slowly, "So for her third matched set she took the tremendous risk of operating with a known address and allowing a series of employees to associate with her over a period of time. Even so, she continued to follow the same procedure she used with the second group. She chose people without relatives, without close friends, even without acquaintances—she thought. People who wouldn't be missed. When that miscarried, she still must have been amply provided with other lines of defense. The police have quantities of information, they have witnesses who can identify her, and the disappearances are as much a mystery as they were the day they happened."

The two students were silent for a moment. Then Kagen said, scowling, "None of that helps us figure out what she was up to."

"No," Laylor agreed. "But if we could lay our hands on her, perhaps the motive would become self-evident." He paused. "What sort of a psychologist with a suspected foreign background would be interviewing a cross section of ordinary Americans to find candidates for obliteration?"

"One out of Edgar Allan Poe," Jill said dryly.

The three of them meditated for a time. Finally the students refilled their coffee cups, and Laylor persuaded them to take rolls to munch on. Again they lapsed into silence, attempting an impossible exercise in logic because the facts had to be deduced before they could start deducing. The result could only be total futility.

Bruce Kagen asked suddenly, "Didn't the Russian secret police make a practice of kidnapping people?"

"The KGB," Laylor told him. "Yes. It had a secret department that specialized in abductions and assassinations. But those victims were political—prominent anti-communists, defectors, people who could be labeled 'Enemies of the Soviet State.' There were notorious cases in the nineteen fifties, and the whole business blew up when a trained assassin named Stashinsky defected to West Germany and confessed everything. It got the Russians a very bad world press, which no doubt was the reason they suddenly began to exercise discretion."

"But that didn't stop them," Jill pointed out.

"Of course not. They simply shifted to the use of local thugs and agents from the satellite countries. But note the emphasis on *political*. Not even the KGB masterminded assassinations or abductions for the fun of it. Such a thing had to be ordered by someone very high up, and it was only done for what the KGB, at least, considered good and sufficient reason—to remove a dangerous adversary or punish someone regarded as a traitor. And of course the KGB is kaput. Done for. Even if it weren't, what possible reason could it have for eliminating three trios of ordinary American citizens who have no political connections of any kind and no special skills or knowledge that would be of any use or danger to anyone?"

"If it had a reason," Jill asked, "would it have hesitated to do it?"

Laylor said slowly, "No, it certainly wouldn't have hesitated. If the KGB had decided for any reason at all that it needed to abduct Americans in groups of three and dispose of them, it wouldn't have delayed ten seconds to consider either the morality or the legality of the action. It was cunning, ruthless, and viciously heavy-handed. It inflicted unspeakable cruelty and death on its own people, or on anyone else it considered an obstacle, whenever it chose to do so."

"But we don't know it's not still doing it," Jill said. "I read somewhere that Russia's foreign agents are still functioning. Let's assume the KGB is and it had a reason. Where would we go from there?"

Her intensity amused Laylor. "I've read that the GRU—that's Russian military intelligence—has continued to steal information about America's military technology long after the Soviet breakup. If it's still in action, the KGB probably is, too, but connecting it with the abduction of three ordinary people in Ann Arbor, Michigan, seems preposterously farfetched. It ought to have more important things to do. On the other hand—" He broke off. He was thinking about Bront's two missing men and the cars that had tailed him from Feinstwaller Manor. "There's no doubt this is the kind of unreasoning, totally ruthless crime that the KGB specialized in," he went on slowly. "Even though it makes no sense to us, we have to assume those responsible thought they had a good reason for it."

"How would we go about checking?" Jill asked.

Laylor was intent on his own thoughts. "Maybe we've been going at this the wrong way. We've been looking for a logical reason for the abductions, but nothing was logical about the KGB. Everything it did had a fanatical irrationality about it. Many of its acts bordered on sheer paranoia.

"Originally it took its cues from Stalin, who was obsessed with imaginary plots. He thought war with the West was inevitable, and of course war justified anything—including the vicious repression of the Soviet people. The confinement of Soviet dissidents in experimental psychiatric hospitals was a scandal that hasn't been fully documented yet. Dissidents also were condemned to death by being sent to mines and factories with low safety standards or by being denied essential medical treatment. They were used for perverted medical experiments that were reminiscent of what the Nazis did in their death camps—doses of radiation, for example, and tests involving drugs and bacteria. They were incarcerated with criminals who were encouraged to murder them. Since the KGB inflicted such vicious measures on its own people, it's no surprise that it didn't hesitate to treat foreign nationals just as harshly whenever its demented logic found a reason for it. Even so, to assume that the KGB is still active here and now, and that it somehow has devised a fantastic use for three groups of three ordinary American citizens, taxes the imagination considerably. I'm sorry—you asked a question."

"How would we go about checking?" Jill asked again.

"We would go to the University of Michigan Library and ask them, please, could we search for a needle in their numerous bookstacks." He paused. The students waited for him to continue. "KGB or not," he said finally, "if Madam is a prominent foreign psychologist, a check of foreign publications makes sense. I suppose her nationality could be almost anything—from Russian and Eastern European to South American or even Arabic. If there's any chance at all this is a KGB scheme, Russia is the place to start." He got to his feet. "Let's do it. We haven't anything better to occupy ourselves with."

"Wouldn't it be helpful to have a translator?" Bruce Kagen asked.

Laylor clapped his hand to his forehead. "It definitely would be helpful to have a translator. I'll see if I can find one."

* * * *

Andrei Zinovyev had himself driven past Feinstwaller Manor three times on Friday morning in three different cars. On the first trip, he caught a glimpse of, and immediately identified, the private detective named Bront, who worked for the attorney Laylor. On the third, he discerned the function of the van parked by the road with a woman selling woven baskets. One trip down the side road that skirted the mansion's grounds was sufficient to identify the concealed watch kept on the drive to the rear entrance.

"*Dourakee*!" Zinovyev muttered. He was referring both to Bront's men, who carelessly allowed themselves to be visible to anyone looking for them, and to the local KGB agents who had failed to see them.

From the basement headquarters in the old house near the campus, he telephoned Cherkasov, Mr. Harriman, at A&B Realty, and told him what he had discovered.

"It doesn't matter," Cherkasov said cheerfully. "What could they possibly see? This is just a real estate office quietly going about its proper business. Eventually they'll get tired watching and go away."

"They're waiting for Dr. Sokolova and her assistants to leave the building," Zinovyev said bluntly.

"Let them wait. Madam can finish her experiments and compile her records and reports. If she needs anything, we easily can provide it. The Americans are not a patient people. Eventually they'll give up."

Zinovyev thought for a moment. If the Americans discovered the secret laboratory, that would be bad, but they wouldn't be able to connect it with anyone except perhaps the vanished personnel of the vanished Z-R Publications. On the other hand, if they discovered the laboratory with Madam, her assistants, and all of her records, that would be disastrous even if they found no trace of the missing Americans used in experiments. Sooner or later the scientists would be identified as Russian, and the KGB connection certainly would be deduced if not proven. He couldn't permit that to happen.

"I'm going to secure the building tonight," he said. "I want Dr. Sokolova and her assistants out of it. They're to finish what they're doing, pack records and anything else that's identifiable, and be able to leave the moment we're ready for them. I'll set up an escape route to Canada."

"The private detectives will be watching."

"We'll eliminate them first. *Believe me, there'll be no fuss.* I'll ask Chicago and New York for the best men available."

"What if there are real police watching?"

"They'll be trespassing without proper authority. Don't you know American law? After the building is secured, we'll turn them loose with a stern complaint. In the meantime, the scientists will be safe in Canada. I'll tell Sarnia to expect them. If those watching are merely agents of the attorney Laylor, as we suspect, we'll take care of them properly.

Cherkasov said weakly, "I suppose Dr. Sokolova will have facilities to dispose of the bodies, but—all those missing people—the publicity—"

"*Eestoukany*! Moron! That's the kind of stupidity that got us into this mess! There won't be any bodies or any missing people. We'll overpower them one at a time, tie them up, and put them in a safe place. Surely in that huge building there is a room remote from Dr. Sokolova's operations where we can hold them. When she and her assistants are safely away, we'll turn our captives over to the police with a trespassing charge. And that will end the matter. Dr. Sokolova may have to wait a year or more to resume her experiments, but when she does, her security will be handled competently."

Cherkasov continued to babble objections. He envisioned a pitched battle around Feinstwaller Manor, and he could imagine the next day's headlines.

Zinovyev shushed him. "I've been in touch with Mr. Hendy," he said. "Dr. Sokolova impressed him. His people have a definite interest in her work. He was alarmed to hear that her security has been compromised, and he'll fly some of his own men in to help out. We'll deal with the watchers one at a time. All you have to do is find us a place where we can hold them until we're ready to turn them over to the police. A&B Realty is responsible for both the building and the grounds, and the police are on its side in this. We might as well make use of them. For once, something about this operation is going to be handled professionally."

"Wait!" Cherkasov pleaded. "The electricity is going to be turned off tonight. Something about repairs to a transformer."

"When will it be turned off?"

"After our closing time. They expect to complete the repairs by dark."

"Where is this transformer?"

"It's on the side road near the drive to the rear entrance."

"We'll start at the other end. Just before dark. Those watching won't be expecting us—their attention will be on the building—and among the trees surrounding the mansion, there'll be just enough light for us to see them. Talk with Dr. Sokolova and call me back. She should plan on finishing her experiments before the electricity is turned off. The night watchmen—are they your own men?"

"No. I hired them from an agency."

"Let them go on doing whatever they've been doing. They may see something. If Laylor's men can avoid them," Zinovyev said caustically, "surely ours can. We want everything to look normal." He hung up.

* * * *

The room was large, brightly-lit, and many windowed. Laylor sat with Jill, Bruce Kagen, and the elderly translator at a corner table confronted by piles of books and periodicals. The students in the room were sending curious glances their way. For one thing, they were an odd-looking study group. For another, staff members fluttered about them at intervals in a way that was highly unusual. Library procedures had proved inimical to Laylor's conception of how best to look for a needle in a book stack, and he had appealed to a friend on the law school faculty for assistance. As a result, the dean himself had personally contacted the director of the library in Laylor's behalf, and this excessive attention was an unexpected by-product.

So the mountain came to Mahomet. Books and periodicals converged on their table from various directions, and they had to suffer repeated incursions from the librarians, who hovered like waiters and waitresses interrupting a meal to ask if the food was satisfactory.

The translator, a tiny, bald man who looked like an impoverished clergyman, printed Russian titles on a scratch pad in neat English letters, added the translations, and then sat back waiting to be asked to do something.

Laylor gazed perplexedly at the titles. *Materialy Soveshchaniya po psikhologii; Voprosy psikhologii; Trudy instituta fiziologii emeni Pavlova; 16 oye soveshchaniye po problemam vysshei nervnoi deyatel'nosti; Tezisy i doklady; Zhurnal vysshei nervnoi deiatel'nosti imeni I.P. Pavlova_* . . .

He leafed through one of the journals doubtfully, scrutinizing the illustrations—graphs, pictures of apparatus, a hazy photograph of what looked like the inside of the mouth of someone undergoing torture.

"What we really need," he announced, pushing the journal aside, "are picture books. No others need apply. Just look for photos of psychologists. Or of psychiatrists, which in our case may be a distinction without a difference. Names won't help us, and I doubt that scientific publications oblige their readers with police-type descriptions of contributors."

The three of them began to turn pages; the translator looked on benignly. Time passed. When they had worked their way through the piles in front of them, the helpful librarians brought more piles.

Jill, who was not a U. of M. student, became disgusted and stalked off to do her own detecting. She returned in a huff. "The main catalog dates from pre-World War I," she said indignantly. "Everything is catalogued under 'Russia'. There's no mention at all of the U.S.S.R."

"You can't expect a tradition-bound institution like a university library to change its cataloging procedures merely because a bunch of political upstarts took over the country temporarily," Laylor told her. "As things turned out, the library was right. There is no U.S.S.R."

"The serials room doesn't even have a card catalog of foreign publications," Jill said. "All they could offer me was pages and pages of typewritten listings, alphabetical by title. The only way to locate journals in Russian would have been to search through the entire list and hope I could recognize the Russian language when I saw a title in the English alphabet."

"Efficiency," Laylor said, "would take the spirit of adventure out of using a library. We're getting everything we need. Relax and let the mountain come to us."

Jill wasn't finished. "The catalog file cards mention portraits, plates, and illustrations. The girl at the desk said never the twain shall meet, illustrations can't be portraits, but when I asked what illustrations I'd be likely to find in a biographical dictionary, she said, 'Oh, *those* illustrations probably would be portraits.'"

"Be merciful," Laylor murmured. "Librarians have to impose order on books, but the publishing industry knows no order."

"It would help," Jill said, "if libraries would stop pretending it does."

An hour and forty minutes after they began, Bruce Kagen shattered the reading room's solemnity with an exclamation. He handed Laylor a slender book in Russian. It was opened to a group photo, and one of the group was a strange-looking, ageless little woman with an ultra-prominent nose and glasses that Laylor knew, instinctively, had to possess unusually thick lenses.

The translator, pleased to finally have something to do, rendered the caption into English. These were eminent Soviet psychiatrists and psychologists, and—yes, the woman—the woman was named Zinaida Sokolova, Dr. Sokolova, she was a graduate of Moscow University, and at the date of the caption she was a member of the staff of the State Scientific Research Institute of Psychology. She had won the Lenin State Prize in science in 1971, no doubt for scientific research, and—her specialty? That wasn't indicated, but obviously she was considered a very capable scientist.

The book was twenty years old. Laylor wondered doubtfully whether that made the woman the right age to be the "Madam" their witnesses had described.

"Never mind that," Jill said. "Her natural sloppiness probably made her look older than she was. The other features are as described, even including the glasses slipping down her large nose."

"We need some good enlargements of this, quickly," Laylor said. "That means removing the book from the library, and my influence has limits. This is a job for Lieutenant Prehn."

He telephoned Prehn. Then he telephoned a friend at the Department of State in Washington to start a different kind of machinery in motion. He wanted to know whether Dr. Zinaida Sokolova, formerly a citizen of the Soviet Union and now probably a citizen of one of the new Russian states, had been granted a visa and was or had been in the United States legally.

When he finished, Prehn had already arrived and was applying his persuasiveness, status, and potential exercise of police powers in an attempt to borrow a non-circulating book long enough to have its picture taken. Laylor left the problem to Prehn and went to tell the translator to look for more material on or by Dr. Sokolova.

"The problem," Prehn announced when he returned, "is that no one here has any authority."

"You have to remember that all librarians have split personalities," Laylor said. "One half wants to collect everything and lock it up for posterity. The other half wants to circulate everything as freely as possible, in which case entire collections would vanish overnight. Whenever anyone is allowed to check out a book, it represents a compromise."

"No one I've talked with has any connection with the half that wants to circulate anything," Prehn grumbled.

Finally, perspiring but triumphant, he received permission to borrow the book. Their first stop was an establishment half a block from the campus. Laylor had noticed a sign in the window that advertised instant copying of photographs. The result was barely adequate, but Laylor dispatched Jill and Kagen with copies to show to a few former Z-R Publications employees.

As Prehn was leaving to look for a photographer who could quickly make clear enlargements, Laylor said to him, "Did you think to check Feinstwaller Manor's electric bills for the times of the other disappearances?"

Prehn ruffled his hair fretfully. "Damn. That would cinch it."

"If it still needs cinching, that most certainly would cinch it."

Laylor returned to his motel. An hour later he received a package of still-damp enlargements from Lieutenant Prehn. He was studying one of them when Jill telephoned to report that three former Z-R Publications employees had positively identified Sokolova as Madam.

"Prehn will need the rest as witnesses for the police lineup," Laylor said. "I earnestly hope there will be a police lineup. Come back here and pick up these enlargements. On the way, you and Bruce can flip a coin to decide which of you goes to Korning Falls, Ohio, and which goes to Nortonville, Indiana. The sooner we tie all of these cases together, the sooner we'll get a maximum effort launched to track this woman down."

"What about Texas, Oregon, California, and Alabama?" Jill asked.

"Indiana and Ohio are closer. If you can get positive identification there, the police, the F.B.I., the C.I.A., the U.S. Immigration and Naturalization Service, and maybe even the Boy Scouts, will be after Madam like rapacious bloodhounds. So let's get moving."

CHAPTER 23

Pavel Derzhavin was operating the control panel. Konstantin Murov, attired in a western-style, broad brimmed hat in imitation of someone he had seen on television, sat beside him scowling at the panel lights that flashed on and off at intervals of several seconds. The subjects were being allowed twelve minutes of rest, but were they asleep? Murov watched for another minute and decided they had dozed off the moment they sat down. He entered figures on his chart, glanced at the timer, and nudged Derzhavin.

Derzhavin, his unruly hair looking more tangled than usual, was glancing over his shoulder at the videotape machine where Madam and the other assistants were replaying, over and over, the maneuvers by which the subjects had escaped the water trap.

Murov nudged Derzhavin again. Derzhavin started, gave his attention to the timer, and at the precise second pressed the gas button. Nothing happened for almost a minute. The outlet was some distance from the subjects, and obviously they were sound asleep. Finally Dolan stirred, glanced about blearily, sniffed disgustedly, and shook the others awake. They got haltingly to their feet and began their cautious movement along the alley, testing the floor with every step.

Murov made another entry in his chart. Then he turned to watch the videotape machine. The subjects' scramble over the rising partition fascinated all of them. Even Madam was clucking her tongue thoughtfully. These subjects were becoming a positive embarrassment. Not only had they triumphed over every hazard, but they still displayed no symptoms of protective transmarginal inhibition—Pavlov's term for neuroses induced by more tension than the brain could tolerate—despite deliberate attempts to intensify experimental stress. Dolan, at least, should have been close to a breakdown, but he continued to exercise leadership, and there seemed to be no limit to his physical and mental resourcefulness.

Konstantin Murov, scratching his head under his ridiculous hat, remarked, "I read about a scientist who developed a laboratory breed of fly that couldn't be killed. No kind of poison affected it. The only way he could get rid of it was by starving it to death. Do you suppose maybe—"

"I suppose maybe he could have used a fly swatter," Madam snapped. "Go and think of something positive. I suggested early in the experiment that these subjects might be resourceful enough to enable us to employ the entire test series before terminating them. Now I want each of you to draw up a program for that. Allow two days—no longer unless you feel you have to. Consider which tests should be repeated and schedule all tests not yet used. Let me have your recommendations before noon."

She got up and went to her office, where she seated herself at the desk and stared blankly at the draft of an unfinished progress report that lay before her. She was tempted to terminate the experiment immediately, but it would have been a cowardly admission that these subjects had defeated her. Further, the notion of intervening in an experiment that was predicated on non-intervention was repugnant to her. Even interfering temporarily, in order to separate the subjects, had seemed like a violation of principle.

She was highly disturbed about a number of things. The local KGB agents had assured her the three subjects wouldn't be missed until long after the experiment had run its full course and their bodies had been properly disposed of, but the police began searching for them almost at once. She herself hadn't grasped the full social significance of the "dates" Americans mentioned so casually, but the local agents should have known.

The police were showing an embarrassing, perhaps even a dangerous interest in Feinstwaller Manor because the subjects had worked there. They announced their search of the building in advance, with typical American stupidity, and she'd had ample time to send Ilya Bychevsky to perform his own search of the subjects' former offices and make certain they had left nothing incriminating, but there could be no doubt that the disappearance of Z-R Publications at the same time its employees vanished had heightened police suspicions. That was another blunder by the local KGB personnel. They had been more interested in expediency than efficiency. Her own recommendations had been ignored.

Then there was the strange incident of the attorney calling on A&B Realty with a forged letter. Madam found that more disturbing than the police search. Fortunately Andrei Zinovyev had arrived, and he soon would have everything under control. She considered him an insolent puppy because of clashes they'd had in the past, but there was no doubting his competence. He was perfectly correct in his assertion that the publishing firm should have been located in another state. She had said as much in her reports.

Wearily she reached for a book by an American psychologist and turned to a section on "survival". Her Soviet colleagues ridiculed all American psychology. They poked fun at its test methods and called it a system of "testology" that had no properly established scientific basis, but Soviet psychology had its own share of silly obsessions. Madam considered them symptomatic of a young science whose procedures of testing and measurement were evolving and maturing through experimentation.

She reflected again on the differences between experiments on animals and experiments on humans. Pavlov had delineated the problem unerringly with his formulation of the first and second signal systems. Experiments on animals too frequently yielded results contradictory to those produced from tests on humans, and such inconsistencies had to be due to the fact that humans could think and verbalize. Even when introduced into an experiment unknowingly, they quickly figured out the role they were being forced to play.

Animals, operating on the first signal system, did not. Pavlov's dogs salivated when he rang the bell that accompanied their feedings. These three subjects joked about a dinner bell, speculated in deprecatory terms as to what sort of food might be offered them, and made insulting remarks about Madam and her assistants. Surely the experimental data obtained under such circumstances had doubtful validity.

The basic purposes of her experiment were to observe the subjects' reactions to simulated war conditions and similar horrors and to determine as scientifically as possible how much stress they could tolerate and for how long. Usually subjects began to lose their mental equilibriums by the fourth day if not earlier. Madam was tempted to let this particular experiment run to a natural conclusion just to discover what limits of endurance these three subjects had because she thought she was on the verge of a discovery.

American psychologists made much of what they called "operant conditioning," or "operant behavior." It was voluntary behavior, behavior on the second signal level, behavior under the mental control of the subjects rather than their reflexes. One American author thought operant conditioning enabled a person to deal effectively with a new environment through the reinforcement of behavior patterns evolved in the old environment. It was a provocative thought. Psychologists had long believed that reinforcement was important to species-specific universals of behavior. Was it possible that there were nationality-specifics of behavior, also reinforced by the national environment?

If there were, could the lawless and unregimented American environment be producing a nationality-specific behavior with superior qualities for meeting contingencies of survival imposed by war? Her superiors thought not, but they had been uncertain enough to ask her to attack the problem experimentally because the question was crucial. Projects Ob and Sosva and the other national experiments that were to follow them were designed to answer it.

The first phase-groups had provided only a tenuous beginning for Project Ob, but already she was obtaining sensational and entirely unexpected results. Now her entire program was threatened by the blundering of local KGB agents. Perhaps the wise course would be to terminate the present subjects and cease operations until the turmoil had faded. She could use the time to work out a new technique for securing subjects. But could she justify the abandonment of an experiment that was yielding such important results?

There was a timid tap on her door. She frowned—her cloddish assistants couldn't run a simple test for ten minutes without coming to her for advice—but she said patiently, "Yes?"

Leonid Sisovsky, Adelle Gernyan's Goon 1, entered with slow steps, his broad face a massive display of gloom. He said, "Were you thinking of terminating the experiment, Madam?"

"That's an alternative that must be considered," Madam answered shortly.

"I think termination would be an error."

She regarded him with tolerant amusement. "Why?"

"Each day this phase yields more results that are both interesting and unexpected."

"True," Madam said.

"And," he went on, "it might be the only phase where we can use the entire resources of our laboratory on the same subjects. If they survive long enough to undergo the entire test program, that alone has important testing implications. No group of Soviet citizens achieved that, and the other American groups didn't do nearly as well."

"True," Madam said again. She was watching him carefully. In the past few days she had begun to enjoy his reactions to her arguments. She went on, "But isn't that also justification for termination? No other subjects have endured a comparable amount of stress over a comparable period of time. We have no data with which to evaluate their performance. What would we gain from further testing?"

Sisovsky frowned. "But isn't it important to be able to use the entire test spectrum on the same subjects? At least we would have their records for future comparisons, and we may learn something about our tests."

"We may indeed," Madam agreed.

They had already learned enormously from these subjects. As a result, some apparatus would have to be redesigned, and some tests were certain to be eliminated entirely. Madam had been especially amused by the way this group reacted to the illusions. Those effects were the creation of a high-ranking non-scientist KGB officer, and she hoped to have the pleasure of showing him a tape of the subjects poking fun at his "zoo". The "zoo" had caused one of the subjects in the previous group to have a heart attack, but Madam agreed with the current subjects that it was silly.

"I have to consider whether to end the experiment and terminate the subjects as a safety measure," Madam said. "It might even be wise to seal off the laboratory and leave the project dormant for a time."

Sisovsky's massive gloom gave way to puzzlement. "Are the police that much of a danger?"

"We don't know. If we err, it should be on the side of caution."

The change in Sisovsky since the experiment began was remarkable. He was actually attempting to use the test equipment inventively, and she hoped eventually to make him her first assistant. There would be plenty of time for additional training before they could risk another experiment, and Sisovsky was teachable.

She wasn't surprised that he wanted to keep the experiment going. And perhaps he was right. Perhaps she overestimated the danger. Aleksei Cherkasov had assured her that the police search had been a routine one, made only because the building was large and most of it was unoccupied.

"Very well," she said. "We'll keep the experiment going for another day, at least. Is your program written?"

Sisovsky smiled. "I'll finish it now."

He left the room, and she returned her attention to the book.

Her phone buzzed stridently. She lifted it but did not answer. Aleksei Cherkasov, Mr. Harriman, said softly, "Andrei Zinovyev has assumed personal responsibility for your security. He asks you to end your experiment, dispose of the subjects, and be prepared to move out tonight. He wants to take you and you assistants and all of your records to Canada."

"He does, does he?" Madam said angrily. "Tell Andrei Zinovyev that the duration of an experiment is determined by scientific considerations and not by his whims. Until such time as he is appointed Director of Project Ob, I will make the decisions."

"One moment," Cherkasov said apologetically. "The electric company wants to turn off the current for transformer repairs. The transformer is malfunctioning, and there are surges of current that could damage electronic equipment and motors. They want to know if they can do it after closing today. It will take them at most two hours. If they start at five-thirty, they can be finished before dark."

Madam said quickly, "Did they suggest five-thirty?"

"Yes. It's a routine matter. The entire neighborhood is affected."

"Ask them if they can make it six o'clock. Let me know at once."

"Five-thirty to seven-thirty, six to eight—does it matter?"

"It matters very much. I must know immediately."

She hung up and waited.

Five minutes later the phone buzzed. She lifted it. Cherkasov said, "No problem at all. The current will be turned off precisely at six o'clock."

"Thank you," Madam said.

"About Zinovyev—"

"Just a moment."

Their apparatus did require a large amount of electricity. Could a heavy consumption of current in a supposedly empty building have aroused someone's curiosity? She had always felt uneasy about that, and a 'routine' request from the electric company had to be viewed with the upmost suspicion.

"For all of our training and experience, we know so little about American customs and habits of thought," she told herself.

American businessmen were ridiculously considerate of their customers' convenience, and if the electric company was willing to accommodate a request for postponement, perhaps there really was a malfunction. On the other hand, Zinovyev was no fool. He wouldn't suggest terminating an experiment and slipping off to Canada without a sound reason.

"What does Zinovyev propose to do about the people watching the building?" she asked.

"He says he'll take care of them."

"I'm sure he will," Madam murmured. If Zinovyev said something would be taken care of, it would be.

"He's bringing in men from New York and Chicago. Mr. Hendy is also bringing in men to help out. Zinovyev intends to capture the watchers and hold them until you and your assistants and your records are on the way to Canada. Then he'll turn them over to the police on a trespassing charge."

"Is there any reason why it couldn't be done tomorrow?"

"He considers it urgent." There was a touch of indignation in Cherkasov's voice.

"It may be. This request from the electric company—"

"But that is routine! That sort of thing happens all the time!"

His sputtering protest heightened her suspicions. Cherkasov had been wrong about everything else. There was too much at stake to permit him to be wrong about this. "Please thank Andrei Zinovyev for his advice. I'll discuss it with my assistants, and I'll let you know as soon as I've decided."

She hung up and went to the door of her room. Pavel Derzhavin was still at the control panel. Her other four assistants were seated around a large table working on their programs.

Madam announced, "The electricity will be turned off for two hours this evening. We'll have to decide at once what to do with the subjects."

They gazed at her blankly. Derzhavin turned and asked, "The electricity? Why? How?"

Madam gestured impatiently. "Some kind of repairs. The electric company suggested five-thirty. I told Aleksei Cherkasov to ask for six o'clock, just to see what the reaction would be and also because we'll need as much time as we can get if we decide to end the experiment." She paused. "It does seem odd, coming at this particular moment, but electric companies do sometimes have to repair things."

She paused again. "In any case, we'll be without electricity for as long as two hours. The question is whether we should end the experiment and terminate the subjects before six o'clock. If we decide to do so, then we must consider what we can achieve in the time that's left and what test we should use for termination."

Four of them—Murov, Borod, Derzhavin, and Bychevsky—began to argue. Each had a favorite test or two that hadn't been used yet. Madam's contempt for them had deepened in recent days. Their carelessness knew no bounds. One of them—she hadn't been able to determine which—had stupidly included chocolate milk in individual containers with the specimens' food ration. He should have known the containers would be used to carry a water reserve. Fortunately they were crushed in the escape from the water hazard, and she'd ordered them removed while the specimens were unconscious. Otherwise, the extra water could have had a serious impact on the experiment.

Madam ignored them and watched Leonid Sisovsky, who was listening silently, his face wreathed with massive puzzlement. His eyes absently followed the subjects on one of the viewing screens. If she had judged him correctly, he was thinking furiously and searching his mind for a means of turning this unexpected development to their advantage.

Finally she said, "Well, Leonid?"

He started. "I was wondering how the subjects would react."

"React how?" Borod demanded sarcastically. "Does it matter? Perhaps we should ask them what test they would prefer for termination."

"React to two hours of nothing," Sisovsky said.

The other assistants turned and stared at him. Madam felt positively aglow with admiration. Never before had an assistant so dramatically justified her high opinion of him.

Sisovsky went on apologetically, "Since the first night, there's been no substantial time lapse when nothing happened. What would they do if the lights went off and there was complete silence that went on, and on, and on? Would they suspect something and try to stay awake?"

"An interesting proposal," Madam said. "I personally think these particular subjects are so exhausted they would drop off to sleep no matter what they thought, but it certainly ought to be interesting. Unfortunately, we wouldn't be able to see what they were doing."

"We don't need to wait until the electricity is turned off to try an experiment like that," Pavel Derzhavin said. "We can give the subjects two hours of nothing when our regular equipment will operate and we can observe them properly."

"True," Madam said, "but we must congratulate Leonid on a most ingenious idea for turning an unexpected setback to our advantage. I agree that this is the wrong time for it, but we can consider including it in future experiments. Right now we have a decision to make. Should we terminate these subjects before the electricity is turned off—and how?"

"For the actual termination, I suggest the lasers," Mikhail Borod said. "I think I've finally got them adjusted properly, and it would be a good opportunity to test them."

Madam nodded approvingly. "That's an excellent suggestion. These subjects are too exhausted to make the test really interesting, but we can consider it. Why don't you lay it out?"

Borod began to trace a route with chalk on a large chart of the maze. Several times he stopped to rub out sections. "They're moving so slowly," he complained. His chalk meandered on—present position, these turnings, work in a test here—

Konstantin Murov was totaling minutes and hours with a pocket calculator. He shook his head. "At six o'clock they won't be anywhere near the lasers."

"So what can we leave out?" Madam asked.

They debated the matter. Borod laid out a new route and included by-passes in case their timing was off. Murov touched the totaling button and studied the result, pouting. He was still wearing his ridiculous western hat. "They should reach the laser alley about five-thirty. The by-passes allow plenty of leeway."

"'Should' isn't good enough," Madam said. "They must reach the laser alley no later than five thirty."

"They will," Borod promised.

"And after that," Pavel Derzhavin remarked lightly, "they can sleep as long as they like."

The others laughed.

Madam turned to Sisovsky, whose large face now exuded a thick aura of gloom. "Never mind, Leonid. It was an excellent suggestion, but I have a presentiment that we'd be wise to abandon this experiment." She said to the others, "Remember—I want the subjects in the laser alley no later than five-thirty, but no earlier than that if we can help it. We might as well get as much use out of them as we can before termination."

When Sisovsky started to protest, she shook her head and spoke firmly. "No, Leonid. No arguments. I don't like this business of turning off the electricity. I want the experiment terminated and the subjects' bodies disposed of before six o'clock."

She returned to her office and picked up the phone. Cherkasov answered with a grunt. "Tell Andrei Zinovyev my experiment will be completed and the subjects' bodies disposed of by the time the electricity is turned off," she said. "We will have our records and personal property packed and be ready to leave by six."

"He might not be finished by then," Cherkasov said. "He can't mop things up until the electricians leave. Do you want some flashlights?"

"We have plenty," Madam said. "If he isn't ready by six, that won't matter to us. We'll catch up on our sleep while the lights are off. These experiments are exhausting."

CHAPTER 24

At a quarter to five, Jill Tabold telephoned from Korning Falls, Ohio. She had flown to Cincinnati and rented a car there, and the chief of police had his station crowded with waiting witnesses when she arrived.

"Are twelve positive identifications enough?" she asked excitedly.

"It makes a fair case," Laylor said. "How positive?"

"No hesitation whatsoever. As you may have noticed, Madam's nose is memorable. So are several other things about her. I've got another twenty witnesses waiting, and the chief will round up more if I want them."

"Thank the chief and tell him we'll reserve the others. We hope they'll have an opportunity to identify Madam in person. Do you want to stay there overnight and come back in the morning?"

"No, thank you. I've already turned down the room Chief Markel reserved for me. It's in a ramshackle old house that advertises 'Tourists Accommodated' but doesn't say how. I'll head for Cincinnati and take a late flight back if I can get a seat. Are you keeping watch tonight?"

"Certainly. This development has no affect on our plans for Feinstwaller Manor. A&B Realty requested that the electricity be turned off at six instead of five-thirty, which is extremely interesting, and I wish I knew why. Their office closes at five."

"Maybe someone wants to work overtime."

"That's what I suspect. I'd like to know who and on what."

"Good luck," Jill said. "Look for me when I arrive."

Laylor hung up and turned to grin at Gerald Wyman, who had stopped looking gloomy. He'd had a frustrating afternoon in the engineering library trying to figure out what might be using all that electricity at Feinstwaller Manor, and he was completely in the dumps when he arrived at Laylor's motel—only to learn that Madam had been identified. This didn't take them a millimeter closer to finding out what had happened to the missing persons, but Laylor didn't have the heart to point that out to him. He told Wyman cheerfully, "At least now we know who we're looking for."

He ripped open a package Ray Bront had left for them. It contained work clothing, heavy shoes, and hard hats for him and Wyman. Bront arrived before they finished dressing. He wore similar clothing and carried an array of tools in a thick leather belt, and he looked as though he had been born to be an electric company lineman.

Laylor told him about Jill's call. "By tomorrow morning, Dr. Zinaida Sokolova will be the number one person on a lot of 'wanted' lists. Did anything spectacular happen while I was improving myself at the library?"

Bront sat down heavily. "I don't know whether to believe this or what it means if it's true. Ed claims our day watch on the building is blown."

"What makes him think that?"

"The same two men drove past three times, slowly, looking the van over. Once they drove down the side road, and people I have on the rear entrance think they could have been spotted. Ed got photos, and I passed them to Prehn, but no one has recognized either man."

"They could have been looking for almost anything," Laylor said.

"Sure. But why would they drive past in three different cars? That was quite a strike you made at the library. How'd you happen to be looking at pictures of Russians?"

"Thank the college kids. One of their wild shots hit the bull's-eye, but all it accomplishes is to put a name on a person the police were already looking for. If she's wise, she's out of the country by now. How sure are you that Feinstwaller Manor doesn't have heavy machinery hidden away somewhere? Did the police search the basement thoroughly?"

"It didn't need searching," Bront said. "It's virtually empty except for the heating plant, which of course is turned off, and a few empty filing cabinets and shelves. Some of the fake antique furniture that had to be moved to make room for the A&B offices is stored there, but that isn't using electricity. There's absolutely nothing down there that would draw a watt of current except when the lights are on."

"The place is outside the city limits. Does it have a well and pump?"

"I never thought to check. Even so—"

"Right," Laylor agreed. "A water pump wouldn't be running all night with the building empty and wouldn't use much current if it did. We've got to look for something big."

The phone rang. Bruce Kagen was reporting from Nortonville, Indiana. "The police had everything ready for me," he said. "I got ten certain identifications from the first ten witnesses. Do we save the rest?"

"We do," Laylor said. "Did anyone have the slightest doubt?"

"No. Madam has this conspicuous nose, you see, and—"

"Right. Stay overnight in Nortonville if you feel like it or come back if you'd rather."

"I'll come back. All Nortonville has is a couple of big old houses that rent rooms to tourists. They probably haven't had any business for years."

"Tell Jill about them," Laylor suggested.

He hung up and dialed Lieutenant Prehn. The lieutenant was out, but a sergeant said Prehn had rushed Madam's photos to police in Texas,

Oregon, California, and Alabama, and a nation-wide search was already underway. Hanging up a second time, Laylor said to Bront, "Where were we?"

"Feinstwaller Manor. The basement. It has some cement block partitions, but they aren't wide enough to conceal anything. The building does have a hell of a lot of electric clocks, but most of them aren't plugged in, and a clock only uses about three watts."

The phone rang again. It was the translator, who had been left at the library to look for additional information about Dr. Zinaida Sokolova.

He sounded triumphant. "I've found two more references to this scientist, both insignificant," he told Laylor. "But I also found two articles by her—authored by her."

"Indeed. The articles might be interesting. What are they called?"

The translator hesitated. "One is entitled 'Sleep Deprivation as a Stress Factor in Inhibition Responses.'"

Laylor made a face. "She'll never sell the motion picture rights. What's the other one?"

The translator hesitated again. "There is a Russian phrase, 'Sila duha,' which means perhaps—" He paused. "Perhaps it would be translated 'strength of mind,' or 'strength of spirit.' This article concerns genetic and environmental contributions to 'sila duha' in test subjects."

"It sounds delightful. Are both articles full of technical terms?"

"Very much so," the translator said, sounding resigned.

"I suppose we'd better have translations anyway. Can you manage?"

"I have a friend in the psychology department who knows some Russian. I can consult him."

"Please do that. And keep looking for more references to Sokolova."

"But of course."

Laylor hung up and turned to Bront. "Now what could that have to do with nine missing persons?"

"Eleven," Bront said with a scowl. "My two missing men are still missing. To answer your question, I don't know. If you two are through fooling around here and you still want to see whether this electricity ploy provokes any response, we'd better get over to Feinstwaller."

Laylor drove; Wyman, pleased that he finally had something to do, took the rear seat. Bront sat beside Laylor and talked moodily about his long vigil of photographing A&B employees and customers. "Thus far, no one has come out who wasn't seen going in. Of course we aren't infallible."

"I suppose it's hard getting clear photographs of people in cars," Laylor said.

"It might be if the cars were driving past, but they have to slow almost to a stop in order to turn in, and cars coming out stop before turning onto the highway. We get two shots at everyone. I'm sure whoever was prowling about in the mansion on Tuesday night is still there. Maybe he spends his days working for A&B and his nights sleeping under one of those pseudo antique beds."

"Could we persuade the police to search the place again?" Laylor asked.

"I doubt it. Prehn is certain the other search was as thorough as they could make it."

"What the devil is using all that electricity?"

Bront looked at his watch. "In half an hour, nothing will be using electricity there. I wonder if raiding the place would accomplish anything."

"If a leisurely and thorough police search failed, what could we accomplish doing it hastily and illegally? Also, there's that alarm system. According to Prehn, it's battery operated."

"Any idea what's going to happen?" Bront asked. "With the electricity off, I mean."

"No. But my hunch about announcing the police search in advance was right. We got a reaction. I have the same kind of hunch about turning off the electricity. We're going to get another reaction, but I couldn't guess what it will be."

They turned into the side road that ran past the Feinstwaller estate and parked where a thick growth of shrubbery shielded the car from passersby. It was a quarter to six when Laylor and Wyman watched from the shelter of a clump of bushes while Bront strolled nonchalantly up the rear drive to the manor. He looked the complete electrician. As he passed the strange-looking vent, he dropped out of character long enough to turn aside and sniff suspiciously. Then he went directly to the electric meter by the rear entrance, took one look, and spoke into the walkie-talkie radio he carried.

"Weren't they supposed to turn the current off at six o'clock?"

"Six o'clock precisely," Laylor answered. "It'll be off for an hour and forty-six minutes."

"I guess you've got your response. It's already off."

"What do you mean—already off?" Laylor demanded.

"Well—maybe not off, but no current is being used. The meter's revolving disk isn't moving at all. I'm looking right at it, and it hasn't shifted a millimeter since I got here."

Laylor jammed his radio into a pocket and ran up the drive with Wyman pounding on his heels. They joined Bront on the loading platform, and the three of them stood staring at the electric meter.

"In this entire building, there isn't even an electric clock drawing current," Bront said. "So you got your reaction. They stopped whatever was going on before the current was turned off."

* * * *

Andrei Zinovyev was waiting in a wooded grove a kilometer west of Feinstwaller Mansion when the message reached him. "The private detectives have moved in around the house," he said to Cherkasov. He chuckled. "Some of them are dressed like electricians. The electricians have arrived, and some of them are behaving like detectives. We can start now, but we will avoid the north part of the property until the electricians leave."

"I still think it would be better to wait until after dark," Cherkasov said.

"The property is heavily wooded," Zinovyev said, speaking patiently like an adult lecturing to a child. "It soon will be dark among the trees. American civilization is urban, which means Americans have no woodcraft, and they'll be watching the building, not us. One at a time and from behind—as American sportwriters like to say, they'll never know what hit them."

* * * *

It was already early Saturday morning in Moscow, where three extremely worried men were working late at KGB headquarters beneath the old church whose name Yuri Fedorenko had already forgotten. Dmitri Abrasinov also was working late, and when he sent for them, they filed into his office like condemned men expecting to have their final appeal denied.

Abrasinov didn't invite them to sit down. "Well?" he said, looking from one to the other. "What plan do you have for my consideration?"

None of the three answered.

"Fortunately for you," Abrasinov said, "I was wrong. It was not too late for action. Dr. Sokolova will complete the current phase of her experiment very shortly, and Zinovyev will have her and her assistants out of the United States before midnight local time. The laboratory will be sealed and Project Ob suspended until it can be safely resumed. At that time I'll give Dr. Sokolova an assistant who can handle security competently. Now all of us can go home. Report to me at five this afternoon, and I'll find something for you to do that's more in line with your abilities."

CHAPTER 25

Adelle was bravely resolved to break the group up at the first opportunity, but none occurred. They were herded through the mock stone village again, and this time they spread out as far as possible and flattened themselves on the pseudo cobblestone street while bullets skipped among them—not ricochets, but bullets, the guns had been depressed—and explosions went off so close to them they were drenched by smoke and fumes. Adelle covered her ears and feared for her hearing.

A piece of beam, blasted loose from a building, landed on Mondor. He started to giggle. Adelle turned her head and stared at him.

He giggled louder. "I think my arm is broken."

From across the street, Dolan's chuckle became uncontrolled laughter. Adelle joined him. She suddenly realized she was not frightened. Bombs screamed down, bullets sprayed around them, explosions went off nearby—and she was not frightened. A bullet singing past her head had no more effect on her than a buzzing fly and less than a mosquito.

When the raid was over, they converged on Mondor, who sat in the street examining his arm and flexing it. When he announced that it hurt like hell but wasn't broken, all three of them roared with laughter.

They moved on, and for a time they encountered no hazard except the gas. They collapsed repeatedly, rested as long as they could, and got to their feet again only when they had to. Even with gas spewing out almost under their noses, one of them sometimes had to shake the others awake. The fluorescent overhead lights felt hotter and hotter. Their last drink of water was a distant memory; their last taste of food was forgotten.

The dinner bell sounded a loud, clear tone that made all three of them jump. They faced each other questioningly. They had been deceived by it several times, so they knew it no longer meant the certainty of water, food, and beds. The only spoken reaction was Dolan's. "The despicable clods," he muttered.

Dolan was still limping; Mondor was nursing his injured arm. Adelle knew her turn would come at any moment. The more she thought about it, the funnier it seemed. And it seemed hilarious that someone would waste all that tear gas just to keep them moving.

Dolan said to her suddenly, "Why do you keep laughing?"

"Because everything is so funny."

"It is, isn't it?" After a pause, he added, "I once read instructions for setting a broken arm. I've always wondered if I could do it."

Mondor giggled. "Sorry about that. Maybe next time."

All three of them laughed.

They dragged their feet rather than shuffle them—not because they worried about traps, but because they were so tired. They had spent days walking awkwardly to test the floor, even after they knew it was a waste of effort, and they laughed about that, too.

Adelle stepped along lightly with dragging feet, and her floating sense of euphoria continued to expand. She was not eating, so she no longer needed to watch her weight. That was funny. Tension had been building within her for days, and now she discarded it like an overcoat in hot weather. Unexpected lights or sounds or odors could be met with giggles. Life-threatening dangers were funny rather than frightening. She had worried about the moment that must come very soon, the moment when they would awaken her to move on and she had to answer, "No." Now she looked forward to it.

They walked past optical illusions, dimly aware of them without seeing them. They instinctively averted their eyes from flashes of light and passed through vile odors indifferently. They absorbed blasts of sound without flinching and almost without hearing. Emerging from another test room, none of them could remember what the problem had been or how they solved it.

They were foot-dragging along an alley they had walked days before when Dolan had still been energetically marking the walls. Suddenly he halted, pointing. Under an arrow were the letters, "RC".

Mondor left off flexing his injured arm to stoop over and peer at them. "Lacks plot like the rest of your writing," he said when he straightened up.

"Idiot!" Dolan thundered. "'RC' means 'Rest Center'. The bell rang—remember? We're headed back toward the kitchen. And water. And beds. Maybe even food. Let's go!"

Limp forgotten, he turned and hurried away. Adelle stumbled after him. She was having difficulty focusing her thoughts, and her mind grappled uncertainly with his words: Water. Beds. Food.

"Soap!" she said suddenly.

Dolan turned a puzzled look on her. "How's that?"

"Soap. There was soap there, too. It'd be nice to wash. Maybe even wash my clothing. We've been wallowing in so many odors that we don't know what our own clothes smell like."

"I suspect," Dolan announced, "that all three of us smell like shit. But then, I haven't been to college."

He laughed. Mondor was shocked into silence.

They hurried on. Water. Beds. Maybe food. The expectation had jolted them back to reality.

At the end of the alley, they had a choice between turning left or right. Now they gave no thought to separating. Dolan peered down the right alley, glimpsed another "RS" with an arrow, and took off at a run. They rushed after him, oblivious to a sudden eruption of explosions, and hurtled through a hissing wall of tear gas without breaking stride.

Dolan was far ahead of them, now, and running. He vanished around a corner. When they reached it, they saw him midway along the alley standing motionless and staring at the wall.

They took their places beside him. It was a section of wall that opened and closed—there were the familiar grooves on either side that guided it as it slid up and down. It was like the dozens of similar sections of wall Adelle had heard swishing out of the floor behind her, cutting off her past. This one had decapitated her future.

It had a small window, and Dolan's expressionless gaze was fixed on it. Adelle and Mondor crowded in on either side of him, and the three of them stared together.

The narrow kitchen stretched before them: sink, faucets, refrigerator, cupboards, chairs, bedrooms. The place had been tidied up since they last saw it. The curtains in the doors of the three bedrooms were neatly drawn. The chairs were lined up along the wall. The small table had been returned to a central position.

Of all the partitions in that fiendishly designed maze, only this one was maliciously supplied with a window. Adelle had not felt thirsty—really thirsty—until she saw the sink with a faucet that was ready to gush water at the turn of a handle. Dolan, face red with anger, eyes glazed, beat futilely upon the window with his fist, but it didn't break or even crack.

"What good would it do to break it?" Adelle asked dully. "It's too small to climb through."

Dolan turned on her. His clenched, bleeding fist was poised as though he meant to rain the next blows upon her.

Mondor dropped to the floor. After a moment's hesitation the others did the same, turning their backs on the one place of refuge the maze had offered to them. Adelle attempted, unsuccessfully, to moisten her parched lips. She felt like weeping, but she also felt too dehydrated for tears.

After a time she looked at the others. Mondor had began to snore quietly. Dolan seemed to be asleep. She slumped over onto the floor, buried her face in the crook of an arm to shut out the relentless light, and dozed off at once.

She awoke to the shock of Dolan's bewhiskered face pressed against hers, of his hands on her body. She twisted, rolled away, faced him with fury.

Dolan's whisper was a hoarse cackle. "We're going to die. What are you saving it for? The worms?" He reached for her again.

The mad gleam in his eyes, the twisted lust of his expression, made her instantly, coldly alert. She had almost forgotten that she despised this man; now her contempt blazed in fierce hatred. She planted a foot in his chest and shoved with all of her strength, bracing herself against the wall. He was on his knees, bending over her, and he fell backward, striking the wall behind him with a reverberating crash. He leaped at her with a roar of rage, and his hands were claws that ripped at her clothing.

His fall awakened Mondor, who took in the situation with a glance and flung himself on Dolan. "You filthy pig!"

"Stop it!" Dolan shouted. "We're going to die, damn it! Why shouldn't we enjoy ourselves while we can? She's been laughing at the two of us as long as we've known her. Now it's our turn."

Mondor jerked Dolan backward and aimed a vicious kick at him. Dolan struggled to his feet, parrying Mondor's wild blows. The two men faced each other, panting. Adelle crept away on her hands and knees.

"Damn it, don't you want to screw her?" Dolan demanded. "We're all going to die, and she's got it coming. The last woman you'll ever have. Are you a man, or aren't you?"

Mondor's reply was unintelligible. Adelle heard the sound of a blow being struck and then another. She got to her feet and hurried away on tiptoe. When she reached an opening into the next alley, she began to run. She wanted to get out of sight quickly and find a place where there was more than one opening so they wouldn't know which way she had gone.

She heard footsteps behind her. At the end of a short alley she took the single exit and ran frantically, her shoes slipping on the cement. Somewhere behind her, she heard Dolan's voice and Mondor's angry reply.

She ran on, but her last feeble reserves of energy had long since been exhausted. Her pace faltered rapidly until she heard Dolan's shouted profanity directly behind her. She managed another spurt. The end of the alley was almost within reach.

Suddenly a tiny beam of light cut through the air, sizzling the few strands of her hair that it touched. Behind her, Dolan uttered a bellowing scream. She flung herself down as light beams crackled above her. Mondor cried out, and both men lay twisted in agony as scream after scream echoed along the alley.

Then the lights went out.

The screams subsided to moans. Adelle edged forward on her knees, gained the end of the alley, and slipped through an opening. She got to her feet and moved along blindly in total darkness.

She made another turn, and the next alley seemed to stretch interminably. Her extended hands were still groping at emptiness when her feet stumbled into something. She fell forward and landed on a steep incline. Instantly she knew where she was. She had somehow circled the kitchen and ended up back in the alleys she had walked ages before when she first arrived in the maze, and this slope she had blundered into in the dark was the chute she had plummeted down when Madam sent her to the basement for a folder on tires. The test room was somewhere nearby. Perhaps she was standing in it, but she could see nothing at all.

She didn't hesitate. The chute led upward, and at the top there was a way out. She began to climb. She slipped badly several times before she learned to grip the side rails and brace her feet against them, but she kept going, hauling herself upward through the darkness, a lunge at a time.

But more and more slowly. "I can't do it!" she gasped. Her heart was pounding; her hands were too weak to keep pulling her upward. When a foot slipped, her grip began to slip, too.

She clung to the chute, resting, and then she tried again. It seemed to become steeper as she climbed higher, and each desperate, upward wriggle required an effort that drained her utterly. Her heart continued to pound. The ache of her leg muscles was torment. The screams of Dolan and Mondor still rang in her ears.

She forced herself to keep climbing. Then she rested until she began to slip backward. Struggling desperately, she inched upward again. She couldn't comprehend what had happened, what blunder or malfunction could have lowered the chute and left the way open to it, but for the first time in days she had a glimmer of hope, of actually escaping from this horrible place, and that kept her going. She knew this first chance would be her last.

When she reached the ceiling, she had to duck to get through the opening. After more slipping and frantic clutching, she moved on. A step. A rest. Another faltering step. A slip back.

Her head bumped against solid flooring. Balancing herself precariously, she felt above her with one hand. The bottom side of the trap was framed in wood, and her fingers followed its outline. She gripped a board and pulled downward, and it opened easily.

Too easily. She lost her balance and almost went backward down the chute. Clinging to the trap with aching muscles, breath coming in tortured sobs, she tried to think. She would have to pull the trap down, descend a short distance to get clear of it, and then climb back. After a struggle to brace and balance herself, she managed to edge downward far enough for the trap to open fully and make room for her. She began to climb again. Twice she slipped and thought she was lost, but she clung to the trap and kept her feet braced against the side rails.

Her hands found the opening, felt the surrounding cement floor. With the last effort she was capable of, she pulled and clawed her way up. She lay for a time half in the trap and half on the cement floor, sobbing. Then she managed to roll over and raise her feet. The trap swung shut under her.

She was in the upper basement, but she was not free. Madam and her goons certainly were nearby, and the moment the lights came on in the maze, they would miss her. The pursuit would be immediate and relentless.

There was daylight outside, and some of it reached the basement through a small, high window. Adelle pushed herself erect and staggered across to the flight of stairs. With the support of the hand railing, she hauled herself up to the first floor.

There was plenty of light there, and the changes startled her. The cathedral doors, which always had been locked, stood open. Inside was some kind of office. Other rooms along the main corridor had been converted to offices. Their pseudo antique furnishings were gone.

She tiptoed directly to the front door—and found it locked. She thought for a moment. Then she went to the nearest office and examined the windows. One was blocked by an air conditioner. The other was screened.

She had heard about the building's alarm system. She wondered whether opening a window would set it off and whether she could break through the screen. She looked in the drawers of the desk for scissors and found none. Finally she went to the window, unlocked it, and tugged at the handle.

She couldn't budge it.

"Get out of here!" she told herself through clenched teeth.

She turned and looked about the office. Her gaze fell on the large desk and its executive chair, and she experienced a shock of recognition. They were hers—the ones she had used for three weeks. Against the wall were two straight-backed office chairs. She picked up one of them, hefted it until she got a secure grip on it, and ran at the window. It crashed through. It also ripped through the screen, slipped from her hands, and dropped to the lawn below, where it somersaulted and landed upright.

Somewhere in the distance a bell began to ring. Adelle quickly kicked shards of glass from the edges of the window frame, climbed up, and eased herself backward through the window. "And never mind a cut or two," she told herself. She balanced on the ledge for a moment and then dropped to the ground. She could still hear the alarm ringing stridently.

She had a banged elbow, a scratch on her hand that dripped blood, a sudden, sharp pain in her ankle, and more bruises than she could count. She ignored all of them and ran. She followed the graveled drive, keeping to the grassy verge where she would make the least noise. Her one thought was to reach the highway.

She had gone almost halfway when a man stepped out of the bushes and intercepted her. He was heavy set but pleasant looking in a rough way, wearing a dark sport shirt and slacks. He bore no similarity to Madam's goons, but he stood between her and freedom. She doubled her fists to fight him off—so near and yet so far. The highway was in sight, and she saw a car pass. She was determined to resist to the end.

Before she could make a gesture of defense, he seized her wrists. "Who are you? What are you doing here?"

His voice was thick and vaguely foreign. He sounded and looked puzzled. She struggled to free herself, and suddenly he exclaimed, "You're—you must be—you escaped?"

His grip tightened. He twisted her around and clapped a hand over her mouth. Until that instant it hadn't occurred to her to scream. Now it was too late. She continued to struggle.

The grip relaxed. A man in work clothing and a hard hat—he looked like a construction worker—had darted from the trees and seized her assailant from behind. As the two men began a violent combat, Adelle sprang free—and before she could take a step toward the road, she was seized again.

Now the woods seemed to erupt men who immediately paired off and struggled with one another. The man with the hard hat, still exchanging vicious blows with Adelle's first captor, was himself attacked from behind, but another man quickly intervened. Adelle had no idea who the combatants were or why they were fighting. She only knew she had been captured again and that her captor had started to drag her back toward the building.

A car moved slowly along the drive and stopped. Three grossly overweight men leaped out, pawing awkward for very large looking revolvers. When they finally pulled their guns free, they didn't know where to point them. They gazed bewilderedly from one fracas to another.

Then one of them saw Adelle. "Hey, you, let that girl go!" he bellowed, pointing his gun.

Her captor swung Adelle around as a shield and tightened his grip.

Gun held level, the fat man advanced nervously. Adelle felt more frightened of him and his gun than she did of her captor. Suddenly that nice young man from the *Chateau Arb* —Gerald Wyman, she had almost forgotten his name—was standing beside her. His sudden appearance seemed like the most astonishing event in that long series of incredible happenings. There was an audible crunch as his fist smashed into her captor's face. The vise-like hands dropped away from her. Her captor toppled backward and hit the ground with a thud, and she collapsed into Jerry's arms.

She didn't notice the police car until it coasted to a stop nearby. An officer calmly applied handcuffs to her fallen captor. Other police cars were arriving, and the officers took charge of the various fights, separated the combatants, sorted them out, and marched some of them away.

Suddenly the man who had first come to her rescue stood beside her and Jerry, and at for a moment she didn't recognize him. He had lost his hat in the fight, and he had a swollen eye and a bloody mouth. He also had incongruously gray hair. "Adelle Gernyan," he said. It was more a surprised statement of fact than a question.

She hesitated. "Yes—"

"My name is John Laylor. I've been looking for you. Where are the others?"

"Inside," she said. "They may be hurt. I'm sure they're hurt."

"Can you show us where to find them?"

"Yes, but—"

She didn't want to return to that building again, ever.

The gray-haired man spoke to a tall, robust police officer. "Still have your search warrant?"

"You bet."

"We've got to get in there quickly. Let's go."

One of the three fat men stepped forward and blustered, "Now just a minute. We're the night watchmen, here."

"Sure you are," the police officer said. "If you have a key, go unlock the front door. Then you can come along and watch."

The gray-haired man said to Adelle, "Are you all right?"

They had started walking back toward the building with Jerry keeping a firm arm around her. She was grateful for the support, for having someone to lean on, because she felt herself beginning to sag. "I'm so tired," she murmured.

"It's all right now," Jerry told her. "It'll soon be over. Just show us where the men are, and I'll get you out of here."

"Tired," she murmured. "And hungry and thirsty. And frightened. I've been frightened for so long. There's a maze—"

"Where?" the gray-haired man asked sharply.

"Under the basement there's another basement. You step on a trap in the floor, and it drops you onto a chute. They got all three of us that way. The maze goes on and on—" She covered her face with her hands.

"It's all right," Jerry said. "You don't have to go back down there. Just show us the trap in the floor. Then we can get the men out."

"It's dangerous. They gas you, and explosions go off, and guns shoot, and just before the lights went out there were beams of light that stabbed and burned. They hit Craig and Kevin."

"We'll get them out," the gray-haired man said confidently.

They formed a small procession of police officers and men in work clothing. The three night watchmen had gone on ahead. The gray-haired man spoke to the tall police officer again.

"That was a well-timed arrival. How'd your minions happen to be here?"

"There was a feel of *organization* about this business," the police officer said. "The more I thought about Madam being Russian, the less I liked the implications. So I posted a couple of men to look on and make certain you didn't get into trouble. When they reported a crowd of heavies moving in to take you from the rear, I called in all the available police in the county. We'll soon have a cordon around the whole place. It looks like a rich haul."

"Good show." The gray-haired man turned to Adelle. "Are Madam and her people in that sub-basement?"

"I suppose. Someone runs it, but we never saw anyone." She shuddered.

"As soon as Adelle shows us how to find this place," the gray-haired man said to the police officer, "I want a car ready to take her to the hospital. I don't think she needs an ambulance, but the men might. Will you send for one and have a car waiting for her?"

The police officer nodded and turned away.

The three worried night watchmen were clustered about the open front door. Somewhere behind them, the alarm was still ringing. They stepped aside without a word and watched the procession file past. Moving dazedly with the Jerry's support, Adelle led the way to the basement stairs. Two of the men in work clothing had flashlights ready, and they went down the steps ahead of her. At the bottom, with Jerry's arm still supporting her, she walked straight across the large room to the trap in the floor. The filing cabinets were gone, but she had no difficulty locating it. She pointed; the gray-haired man got down on his knees and searched the floor with his hands. He found the edge of the trap and pushed down on it. One of the men with flashlights held it open with his foot and pointed a beam of light down the chute.

"You climbed up that?" the gray-hair man asked.

She nodded.

"You've got gumption. Now it's off to the hospital for you. We can handle it from here."

Adelle said worriedly, "Craig and Kevin—the beams of light stabbed and burned them. They were screaming." Her voice sounded strangely faint to her, as though it came from an enormous distance.

"We'll get them out. Take her to the hospital, Jerry. There should be a police car waiting. If there isn't, get one. Charlie—make sure an ambulance is on its way for the men. Then see if there's a long extension ladder anywhere about and send for one just in case there isn't. It must be possible to climb that thing, since she did it, but I'd hate to have to carry an injured person out of there."

"There's got to be another way in," one of the police officers said.

"It's a maze," Adelle protested. "There isn't any other way. We walked for days."

"We can't waste time looking for one if the men are hurt," the gray-haired man said. "Ed, you stay on guard here. Half of you follow me. The rest can search the place and see if there's another entrance."

He lowered himself into the opening, let go, and vanished down the chute. A police officer followed him.

Jerry gently helped Adelle back up the stairway. The man called Charlie followed them. The alarm was still ringing when they got upstairs, and she mentioned it worriedly.

"All that does is call the police," Charlie said with a grin, "and the police are already here."

Jerry helped her into the waiting police car and climbed in beside her. Charlie stood and waved at them as the car moved away.

CHAPTER 26

For several hours, Mikhail Borod had been patiently maneuvering the subjects toward the laser alley. The other four assistants were observing intently—something that rarely happened. Subjects' actions and reactions at termination were always interesting, and this first use of the laser alley promised a spectacle they didn't want to miss.

Only Leonid Sisovsky seemed to have given any thought at all to the value of the lasers as a testing device, and he was commendably dubious about them. It was another apparatus inflicted on the program by the GRU, which, like the KGB, had gone underground with its most precious secrets, hibernating until the military programs of the various new Russian states had become stabilized along lines the GRU approved of. Madam agreed with Sisovsky. A highly secret military device had no place in a psychological testing program. She had to concede, however, that information of substantial military value might result, and that was what the GRU wanted. At the present time, there were few places where such devices could be tested.

The fact that the experiment had the full and eager attention of her assistants gave Madam no satisfaction at all. They were demonstrating rank sadism rather than scientific interest. Tests likely to inflict disabling injuries or death on all of the subjects simultaneously were avoided in the early stages of an experiment. A group had to function long enough to provide a fair return of experimental data on the investment of time and money. Occasionally one member of a group was lost early, but this tended to make the survivors wary enough to prolong the experiment. On the final day, when the experiment was about to be terminated anyway, no such restrictions applied. She had to watch alertly to make certain the rigors her assistants inflicted so gleefully had scientific value.

Soon the subjects would be routed past the kitchen, which they would view through a window. They were exhibiting severe dehydration symptoms, and that glimpse of a source of water, so near and yet so far, should produce valuable thirst drive data.

They would be allowed ten minutes rest there to make them as alert as possible for the climactic test. Then the route would take them directly to the laser alley and termination.

They were so exhausted that they showed no reaction at all to the sound effects of a simulated air raid, and yet their feet continued to cautiously test the floor for traps. It fascinated and perplexed Madam that such an unnatural motion could become a firmly ingrained habit so quickly.

She deeply regretted the necessity to terminate. At long last the subjects were showing positive indications of experimental neurosis. Even more intriguing was evidence of the third state of protective inhibition, Pavlov's ultra-paradoxical state, where positively and negatively conditioned responses switched places. The subjects were actually laughing at dangers that should have terrified them. They could have survived another day physically, and in a matter of hours their experimental neurosis would become intense. The girl seemed on the verge of lapsing into withdrawal amnesia.

There could be no doubt, however, that the police search and the watch on their building signified danger. The exposure of their scientific activities would be an inconceivable disaster. Madam's innate caution told her it would be far better to sacrifice one day of one experiment than to risk the project.

The subjects were emerging from a test chamber. Borod had deliberately made the test simple to avoid wasting time there; but he was running well ahead of schedule, and from this point he would make no effort to hurry them. They were stumbling haltingly in the direction of the kitchen, and both Madam and her assistants watched with growing excitement as the subjects discovered Dolan's markings and grasped their significance.

Konstantin Murov, who was controlling sensory effects, opened his entire arsenal on them as they frantically floundered toward the imagined refuge and refreshment. They ignored all of it. Even a length of alley filled with tear gas could not make them hesitate. Finally they stood panting before the kitchen window.

As Madam had predicted, it was Dolan who lost control. She watched ecstatically while he vented his insane rage upon the window. It was dramatic confirmation of the accuracy of her classifications. Pavlov had demonstrated many years before that Strong Excitatory types invariably broke down first.

Adelle Gernyan seemed to have snatched herself back from the withdrawal amnesia she had been succumbing to. She reacted with calm logic, and finally all three subjects composed themselves for sleep. Madam found herself admiring the girl.

She ordered Murov to desist with his sensory effects. "You're fifteen minutes ahead of schedule, and the more rest they have before they reach the lasers, the more interesting the final test will be. The only important thing now is to have them in that alley by five-thirty. That gives us ample time for termination before we lose the electricity at six."

"I'll have them there," Borod said with a grin.

Borod and Murov remained at the control panels. The other assistants drifted away. Madam went to her office and began writing a description of the subjects' reactions. She had been forced to design tests that concentrated on gross stress reactions rather than on behavioral disorders produced by genuine experimental neurosis, and it pleased her immensely to achieve such a striking validation of her program.

She had worked for several minutes when the alarm bell announced an event of special interest. She leaped into the control room just in time to witness Dolan's clumsy attempt to rape the girl.

She watched with fascination, and the off-duty assistants gathered around and stared incredulously. All of them had been expecting something like this throughout the experiment, and the way the girl kept the men in check had been a constant source of amazement and frustration.

But now that barrier, too, was broken. The breakdown came just in time and almost too late.

"Are you recording?" she demanded.

Borod answered irritably, "Of course," but Madam went herself to make certain that the video tape machine was recording all channels. Then she turned to watch the developing drama.

Mondor had leaped to the girl's rescue and attacked Dolan. In their weakened condition, they probably couldn't have injured one another seriously, but they certainly were trying. All of the enmity concealed beneath days of light banter had exploded into open rage. It was a slow motion fight, but their bitter hatred was real.

While they fought, Adelle crept away on hands and knees. Then she got to her feet and ran. The alley openings already had been arranged, and she ran directly toward the lasers. Everything happened so unexpectedly and so suddenly that she reached them before Borod could react.

"Wait!" Madam called.

The men were in pursuit. If the lasers started before all three were in the alley, the men would be warned off and the test ruined. If the lasers were delayed, Adelle might reach the end of the alley and be shielded from the beams, which had a high-angle mount.

Barely in time—with Adelle already two-thirds of the way through the alley—the men entered the alley in pursuit, the opening closed behind them, and Borod turned on the lasers. The girl dropped to the floor when the first beam snapped past her. The men weren't so quick. Dolan was struck in the shoulder, and he spun around and fell, screaming. Mondor was hit twice before he collapsed.

Although seriously wounded, the men didn't panic. Their pain must have been hideous, but once on the floor, they were wise enough to lay motionless and let the laser pattern develop above their heads.

"Interesting," Madam murmured. "How long before the beams drop?"

Borod's eyes were on his timer. "Ten seconds."

The searing streaks of light turned downward in a pattern that would search the floor from one end of the alley to the other. Almost immediately Mondor was hit again, this time in the leg. The girl remained untouched, but the pattern was moving toward her, and the return sweep would finish her as well as the two men. The experiment's final test was seconds from a successful conclusion.

Abruptly all of the lights went out. In an instant the instruments died, the screens blackened, and the laser pattern halted.

Madam heard a click from the control panel. Borod had switched the laser cycle off. The test was ruined, and there would be no point in attempting to restart it when the electricity came on.

Madam glanced at her luminous watch. "It's only five-thirty," she announced disgustedly. "They turned the electricity off too soon."

Someone produced a flashlight and shined the beam on the control panel. Borod, frowning over his banks of switches, tried various combinations and finally gestured hopelessly. Nothing worked.

"It doesn't matter," Madam said resignedly. "We can complete termination after the electricity comes on again. Was the girl hit at all?"

None of them knew for certain.

"Was an exit left open at the end of the alley?"

"It was," Borod said. "I don't know whether the subjects could see it, but this group sometimes seemed to sense things, and if they'd suspected the alley had a dead end, they might have turned back and wasted time for us. I left an exit open to keep them going."

"It doesn't matter," Madam said again. "I'm sure the men aren't able to walk, and even if the girl wasn't hit, she can't go far. She'll probably lie down in the next alley and sleep. We'll wind things up as quickly as possible after the electricity comes on. If you have suggestions for that, let me have them. We got almost as much as we were likely to from the lasers, so this is no great loss. All three subjects were on the floor, and they wouldn't have moved again in any case, so the only failure was in not terminating them. Make a note—the cycle should run more slowly. At the speed you were using, the subjects dropped to the floor and remained there. A soldier would react the same way to machine gun bullets. The subjects should have the illusion that the beams are random and can be avoided."

"Very well," Borod said. "That's easily done."

"Next time, we'll give the lasers a brief test early in the experiment. If the subjects know something deadly might be lurking in any alley, that certainly will heighten stress. Now that we've seen them in operation on real subjects, I want you to think about other uses we can make of them."

She turned, cautiously circled the table—the flashlight was still aimed at Borod's control panel—and started for her bedroom. "The electricity may be off for as long as two hours," she said. "Why don't all of you rest? There'll be nothing to watch or do until it comes on again, and then I want the subjects terminated quickly. We have a full night ahead of us. Leonid—where is Leonid?"

The flashlight flicked about. Leonid Sisovsky was missing.

"He's probably trying to do something about the electricity," Borod said.

Madam chuckled. "He *was* intent on that laser experiment. I thought he understood that the electricity was to be turned off outside the building. They were turning it off for the whole area. Probably that meant the shopping mall, too."

"The shopping mall would have its own transformer," Borod said.

Madam sighed. "We should know more about these things. Stupid of the electric company to turn the current off too soon, but there was no harm done. We'll finish quickly when it comes on again. Everything is packed except these final tapes, and we've all had a long day. Let's rest."

Bychevsky found another flashlight for her, and she went to her room, took off her lab coat, and laid down with a blanket over her. She was feeling oddly frustrated. She had sacrificed her scientific principles to security and ordered a fascinating experiment terminated, and in some strange way these subjects seemed to have triumphed again.

But this really was the end. She refused to entertain for an instant Bychevsky's nonsense about indestructible laboratory specimens, and not even her frustration could diminish the satisfaction she felt at having typed the subjects so accurately. Dolan's breakdown had been a moment of jubilation for her. Individually, the selections had been perfect. It was in the combination that something had gone wrong. Some mysterious alchemy—for she could discern no scientific basis for it—had made the whole radically different from the sum of its parts. She would have to study and restudy the records on this experiment.

A flashlight beam cut through the laboratory control room. She called through her open door, "Is that you, Leonid? Where were you?"

"Looking at the electricity box. Something is wrong."

She chuckled. "We've known for hours that this was going to happen. Unfortunately, the electric company turned it off too soon."

"No." Sisovsky was standing in her doorway. "There is something wrong in this building. A short circuit. When I pushed the main circuit breaker back, it jumped out again. I wondered if the lasers in addition to all the other equipment overloaded the wires."

Madam thought for a moment. "The lasers really don't take that much electricity, so I don't think we were using more than usual. Anyway, there's nothing we can do about it now. The electric company will be turning the power off very soon, if it hasn't already, and we won't be able to check things until it comes on again."

"I still think it was the lasers," Sisovsky said. "Everything was all right until we turned them on."

"Whatever it was, we'll get it taken care of when the electric company finishes. Don't worry about it. Get some rest. We'll terminate the subjects as soon as the electricity comes on if any of them are still alive."

Sisovsky turned obediently, and his flashlight vanished down the hallway. Madam lay back with her eyes closed, wondering whether Zinovyev could have turned off the electricity early for some purpose of his own. He was superbly efficient and resourceful, but he also was stubborn and impulsive.

"He wouldn't dare without asking," Madam murmured. "He knew we were terminating the experiment."

Finally she dozed off. She awakened suddenly and sensed Sisovsky's presence in her room again. She spoke without bothering to open her eyes. "I told you not to worry, Leonid. Everything will be all right."

A strange voice answered, and she sat up quickly and stared.

It was a police officer.

CHAPTER 27

Mondor lay on his back. Plastic tubes drooped down to his arm from the two intravenous bags suspended above him. His chest bulged with bandages—the tracery of having a lung patched. A leg and an arm also were bandaged. He didn't recognize Laylor—he had been unconscious throughout the torturous process of getting him up the chute and on his way to the hospital. Dolan performed an introduction, and Mondor's eyes flickered with momentary interest before they closed again.

Dolan had one massive bandage that swathed his shoulder and patches on an arm and a leg. His bed was cranked into a sitting position, and he had been reading when Laylor walked in. After carefully placing a book mark, he offered Laylor the room's one available chair with a wave of his hand.

A barber had been there ahead of Laylor. Despite Mondor's pallor, he looked—and probably felt—much healthier minus his smudge of whiskers; and Dolan was no longer the shaggy creature he had been in the maze. His beard had been trimmed and its overflow removed.

Dolan plainly was chafing under the hospital regimen. He stretched, manipulated his injured shoulder with a grimace of pain, and then remarked to Laylor, "You don't look as banged up as you did the last time I saw you. How's the eye?"

"Much better," Laylor said. His mouth had healed quickly, but he still had a splendid shiner.

Dolan hesitated and then asked, "How is Adelle?"

"Recovering," Laylor said. "She's gone home."

"I sent her my apologies, but I don't think she accepted them." Dolan heaved a sigh and then grimaced again. "Of the three of us, I never would have thought I'd be the one to go off the deep end that way. Something short circuited. I was convinced we were going to die, you see—"

"You were," Laylor said. "Another minute or two, or maybe a few more seconds, and you would have."

"But we didn't," Dolan said. He sighed again. "So Madam was a Russian agent."

"She'd be deeply offended if she heard you call her that. She considered herself a scientist conducting a rigorous and carefully-planned experiment. The information she was after had profound military implications, and her experimental subjects were humans whom she 'sacrificed'—as scientists say when they kill their laboratory animals—but all of that was incidental. Madam has a high degree of scientific detachment."

"Yeah. The Russians ought to give her a medal."

"They already have."

"No kidding!"

"The Lenin State Prize in Science. I don't think that's one of the big ones, although it makes her officially a 'Lenin Prize Laureate.' There's nothing surprising about her scientific detachment. She's an officer of the KGB, which has a notorious history of murder, abduction, and torture, and ran so-called 'mental hospitals' where psychiatry was perverted to destroy the minds of political prisoners. It's no coincidence that Madam is a former director of one of those hospitals."

Dolan stared. "I'll be damned. I thought the KGB had been disbanded or something."

"It was, but it had deep roots around the world, and at least some of its vast network of agents survived. We don't know how many of its projects are still flourishing the way Madam's did. Right now a lot of officials in a lot of countries are worried about that."

"I suppose she had no compunction at all about performing experiments on Americans after what she'd done to her own countrymen."

"None whatsoever," Laylor said. "In fact, she used Russian citizens as controls and tried all of her tests on them before she came to America. And she sacrificed the Russian citizens just as she planned to sacrifice you. She and her assistants called it 'termination'."

"What was she after?"

"That's complicated. How long has it been since the United States has had first-hand experience of war?"

"Leaving out Grenada and Lebanon, which I would, and writing Panama and the Desert Wars off as training exercises, I suppose Viet Nam was the most recent. Of course Afghanistan was real enough to those who fought there."

Laylor shook his head. "First-hand experience. When was the last time a war was fought *here*? When did American civilians last experience warfare?"

Dolan reflected. "Damn. The Civil War?"

"Right. And that was mostly fought in a few southern states. In the meantime, European civilians have experienced a series of wars, two of them devastating. There's plenty of data about how they react to the horrors of modern warfare and none at all about Americans. Such information would be worth far more to a foreign power than statistics about the atomic arsenal or plans for a new missile. It might even be priceless. The next major war will be won by the government whose civilian population has the most determination to endure."

"I suppose so," Dolan said with a frown, "but what foreign power was Madam collecting information for? Surely the Russians have other things to think about these days than war with us."

"Whatever survives of the KGB is conducting business as usual. Preparing for some future war is part of that business. Madam was collecting psychological information about us. How soft are we? How much can we take? How resourceful are we under adversity? Will we help one another, sacrifice for one another in times of crisis? Things like that, though she expressed them in scientific lingo and measured them with carefully planned scientific tests. There's a Russian word, 'vynoslivost,' which is concerned with physical endurance, and there are terms 'sila duha' and sila voli,' which signify strength of mind and will power. Madam is an expert in testing such things, and she devised something she called the 'telo-um test,' the body-mind test, to experimentally measure fortitude, endurance, tenacity, the will to survive, capacity for suffering, physical and mental tolerance, stamina, resourcefulness under extreme duress, and so on. She was administering a telo-um test to you. In doing so, she was evaluating the resolve and purpose of the American people and their capability to survive a war."

Dolan was regarding him incredulously. "Did she actually believe she could pick a few people at random, run them through a chamber of horrors in a sub-basement, and then predict how the entire American population would react in time of war? You'd think the Russians, of all people, would be aware that war has an emotional impact and that populations have reserves of fortitude, endurance, tenacity, and all the rest of it, that can be drawn upon in moments of crisis."

"Well—the test specimens weren't picked at random. They were selected with meticulous care, and whatever you may think of Madam's moral outlook, as a scientist she definitely knows what she's doing, especially in conducting tests on humans. She devised methods of adjusting her test data to allow for the artificialities of a laboratory situation."

"I'll bet she did," Dolan said angrily. "She probably thinks a guess becomes a scientific fact if it's adjusted enough."

"It was the GRU, the Russian military intelligence organization, that requested Madam's experiments. Its bigwigs thought the information she turned up would have incomparable military value. Madam had an open-end expense account."

"Really? I thought the Russian states were having financial problems. Where'd the money come from?"

"The KGB had its own resources, and there's a Near-Eastern flavor to the agents we captured. American intelligence organizations will have a great time sorting it all out."

"So the Russian military was behind this," Dolan mused. "I'll be damned. All military establishments think alike. I remember blasts of publicity about the Pentagon conducting experiments on humans. In fact, the three of us wondered whether the Pentagon could have put Madam up to doing her stuff on us."

Laylor smiled. "In America, such things result in scandals and law suits. In the Soviet Union, there were no exposés of KGB activities except by a much persecuted underground. The horrors KGB agents perpetrated on their own people are simply unbelievable. It requires a strong stomach just to read about them."

Wincing with pain, Dolan eased himself back against the pillows. "I wonder if you could arrange for us to perform a few tests on Madam and her goons. Slivers under the fingernails, cigarette lighters on their bare feet, some fancy work with the drill while they're strapped to a dentist's chair—I'd promise to perform all of it scientifically and videotape their responses for later study. I'd enjoy studying those responses. Lucky thing for us you had that inspiration about the electricity. It went off just as the lasers were about to finish us."

"It was a bit more complicated than that," Laylor said. "Are you prepared for a shock? Adelle saved your lives."

"I know she did. She climbed out and got help."

"She did more than that. She got the electricity turned off half an hour before Detroit Edison was scheduled to do it."

"How?" Dolan demanded, eyes wide open.

"One of Madam's assistants, a man named Leonid Sisovsky, fell in love with Adelle. He had to take his shifts at the laboratory controls day after day, and inflict various torments and indignities on the object of his affection, and listen to Madam and the other assistants poke fun at her reactions, and finally he had enough. He tolerated all the rest of it, but he wasn't going to have her raped. He thought both of you were after her, and while the others were gloating over your moral disintegration, he used another control console to open an escape route and release the chute, and then he slipped up to the first basement where the circuit breaker box is located and pulled the master breaker. Of course that turned off all the electricity in the building. He didn't expect Adelle to climb out—he doubted that she could. Like Madam, he underestimated her courage and determination. He had a vague hope that the chute might divert you and Mondor and keep her from being raped. He left just as the lasers were starting, so he didn't know how seriously you two were wounded. After he'd done all that, he went back and told Madam he'd looked in the box and there was some kind of short circuit. That was to keep her from sending someone else to look. She decided there was no point in trying to have it fixed before the electric company finished its transformer repairs."

"I'll be damned. One of the goons. Can you describe him?"

"Young. Blond crew cut. Blue eyes. Round face. Beefy build."

"Goon 1!" Dolan exclaimed. "He's the one who was always hanging around Adelle's office."

"That was his job. Each of you had an assistant watching you. In fact, studying you, because all of them are psychologists."

Mondor spoke weakly, but there was no mistaking the disgust in his voice. "If I understand what you said, the thing that really saved our lives was this oversized baboon reverting to type and trying to attack Adelle."

"Roughly that's what happened," Laylor said. "It wasn't Sisovsky's first attempt to sabotage the experiment. The day you were abducted, he tried to get Madam to postpone it. He intended to warn Adelle about it in any case, but Madam chewed him out so thoroughly he lost his nerve. Even so, he tried to make things easier on you throughout the experiment, but there really wasn't much he could do. Another assistant or Madam herself shared the controls when he was on duty, and all of them watched the more strenuous tests. He worked out a plan to save Adelle from the lasers—he thought he could manipulate them so she wouldn't be hit—but Madam let an assistant with more experience run the experiment. He was about to give up hope when Dolan's attack inspired him to turn off the electricity. Of course he had no tender feelings whatsoever for you two—especially after that finale."

"Yeah," Dolan said. He sighed deeply. "Stupid of me. I haven't much tender feeling for myself except where a laser hit me. Say—about those lasers—"

"Our military intelligence finds them extremely interesting and requests that we don't mention them."

"If I'm asked about my peculiar scar, what do I say caused it?"

"A meteorite," Mondor muttered. Then he straightened up and opened his eyes. "If I'd managed to choke this anthropoid misfit when he was after Adelle, look at the pain and suffering he would have been spared."

"Yeah. Stupid of both of us." Dolan brightened. "But it did get us out. I have that consolation. If I hadn't lost my cool, I'd be dead. So would this lobster."

Eyes closed, Mondor grunted noncommittally.

"You're entitled to one more consolation," Laylor said, getting to his feet. "Madam chose you because you were likely to lose your cool."

"How's that again?"

"You were chosen to be one of the subjects because you're the type most likely to become unhinged under that kind of treatment."

Dolan said incredulously, "You mean—she knew in advance?"

"She thought she could, and you proved her right. According to Sisovsky, you made her a proud scientist."

"I'll be damned. I'm going to devote my next novel to an expose' of psychology."

"But psychology is neither good nor evil," Laylor protested. "It's whatever psychologists make of it."

"I don't like what Madam made of it. All right—I'll populate my novel with evil psychologists and have all of them die horribly. Mondor—give me some gruesome diseases to kill psychologists with. Bubonic plague, cancer, Bright's disease, tetanus, beriberi, elephantiasis—"

"Try lasers," Mondor suggested.

They were arguing the point when Laylor left.

* * * *

Adelle Gernyan, tastefully attired in a quilted dressing gown, sat in a chair by the window absently gazing at a bleak view of another wing of her apartment building. On a tray beside here was a glass of juice with a straw. She had another visitor, Gerald Wyman, who sat across the room on a hassock and watched Adelle like a hen brooding over one of its chicks.

One of Wyman's hands was heavily bandaged. He'd had a week of total frustration in his attempts to help find Adelle, and when the chance finally came for action, he substantially overdid it and broke his hand on the face of her captor. He hadn't noticed that it was broken until he got Adelle safely to the hospital. The KGB agent he hit was under police guard in a hospital room down the corridor from Dolan and Mondor with a broken jaw. The agent's face was far more heavily bandaged than Wyman's hand, and in Wyman's view, it had been a fair exchange.

He had just refilled Adelle's juice glass and tried, unsuccessfully, to convince her that she should eat something. If she had dropped even a vague hint that she craved a snack from Win Schuler's Restaurant in Jackson—a sixty mile round trip—he would have left at once to bring her one.

Adelle, remembering how banged up Laylor had been the last time she saw him, immediately asked about his face. Laylor slyly directed her concern where it properly belonged by asking Wyman how his injured hand was.

"I've been visiting Dolan and Mondor," Laylor said.

"How are they?" Adelle asked.

"Dolan is well enough to feel contrite. Mondor was much more seriously injured, and he's had a rough time. He's still weak, but he's recovered enough to be able to argue with Dolan."

She turned and smiled at him. "He would do that on his death bed. What do they find to argue about?"

"When I left them, they were selecting diseases to kill psychologists with. They'll both be up and around soon."

Adelle returned her gaze to the window. She had a quiet kind of beauty, Laylor thought. Much of what masqueraded as feminine attractiveness in these turbulent times was really an animated youthfulness. Even after her scarring experiences, or maybe because of them, Adelle Gernyan had a serenity of loveliness—not because of her youth, or her beautiful long hair, or her perfectly formed face, but because of an inner strength and beauty of self.

She mused, "I wonder if I should visit them."

Gerald Wyman growled something unintelligible.

"Craig saved my life more than once," Adelle said. "Kevin did, too. We all worked together, but Craig was the leader. He reacted so quickly to things. Sometimes he knew what to do and was already doing it before Kevin and I realized what was happening. I really should visit them."

Laylor made no comment. This was a deeply personal decision for her, and he was confident that the answer she found would be the right one.

She said slowly, "I feel as though I'd been dragged in filth and it won't wash off. The whole experience was filthy."

Laylor nodded. "That was part of the experiment, of course. To observe your reaction to a humiliating situation. War is both filthy and degrading. The thin red line of heroes, the charge in shining armor—that sort of thing belongs to the fiction we call history. War has always been filthy, and man's ingenuity has made it progressively worse. The heroism of the next war will be that of civilians starving in ruined cellars, probably radioactive. At least Madam spared you the radioactivity, though if she'd thought of a way to manage it, I'm sure she wouldn't have hesitated."

"Being observed all the time was the most humiliating thing of all," Adelle said. "Knowing that everything we did and said was probably watched and overheard—now, knowing that we were watched, and overheard, and even videotaped—"

"Yes," Laylor agreed soberly. "But you're young and healthy, and you have a stamina they didn't expect, both physically and morally. The doctor said all you needed was a meal and a good night's sleep, but he's no psychologist. Few doctors are. I'll send you one if you like, but I don't think the filth will stick for long. Time has remarkable cleansing powers."

"What will happen to Madam and her goons?"

"The police have found the bodies of the other people they abducted, so they'll be tried for kidnapping and murder. The list of charges could be much longer, but with solid evidence on six murders, plus a confession from one of the assistants, the prosecutor isn't likely to waste time on lesser offenses. The KGB agents and the terrorists are another matter. It was a rich haul, and a couple of the fish we hooked were surprisingly large sharks, but of course all of them claim ignorance of Madam's activities. Thus far the only charges against them are for passport violations and brawling with the police, but Lieutenant Prehn is confident other things will turn up."

"Will I have to testify?"

"Probably, but only to describe what happened to you so the jury can better understand the fate of the murdered people. You can leave the explanations and interpretations to the attorneys."

"They won't get off because of diplomatic immunity or some such thing?"

"Absolutely not," Laylor said. "Officially, none of the new Russian states are willing to acknowledge their existence. The present leaders claim to know nothing about them, and that may be true. The KGB could have been acting entirely on its own. Even so, this is causing a considerable diplomatic upheaval, as you know if you saw this morning's paper."

"Jerry wouldn't let me read it," Adelle said, smiling. "The only sections he gave me were the comics and the women's pages."

"Spies have a lonely fate if they're caught, and the notoriety Madam has achieved would have made the Russians disown her in any case."

"Was the real estate company in it, too?"

"The company and its employees are genuine. The owner and some of the higher-ups are in it considerably above their ears. They also own Feinstwaller Manor—they have for years. Their silly goofs—such as operating Z-R Publications in the same building as the laboratory—were probably due to overconfidence. The KGB has never thought highly of us naive Americans. In retrospect, though, they weren't being as stupid as it seems. They might have got away with it if your Goon 1 hadn't fallen for you."

"Then there would have been nine bodies," Adelle said soberly. "And how many more?"

"I don't know. Only those who have looked through Madam's records know how many people she 'terminated' in the Soviet Union before she came to America, and thus far they aren't talking about it. Fortunately she won't be conducting any more experiments in either place. You and a lot of others, Russian and American, can be grateful to your Goon 1. He'd had enough, and he wanted to be caught. The Soviets have never learned to cope with the innate decency that keeps coming to the surface despite the vicious training they inflict. The same thing happened with the KGB assassin, Stashinsky. After a couple of murders, he couldn't take any more. Are you going to visit Mondor and Dolan?"

"Yes. But not today."

"If you do, I'm coming with you," Gerald Wyman announced.

She gave Laylor her wisp of a smile. "I'm sure I can handle a pair of invalids. I never thought of them as people, you know. They were two men I disliked, and it relieved the monotony of that stupid job to exchange insults with them, but they might have been robots for all I thought about their feelings. I'll go and thank them. I'll thank Leonid Sisovsky, too."

"And then what?" Laylor asked.

Adelle smiled again. "There was a check waiting for me when I got home, and the bank says I have another coming. That's droll, isn't it? I can convalesce in good conscience and without damaging my bank account. I earned it. After that, Jerry thinks he can find me a job where he works. I'm a highly skilled typist, especially with numbers."

Laylor got to his feet and handed her his card. "If that job doesn't work out, or if you think you'd like to type legal papers, come and see me. If working in Detroit doesn't appeal to you, I know some Ann Arbor attorneys."

"Thank you. We all thank you for investing your time and money in such a forlorn cause. You've been working on the disappearances for more than a year, haven't you?"

"Off and on," Laylor said. "Never very effectively until the end."

"What are *you* going to do?"

"Make a phone call. To the friend in Indiana who started me on this. Then I'm going to take six photos down from my motel room wall and offer fervent thanks that I don't have to put up three new ones." He paused with his hand on the door knob. "Dolan and Mondor will enjoy seeing you, and Dolan will feel much better about everything. I'm glad you're going."

"I'm sure I'll feel much better about everything, too."

Laylor took his leave of them and strode down the hall to the elevator. He was thinking that Adelle Gernyan and Gerald Wyman made a handsome couple. He wondered how things would work out for them. Unlike Madam Doctor Colonel Zinaida Sokolova, he risked no predictions concerning human relationships. He knew just enough about human nature to be aware of his ignorance. Zinaida Sokolova knew too much to be aware of hers.

She had read implacable enmity into the insults Dolan, Mondor, and Adelle exchanged, not being able to understand that these were only a mental exercise that helped relieve the tedium of the senseless work they were engaged in. All three of them were intelligent enough to recognize and respect ability and intelligence in others, and when they were tossed into a stress situation together, they made a formidable team.

And of course Madam knew very little about love or infatuation, which—Laylor reflected—really did make the world go around. Or bring a lot of things to a smashing stop.

As for himself, he felt a strange emptiness. He had lived with a hopeless problem for more than a year. Suddenly it wasn't there any longer. The satisfaction he should have experienced was lost in the awareness that he had nothing to take its place.

Nothing but a telephone call to make and the photographs to remove from his motel room.

"But I'll have a few souvenirs," he told himself. "I can keep the photos—all nine of them." Eleven, counting Bront's missing agents, who probably would never be found. The dimensions of a man's life, he thought, could be measured by the keepsakes he refused to part with.

He got into his car and slammed the door.

* * * *

From Adelle's sixth floor window, she and Wyman watched him leave.

"What a good man," she murmured. "He radiates goodness. It's cleansing just to come into contact with someone like that. All that work and money and time invested merely because he was so concerned about the victims. Our society needs more people who worry about victims. And now everything is ended for him."

"Not ended," Wyman said confidently. "He'll find more victims to be concerned about. He's that sort of person. After an ending, there's always a new beginning. I was wondering…" He put his arms around her.

"What?" Adelle asked, looking up at him.

"Things got pretty thoroughly messed up for us, and we need a new beginning, too. There's a student recital at the university next Sunday afternoon. Violin instead of piano, but I hear he's very good. Do you think you could arrange to be well enough to go?"

"I certainly could," she said. "I positively guarantee it."

"And on your new job, whatever it is, will you promise not to perform any errands in basements without taking me along?"

"I'll guarantee that, too," she said, smiling. "It'll be a long, long time before I perform any kind of an errand in any basement. And if I ever again stand you up for a date, will you promise to immediately call out all the police departments in the area and the national guard?"

He nodded gravely. "Also all the fire departments, the FBI, and the Federal Marshalls. I won't hesitate an instant. Of course I promise. I like making promises to you. I'm even going to like keeping them."

He kissed her.

www.ingramcontent.com/pod-product-compliance
Lightning Source LLC
Chambersburg PA
CBHW050419260626
47156CB00003B/1079